D0808820

Mil Millington is the creator of the cult website www.thingsmygirlfriendandihavearguedabout.com and co-founder of www.theweekly.co.uk. He writes for various newspapers and magazines and was named by the *Guardian* as one of the top five debut novelists for 2002. Mil's two previous novels, *Things My Girlfriend And I Have Argued About* and *A Certain Chemistry*, are also available in Phoenix paperback.

By Mil Millington

Love and Other Near Death Experiences
A Certain Chemistry
Things My Girlfriend And I Have Argued About

LOVE AND OTHER NEAR DEATH EXPERIENCES

MIL MILLINGTON

PHOENIX

A PHOENIX PAPERBACK

First published in Great Britain in 2006
by Weidenfeld & Nicolson
This paperback edition published in 2006
by Phoenix,
an imprint of Orion Books Ltd
Orion House, 5 Upper St Martin's Lane,
London WC2H 9EA

1 3 5 7 9 10 8 6 4 2

A CIP catalogue record for this book
is available from the British Library.

ISBN-13 978-0-7538-2117-6
ISBN-10 0-7538-2117-6

Printed and bound in Great Britain by
Clays Ltd, St Ives plc

The Orion Publishing Group's policy is to use papers that
are natural, renewable and recyclable products and
made from wood grown in sustainable forests. The logging
and manufacturing processes are expected to conform to
the environmental regulations of the country of origin.

www.orionbooks.co.uk

To second chances, generally.

ONE

Hello. My name is Robert, and I haven't been dead for sixty-three days now.

TWO

'Silver or gold?'

'Silver,' I replied. 'Or gold.' I peered hard at the samples in the catalogue again. 'Or silver.'

'Which?' asked Jo.

'Which do *you* like?'

She sighed. 'I want to know which lettering *you* like. I'm not sure.'

'Me neither.'

'Come on, Rob, I can't do this all on my own.'

I peered even harder at the catalogue of wedding stationery.

Why did we need to have place cards printed for the guests at all? Couldn't we just use Post-its or something? Or even let people sit wherever they felt like. I understood that the heel of hundreds of years of finicky tradition was on our throats at the church (put an aunt in the wrong pew and the whole place might explode into a brutal chaos of arguments, jostling and unfathomable hats), but the reception didn't need to be so tightly policed, did it? We didn't need to decide about every single detail of every single thing, surely?

'Couldn't we just use . . . ?' I began. Jo's eyebrows climbed higher and higher up her forehead as she waited for me to complete the sentence; finally, they reached an elevation that seemed to say, 'If the next word out of your mouth is "Post-its", then you'll die where you're sitting.' I waggled my hands about a bit. '. . . ushers?'

'For God's sake, Rob – be serious.'

I imagined my face looked pretty serious already, but,

for Jo's sake, I took a shot at getting it to look more serious still.

'This is the biggest day of our lives, babe,' she went on. 'Everything should be *perfect* – we won't get a second chance if we get it wrong. Let's get everything sorted in good time so there are no last-minute panics.'

'It's only just October. We've got nearly another three months yet. I mean, we could panic six weeks from now and it'd still be OK, wouldn't it? It wouldn't be anywhere near the last minute, even then.'

'Silver or gold, Rob?'

'Ohhhh, I—'

'Just say which one you like best.'

'I don't know.'

'You must know.'

'Why? Why must I know? *You* don't.'

'I do. I know which one I like best. I simply want to see if you like that one best too.'

'I'm easy. Let's just have the one you want.'

'But I want to have one we both like.'

'Well, which do you like?'

'I like them both.' She shrugged. 'But I prefer the silver.'

'Phew.' I relaxed. 'Me too.'

'Do you? The silver? God – *why*?'

'What? What do you mean, "Why?" The same reason that you like it, I suppose.'

'I don't like it. It's awful. I like the gold.'

'But you just said you liked the silver.'

'I was testing you.'

'*Testing* me? Why would you *test* me? Why would *any-body* do that? Why would anybody *test* someone over the colour of the lettering on a wedding-reception place card?'

'Because I wanted to see if you liked the same thing, or if you were just going along with what *I* wanted.'

'What does it matter? What . . . hold on – why did you

say "Silver", then? How did you know that to "test" me, you'd need to pick silver?'

'Oh, it's obvious. I know you, babe – I knew you'd prefer the silver.'

'Christ all shitting mighty! So you knew what *you* wanted, *and* you knew what *I* wanted too – and yet we've still been sitting here for the last thousand years having this discussion. Why are we having this discussion?'

'Because I want to discuss the wedding *with* you: it's *our* wedding. When two people are getting married, they should both be sure about everything, shouldn't they?'

'Jesus.' I closed my eyes and slapped myself on the forehead: astonished at how, despite my best efforts, I was unable to escape this conversation. A decision that I – that even *I* – hadn't seen coming, now had me in its jaws and wouldn't let go. 'Jesus.'

When I opened my eyes again, Jo was looking down at the catalogue far too intensely, even for her. She'd tilted her head so that curtains of gently layered, mousy-blonde hair had fallen forward to cover her face: she was hiding in her bob. I let out a long sigh.

'I'm sorry. It's just, you know . . . *Jesus.*'

'I . . . It's not just about the lettering, Rob. I thought that doing it might help too.'

'Help?'

'You know, babe.' She looked up and laid her hand on my leg. 'Help *you*.'

'What are you talking about?'

I knew what she was talking about.

'Just,' she said, 'that . . . well, that it'd help you to work your way back up. Like lifting weights or something. You begin with light things and it builds up your strength; then you can move on to the heavier stuff. And so on.'

'I have *no* idea what you're talking about.'

I knew what she was talking about.

'I thought it might help if you . . . oh, I don't know. If you "eased yourself in" with some unimportant decisions.'

'There *are* no unimportant decisions. How many times do I have to explain this? That's the whole bleeding point – there *are* no unimportant decisions.' Already, I could feel myself getting angry.

'Right . . . So we'll go with the gold, then,' Jo said, after sitting there for a few moments of watching me try to get my breathing under control. 'The gold.' She grinned. 'I don't suppose you'd like to pick a font?'

'You sod.' I laughed, and it washed some of the tension from me.

Jo put down the stationery catalogue, and picked up a different catalogue. Jo had an impossibly extensive collection of catalogues.

'Have you spoken to Pete?' she asked, glancing through the pages. (They turned slowly – regally – each heavy leaf causing a slight breeze. I didn't need to look inside; just the sound of the pages moving told me that whatever was on them was damagingly expensive.)

'Yeah, you know I have. We went out for a beer last night.'

'Tch – I don't mean have you spoken to him generally, you fool; I mean have you spoken to him about the hotel?'

'About . . . the . . . hotel . . .'

'About asking the hotel if they could fit another two tables in the reception room.'

'Oh, *right*, about that . . .'

'Have you?'

'No.'

'*Rob*.'

'I forgot, OK? We had other stuff to talk about; I got side-tracked.'

'What other stuff?' Jo prodded me with a pair of light-blue eyes that she kept in her head for this purpose.

'Um . . . well, the beer was a bit suspect, for a start – I remember we had a long debate about whether the barrel needed changing.' Jo looked like she didn't quite grasp how this debate could be devilishly complex enough to occupy most of an evening. Jo didn't spend *nearly* enough time in pubs. 'Anyway, you could call the hotel and ask yourself.'

'I don't want to step on Pete's toes – dealing with paying the people at the reception venue is one of the best man's jobs.' She nodded reverently towards the mantelpiece. On there was our copy *of Arranging Your Wedding*, lying where it could be referred to at any time, day or night. It contained a ruthlessly comprehensive list of what *had* to be done, and who *had* to do it. To overlook or (unthinkably worse) ignore the edicts of *Arranging Your Wedding* was not simply careless, it was indecent – your own outraged guests would stone you to death; I had little doubt about that.

'Ha!' I replied. 'Don't worry about his toes. Pete would gladly offer up the whole of both of his feet for stamping on here. Trust me – you go ahead and call the hotel.'

Poor Pete. Asking someone to be your best man is rather like letting a mate know that you think he is admirably resilient by abruptly pushing him down some stairs. Yes, it signifies that you regard him as a good friend and also think he's competent and reliable, but it does so by giving him an utterly miserable pile of work to do (the 'Best Man's Responsibilities' section in *Arranging Your Wedding* dwarfs most of the others). Worse still, you're compelling him to give a best man's speech: little can match the misery of knowing you have to give a best man's speech. It's a gold star by the male character that the tradition has been endured all this time – imagine the fuss if a woman were told that, just because she happens to be the bride's friend, she has to stand up in front of a room packed with people – at least half of whom are complete strangers – and give a speech in which she's *expected by everyone* to be funny, and original, and risqué – but not so much as to cause offence – and to reveal something embarrassing about the bridegroom – but not *too* embarrassing; something just embarrassing enough – and then to end on a wonderfully touching note.

As it happens, taking the poisoned chalice of being my best man was an act of even greater than usual nobility where Pete was concerned, because Pete and Jo had been engaged at one point. Oh, it was quite a time ago now – they'd split up well before Jo and I became an item – and I'm not suggesting that Pete still carried a torch for her or anything like that. No, I'm not worried that he'll break down in the middle of the speech sobbing, 'It should have been me, Rob – *it should have been me!*' (In fact, when I first started seeing Jo, I rather sheepishly asked Pete if he was OK with it. I didn't really want to ask, to be honest – I'd have preferred to avoid the embarrassment I knew we'd both feel because of my raising the subject – but Jo had insisted I do it, so that *she* wouldn't feel uncomfortable. Anyway, he put my mind at rest by the traditional method of (a) saying, 'What's it's got to do with me? We're not together any more. You are *such* a poncey twat, Garland,' (b) our both then getting so pissed that I woke up in a bus shelter, surrounded by Monday-morning commuters, and in a sexually compromising position with a set of temporary traffic lights, and (c) never mentioning it again.) I mean that he can't help but be aware that, if things had gone a little differently, *I'd* have been the poor bastard doing the best man's job for *him*.

Hmm . . . if things had gone a little differently. Now *there's* a phrase.

Jo gave me one of her looks.

'OK, OK,' I said. 'I'll give Pete a call.'

'When?'

'Later.'

'Why not now?'

'OK, I'll do it now.'

'Right.'

'Right . . . Mind you . . .'

'Erghhh.'

'No – listen – no, it's teatime, isn't it?' I said. 'Pete's probably only just got in from work – all tired and sweaty from brutalising sickly English schoolchildren. It's not really fair to dump another job on him when he's barely got through the door, is it?'

'OK. You're probably right, there.'

'Am I? Or do you . . . ?'

'*You're right, there*, Rob.'

'OK. Sorry.'

'Call him later, babe . . . but call him tonight, yes?'

'Yes, I'll call him tonight.'

I sat in the spare room and looked at my mobile phone. I'd been up there for three hours now. Jo had remained downstairs after tea to, oh, perhaps – and I'm guessing here, admittedly – 'go through catalogues', and I'd come up to the spare room to 'sort out some music for the show tonight'. In fact, I wasn't choosing music at all; I was just aimlessly sifting through the CDs. Keith, my producer, would have got a playlist together, so there was no need for me to pick tracks. Still, I *used* to pick them anyway; I'd infuriate him by arriving at the last moment and rewriting his list – enthusiastically inserting songs from my jagged carrier bag full of CDs. Now, I didn't. Now, I just turned up at the studio and played whatever he'd chosen. Now, I came up to the spare room each weekday evening and moved the CDs through my hands in nothing more, or less, than an unthinking, soothing rhythm – like rosary beads.

I scrolled through the phone book on my mobile. There was Pete's entry: a key press away. He could be out jogging, though. Pete wasn't mad, you understand – it was simply that he was a sports teacher. So, he pretty much *had* to exercise, attend a gym and so on; I wouldn't like you to think that Pete was the kind of person who jogged for fun. Anyway, I knew he went for a run of an evening, and that he took his mobile phone with him. Suppose my ringing his number alerted a group of thugs to the fact that Pete was carrying it. It was dark, and Pete – though an athletic six foot two – could well be near-exhausted from his run. He'd be alone and possibly in a secluded area of the park too. Hitting the speed dial now might make him a target for a mugging. If I carefully *pressed* the individual numbers, however, that could allow enough time for Pete to be out of earshot, and thus out of danger, before his phone rang. Or perhaps *that* would place him in danger instead. Perhaps the group of pre-datory crackheads lay farther along his path. If I used his phone book entry *right now*, we'd have finished talking, and he'd have put his mobile back out of sight before he reached the brooding, bellicose junkies . . . but slow, methodical, manual dialling on my part would mean it was still temptingly in his hand as he passed the drug-addled, disaffected motorcycle gang with their Stanley knives and make-shift iron-railing spears.

How did I know which was right? How do you *ever* know which apparently trivial decision will remain trivial if you go one way, but will lead to unimaginable horror if you go the other? What are the rules?

'Bye!' I shouted, as I began to leave for the radio station.

'Hey – don't I get a kiss?' Jo called back from the living room.

I dashed in – glancing obviously at my watch – and

tagged her lips with mine before heading once again towards the door.

'Did you phone Pete?' she called to my fleeing back.

'Mmmrrrrnnommm,' I replied, reassuringly.

'What?' she queried – she was still in the living room, though, and I was in the hallway now. I could pretend I hadn't heard that. It's part of Common Law or something: a traditional thing – like the police not being able to try you for the same murder twice, say. If you've managed to put a door between you, or you have a tap running, or the TV is on, or you're reading something, then you can say you didn't hear. Everyone accepts that. And I was in the hallway now.

'What?' she repeated – suddenly standing a few feet behind me in the hallway too; getting there before I'd managed even to open the front door properly. Christ, but she was nippy across a living room when she wanted to be.

'I . . . erm . . .'

'*Rob.*'

'I meant to, Jo, honestly. I *wanted* to but . . .'

'Did you? Did you really want to?'

'Yes. Of *course*. Look – I've got to go—'

'No, stay here. We need to talk about this.'

'I can't, I have to get to work.'

'This is important, Rob.'

'If it's important, then it'll still be important tomorrow morning.'

'I need to get this sorted out *now*.'

'I need to leave for work *now*. Whatever you want to talk about we can talk about later, but the radio station can't just casually start my show an hour late because I was talking to my girlfriend in the hallway.'

'Five minutes. That's all it'll take.'

'It's never five minutes.'

'What isn't? You don't know what it is.'

'But I know it's "five minutes" – and I know that what-ever you introduce with the words "five minutes" never comes in at under an hour.'

'OK – just go then! Just piss off and do your show!' She turned around and stomped back into the living room.

Awww – crap. Now we'd crossed a line. If it had reached the point where she'd told me to go, then I'd genuinely be in the shit if I went. I blew out a lungful of defeated air and shuffled into the living room after her.

She sat on the sofa and ignored me, flicking through a magazine so viciously that she was slapping the pages rather than turning them.

'What is it?' I asked, wearily.

She continued to ignore me.

'OK,' I sighed. 'If you won't tell me what the problem is, then there's no point my being late for work.' I turned and began to go back to the front door. 'I'll see you tomorr—'

'Do you still want to go ahead with it?'

Damn. Perfect brinkmanship. It was undoubtedly right on the edge, but my trailing heel was *just* her side of the door frame, and I was, in any case, still talking (which meant I accepted we were still within talking range). She'd got me.

'Go ahead with what?' I replied, leaning back into the room.

'You know. Go ahead with the wedding.'

'When have I *ever* said that I didn't want to go ahead with the wedding?'

'Maybe you're scared to. Or, um . . . embarrassed. Maybe you think that you're obliged to go through with it now; that you've had second thoughts, but it's too late to back out.'

'Tch.'

'Maybe the reality of it is finally dawning on you, and you're frightened of commitment.'

'Frightened of commitment? Oh, please. Did your brain just get replaced by a *Cosmo* test?'

'Some men are.'

'One in ten million – all the rest aren't "scared of commitment"; they simply don't want to commit to a particular woman . . . and it just happens to be the particular one who's filling in the test.'

'You haven't said, "No".'

'OK. "No. I am not scared of commitment." '

'You haven't said that you still want to get married.'

'Oh, for Christ's sake. "I still want to get married." Satisfied?'

Jo had put the magazine aside. She looked down at her hands and began to turn her engagement ring round and round on her finger. 'People fake madness to get out of the army.'

'Is being married to you going to be like a war? Because, if it's not, then every single bit of that sentence is nonsense. I'm *not* trying to get out of anything, I'm *not* faking anything . . . and I'm *not* mad.'

'I didn't mean exactly—'

'I'm *not*.'

(I'm not. Honestly.)

'Not completely raving – you know that's not what I meant . . .'

'Oh, I *see* . . . Only a *partial* lunatic. Well, why didn't you just *say* that? Yes, of course, I'm thirty-or-so per cent deranged, but—'

'You're . . .'

'Yes?' (I challenged her with great bravado.)

'You're . . . not like you were.' (And got what I deserved.)

I ran my thumb along the edge of the door frame, scarring the wood with my nail. The room seemed tight, as though the air in it had hardened around me like a constricting skin: I felt shrink-wrapped.

'I see things now,' I replied – quietly, but with a good deal of passion. 'Things I didn't see before – things most people tune out to protect themselves.'

'There you go, babe. That's what I mean. Who says stuff like that?' She counted off on her fingers. 'Mad people, Stephen King characters . . . who else?'

'People who see things say it. What am I supposed to do? I've discovered something.'

'Something *good*?'

'That's not the point. Should Captain Cook have kept quiet about finding Australia because we've ended up with Russell Crowe?'

'This is worse than Russell Crowe, Rob.'

'Well – now you're just talking nonsense . . . And, anyway, it's irrelevant; because you can't *un*know a thing once you know it.'

'You could see someone.' I noted that, tellingly, she couldn't look me in the eye as she said this. She raised her head. 'You could talk to someone.' Jesus, she *could* look me in the eye as she said it. That was even worse. 'A therapist or something.'

'I do not need to see a therapist.'

'You can't function.'

'I *can*.'

She stared at me.

I made a vastly exaggerated 'What?' expression. And then jogged on the spot while sweeping the tips of my index fingers out to the side, then in to my nipples, then out, then up to my nose, then back around again. That showed her. I came to a halt and flung my arms wide, triumphantly.

'I have a number you can ring,' she said.

I exhaled heavily and let my head drop.

'My mum gave it to me.'

'You've been telling your *mum* I'm mad?' I asked, not very quietly.

'I didn't say that. I just said I thought—'

'Did anyone use the word "mad"?'

'I—'

'Did anyone use the word "mad"?'

'Maybe. OK? Maybe Mrs Williams or someone used it but—'

'Mrs Williams?'

'What?'

'What was Mrs Williams doing there?'

'She'd come with Susan and Pam and Aunty Barbara – we were discussing the wedding.'

'*Jesus.*'

'What now?'

'Why don't you just do a "Rob's Barking" poster campaign?'

'It's nothing to be embarrassed about.'

'I'm not embarrassed – I'm bleeding *astounded*. I can't believe that you've gone around telling your friends and family that I'm mad.'

'Christ!' Jo stood up. 'I didn't need to *tell* them that you're mad!' She sat down again abruptly, lowered her voice, and waggled her finger in the air. 'Not that you *are* mad, obviously . . . I meant I didn't need to tell them that you needed a little help.'

'I don't need "help".'

'You lock up, Rob.'

'Not all the time.'

'What about yesterday when you stood in Safeway until all the ice cream had melted in the shopping bags because you couldn't decide which door to leave by?'

'OK. That was a time I *did* lock up a bit, yes. I admit that.'

'I still can't get the stains out of the cushion covers you bought.'

'Hey – *you* wanted raspberry ripple, so don't blame me for that.'

She began to fiddle with her ring again.

'Rob . . .' She sighed. 'Look – Rob – this is either some kind of subconscious thing – your way of dragging your feet because you don't want to get married anymore – or it's got nothing at all to do with the wedding.'

'You know it hasn't. You know what it's to do with.'

'OK, OK. Well, if it really *isn't* a sign that you don't want to marry me, then you need to deal with it . . . or *I'm* not sure I can marry *you*.'

She looked up at me. I couldn't think of anything to say.

'I love you, Rob, but we can't go on like this. I've waited – hoping things would improve if I gave you time – and I've tried to help you get over it too. But it's not getting any better, is it?'

'I . . .'

No – still nothing there.

'If you love me, Rob, you'll do something. Do *something*. You're ill. And, before we can go ahead with something as important as getting married, you need to get well.'

I looked down and spoke very quietly.

'I'm not ill . . . I just *see things*.'

Rob's Story

*I'm not sure where to start. And that's part of it, you see –
where do you start? What moment do you choose? How
can you possibly know where the start is? Ffffff . . . OK, I
suppose – just to keep things manageable – I'll start at the
point where I didn't buy a hotdog.*

*I'm very fond of the hotdogs you get from those mobile
street stalls, and often buy one if I'm passing. I regard them
as part food, part heroic trial of one's mental toughness.
They taste great. The task is to focus only on how great
they taste: exclude the weak, cowardly thoughts about
their being sold to you by someone you'd probably be
uncomfortable sitting next to on a train, or that the 'meat'
in them was surely gathered by blasting the most stubbornly adhesive matter from the bones of animals using
high-power water jets; jets wielded, moreover, by the
calibre of individual who'd want to do that for a living.
It's a test of will.*

*Except on this day, I didn't buy a hotdog. I almost did.
As I was walking through town, I saw the hotdog stand
and went over to it, fully intending to buy a hotdog, but an
instant before I got there a bunch of football fans slipped
in just ahead of me. If any one of the four of them had
delayed the others – checking he had his ticket, pausing to
call goodbye to his girlfriend, hesitating when crossing the
road – by even a single second then they wouldn't have got
there first. If their team hadn't been playing in the city that
week, they wouldn't have been there at all. (I don't follow
football – because I'm not an idiot – but I'm sure the*

circumstances that led to their team being there on that Saturday were pretty complex and uncertain.)

I sighed, said, 'Wankers' to myself and, braving the injustice of it all with great elegance, waited behind them in what was, now (wankers), a queue. I glanced around absently while they individually and collectively struggled with the question of whether they wanted a hotdog or a burger. That's when I noticed the discount shop just a few yards along. It was one of those places that doesn't sell anything in particular, but rather sells pretty much everything, discounted. They had some towels in the window: three for a fiver. Yeah, I know, that's what I thought. Can't grumble at three for a fiver, can you? I mean, they'll probably be rubbish, but at three for a fiver they'll still be good value, right?

Now, I'm not the kind of bloke who's always on the lookout for bargain house wares, I'm honestly not. But, just that morning, I'd thought, 'We could do with some more towels,' as I'd walked, dripping wet from the bleeding shower, around half the bleeding house, trying to find a bleeding towel. Even armed with that information, however, if I'd have been a second quicker to the hotdog stand, then I doubt that the towels would have caught me. They don't like you going into shops when you're eating a hotdog, so I'm sure that, had I seen the towels after buying one, I'd not have bothered hanging around until I'd finished it. Even if my attention had briefly flirted with failure and drifted away from the all-consuming taste of my hotdog enough to notice the towels at all, I'd have gone, 'Oh, towels . . . Wow! Three for a fiver! I must tell Jo about that,' and carried on walking. But, as it was, I was standing there separated from my hotdog by four morons who didn't know what they wanted to eat, and so I left them to it, went into the shop, and bought some towels.

They were rubbish.

'*These are* rubbish,' *said Jo.*

I was, obviously, prepared for this. '*They were only a fiver.*'

'*You paid a fiver for these?*'

'*I couldn't find any towels this morning.*'

'*What? Did you look in the towel drawer?*'

(We had a 'towel drawer'?)

'*Yes. Of course I did.*'

'*No you didn't.*'

'*I did. There weren't any there.*'

Jo laughed. 'Sure.'

'*There weren't.*'

'*Right. OK – let's go upstairs now and you can show me how you looked.*'

'*Don't be childish. That's not the issue anyway. We're discussing* these *towels.*'

'*Yes, we are. You're taking them back to the shop.*'

This suggestion was so preposterous that my voice instinctively went falsetto as I replied. '*I can't take them back to the shop.*'

'*Take them back on Monday.*'

'*I can't.*'

'*Yes you can.*'

'*I* can't. *I'm driving over to Sedgely to interview Billy "Lips" O'Connell on Monday.*'

'*You'll have plenty of time to take them back in the morning, before you go there.*'

'*I can't take them back – they were a* fiver.'

'*So?*'

'*So, how does it make me look if I kick up a fuss about some three-for-a-fiver towels?*'

'*Make you look to who?*'

'*To the woman in the shop. I'll look like some penny-pinching git.*'

'What on earth does it matter what she thinks? And, anyway, do you imagine that right now she's under the impression that you're a sophisticated, independently wealthy playboy? Eh? On the evidence that you came into her shop and bought three towels for a fiver? You surely can't be afraid that taking them back now will shatter her illusions.'

'It's embarrassing.'

'It's a fiver. Throwing away money is throwing away money, babe, it doesn't matter how much it is. And, anyway, I've had my eye on some towels, as it happens – I spotted them in the Ikea catalogue. Nice towels. Made from proper material, and not covered with a pattern that requires their labels to include an epilepsy warning. We have enough towels to be going on with until I can get them. We do not need to spend five pounds on rubbish towels in the meantime. Take them back.'

'I can't take them back. It's not just the money . . . they're towels.'

Now Jo stared at me with an infuriatingly contrived expression of confusion. 'What do you mean?' she said. 'We haven't used them.'

I sighed, explosively. 'They're towels.'

'I know.' The look on her face was holding fast. 'So?'

'Oh, come on – don't take the piss, Jo. You know what I mean. No man would ever return towels. It's bloody obvious to everyone – if I turn up holding a bag of towels and asking for my money back – that my girlfriend has made me do it. I might as well march in and announce, "Hello, everyone! Yes, that's right: I'm whipped!" '

Jo roared with laughter. Even worse, she leaned forward and kissed me on the nose.

I gave her my most pleading eyes. 'Can't you do it?'

'No, I'm at work on Monday.'

'Later in the week, then.'

'Rob . . .' She placed her hands on my shoulders. 'Every man at some time faces a moment when his courage is tested to the limits – landing on the beach on D-Day, helping women and children into lifeboats as the Titanic sinks under him . . . it's in that moment that he defines himself. For you, that moment is taking some towels back to a discount shop on Monday, OK?' She clicked her teeth and gave my shoulders a comradely little shake. 'God be with you.'

'You're the funniest woman ever. Really – it's killing me to keep a straight face right now.'

I went out to the pub with Pete in the evening. We had a few beers, and I told him about the ridiculous way that Jo was making an issue of all this. He agreed with me that it seemed rather unreasonable. It was my five pounds, after all – I could do what I liked with my own money, surely? It wasn't as if I'd sneaked a fiver out of her purse, or blown ten thousand pounds earmarked for a tiny child's liver transplant on prostitutes and cheese. Justice was clearly on my side in this matter.

At half eleven on the Monday morning I took the towels back to the shop.

It was even more embarrassing than I'd imagined. The woman behind the counter rubbed it in by giving me my money back immediately and without any sign of annoyance. Evil. If she'd been difficult I could have put my foot down or something – made it clear that I knew my rights and couldn't be messed with – I'd rehearsed a little righteous indignation routine in the car, in fact. She didn't show me that mercy, though. She just refunded my five pounds with a kind of bored efficiency; leaving me with nothing to display except the unmistakable actions of a tightwad who was completely dominated by his girl-friend. I stuffed the note into my pocket and fled the shop, hot-faced.

Actually, the sheer, hammering shame wasn't the only reason I had for hurrying away. I was supposed to meet Lips O'Connell at the Bird Dog pub in Sedgely at twelve. We were going to do a feature on him for the show. Lips was a bit of a local legend . . . well – he was local, at least. For thirty years, his trumpet playing had been the driving force in the O'Connell Nine (a seven-piece. That was the joke, you see. Ahh – thirty years old and still funny). A bit too Dixieland for my tastes, but never mind: I was going to meet him in the pub, listen to the lunchtime set, and then record an interview with him right there in the bar when he'd finished. Except, earlier, I'd got caught up in a traffic jam in the city centre (burst water main), and I was now running about half an hour late; if I didn't hurry I was going to overshoot the time we'd arranged to meet by so much that I wouldn't arrive until after their set had begun – which would look very sloppy and, worse, bad-mannered. And all because I'd had to take some bloody towels back.

As I hurried to the car park, I pulled out my mobile and gave O'Connell a call.

'Billy? Hi, it's Rob from Central FM here.'

'Hello, there. How am you doing, Rob?'

'Crappily, I'm afraid. Sorry, but I'm going to be a bit late, mate. I had to take my girlfriend to the hospital.'

'God – is she OK?'

'Yeah, yeah, it was just . . . you know, her legs or something.'

'Her legs?'

'Yes. We thought they were broken. But it turns out they're fine . Anyway, never mind about that, I just wanted to apologise for the delay. I'll try to be there for the start of your set, though.'

'OK, mate – bosting. I'll see you then.'

'Yeah – see you then.'

Forty minutes later it was absolutely clear that I wasn't going to get to the Bird Dog before O'Connell went on stage. I decided to give him another call, to at least say sorry again and wish him good luck with the set. Flicking my eyes up and down between the road ahead and my phone, I searched for the Last Number Redial. I skilfully found it after only a couple of near misses with the central reservation, but when I called I was put through to O'Connell's voicemail. 'Bugger,' I thought, 'he's turned his phone off because they're getting ready to play: I'm even late for apologising for being even later than I'd previously apologised for.' It was about a quarter past twelve.

At just after half past twelve I stood watching a woman scream.

Her hands were attacking her own head – they were clawing at it and pulling her hair. She looked insane – exaggeratedly insane, like an am-dram actress playing insane in a self-consciously gothic play. The sheer volume of her screams was the most unbelievable thing, though. Guttural and shrill at the same time, they stabbed into my eardrums; I could feel muscles somewhere inside my head flinching, trying to shield my ears from the penetrating attack of her cries. She continued to scream, and I continued to look at her with a kind of surreal disinterest. I simply didn't know what else to do.

The Bird Dog had stood at the end of the dual carriageway. It had stood there. A tanker speeding along the road (impatiently overtaking the coach in front of it before the two lanes became one) had lost control, swerved, mounted the pavement and smashed into the side of it like a 10-foot-high, 70-mph, 40-tonne sledgehammer. Anyone not killed instantly by this impact would have had a fraction of a second to contemplate their good fortune before they were killed by the two storeys above collapsing down on top of them.

I stood in front of what was now little more than a chaotic hill of bricks – like a heap of shattered teeth – and watched the woman next to me scream. The tanker was leaking. It was leaking milk (calcium – good for your bones). I peered down and saw that the ground was white all around us. 'Christ, I bet that's going to reek – a great pool of milk left out in this sun,' I remember thinking.

Everyone who was in the Bird Dog that afternoon died. I should have been there – I'd had an appointment, even – but I wasn't. I was alive because I was taking some towels back that morning, because they were rubbish. Or was I alive because I hadn't waited to buy a hotdog on the previous Saturday? Or was it farther back? Was it back when I'd decided to go to the city centre at all? Or when I'd decided to have a shower rather than a quick wash that morning? Or farther back even than that?

What trivial decision had saved my life?

THREE

Keith was eating a tangerine. Before he popped a segment into his mouth, he teased off each flaccid white vein of pith – grabbing one end between his thumb and index finger, and then slowly tearing it away. To someone who didn't know him, it might have looked fussy. I did know Keith, so I knew that really it wasn't finickiness at all: he was torturing the fruit.

Central FM had introduced a no-smoking policy about ten months ago. This had hit Keith – who'd become a radio producer in the first place specifically so that he could sit around smoking all night – very hard indeed. In theory, he could pop out into the car park for a quick cigarette if he was desperate, but it was two floors down and, as we were in Birmingham, when he got there it would almost certainly be raining. At first, he'd used sweets as surrogate cigarettes. Every evening, he'd munched his way through the show; plugging his nicotine receptors with sugar. A few months and 14 lbs of fresh stomach fat later, he'd bitterly switched from sweets to fruit as a way to occupy his mouth from midnight until 3 a.m. He hadn't lost the weight he'd put on, but at least he wasn't gaining any more – though at the cost of now having near-constant diarrhoea. And he didn't even like fruit very much. Thus, each night, he tormented his edible victims as much as possible before putting torn parts of them in his mouth. Grinning with malice, he'd skin apples using a penknife; he'd rip at a cherry with his incisors until the flesh hung gory from the stone, and then suck it clean; I've seen him do things to a peach that would drain the blood right out of your face.

24

Keith was the Dr Mengele of pulpy reproductive-seed plants.

'Hi.' I nodded to him and Jenny (our assistant, researcher, engineer and anything-else-that-needed-to-be-done doer) as I loped across the room. Keith grunted; Jenny was too busy checking something on a clipboard to answer with more than a raised hand. I sat down and pulled thoughtfully at my lip, while Jenny continued to work and Keith continued to eat. No one spoke until Jenny said, 'Five minutes,' at which point I got up and walked through from the control room into the adjoining studio – picking up the playlist from in front of Keith as I did so. *Keith*'s playlist. Compiled by him alone, and which I couldn't help but feel he deliberately made me walk over and collect nowadays: like a beggar.

I slid on my headphones; the tail-end of the show before mine – K. K. Lee's Nineties Classics – was coming through on them. On the desk in front of me Jenny had put a bottle of water, a Styrofoam cup and the night's overall running order. (Keith had also put little notes by the side of some of the tracks on the playlist – generally the date when the performer of them had died.) K. K. wound up and, as she always did, whispered in her huskiest voice, 'Remember, the night is just beginning . . . and here to take you on into the rest of it is Rob Garland.'

'Thanks, K. K.,' I said – knowing her headphones were probably off even as I spoke (the night might be just beginning for me, but she was already heading home to eat a bowl of cornflakes while watching the episode of *ER* she'd videoed, before shuffling straight off to bed). 'Hello again, everyone. This is Rob Garland, and this is Jazz Central, and *this* is Woody Shaw, and *this* is "Imagination".' The track began.

'Nice "This" work there, Rob,' Keith said via talkback.

I looked up through the big, plate-glass window to where he and Jenny were sitting and made a gesture.

Building on my impressive opening, I sparkled along until the second news bulletin at 1.30.

It was only a five-minute report, but I'd pre-recorded a lengthy Joe Henderson retrospective to run right after it, so, rather than sit pointlessly in the studio, I went back into the control room to stretch my legs and get a coffee.

Jenny was concentrating on fiddling with sound levels and didn't look up. Keith didn't appear to be doing anything at all except ignoring me for its own sake. I walked past them both, went over to the drinks table, and picked up a new Styrofoam cup from beside the hot-water machine. Next to it there was a small plastic bowl containing single-serving sachets of instant coffee and those teabags that affect grandeur by being on a bit of string.

I stared at this bowl.

Should I have a coffee? Or a tea? Coffee gives you more of a lift; perhaps that millisecond advantage – the minuscule difference in my reaction speed – will prove crucial later. Maybe, if I have a coffee now, then I'll escape otherwise certain death because of the tiny, but vital, edge I possess.

Yes.

Unless, of course, it's the extra jitteriness that comes from having a coffee rather than a tea now that *causes* me to make some kind of mistake or slip or twitch or jerk or something that brings about a fatal situation which otherwise wouldn't have occurred. Though – obviously – it could be that the critical thing isn't whether I have coffee or tea; all that matters is that I have *something*. That way, when an unforeseeable set of circumstances leads to the hot-water machine being knocked over in a particular way at some point after this decision I'm making right now, then the cascading water will be shy of the very cupful that would have reached a piece of wiring or section of exposed circuitry and instantly arced crackling death out to whoever was in the wrong spot. The important thing, then, is to have *something*. Something that will eliminate the fatal cupful of water. That causes the short.

Or . . . that puts out the unseen electrical fire before it has a chance to take hold.

Damn. What's more likely? Death due to fire or death due to electricity? It has to be fire, right? Fire is the bigger killer. Statistically, you stand a far higher chance of being killed in a conflagration than by electrocution. If you're going to play the odds, then the smart move is to dodge a showdown with flames and face off against the mains instead. Definitely.

But electricity can take you out, literally, in a flash, can't it? You don't stand a chance. Whereas, surely, we could all evacuate the building safely if a fire started in this control room. We'd have enough time. It wouldn't catch us out.

Except, it *does* catch people out, doesn't it? It catches them out all the time. It catches people out precisely because they think it won't. Or because they're a tiny bit too slow through not having enough caffeine in their blood. Or a tiny bit too cocky or panicked because they have too much.

I noticed that I was breathing harder than was really necessary for the physical exertion of standing perfectly still looking at a small bowl of potential beverages. I also noticed that I'd involuntarily crushed the Styrofoam cup in my hand. Should I get another one? Or should I leave it?

I slowly turned away from the table – 'slowly' because doing so required a quite extraordinary effort of will. Jenny and Keith were still sitting there at the control desk.

'Do you think I have a problem?' I asked the back of their heads, at last.

'God yeah,' Keith replied, without looking round.

Jenny did swivel to face me. 'Are you OK, Rob? Do you need to take a break? Personal issues or something?'

'He's fine,' said Keith.

I peered down at my split and crumpled cup. 'Jo says I can't function.'

'Ugh. Rob, for Christ's sake – share *less*,' Keith replied.

'What about Viagra?' asked Jenny, leaning forward towards me slightly. 'Or there are these pumps you can get fitted – when you want to do it, you squeeze them and they inflate your thingy. I saw a documentary.'

'Jesus, Jenny,' whined Keith, 'I'm trying to eat a lychee here.'

'So? How am I putting you off? Rob's thingy doesn't look like a lychee, does it? Does your thingy look like a lychee, Rob?'

'No.'

'There you go, Keith, there you go. So, if you're thinking about putting Rob's thingy in your mouth, then you're thinking about putting Rob's thingy in your mouth – and you're simply using me and that lychee as an excuse.'

Keith dropped his lychee back into the bag.

'Actually, I—' I began.

'Do you need to go home and be with Jo?' Jenny cut in. 'I think that's probably a good idea. Talk it through. Take some time out. Sensual massage.'

'No, listen,' I said. 'I didn't mean that I can't function *sexually*.'

'Really?' asked Jenny, sympathetically. 'Are you *sure* you didn't mean that, Rob? Don't take any notice of Keith and his stupid lychee insinuations.'

'Are you watching the time, Jenny?' said Keith.

'Yes. "Shade of Jade" is going out now. 7 minutes 42 seconds of the segment still left to run. I'm on top of everything if Rob's got to go.'

'He is not going *anywhere*, Jenny.'

'For God's sake, Keith. This is Rob's sexual health we're talking about here. He and Jo are getting married in December – what kind of life do you think they can look forward to together if—'

'I *really* did not mean sexually, OK?' I reaffirmed. 'Hard though it clearly is for both of you to believe, can you just take it on faith that I have no problems in that area? All right?'

'See?' Keith said to Jenny. 'Give it up, woman.'

She ignored him entirely and asked, 'Well, why do you need to leave, then, Rob?'

Keith sighed with theatrical exasperation.

'I don't need to leave,' I replied. 'I just asked if you thought I couldn't function. I'm aware I've been a bit . . . you know – since the crash . . . but I *function*, don't I? I still manage to do the show.'

'Tch. All you have to do is mumble a few things into a mike every other track,' Keith said, allowing himself a little laugh. 'I get everything ready, and Jenny makes it work on air.'

'And you do . . . you know . . .' Jenny let her tongue loll out of her mouth and her eyes lose focus, '. . . "drift off" every so often.'

'Jenny has to start the next song early to cover,' added Keith.

'OK . . . maybe. Maybe I do experience that drifting problem sometimes.' I wriggled my shoulders uncomfortably. 'I don't do that very much, though, do I? It's not a big thing.'

'It's not a big thing if you present a late-night jazz show,' Keith admitted with a generously encouraging nod. 'But I'm fucked if I'd want you as an air traffic controller.'

'So – what? What are you saying? Can I function or not?'

'You can function as a local radio presenter,' replied

Keith with a shrug. 'But, very possibly, being a local radio presenter is the only thing you function well enough to be.'

I flopped down into a chair. 'Honestly?'

'We're only saying this because we care,' soothed Jenny.

'I don't care,' added Keith.

'Christ . . . I didn't think I was *that* . . .'

There was silence for a few moments. Then Jenny spoke to me. 'Five minutes, Rob.' I nodded, but didn't move from where I was. 'Perhaps I should—' she began.

'No, you shouldn't,' said Keith. 'He'll be fine.'

'I'm only thinking of the show, Keith,' she replied.

'Give it up.'

Finally, I brought my thoughtful little pause to an end and started to shuffle towards the studio. But then I stopped again.

'Keith,' I said, 'I'd like to do something new tonight.'

'No,' he replied, immediately.

'You haven't heard what it is yet.'

'I don't need to. It's a bad idea.'

'How can you possibly say that without hearing what it is?'

'Because our demographic is, self-evidently, people in the West Midlands listening to post-bop on the radio from midnight to three a.m. This is not a thrill-seeking demographic, Rob. It's jazz trainspotters, people trying to get to sleep and the clinically depressed. You start getting interesting and you're just going to alienate our listeners. Stick to the format.'

'But . . . but I think doing this thing would help *me* too.'

'Would it?' said Keith, nodding slowly. 'You see this, Rob?' He swept his hand up and down, indicating his own head. 'Is this, do you think, the face of a man who gives a fuck?' To emphasise the point, he then popped the lychee into his mouth and showed me his teeth cutting it in half.

'Keith—'

'*Stick*,' he spat the word quickly into the path of my sentence, paused to eyeball me seriously, then continued, 'to the format. Don't piss me around, Rob. You don't want to get on the wrong side of me, not when everyone knows we're carrying you here. You'll be out on your arse. I promise you.'

I watched him carefully and comprehensively castrate me via the proxy of a fruit.

'Three minutes,' said Jenny.

I let out a defeated sigh and dragged myself off into the studio.

My headphones back on, I listened to the end of the Henderson insert and sagged over the desk, watching Jenny through the window. She raised her hand and counted down the last five seconds, pointing towards me on the 'zero'.

'Joe Henderson,' I said. 'Great stuff. And we have some more great stuff coming up shortly – Bobby Watson and Joe Lavano are both waiting in the wings . . .' I looked at the crushed cup – which I was still clutching tightly in my clenched fist. Calmly, I let my hand open and watched the Styrofoam bloom a little in my palm. 'But first . . .' I took a breath and tossed the cup towards the waste bin. 'But first, I'd like to do something a bit different. Let me stop the music for a while here, because I want to tell you about something now.'

On the other side of the glass, I saw Jenny's mouth move through the shapes of 'Keith?' as she looked across at him, questioningly. Keith's own mouth opened and closed but, I was sure, didn't emit any sounds. He was sandbagged by frantic inaction: completely unable (and I can't express the sheer delight that this irony gave me) to decide what was the best thing to do. I continued to talk and, after I'd got a couple of sentences farther along, he did stab a finger down on to the control panel and begin to say something.

However, when I saw him start the movement, I reached up and pulled off my headphones, so I only caught 'You cu—'!' and therefore can't possibly imagine what he might have wanted to tell me.

Whatever else he might have done after that I don't know, because I closed my eyes then. I closed my eyes and I talked about what had happened with Lips O'Connell. This wasn't news, of course; the crash had been a big story locally at the time. I'd mentioned on air that I was due to meet him the day he died too, during the tribute show we'd done. But O'Connell was merely a supporting actor in what I was saying now. Now, I was talking about me. I was speaking about my feelings, about how the events had affected the way I looked at things. It was truly cathartic – you can't get much farther away from keeping things bottled up inside than broadcasting them live on a radio show. I carried on until the news bulletin at 2.30.

Keith let me. He'd obviously decided that allowing me to continue was marginally less disastrous than taking me off air mid-show. However, as soon as I allowed them to break for the news, he erupted into the studio.

'You,' he said, backing it up with a jabbing finger, 'are *so* fucked.' He sucked in air between his teeth – I suppose pulling a breath into himself in the same kind of way as one might blow one out over a pan of milk as an emergency way of stopping it boiling over. 'I'm going to see to it that you get an even shittier slot than this, Garland. You think there are no shittier slots than this? Well – think again. How does Songs from the Shows at one a.m. on a Sunday strike you? And the only reason I'm not having you removed from this studio right now is that it'd mean Jenny stepping in. If she were a single, *tiny* iota less desperate to do this show, then the pleasure I'd get from not letting her wouldn't be worth my keeping you on air for one more second.'

'Sorry, Keith. It was something I just had to do.'

'You're a wanker.'

'Yes. I know. Sorry. After the news we'll go back to the format for the final half-hour.'

'Wanker.'

'Yes . . . Sorry.'

After the news I continued to talk about the crash and the questions it had raised for me. I think one of the blood vessels behind Keith's eye burst at around a quarter to three.

When the show ended I crept into the control room looking sheepish. In fact, I didn't feel sheepish – I felt *great*: better than I'd felt for a long, long while. But I thought it best, politically, not to swagger. Though, I probably could have swaggered, as it happens, because Keith pointedly didn't look at me – even when he began to speak.

'You can see the week out, Garland,' he said, evenly. 'It's unprofessional for us to abruptly redo things after the week's started. But I'll be going to Bill and I'll be asking that, come next Monday, this station be Rob Garland-free. I'll be suggesting you get fired for unreasonable behaviour and breach of contract. If I can swing it, I'll also be advising that we slip Geoff The Security Guard a few pounds to take you out into the car park and give you a fucking good kicking.'

'Maybe you're being a little harsh, Keith,' Jenny said, trying to pacify him. 'I mean, Rob's not normally like this – and I'm sure he's got it out of his system now. Right, Rob?' She lifted her eyebrows at me.

'Cock to that,' replied Keith. 'I'm the producer, Jenny; he *completely* trampled on my authority. I can't have someone on air who just ignores me if he feels like it.'

'But Bill might—'

'Bill runs the station and Bill will accept that a presenter who – against the specific instructions of his producer – uses a show for his own reasons might say *anything*: slander, personal vendettas, who knows what? And it's the station that'd have to face the legal consequences of that. Bill will back me up.'

'But—'

'Jenny? Would you like to do the show from now on?'

'Yes,' replied Jenny, instantly.

'Well . . . you're not fucking going to. And Rob's screwed. And I'm the producer. Is everyone clear about the situation now?'

I let out a long breath. Not for any particular reason – just as a kind of full stop, to mark where I thought the end of the night was. 'I'll see you tomorrow, then, Jenny . . . Keith,' I said, and left.

I don't know what phrase you use for the opposite of a pyrrhic victory, but that's what I felt this was. It was a thoroughly splendid disaster. I had no doubt at all that this was the best bad move I'd ever made and I was, frankly, damn pleased with myself.

FOUR

Do you know how I walked to my car? Jauntily. I swear to God: 'jauntily'. I'd completely flushed my career, but I felt wonderful. If unburdening myself – admitting my problem as publicly as it was possible for me to do – had somehow killed the demon by exposing it to the brightest available light, then even being unemployed and unemployable would be a reasonable price to pay. It was more than reasonable, in fact; it was a bargain – because it paid for me to buy back my entire life. I was the Rob Garland I'd been before. Ready to move on. Ready – and fit – to marry Jo and for us to live a carelessly normal, utterly bog-standard, blissfully mundane life together without a doubtful thought passing through my head ever again.

As I walked along, I puffed misty little breaths up into the cold night air and pretended to be a train.

Central FM's car park was big enough to take two cars. The only reason it was called a car park at all, rather than 'a small driveway', was that a genius had put up a sign that said 'Car Park' – it was a bit like laying laminate flooring in your living room so that there's accidentally a two-inch height difference where the surfaces meet in the middle, and addressing this problem by simply referring to the higher area as 'the mezzanine'. Managing to get a space in Central FM's car park was such an astonishing achievement that, had I ever done it, I'm sure I'd never have moved my car again – I'd have just left it where it was, in triumph, and walked home. Because, as usual, there wasn't a place free when I'd arrived, I'd done what I always did and parked my car out on the street in the nearest available space. Sometimes this meant parking several hundred yards away from the station, but there wasn't really any choice about the matter (and, on one level, it was quite exciting, in fact: to park your car out on the street at night in Birmingham and find it still there when you return a few hours later always gives you a surprised little thrill). This night, however, I'd managed to find a place reasonably close.

I walked out of the car park on to the pavement and reached into my pocket for my keys as soon as I'd turned to head down the street. I'd jangled them in my hand for only a moment before I was already close enough to aim at my car and – *nya-eeep!* – turn off the alarm. There's something about setting or unsetting a car alarm that makes you look around. I don't think the impulse is as fully formed as expecting to see a lurking youth punch his palm and spit, 'Drat!' when you set it, or a group of joyriders whoop, 'Now!' and make a dash for your suddenly vulnerable vehicle the second you disable the thing, but it's certainly that kind of notion rippling up indistinctly from your subconscious. So, instinctively, I followed my switching the alarm off with a quick glance back up the road.

That was when I saw him.

Instantly, I knew he wasn't right. It was after 3 a.m. in a part of the city where only returning jazz radio presenters had any call to be on the streets at that time of day – so that alone immediately made me suspicious. That was the least unsettling thing about him, however. A more uncomfortable aspect of his even being there at all was that he'd obviously been waiting by the station, in the darkness of the micro car park. He was walking out from it on to the street, exactly as I had just done. The only reason I could imagine for his being there was that he was attempting to break in to one of the cars. And that would have been fine (better than fine, actually – I think one of them was Keith's), if he'd hidden as I'd walked past and then carried on or – panicked by my appearance – bolted off up the street as soon as I was far enough away. But he was neither running nor hiding: he had come out of the car park and was, at a calm but brisk pace, following me down the road. Glowering above even these two shivery truths, though, was the signalling wrongness of the fact that he was wearing camouflage fatigues. Who wears camouflage fatigues in the street except for the worryingly disturbed? Everyone knows that they are the chosen uniform of the mad.

So, a psycho was coming after me in the semi-darkness of a deserted road in the early hours. Worse still – a big psycho. Not one of those psychos who read SAS books and fill their rooms with replica weapons, but who are – tellingly – seven stone, four foot six and can be disabled, if not killed outright, by merely knocking their inhaler from their hands. No such luck. This was a big psycho. Tall, heavily built, and his head (just in case there was any doubt he was a nutter) shaved so that only a short, psycho-bristle covered it.

Oh, and he was clearly peering right at me too – he wasn't even making any attempt to hide this fact. Looking back, even across the distance that divided us and in the poor light of the street lamps, my eyes connected directly with his, and he deliberately held them.

Continuing to walk, I turned back around towards my car. My mind sped through the possibilities. If someone grabs you from behind, in a neck lock, then you stamp your heel down hard on the mid-section of their foot while simultaneously pulling their arm away – using the awkward twisting of their wrist joint to force them to yield. Knife attack? Grab the person by the hand and elbow of the attacking arm, and push both inwards – the way muscles are arranged means that they have no real strength in that direction, so one can compel even an assailant who is physically much stronger than you to drop the weapon. A face-on attack, of course, you meet with a sharp, upward blow using the heel of your palm – driving the attacker's own nasal bone into his brain and killing him instantly. The only questions were 'What was my best move?' and 'When was the best time to make it?' I felt there was no point waiting for him to snatch the initiative. I should move first – act, not respond; see that the situation played out on *my* terms.

So, I screamed as loud as I could and ran like fuck for my car.

I was at the driver's side door in seconds, but it was a million years later than I would have preferred. If I'd thought that I'd terrify the Camo Killer into a scrambling retreat by unexpectedly racing down the road away from him shrieking like a six-year-old girl, then I was wrong. He was obviously made of sterner stuff than that. Not only wasn't he taking the opportunity to escape, he had now actually started to race after me. My eyes bulging, I stared at him over the top of my car and screamed at F# above top C one more time, just to show him I meant business . . . But he kept on coming.

Using what appeared suddenly to be someone else's fingers, I fiddled frantically with the door – furiously wondering why Renault, it seemed, had decided to produce a car with a millimetre-wide lock that needed to be opened using a key the size of a hover-mower. While I stood there, fumbling, Camo Killer hammered along the pavement; he was now only a few steps away. My bowels plummeted to the earth's core.

Finally, I somehow managed to thread the shuddering key into the minuscule hole. A twist, a pull and a leap, and I was inside the car. I slapped down the peg on the door to seal myself in, and started the engine. Only then did I allow myself a glance in the rear-view mirror. Bizarrely, my would-be murderer was nowhere in sight.

Thwump!

Ahh . . . that would be because he was just rounding the car so he could throw himself on to the bonnet, then. Glad we cleared that one up.

He was leaning forward on the front of my car now; his arms stretched straight down in front of him, supporting his weight – rather like the commanding position you'd see a politician take up behind his plinth when announcing a new plan he'd drawn up to reject asylum applications more quickly. His eyes were wide and searching, and flooded by a look that was vivid with intensity and the colour of brain crazy. The pure shock and fear of seeing him suddenly there made me snatch in air and jerk backwards – I hit the headrest and bounced forwards again. The whole time I couldn't look away from his eyes. All this took perhaps only a couple of seconds, but it felt like long, icy minutes of him locking my gaze to his. It reminded me of the way, in films, Dracula's sinister power holds the eyes of his virgin victims.

Oh God! Maybe it was sexual!

Maybe he was going to shag me. Then drink my blood. Christ – he was going to shag me then drink my blood! Shit. *Shit*. This wasn't fair. This simply wasn't fair – I'd *just* got my life sorted out, and now a nutter was going to shag me and then drink my blood. *God*, but I hate Birmingham.

His mouth began to move – he was going to say something ('Graaahhhhh!' possibly, or maybe, 'Shag!' then, 'Blood!'). I leant forwards slightly, transfixed – my own mouth dropping a little as his opened, in involuntary reflection. The car engine was a deafening, ragged howl (I was in neutral, but my foot was panicking down hard on the accelerator). Above this shuddering, ear-stabbing noise, Camo Killer's voice roared through the horribly fragile barrier of the windscreen, right into my face: 'What's your name?'

Not really what I'd been expecting him to say, I must admit. In fact, it threw me so much that I drew in a breath to shout back, 'Rob!' But then I caught myself, and was heading towards, 'Who am *I*? Who the fuck are *you*?' before I remembered that he was a madman bent on shagging and killing me. *Of course* he hadn't said anything that I'd expected him to. That's how nutters function. They say, apropos of nothing, 'Have you got my aunt's sofa?' And then they stab you. Because they're nutters.

I clamped my mouth shut and wrenched the car heavily into reverse. I'd like to say that, even with my life in the balance, my basic humanity compelled me to send the car backwards rather than going forwards and running him over. But the reality was that reversing simply seemed the direction that was the most obviously and immediately *away*. My favoured option, were it available, would have been to have reversed, but at the same time machine-gunned him to death with heavy-calibre weapons mounted by the wing mirrors.

Once in reverse, I flinched my foot off the clutch and the car lunged back so quickly that my head flew forwards and hit the steering wheel, right where my hand was gripping it. Thus, hurting both my head and my hand. I really was having no luck at all tonight. The agony only lasted for a flicker, however, before the natural painkiller of distracting, constricting terror swept it aside as I realised that I'd pulled back too frantically and stalled the car. The silence of the engine shook me by the ears and – my breathing jammed into the 'off' position – I twisted at the car key damn near hard enough to snap it as my own voice screeched in my head, '*Don't snap it, you stupid fucker!*'

Camo Killer had been briefly unbalanced as the car he was resting on had leapt away from under his hands. He didn't go as far as to fall, or even have a good stumble (which, I thought, would have been the decent thing to do), however. He merely lost his physical equilibrium for a moment, and was then back in control – and beginning to come towards me looking, it's safe to say, 'miffed'.

I wrung the key in the ignition again. He marched forwards, but not to the position he'd occupied before; he came round the side of the car this time, heading towards my door. The engine caught. He'd started to crouch down, so as to be the same height as my window – he was so close now that I could see the folds of fabric curling around where the powerful bulk of his upper body untidily distorted his camouflage top. He reached out to my door handle – but then he seemed to be snatched away. Really, of course, he stayed where he was, but I'd got the car moving once more and sped backwards.

I reversed, so fast that I was barely in control, for about fifteen yards and then knocked the engine into first. I wasn't about to take the time to do a three-point turn. Instead, I swung around in a semi-circle, mounting the pavement with a vertebrae-kicking crunch halfway through the manoeuvre. When I was safely heading in the opposite direction, I looked (not trusting the rear-view mirror again) over my shoulder to check on Camo. He obviously saw me do this because, standing calmly in the middle of the road, he stabbed his finger at me and shouted something, but I couldn't hear what it was.

I turned away from him, and my face folded with concentration as I tried to match the shape of his mouth to an actual sound. 'Larks'? Why would anyone shout 'larks'? Does he think the birds are out to get him? Is that the root of his madness – some kind of avian persecution complex? Christ – now that really *is*— My eyes paused on the dashboard. 'Lights.' I switched on my headlights. Right. OK, fair enough – even murderous psychos are concerned with road safety at some level, I suppose.

I pulled out my mobile and rang Central. Luckily, Jenny was still in the studio.

'Jenny? Listen – there's some kind of freak outside the station.'

'What kind of freak?'

'A weirdo in camouflage gear – he was hiding in the car park. He followed me down the street and jumped on to my car.'

'God – are you OK?'

'Yeah, I'm fine, but he might hang around there. Be careful. Have Geoff leave the security desk for a while and escort you to your car.'

'Right . . . Um – Keith's already started down . . .'

'Ahh . . .'

'Well . . . I should warn him.'

'Yes. You should.'

'Yes . . . I mean . . . We have to warn Keith, yeah?'

'Absolutely.'

'Because we wouldn't want him to be attacked by a maniac, would we?'

'No. Not at all.'

'So . . . I'll go and do that straight away, then, Rob.'

'Straight away, Jenny. Yes.'

'Rob . . . ?'

'Yes?'

She paused for a few seconds. I paused with her.

'Oh shite,' she said, at last. 'It's like that moral dilemma of whether you'd kill Hitler when he was a child . . . OK, OK. I'm going to warn Keith now – I just hope history forgives me.' She hung up the phone.

FIVE

I didn't know whether to tell Jo everything as soon as I got back to the house. I mean, I thought it was pretty newsworthy: being psychologically reborn *and* escaping from a berserk assailant all in the one night. But, against this, one had to weigh the fact that Jo could be, well . . . 'irritable' if you woke her up early. She could be really quite strikingly irritable. And it's a bit crap to evade a psychotic attacker, only to go home and get killed by your girlfriend.

Aware of this, I crept into the bedroom and tried to decide whether I should rouse Jo or not. I moved around the bed, looking down at her lying there in deep, mouth-open slumber; a soft motor of steady snoring ticking over at the back of her throat. I was still considering my options carefully when I tripped over some shoes and fell into the wardrobe.

'Fuck!' *Thud!* 'Fuck!'

'Nnerr . . .' Jo stirred. She raised herself up on one elbow and did a sloppy approximation of peering around the room (her eyes remained closed and her head didn't so much rotate as fall from one position to another, as though her neck had been de-boned). She looked a little like a newly born mouse sightlessly sniffing the air.

'Oh,' I said, upbeat with surprise. 'You're awake, then?'

'What? I . . . Was there . . . ?' She was groping for her brain's 'on' switch. 'What time is it?'

'I'm not sure. But anyway, as you're still up, I've got something to tell you.' I took a big, deliberately audible breath, by way of a drum roll. 'It's OK, Jo . . . It's all going to be O – K. I've taken hold of things and turned them

43

around. You said I needed to change, and I have done. I changed tonight. I thought about what you said, and how much I wanted to make things right, for us. I attacked the situation head on . . . and I beat it – faced it down. Everything is OK now.'

'Jesus fucking Christ! It's quarter to four!'

'And I was attacked in the street.'

'It's still the middle of the bastard night!'

'I love you.'

'What the fucking hell are you talking about at a quarter to four in the fucking morning?'

Out of bullets, Rob – retreat!

'I think I'll go downstairs and put the kettle on.'

I fled to the kitchen while Jo was still scaling the ragged horror of being woken up in the vicinity of 4 a.m. – when her mind had finally climbed over this frustrating mountain, I didn't want it to immediately find me standing on the other side.

While I hid out, I made myself an Irish coffee. It was a Rob's Irish Coffee: get half a mug of whisky, a spoonful of instant, top up with hot water and add some cream (if you have it). (If not, milk.) (And, to be honest, you can pretty much do without the milk too.) I was in the dining room, hunched over my mug like someone inhaling a cold cure, when Jo shuffled in. She was wearing her lilac Next pyjamas with the kitten on the front, and her hair appeared to be in some distress.

She rounded the table and flopped heavily into the chair opposite me, then pulled my coffee away to in front of her, and blew on it. 'So . . .' She took a sip, thought hard for a moment, then repeated, 'So?'

'So . . . I've sorted myself out,' I replied.

Her hand moved up to intercept a clump of hair that had fallen over her face; she caught it and imprisoned it behind her ear. She stared at me and nodded, wordlessly.

'I have, Jo,' I said.

'How? Tell me what happened. Oh, and please go slowly – keeping in mind that I'm still legally asleep.'

'Well, you know how you always say people shouldn't keep things bottled up?'

'Do I?'

'Don't you?'

'Fuck knows. Maybe. It's four in the morning. Remembering where "downstairs" is took me five minutes.'

'Well, whatever. I think you say that. And, even if you don't, loads of people *do*. They're forever saying it.'

Jo did one of those yawns that are so huge that they make the bones in your ears click. I took this as a sign to press on swiftly.

'Anyway. I thought, what better way to more conclusively not bottle something up than to talk about it on a radio show? Just go in there, sit down by the mike, and let it all out.'

'And Keith was OK with you doing that?'

'Hold on, I haven't finished telling you about this. So—'

'On a jazz-music show?'

'So, that's what I did. I told the whole story. What had happened. How it had made me feel. The questions it had forced me to ask myself. It was wonderful, Jo. *Freeing*. A talking cure. Saying it out loud, publicly, was like shedding clothes – a bit scary at first, but as I cast them off I felt more and more light and unencumbered. I can think clearly now; I've washed the mud from my mind.'

'Are you sure?'

'Positive.' I reached across the table and picked up her hand. 'I'm back to normal, thank God.'

She gave me a sleepy smile. 'You were never exactly normal, babe.'

'Well, I'm back to the slight deviant you agreed to marry, then.'

Jo smiled again and squeezed my hand. We sat there for a moment. Happy.

'Oh,' I went on, finally, as I rose from the table, 'but Keith says I'm probably fired. Do you want a biscuit?' I was heading for the kitchen.

Jo's hand whipped out. She caught me before I reached the door – grabbing the inside of my leg from behind. 'What? You got *fired*?'

I looked back at her. 'It's not important,' I replied.

'Then why are you crying?'

'I'm not crying, it's just . . .'

'What?'

'It's just that you pinched the skin on the inside of my leg, OK?'

'Jesus.'

'Hey – it makes your eyes water, getting pinched there . . . Don't look at me like that – it really bloody hurts, Jo. Shall I pinch *you* there?'

'Never mind about that. What's this about you getting fired?'

'I didn't say I was fired.'

'You did.'

'No, I didn't. I said I was *probably* fired.'

'How probably?'

'Um . . . *very* probably.'

'Oh, my God.' Jo turned away from me, back towards the table. I returned to my seat so that I could face her. She was sipping from the mug of coffee, and her eyes were unfocused by deep thought.

'Look, Jo . . . Keith is going to try to get me fired, yes – but there's absolutely no guarantee he'll be able to do it.' She peered at me questioningly. 'It's just as likely,' I continued, 'that he'll only be able to have me cut back to a single slot a week.'

'Oh, my God.' Her eyes had gone again. 'That's the end of the wedding, then. There's no way we can pay for everything now.'

'No – it'll be OK,' I said.

'Tch. We can barely afford it as it is. What chance have we got if you're not bringing in a proper wage?'

'It'll be tight, yes, but we'll manage. Don't worry. Though . . . maybe it would help to delay it. Just for a little while.'

Her eyes were right back now. Not just right there in her head, but burrowing into mine too. 'Is that what you want?'

'No, no. It's not what I want, but . . .'

'You're *sure*? You're sure that this isn't simply a way of you sabotaging the wedding?'

'Sabo—?'

'Subconsciously, I mean. Having second thoughts about us, and – instead of facing them head on – acting . . . well, so as to bring about a situation where the wedding has to be put off, maybe forever, but it seems like it's not your fault.'

'Jesus, Jo – no. Not at all.'

I was pulled, for some reason, in three different directions: (1) wanting to reassure Jo, (2) being angry with her, (3) feeling childishly embarrassed. The result of this interaction was a very curious and subtle blend of emotions, and, instinctively, I conveyed the complexity of it by shouting.

'If I hadn't done what I did tonight,' I continued, 'I'd still be in a mess mentally and there'd have been no wedding anyway. Can't you see that? Cheer up – we were fucked either way.'

'Right. So that's the bright side, is it?'

'Well . . . yes . . . Oh, and I count not being sodomised and killed as something of a plus too.'

'Keith threatened you with buggery and death?'

'No, no, I— Well, actually, I think he did at one point – he was behind the glass in the studio and I could only see the actions he was making. But I meant the nutter who attacked me.'

'*What?*'

'The one outside the station.'

'*What?*'

'I told you. I told you upstairs that someone attacked me.'

'I didn't hear that.'

'Well, I said it.'

'Did you say it right after I was wrenched out of a deep sleep by the sound of you shoulder-charging a wardrobe at four a.m.?'

'Then, or thereabouts.'

'Well, it obviously didn't register, did it? So, what the hell happened? Are you hurt?'

I looked down at my knuckles, which *were* slightly sore; I rubbed them and grimaced. 'No,' I said. 'I'm fine.'

Jo reached across and took hold of my hand again – this time examining it carefully.

'Did you punch him?' she asked. She was, despite herself, quite impressed – I could tell by the tone of her voice.

'What? Oh. No. Not exactly.'

'What do you mean "not exactly"? What happened to your knuckles, then?'

'I head-butted them.'

'You head-butted them?'

'Yeah. My hand was on the steering wheel, and I head-butted it while I was trying to reverse away from the guy in panic.'

'Right,' she said (the impressed tone not especially noticeable in her voice this time).

'I head-butted it *really hard*,' I said, aiming to claw back a little admiration.

'I see.' Jo gave me my hand back. 'So, who was it who attacked you, then? What happened, exactly?'

'I left the station and I think he must have been waiting for me. I spotted him, though, and made a run for my car. He came after me, but I got inside just in time. He jumped on the bonnet—'

'Jesus – he jumped on the bonnet of the car?'

'Yes. Well, kind of leaned on it – you know, *abruptly*.'

'OK.'

'And heavily. Abruptly and heavily. Then he ran around to the side of the car and tried to get in my door. I *threw* the engine into reverse, *screeched* backwards—'

'Head-butting your hand.'

'No – that was a little earlier.'

'Earlier?'

'Yeah, well, I'd actually tried to reverse away before he came around to the side. But I stalled the car.'

'Right. So you head-butted your hand and stalled the car, and then—'

'And then I *threw* the engine into reverse, *screeched* backwards and *flung* the car around to face the other way – that's right.'

Jo twisted her lips in thought. 'Do you think he was a stalker?'

'A *stalker*?' I asked, confused.

'You said he was waiting for you. Do you think it was some kind of obsessive fan?'

'No. No, I didn't mean he was waiting for me specifically. I just meant that I thought that he was probably waiting for someone to leave the station, and that person turned out to be me.'

'Are you sure?'

'Yeah.'

'Only it'd be useful to have a fan, wouldn't it?'

'I *do* have . . . I mean, there are a few people who've written in to the show. One guy has written in three times.'

'That's not exactly dazzling, is it, Rob?'

'I'm a jazz presenter. It's not about me, Jo – it's about the music,' I said, a little defensively.

Jo patted my hand and said, 'Yes – of course it is, babe.' Which made me feel a good deal less better. 'It'd be something you could use, though, wouldn't it?' she continued. 'If they're thinking about firing you, then having a stalker in your corner would help no end. It'd suggest that you had a real connection with the audience – the station might be wary of losing that.'

'Not as wary as I am about the prospect of being buggered and killed.'

'Why do you think he wanted to bugger you?'

'It was just a feeling.'

'Hmmm.'

'And, anyway, he definitely wasn't a stalker.'

'How do you know? How can you say for sure that it wasn't you, specifically, that he was waiting for?'

'Because I've just remembered that he shouted at me. He shouted, "What's your name?" It was above the noise of the engine, but I'm sure that's what he said. If he's completely obsessed with me to the point of murderous, sexual frenzy, but he's still got no idea what I look like, then he's either the world's most incompetent stalker, or he seriously needs to get his priorities sorted out. He'd only have to write to Central enclosing a stamped, addressed envelope and they'd have sent him a publicity photo.'

'OK . . . maybe. But then, publicity photos aren't very good likenesses, are they? He might not have been sure it was you. You do look . . . you know.'

'What?'

'You look different in your publicity photo.'

'You were going to say "better", weren't you?'

'Well, it's a publicity photo – it's designed to show you looking good.'

'And I don't look good otherwise? I look so far from good, in fact, that I wouldn't even be recognised, you mean?'

'I didn't say that.'

'Well – I looked good enough for him to want to bugger me.'

Jo didn't seem to know what to reply to this. One to me, I reckon.

'Look,' she continued after rubbing her forehead a little, 'all I'm saying is that he still *could* have been a stalker, and that having a stalker wouldn't be *completely* negative right at this moment.'

'OK.'

'Did you call the police?'

'No. I phoned the station and warned Jenny, but I didn't think there was any point calling the police. They wouldn't do anything. They *couldn't* do anything, for that matter. Even if they found him, what could they charge him with? Actually? "Running after someone"? "Leaning forcefully on the front of a person's car"? When there are gangland shootings happening here all the time, how much of a sentence do you think they'd hand down to someone for "being pretty scary"?'

'I suppose so.'

We fell into silence for a while.

'But who cares?' I said, brightening. 'That's minor stuff. Some nutter – and my job – are peanuts compared to me getting myself sorted out. My head's right now. That's more important than everything else put together.'

'Yeah,' said Jo, still a little downbeat. Then she smiled.

'*Yeah* – you're right, babe. Of course you're right.' She leant across the table and kissed me. 'Come on – let's go to bed.'

I put my arm around her, and we went upstairs and had some really very satisfactory sex; after which I slept better and deeper than I had in weeks.

SIX

The next day Jo came into the bathroom while I was standing there about to have a shower. Or about to have a bath. I'd been standing there for a little over an hour and a quarter.

SEVEN

I arrived at Central FM that night with only a few minutes to go before the show started. Keith had called my mobile several times, but I could see it was him on the caller display and so I didn't answer. There was no point listening to him shout at me to hurry up or call me a twat, because I didn't want to hurry up, and I knew I was a twat. And it wasn't as if he could get much more pissed off with me, so my not answering the phone hardly mattered on that account.

When I'd gone to sleep, I'd thought I'd be sitting in the studio in an impregnable bubble of happiness today. Yes, Keith would still be grim and vindictive, and, yes, I'd probably soon be looking at rather fewer running orders and rather more unemployment-benefit forms, but that wouldn't matter. I'd be in my own contented shell, and nothing would be able to touch me.

But that dream had collapsed. Now Keith was crap, my life was crap, and I was crap. The best I could do was to try, for as long as possible, to keep it down to only two of those elements being in my face at any one time. Also, and unconnected to the fact that I was deliberately dragging my feet, I'd been late leaving the house. Jo, suddenly noticing the time, had needed to march upstairs and intervene in my underpants selection – which had by then clocked up thirty-five minutes and was still going nowhere.

I wasn't wearing any socks at all.

When I'd gone to sleep, everything was going to be all right . . . but, all too quickly, I'd woken up.

I was poring over my own misery so completely that I

was inside the building that housed Central FM before I remembered about the nutter from the previous night. Had he been waiting for me – like a stalker, say – he'd have had no trouble; he could have pounced, knocked me to the ground and eaten most of one of my legs before I'd even begun to focus on anything but the general shittiness of my broad personal circumstances.

Geoff, the security guard, was sitting behind the reception desk, reading a newspaper (the receptionist herself left at six). I paused in front of him as I walked by. 'Geoff? Was everything OK here last night?'

'Yeah.' He carried on reading his paper and didn't look up.

'Right . . . Only I had a bit of trouble . . .'

Geoff turned to the lifestyle section.

'I had a bit of trouble. And I phoned back here to tell Jenny.'

'Yeah.'

A good ten seconds ticked by.

Geoff continued. 'She told me. I escorted her to her car. And had a look around. No one about.'

'OK . . . Thanks.'

Looks like the guy last night was simply some random, opportunist nutter after all, then. He must have moved on after I'd got away from him, and was now most likely back where he'd come from. Walsall, probably. I thanked Geoff again, and made my way up to the studio.

'Where the fuck have you been?' Keith shouted the instant I walked in through the door. He jumped to his feet – lacerated strips of tangerine peel flying from his lap and scattering across the floor as he did so.

'Nowhere,' I shrugged, in the manner of a sullen fourteen-year-old.

'Christ. I . . . Oh, never mind. As long as you're here, that's all that matters.' He came over and gave me a hug.

Well, *this* wasn't right. This wasn't right at all.

Keith leaned back from me, smiling warmly – as though I were a beloved son returned at last from the war. His arms were outstretched and his hands fastened to the sides of my shoulders. He gave me a friendly little shake.

'Er . . . Keith . . .' I said, cautiously. 'Have you found Jesus?'

Keith laughed like someone in a musical, and gave me yet another friendly little shake. 'You've no idea, have you?' he said.

'About what?'

'You're a star, mate – that's what.'

I looked over at Jenny. She smiled at me too; though, unlike Keith, it wasn't scary when she did it. 'What's he on about?' I asked her.

'You've become a bit of a celeb on the Net, apparently,' Jenny replied.

I instantly had a vision of dozens of photographs of me naked having been plastered all over some seedy Website. Before I could stop it, the idea tragically gave me a tiny thrill. Except, as far as I knew, there weren't any photographs of me naked in existence. And, really, it's the kind of thing I think I would know about, if there were.

'What?' I said.

Keith took over. 'It seems that someone who was listening last night started talking about you on one of those Internet chat things. People began to visit our Webpage to listen to the archive of the show. Word spread, it was picked up by sites that do listings of interesting links, and it got mentioned in some . . . um, what did Danny say they were called, Jenny?'

'Blogs.'

'That's it. They're like online diaries or something – nerds talking to themselves in public. Anyway, the upshot is that you've become a little bit of a phenomenon. Our site's had a crazy amount of visits – from all over the world. More people have accessed the online archive of last night's show in the past day than would have listened to you here in an entire week.'

I nodded, thoughtfully. 'Right.'

Well, that was good. I mean, even considering that my weekly listening figures rarely peaked higher than the bottom reaches of 'miserable', it was still good to have topped them, online, in a single day. I was popular. And, because I was popular, Keith was happy with me. I'd been wretched all day and, to be quite honest, I was settled in now. It wasn't easy to let go – I'd got it nailed. There was a good deal of inertia urging me to remain comprehensibly fed up, but I was finding it hard to devise a way of characterising this new information in a fashion that didn't make it look like Good News.

'Three minutes,' said Jenny.

'God!' Keith cheerfully started to bundle me through the control room, in the direction of the door to the studio. 'Quick, Rob – get in there and let them have it. We expect *masses* of people to be listening to the show streaming via the Webpage tonight.'

'OK. Um – great.' I was a bit flustered by all this – quite excited, obviously, but a little wrong-footed too. 'Is everything ready? Where's the playlist?'

'The playlist?' said Keith, as though I'd made a bizarre and funny request.

'Yeah – is it already in there?'

'No.' Keith smiled indulgently and looked at me like I was a little slow. 'No, of course not. There isn't a playlist. There isn't even a running order, really. You just go in there and do exactly what you did last night – what you did for the final half of the show.'

'But . . . I didn't do a show for the final half of the show,

Keith. I *stopped* doing the show and just . . . you know . . . talked about the problems I was having.'

'Yes – that's it. Do that again.'

I looked across to Jenny. She was staring down at the control desk, hard. I looked back to Keith.

'Do it *again*? Never mind the fact that last night you wanted to have me physically injured for doing it at all – even if we ignore that – how could I possibly do it again? It was a cathartic thing. I did it to get everything out of my system and start afresh. How can I do that *again*?'

Keith could have replied that I could easily do it again, as it had strikingly failed to work the first time. Luckily, though, he didn't know that it hadn't worked – and I wasn't about to offer him that piece of information right now, as whether it had worked or not wasn't the point. Not that I was precisely sure what the point was. But I was sure what it wasn't. And that wasn't it.

'Just . . .' Keith waved his arms about a bit, illustratively. 'Do.'

'I can't.'

'You *have* to.'

'What do you mean, I have to? I present a jazz show. Line some songs up and I'll do the show: the same as I've always done.'

Keith wasn't smiling any longer. 'No, you won't. Do you imagine people will be listening in tonight to admire Wallace Roney's trumpet technique? Do you think a single one of them gives any kind of a fuck about Mulgrew Miller? This buzz we've got going started because they heard you losing it on air – not because of some bloody jazz instrumentals and a bit of tedious chatter.'

'But—'

'In the Internet chat rooms, they were having bets about whether you'd break down entirely before the show ended.

One guy was certain you'd start speaking in tongues at any moment.'

'But I don't—'

'We've got thousands and thousands of listeners out there just waiting for you to start spilling your emotional guts again. What do you think will happen if we give them a nice bit of piano playing instead?' As he said the listeners were 'out there', Keith pointed towards the door. I looked over at it, and couldn't help imagining suffocating numbers of people all crammed together on the other side – jostling for the keyhole, packed into the corridor, bulging in the stairwell, jamming the reception area, carpeting the car park, and flooding over the street outside the station.

'But I can't, Keith.'

'One minute,' said Jenny.

Keith gripped me by the shoulders again, but this time there were no smiles and no friendly little shakes. 'You *can* and you *will*, you selfish shit-stick. This is my chance, Garland. I'm forty-one years old and I'm stuck producing pointless shows at a ludicrous local radio station. Half of our airtime is taken up with adverts for bloody car-finance packages – I have "terms and conditions apply" burned into my brain; it repeats over and over in my head whenever I try to get to sleep. Every fucking time I close my fucking eyes: "Ask for written details." I help third-rate presenters make third-rate shows that are really just a way of keeping the frequency open so that we can broadcast adverts for bloody car-finance packages. And do you know how we get away with it? We get away with it because no one cares. Virtually no one listens, and those who do, don't care. Well, here's my chance to leave all this shite behind. If this show can make some news – create a bit of a stir and get a following – then I'll have a profile. I'll be able to get a job at a decent London station – maybe even a *national*.'

Keith began to bundle me through the door into the

studio. 'You're not going to blow this for me, Garland. If you want to keep not only your job but also your testicles, then sit down and give them what they want: voyeuristic, soul-baring, mad-as-a-fucking-hatter-ness.'

He pushed me towards the desk, and slammed the studio door closed – I thought for a moment that he was going to stand on the other side, guarding it. But he didn't. Instead, he jammed it shut with a chair.

On the surface in front of me were two piles of papers. One set had details of the phone calls about last night's show that the station had received during the day, and the other was a printout of the emails. I gazed back and forth between them in panic.

When I looked up, Keith and Jenny were both staring at me intensely through the glass. Keith was tearing the top off a plum with his teeth – like a soldier pulling the pin from a hand grenade. Jenny was counting me down from 'five'.

EIGHT

'And do you need to pee all the time?'

'No, Linda, I—'

Linda didn't let me finish. Linda was calling from Gornal and there was no stopping her.

'Don't you? Really? Only since my George died, that's the thing I've noticed the most. I used to go four, perhaps five, times a day – you know, average, like – but now. Well . . . Sometimes I have to go that often just during *Monarch of the Glen*. It's almost as if, when my George passed over, he took some of my bladder with him. I can't think why that would be. What does that mean? What do you think that means, Rob?'

'Er, well, I—'

Linda started up again. I sighed, leaned back, and decided to let her get on with it until she was stopped by Keith cutting her off, by the show ending, or by a sudden need to visit the lavatory.

Keith had arranged things so that we had become a phone-in show. Possibly it was because he was worried that I might dry up – and, if that happened, he didn't want to lose listeners by playing any jazz – or maybe it was because he thought that the kind of people who call local radio stations at 1.30 in the morning might tip me over the edge into entertaining hysteria. Probably, it was a little of both. In fact, the callers were by no means all from our area. The audience listening via the Web meant we were getting calls from all over the country, and emails from all over the world. Interestingly, however, though the audience was now both far larger and also global – spanning all manner of locations, time zones and cultures – nearly everyone who called or emailed was still precisely the kind of person who would call a local radio station at 1.30 in the morning.

These people hadn't got a clue.

They didn't understand what I'd said – let alone what I was experiencing. They were telephoning the show and telling me that someone they knew had died at some point during the past fifty or sixty years. Or they were telling me about meaningless coincidences that had happened to them – 'And, do you know, it turned out that they were *my* sunglasses . . . Makes you think, eh?' – or, more often, had happened to a friend's brother-in-law or someone they'd met on the train or a bloke in Korea they'd read about in the *Daily Mirror*. The ones who were emailing were largely the same, except that they were also frequently telling me that I was a fucker.

I'd tried restating my situation, but those who didn't simply ignore what I was saying completely actually became combative; rational thought seemed to anger them. In fact, during the entire three hours of the show I received only one piece of feedback that wasn't utterly wearisome. And that wasn't because it was interesting or informative or helpful – it was because it was a little unsettling.

It was from someone called Beth, it had arrived early in the morning (after last night's show), and she said she could help me. If a complete stranger turns up and says they can help you, you're immediately uneasy, right? So, even as I'm reading the email, I'm instinctively checking that my wallet is still safe. Beth didn't make me feel any less tight around the shoulders by then telling me that I was in danger. The words she used, in fact, were 'Your life is in danger', which made it even worse. It made it more specific than general 'danger', somehow; it pinpointed the danger in a depressing location – if something of mine is going to be in danger, then I'd rather my life weren't that thing, really. The tone of the email was the third shivery thing. First of all – though she didn't give anything that could be confused with actual details – it was clear that she didn't mean my life was in danger in some kind of spiritual fashion. She didn't fear for my chi or anything like that: she meant that I was at practical, physical risk. The other thing about the tone of the mail was that it was very measured. It didn't rave or rant, the grammar and spelling were correct, and it was coherently structured. It didn't read like the foaming of an Internet weirdo; it read like medical notes. It read as though a hospital consultant had examined me, made a considered diagnosis – 'Life in danger' – and then written it up in my records for the junior doctors to refer to. The confident but calm authority of the voice made it hard for me to close my mind to it.

The final disturbing thing about this email was that it had come directly to me.

That's to say, Beth hadn't emailed the Rob Garland address that was given out for general show feedback – the address to which all the other emails that had come in that night had been sent. Beth had sent it to my private Central FM address. I used this address as my own, personal account now, but it had been set up originally for internal mail. Everyone here had a private Central FM email address – so that company info, exchanges between staff and so on didn't get dropped into the same account that the listeners, the public generally, and everyone everywhere with *Ch3@p Vl@gr@!!!* to sell had access to. Somehow, she knew my private address (sadly, her email had come from a standard Webmail account – rather than from a work address – so I didn't have a clue where she was).

The final words in the email were 'I know what it's like.' Had the mail begun in that way, it would have been an unremarkable sentence. Practically everyone who had contacted the show had opened with, 'I know how you feel, because . . .' before going on to tell me how they'd had a budgie that had died, or how they'd gone on holiday to Tenerife only to discover that their hotel room had been double-booked with someone who'd sat just two rows behind them in primary school, or how they were so confused by the pace of life nowadays and that they blamed these new ten-pound notes, computer games and Europe. Somehow, though, having it right at the end – and standing alone – gave it weight. It was neither clamouring impatiently for attention nor overeager to convince. It left things unspoken. Because it just 'knew'.

As I said, this email made my skin prickle a little, but it intrigued me too. I think I might have replied immediately – except I couldn't do that. Central FM's half an inch of a second-hand shoestring budget hadn't yet allowed the station to get around to installing networked PCs in the studios, as was standard in virtually every other station in the First World. The computer with Internet access was in the control room – Keith went through the emails, printed them off and (just in case I'd try to make a break for it if given the chance) pushed them under the door. I'd read the email, been a bit creeped, then rather curious, and then, thinking about it, had asked Keith over talkback, 'Hey, Keith? How come you can access my private email account, you bastard?'

Keith replied, 'Does it make you feel angry? Good – use that.'

I looked up at the clock. The show was almost over. Three hours of my life had gone. Linda, I discovered as my mind drifted back to earth, was now talking about spirit

64

mediums. I had no idea how she'd got there, and, quite honestly, I didn't care.

'Linda . . . ? Lin—' I attempted to interrupt. 'Lind— . . . Linda – *shut up, you idiot woman!* What are you going on about? Are you a *complete* moron? I don't need a medium. When have you ever heard someone who claims to be speaking to the dead say anything useful? They always say stuff like, "He's telling me . . . you have a picture on the mantelpiece. Have you got a picture on the mantelpiece? Have you, Beryl? Yes. Yes, he can see it. He's telling me." What the hell is the sense in that? If I'm getting a message from beyond the grave, then tell me something useful. Tell me about the mechanics of exist-ence, so I can use the knowledge to take practical actions. Don't say, "It's very comfortable here," or, "Your grand-dad loves you," and certainly don't start telling me what my own house looks like – I *know* what my own house looks like; why are you reaching out from the afterlife just to tell me what my own house looks like? You know, almost as though the medium were merely performing some age-old party trick. But it fools you, doesn't it, Linda? It fools you, and thousands of others – and I suspect some of the "mediums" even fool themselves into believing it. And you know why? Because you only hear what you want to hear, and you want to hear it so much that, in your heads, *everything* sounds that way. I tell you about my problem, and you come back with rambling nonsense about mediums and dead pets and aliens.' In fact, I didn't recall anyone mentioning aliens. But, it was surely only a matter of time, and, in any case, I was angry as a wasp and in gear now. 'Don't talk to me about this rubbish when I could be dead at any moment. I could be dead this time tomorrow because I wore a blue jumper, or dead because I didn't wear a blue jumper, and I've no crapping, crapping, *crapping* way of knowing which jumper it is I should wear. No one is giving me any help here. You're all useless! You're all useless, and I hope you die!'

I tore off my headphones, pushed my chair away from the desk and sat there, taking deep breaths.

After two or three seconds, I felt I'd regained my composure enough so that there was a less than even chance of my running around the studio shrieking incoherently and tearing at my clothes. I looked up and saw Keith and Jenny both staring at me through the glass. Jenny's face was set, unmoving, into something between astonishment and fear. Keith looked and me, raised his eyebrows hopefully, and tapped his wristwatch. I glanced across at the clock again, then shuffled back to the desk and put my headphones back on.

'OK,' I said with professional easy-going cheeriness. 'This is Rob Garland winding up for tonight. Taking you through to breakfast is Tony Whyman. Are you well tonight, Tony?'

'Yes,' I heard Tony reply in my headphones, speaking from the studio on the other side of the building. 'I . . . Yes,' he added. Then Simply Red started playing.

'Brilliant!'

Keith had removed the chair that had been jamming the door shut and allowed me into the control room once more. He was now leaning back against the mixing desk beaming and showing me two ecstatically up-pointing thumbs. 'Brilliant! OK, it sagged a bit in places – we need to work on that – but we had enough weirdoes calling up to keep people interested, and the way you completely lost it at the end there . . . *Brilliant*. Roaring, hectoring, threatening to murder everyone—'

'I didn't threaten to murder everyone.'

Keith waved a dismissive hand at the nit-picking. 'Threatening to murder them, wishing them all dead – whatever. The point is, it was great radio.'

'I'm going home now,' I said.

'Yep. Sure . . .' Keith jumped forward and put his arm round me as I walked to the door. 'You get yourself back home. Have something to eat. Recharge your batteries. Maybe, you know, sit around for a while and brood on stuff . . .'

'Goodnight, Jenny,' I called without looking back.

'Bye, Rob,' she replied.

I walked all the way out of Central FM with my jaw locked tight and each of my footsteps an I'm-making-a-point-here stamp. When I got to the street, I looked down at my hands – held them, palms upwards, in front of me – and saw that they were shaking. Their involuntary movements, and their unnatural colour in the sodium street lights, made it feel as though they weren't really mine. I briefly wondered if they'd go for my neck (I'd seen enough movies to know that if, somehow, you'd ended up with someone else's hands, then it was pretty much inevitable that they'd turn out to be the hands of an executed strangler).

I dared them to make a move towards my throat. *Dared* them. I wasn't frightened. My hands weren't shaking with fear; they were shaking with anger – *revving* with it. I wasn't entirely sure who I was angry with – Keith, the listeners, everyone in the world, myself . . .

No, it was Keith. Keith's a cunt.

The others on the list were definitely in with a chance, though. Especially me – I was even more useless than everyone else. Everyone else was useless in a kind of uncomprehending, bovine way; I was useless even though

I could *see* I was useless. What a thoroughly useless prick. I stopped examining my quivering hands and instead made a fist with the right one and slammed it hard into the palm of the left. No, I wasn't frightened – I was just very, *very* angry.

That situation reversed itself amazingly quickly during the next twenty seconds.

NINE

I didn't hear him. I didn't hear him at all. The first I knew that he was there was when his hand came down on my shoulder.

Perhaps one reason I didn't hear him was that some thoroughly annoying car headlights distracted me. They came on – dazzlingly (is there *anything* more instantly aggravating than car headlights shining in your eyes at night?) – almost as soon as I got out on to the pavement. The car started up and began pulling across the road towards me. My guess was that the person in it was lost. He'd probably been sitting there weeping over an A–Z, never expecting to see anyone he could ask for directions at this time of night, but then had seen me and decided to plead with me to tell him where the council had hidden the M6. Well, shining his headlights into my face – on top of the mood I was in anyway – wasn't doing him any favours. I'd already almost decided that I'd misdirect the irritating git: a few casual lies about which way he should turn, and he'd be on the ring road – where, a few million years from now, archaeologists would find his fossilised remains. He was heading towards me at quite a pace but, suddenly, with a screech of tyres, he pulled up – stopping, with his engine running, in the middle of the road.

I paused, wondering what he was doing.

A moment later, the car started off again. At first, I thought it was coming towards me once more, but then it swung away and sped off into the night. What was that about? It was almost as if the driver had been scared away – had suddenly seen something that made remaining lost in

Birmingham preferable to pulling over where I was standing. Maybe the expression on my face conveyed exactly how pissed off I was with the world.

That's when the hand touched me. I spun around instantly – causing the huge, heavy fingers to lose their grip on my jacket as it twisted away from them. For the briefest instant, as I stood there looking at the hand's owner, I thought that this lightning swirl out from under his grasp – the instinctive immediacy of it, its recoiling-elastic speed – might be a factor in my favour. Maybe he'd mistake it for a sign of martial-arts training. Maybe he'd think me a ninja. But then I allowed for the fact that, as I'd whipped around, I'd also squealed, 'Aeei – fuck!' and put my hands up in front of my face like I was someone's mum panickingly trying to protect herself from the scary approach of a football. I don't believe ninjas do that.

He was dressed exactly as he had been the previous night: camouflage gear and boots. The combat jacket looked a little too tight for him – as though it had been an impulse buy; purchased without taking into account the amount of steroids he intended to inject later in the day – but otherwise his was the immaculately turned out look of a paramilitary maniac. The martial neatness was obviously part of the thing for him. ('I bet you put that stuff on to have a wank, don't you?' I'd certainly have said with a sneer. Had I been safely talking to him from Canberra via satellite.) What's more, he was not only broad and mad; he was also tall and mad. Standing close, facing each other as we were now, he was looking down from perhaps five or six inches above me. So, he was broad, tall, mad and right here. I assimilated all these things in the time it takes to blink. I rapidly absorbed the image, gathered all the information, and converted it into a sensation of icy coldness in my testicles.

Though I'd twisted around to face him, and taken a

couple of steps backwards, Camo Killer hadn't moved. Now, he peered at me for a motionless moment (I noticed that his face was surprisingly young), and then he began to move forwards.

'Please don't bugger me,' I said.

He pulled up abruptly at this. Then, slightly uneasily, shifted his weight from one foot to the other, and back again, before shrugging the reply, 'K.'

There was then a rather awkward pause – as though we'd hit a pothole in the etiquette. We were both a little stymied. I'd asked not to be sodomised, and he'd agreed to that request – so we had, you know, sort of made a connection there. I sensed that we found ourselves in that difficult social no man's land, where it was no longer clear whether it was the done thing to move right on to his savagely murdering me, or whether we ought to have a chat about what we'd each last seen at the cinema first. *I* had no idea what to do at all; if I tried to run away now – after he'd shown goodwill by taking anal rape off the agenda – would that be bad form?

He came to a decision much quicker than I would have, and moved towards me again. At the same time asking, in a strange voice, 'Who are you?' I instinctively pulled away from him, but found myself up against someone's garden wall – the sharp edges of its topmost bricks hit me in the small of my back. I was trapped and scared, and was so focused on these two things that I automatically, unthinkingly, replied, 'I'm Rob Garland.'

Fuck. What an *idiot*. He knew my name now. Even if I got away, he knew my name and could track me down. If – somehow, incredibly – I escaped tonight, that wouldn't be the end of it. In six months' time there'd be a window catch jemmied in the pitch-black night, and he'd slither into my bedroom. Defeated once, all sodomy assurances would be withdrawn – you could bet on that. I'd be wrenched out of an innocent sleep to find myself being buggered to death. Oh, Jesus. *Jesus*. When he'd asked who I was, why the *hell* didn't I reply, 'I'm Keith Jennings'?

His hand reached out – heading for my groin. I watched it coming in the famous slow motion that's produced when terror presses its retarding thumb against the wheel of time; I didn't even try to stop it. I don't think I was quite paralysed with fear – it was more that I was transfixed by it. I was horrifically fascinated in the same way that you can find yourself completely unable *not* to stick the tip of your exploring finger into the jagged hole in your tooth that's home to a naked nerve ending. I was, therefore, grateful, and surprised – and very, very grateful – when Camo Killer's hand stopped by itself, some ten inches away from my genitals. It froze there. Reaching out, but unmoving in the air. Did he expect me to move my groin up to meet it? 'Well . . . *that's* a bit presumptuous,' I thought. 'OK, I may be—' Then I realised that he was offering it for a handshake.

'I reckoned it was you,' he said. (Again the strangeness in his voice. An accent? Yes. He wasn't local – he wasn't even English.) ''Specially when I heard you speak . . . I've been listening to your show.' The accent was American. (Or Canadian. Is there any difference?) He smiled slightly.

His hand was still waiting there, and I tentatively reached out and shook it. 'Right.'

'I tried to speak with you last night.'

'I recall.'

'You're kind of nervy, ain't you?' He grinned. The fucker.

'No, in fact.' I leaned forwards a little. Not exactly towards him, but away from the wall behind me enough to reduce the possibility that the force with which I was pressing back against the top edge of it might actually sever my spine. 'I'm not usually nervous. I've just been having an . . . *unsettling* time lately. Things had been a bit up and down all over, and, in those circumstances, it's only natural that I'm not going to be happy as Larry if some huge twat in combat gear starts chasing me down a deserted street at three o'clock in the morning, OK? Chases me down the street, and then jumps on the bonnet of my car.'

'Ha – "bonnet". That's so *cute*. Anyways, I didn't jump on it.'

'Yes, you absolutely almost did . . . And then you creep up—'

'I didn't cre—'

'*Creep* up on me again tonight. I'm not *nervy*; I'm just understandably wary.'

'Well,' he said, beaming, and grabbing my hand to shake it again, 'you relax. I ain't going to hurt you.' Then, he brought up his other hand and clasped that over mine too. His mouth still smiled, but his eyes had become almost sad now. He lowered his voice and spoke as though the words needed to climb over a good deal of emotion to make it out.

Oh hell – he *fancied* me. Buggery was right back in the bleeding picture again, then.

Zach's Story

Man, I . . . All right: facts, yeah? Here's the intel. My
name is Zachary Patrick Thufvesson – Swedish father,
Irish mother – I'm twenty years old, and I'm from O'Neill,
Nebraska. So, OK, I enlisted straight out of high school. I
always knew I wanted to be in the army. My mother said
I should study; go get some qualifications. You know,
maybe do a deferred enlistment and have the military pay
my college fees. But I didn't want to wait; I knew what I
wanted to be, so what was the point hanging around in
school any longer? I'd been hanging around in school long
enough already. Still, to make her happy, I said I'd start by
signing up for just two years. Then, that was it. I was off,
man – MOS IIB – eleven-bravo – infantryman . . . Grunt.

And it was way cool.

I know some people are, like, not able to cope with the
demands and stuff, yeah? But for me it was a real experience and a real good opportunity for growth. I've always
been totally goal oriented. I, kind of, see a thing, and go
after that thing. And, if it don't work out, I sit there and re-
think the situation and go at it another way and stuff. You
know what I mean? I like the challenge, and I don't quit
until I've achieved whatever it is I'm trying to do. The
army is good for that. You have clear objectives and lots of
ways to stretch yourself physically, mentally and psychologically. And the guys you're there with? They're special,
man. They're not like your friends, not like people you
hang out with – they're your brothers. Really, they're your
brothers.

I got myself a new family. There was me, Joe, John and

Kyle – and we'd be on patrol together, or training, or playing softball, or, whatever, just sitting around talking, you know? When you're together so much, and you're facing the same things and looking out for each other, then you get to know people. Really know them – maybe more than you know yourself, even.

We were part of the peace-keeping force. Bosnia. For sure, the war was over long before we arrived, but there was still enough there to make the hairs on your neck prickle. You'd be in a village and every house would have ordnance scars on the walls – people living in homes covered in bullet marks and stuff, you know? Or, sometimes, one of the houses would have taken a shell direct, and only half of it would be left. It'd be all hollow, and with the broken beams and whatever sticking out – like the carcass of an animal that's died a while back, and it's been eaten out, and you've got the ends of its ribs exposed where the hide's come off. Most of the folks there just wanted to get on with their lives, but you always knew that you might come across someone with issues, or someone who'd done something in the past and would panic when he saw us approaching – thinking we'd come to get him, maybe. And, well, there's an angry, scared guy, and then there's an angry, scared guy with a bunch of rocket-propelled grenades in his basement, you know what I'm saying?

So, this one day, me, Joe, John and Kyle were out in a Humvee. We were just checking roads – sometimes the map tells you there's a road there, but there ain't one anymore; say, it's cratered and impassable now, or whatever. We'll do a tour and mark stuff so we can update the map back at base, or maybe try to fix the problem. So, right, we're driving down this track – it's no wider than our vehicle; we're brushing against the hedges on both sides. Then, suddenly, there's a fence. Just like that – right across the track. We figure the local farmer has put it there to keep his livestock in. On the one hand, it's good to see people reconstructing and moving on and thinking about everyday stuff, but on the other, he's, you know, built a fence across the road. Joe – Joe's the driver – Joe's like, 'Oh, come on, man,' because, as I said, there's no room to turn. He's now got to reverse the Humvee back along a narrow, winding track for like a half a mile or something until there's somewhere with a little space to manoeuvre. We all get out: Joe's whining, and Kyle's checking the GPS so he can mark the fence on the map, and John's stretching his legs – he finds a blackberry bush and starts popping them in his mouth; they can't have been ripe – must've been sour as hell: John'd eat anything.

Me, well, I'd been playing a computer game all the previous evening. I mean all *evening*. I was set on beating this thing. Kept losing, and starting again, and losing, and starting again. In the end, I wasn't even enjoying it; I just couldn't bear to leave off – like it'd be a personal defeat or something. Anyways, staring at all them jerking pictures on the screen for hours and hours must've strained my eyes, because I got myself this real bad headache. I thought that a good night's sleep would cure it, but the darn thing was keeping me awake – like it was determined it was going to hang in there. It took a long time and a whole bunch of Advil before I finally managed to get some shut-eye. Next morning – which is, like, this morning, you know? – I got no headache, but I was real, real tired. At breakfast, before we went out on patrol, I had four cups of coffee to try to kick my eyes open. It worked well enough, but now, an hour or so later, I seriously needed to use the bathroom. Just beyond where we'd stopped, there was a group of trees, so I climbed over the fence and jogged into them to, well, answer the call.

So, I was relieving myself behind this tree. My . . . you know, ran down the bark, then back toward me; I looked down where it was heading, and I shuffled to the side a ways to avoid it. Know what the biggest danger is out there? In Bosnia? UXO: Unexploded ordnance. Mortars, shells, bombs – there's over a million mines still buried in that country, and no one knows exactly where they are. But I'd certainly found one of them. Yeah. One of them was right under my boot.

I don't mind telling you that I was scared, man. It was lucky I was already taking a pee, I reckon, or I might have peed myself anyhow. I mean, for sure, I could see by the fact that I wasn't dead and my leg was still there that the mine hadn't gone off. That was definitely a positive. It didn't mean it was a dud, though. Maybe it was the kind that detonates when you take your weight off of it, or maybe it was timed, or maybe it was just a mite faulty – a wire half-broken or a trip partly jammed – and the extra disturbance of me moving away would be just the nudge it needed to explode back into life – and for me to explode out of it.

At first, I was frozen, you know? Frozen with panic. Then, I got control of myself and decided that the best thing I could do was to stay perfectly still. Which is what I was doing anyway, being frozen with panic and everything. So, in real terms, not a lot changed, operationally. I'm thinking what to do next, when I hear Kyle call to me. 'Zach! Come on, man – we're heading out.'

'I can't move!' I call back.

'What?' he asks.

'I can't move. I'm kind of standing on a mine.'

'A mine?'

'Yeah.'

'All right . . . All right – don't move.'

'OK.'

I hear him tell Joe to radio back to base and request support, and then he shouts up to me again. 'Zach?'

'Yeah?'

'Don't move.'

'I am.'

'No – don't!'

'No, no . . . I meant I am *not moving*.'

'Right. Good. Keep doing that – I'm coming over to take a look . . .'

'No, man – stay there!' I shout back to him. 'There's nothing you can do, and, if this thing goes off, I don't want it taking you out too.'

He pauses for a couple seconds, then he calls, 'I'm in command here, Zach, I think I need to—'

'I know you're in command,' I cut in. 'And I also know what a mine can do to a person. And I know you have a wife and a kid . . . send Joe up here.' There's a silence, and, despite the fact that I'm standing alone behind a tree in Bosnia with my foot on an explosive device, I can't help laughing. 'I'm kidding, Joe – I'm kidding,' I call out.

'You are such *a jerk*,' Joe shouts back, and he's laughing, but I can hear in his voice that he's worried too.

'Look,' I say, 'I'll be happier waiting for the experts than for any of you coming up here and starting to poke around. None of you are qualified to disarm mines – it could turn out to be kind of a steep learning curve, you know? And . . . well . . . if the thing just decides to go off, then that's that. I'm sure I'm going to get through this, but, if I don't, there's no sense any of you coming with me, right?' There was no response right away, so I called out again. 'Right?'

That's when I heard the engine and the noise of the impact. At first, it, like, completely threw me. I hear this huge bang, and so, obviously, the first thing I think is that the mine's gone off. Except, it clearly hasn't, because I'm looking down at my leg, and I'm not looking down at it *from the top of a tree or anything. Then, I realise that the sound came from back down on the track.*

I call out a few times, but there's no reply. I can't see what's happened. It might sound strange, but I swear to you it's true: the hardest thing I've ever done was not moving then. I knew there was a pretty good chance that, if I did move, then the mine would go off. But to just stand there, unable to see what had happened, was so tough, man. Then, after a minute or so of me calling, I heard a voice. But it wasn't Joe or John or Kyle's voice; it was Bosnian. I couldn't understand what the guy was saying, but I could hear that he was in a bad way. I shouted to him, but he just carried on talking to himself.

Not long after, the chopper arrived. They'd come with a mine specialist, and also brought along a medic. The mine guy eventually freed me – turns out that the mine hadn't been primed, though they found half a dozen others buried among the bunch of trees that were set, and would have taken me out in a second if I'd trodden on one of them. So, I didn't need a medic at all, luckily. The medic treated the Bosnian truck driver. It was too late for a medic to be of any use to Joe, John and Kyle.

The Bosnian was making a delivery of animal feed, and was drunk. He'd come careering along the track (the wrong track, as it turned out – he'd taken a false turn), rounded the bend and smashed right into our stationary Humvee. John and Joe were standing behind and were crushed between the two vehicles – they died instantly, the medic reckoned; maybe didn't even know a thing about it. Kyle was in front of the Humvee, and was hit by it as the Bosnian's pickup pushed it forward. Massive internal injuries. Maybe he remained conscious for a while – so he'd have lay there listening to me calling; heard me shouting out for them to tell me what had happened – or maybe he hadn't. There's no way we'll ever know about that.

We were soldiers, you know? They were soldiers. Sometimes you're going to lose someone. In war, sometimes the guy next to you is going to fall. You accept that. You prepare for it. You pray it don't happen, and, for sure, you don't think about it all the time, but you prepare a place somewhere inside: a place to put it if it does. If Joe or Kyle or John had taken a bullet, or gone up to the trees themselves and stepped on one of those live mines that I missed, then it would have been bad – real bad – but I could have accepted it. But to get taken away by some drunken Bosnian in a pickup full of pig feed? That's not right. I couldn't see how that was right. It was stupid. Just stupid, man – you know what I mean?

And it got to me. Losing my brothers – losing them like that – messed my head up. I had a few months to serve, and I got through them somehow, but . . . well, no one was busy suggesting I be given any nuke codes, if you know what I mean. When my time was up, I left. I'd always meant to re-enlist immediately, but that was over now; I just sat in my exit interview and said, 'I'm out.' And my CO – who'd normally try to persuade people to sign up again – replied, 'I'll do the papers.'

Then, I went home to O'Neill, where I totally lost it.

At least I had some, you know, structure in the army. I had something telling me what I needed to do, a plan to follow. Back home there was just me, and I fell to pieces, man. I plain fell to pieces and scattered across the floor.

TEN

Zachary Patrick Thufvesson rubbed a big hand over the top of his head, raking his cropped hair with his fingers. He stood there, not saying a word, and stared down at his boots, and I felt sorry for him.

'I know,' I said.

He looked up at me, and nodded.

In a way, that almost seemed enough – I didn't need to say anymore. At least, I didn't if he believed me. It was the same as with that email I'd read earlier in the night that had ended with 'I know what it's like.' The writer gave no details of *why* she thought she knew this – as practically everyone else who had contacted me had done. But she didn't need to. Because I believed her. Possibly the very fact that she *hadn't* tried to convince me made me believe her. Saying, 'I know,' just now made me realise what was really so – paradoxically – unsettling about that email: it was unsettling because it was comforting. Being told my life is in danger certainly flicked the nose of my attention, but what grabbed its whole face and held it was the feeling that another person understood what it was like. The wonderful sense that I wasn't alone; that there was someone else out there like me. The really unsettling thing about that email had been the releasing solace of a message that was warning me that I might die.

I wanted to pass the comforting part of that feeling on. 'I know,' I repeated, gently. 'I understand just how you feel, Zachary.'

'Zach – everyone calls me Zach.'

'OK – Zach. I understand, Zach. You're, um . . . "lost",
aren't you?'

'Well . . .'

'You're wondering what tiny, seemingly insignificant
thing you did actually saved your life. Deciding to play a
computer game? That extra cup of coffee? What was the
crucial moment where you chose A, not B, and unknow-
ingly set yourself on a course that bypassed death? And
you're wondering how on earth you're supposed to know
the next time you're at one of those moments.'

'Um, no . . . That's not really it.'

'Oh. Are you sure? Oh. OK, then. Well – right. *Yes*. I
suppose you're feeling guilty, then, right?'

'Guilty?'

'Yeah – you *told* the friends to stay where they were.
Told them not to come over to you – and staying where
they were meant they got killed. Hell, Zach – *don't blame
yourself for that*.'

Zach looked at me like I was a bit of an idiot. 'I don't.'

'Don't you?'

'No. Of course not. I was standing on a landmine. You
think I should have said, "Hey, guys! Come and look at
this!"?'

'Well . . . I just meant – if you'd have known how things
would turn out . . .'

'How could I have known that?'

'You *couldn't* have – that's the point.'

'What point?'

'The point of why you shouldn't feel any responsibility
for their deaths.'

'I don't.'

'None at all?'

'No.'

'Fuck – I would. You're a bit self-centred aren't you?'
I'd never cut it at the Samaritans.

I was about to continue consoling him, but Zach was keen to speak. Chirpily keen, in fact.

He grinned. 'I was all confused about "Why?", Rob. That's what tore at me, you know? What was the point? What was the meaning of this? I knew that it wasn't in my control – but life has to have a *meaning*, right? I fell around for months not having a clue what was going on; not having the smallest idea what was happening, and how I fitted into it.' He laughed at the memory. 'Man – I was a complete basket case.'

I smiled back at him. I knew that feeling.

'A *total* psycho,' he said, laughing louder.

'Yeah.' I was laughing too now.

'Hahaha . . . But that all ended when, one day – out of the blue – I suddenly realised the truth.'

'Which was?'

'That I'd been chosen by God.'

My hand slipped into my pocket and felt for the car keys. What was it? About ten yards away? If I made a run for it – without warning: just dashed off abruptly – maybe he'd be too surprised, and I'd manage to get there and lock myself inside before he had time to react.

No, that wouldn't work. He'd be too quick. I bet he trained his reflexes – probably at night, in forests, in the nude.

The expression I'd had a few seconds ago was now riveted on to my face as a static thing – like the grin of a ventriloquist's dummy. Zach was staring at me: beaming and looking like he expected a reply.

'Hahaha,' I said. I was aiming at a good-natured, non-committal and, above all, un-provocative laugh that conveyed nothing more than 'Well, well, well, eh?' I actually produced a flatly manic thing that was as taut as it was unnatural. If anyone had been watching the pair of us at this moment – Zach, smiling and open; me, rigid, wide-eyed and cackling in an eerie monotone – they'd have probably thought that *I* was the lunatic.

'Who else,' continued Zach, 'could have arranged it so that I'd be *stuck* away from everyone, in the cover of the trees, at that moment? To have seen to it that *I* wouldn't be standing by the Humvee too? Who, Rob? Who but the Big Man? Right?'

'Yes,' I said, gently edging away. 'Now you say it, it's *obvious*.'

Slowly drift towards the car, Rob. That's it. Slow and steady.

'But there was a problem,' Zach said, waggling a finger in the air.

'A problem?' I echoed – serving up a 'Surely not?' expression, with a side order of 'What *can* that be?' you've-got-me bewilderment.

'Yeah. For sure, I'd been chosen by God . . . but what *for*?'

'Well, you know . . . does it *matter*? It's just nice to be picked, really, isn't it?'

'No, no, there had to be a reason. There's a reason for everything, isn't there? Why had God saved me?'

'Hmmm – it's a thinker all right.'

I was managing to inch along, getting nearer and nearer to the car; but, tragically, this didn't mean that I was getting farther and farther away from Zach. As I moved imperceptibly down the road, he moved imperceptibly along with me, always maintaining the same distance between us.

'I had a bunch of money saved from my time in the service, so I sat down with my folks,' I tried to picture Zach's parents. All I could see was his mother: she was stuffed and in a rocking chair in the attic, 'and I hammered things out.' ('Hammered'? Sweet *Jesus*.) 'OK, I'd gotten

84

my head together now . . . but I couldn't settle until I found out what the Lord wanted me to do.'

My fingers finally touched the door handle on the car. I carefully peeled the keys from my pocket, keeping absolutely unbroken eye contact with Zach all the time – in the hope that this would somehow prevent him from noticing that I was making preparations to flee in terror.

Cack.

I'd parked the car legally.

It was facing in the direction of traffic, which meant that the driver's door was on the other side – away from where we were on the pavement. Should I try to work my way around, hoping Zach would be too busy with his personal update of the Bible to realise what was happening? Or should I simply open the passenger door, scramble in, lock it, and crawl across to the other seat? The second option seemed better, because it got me into the car quicker.

'I decided,' continued Zach (sufficiently enthusiastic about what he was saying that he seemed unaware of my fiddling with the car door behind me), 'that the logical thing to do was to return to the place where God had selected me.'

'Yes,' I nodded. (Come on, come *on* . . . get in there and unlock, you bastard – how difficult can opening a locked car door in secret behind your back while in mortal terror possibly be?) 'That does seem like the logical move.'

'So, I caught a plane— Bosnia is in Europe, you see.'

'Ah.'

'Ha – sorry, man. You knew that, right?'

'Well, I had heard *something* . . .'

'OK, so I caught a plane to come over to Europe . . . but, guess what?'

'Fuck!'

The key had not only refused to sink home properly – yet again – but this time it had skidded away abruptly, causing my hand to jerk downwards, catching a passing knuckle agonisingly on the lock as it did so. If I survived this night with 'Zach the Mad: Servant of the Lord', I was getting a car with electronic central locking, never parking legally again, and, now I came to think about it, having a lot more sex with Jo.

Zach peered at me deeply.

'Fuck!' I quick-thinkingly repeated. This time nudging the inflection away from a cry that indicated frustration and unexpected hand injury, and into one that spoke of excited fascination. 'Fuck! Go on – *please.*'

'Um . . . well . . . OK, so – guess what? Something made me decide not to buy a ticket direct to Sarajevo. I deci— Oh, Sarajevo is—'

'The capital of Bosnia. Yes, I know.'

'Right – for sure – sorry. Of course you do – you're European, ain't you?'

'I . . . Yes, that's it – go on.'

'*Something* made me decide to go through Europe on the way. Now, I'm not saying that I actually heard the voice of God telling me to do this . . .' He laughed.

I laughed in reply. *Christ.*

'No,' he continued, 'it wasn't that obvious . . . but I *did* think that this journey across to Sarajevo would be a kind of pilgrimage. That's the very word that came into my head, Rob – *pilgrimage* . . . It certainly makes you think, doesn't it?'

'*Oh* yes.'

'So, I flew to Edinburgh, Scotland. Cool place – they have this big castle, you know? And lots of other neat stuff. I was talking to a waitress there, and she said there are ten branches of Starbucks in the city now too. So, it's like this really amazing blend of the ancient and the modern.'

'Wow.'

'Yeah. Anyway, I stayed for a while, and then caught the train down to London. But – guess what?'

'What?'

Had I bent the key? Maybe I'd bent the key during one of my frantic and failed attempts? It didn't seem to want to fit in the lock, however much I panicked at it. Perhaps I'd never open the door. Perhaps I'd try and try until Zach finally became violent and killed me or, possibly even worse, trapped me here listening to him forever.

'You'll never guess,' Zach assured me, with a grin.

'OK.'

'This is *really* going to freak you out.'

'OK.'

'*The train was delayed at Birmingham!*'

'No!'

'I *swear* to you, man. I was sitting there and they announced that there was a fault with the overhead power cables or something. What are the chances?'

'Incalculable.'

'So, for sure, I knew that was a sign to get off at Birmingham. Which I'd never intended to do, obviously, because there's nothing here. But then it gets even wilder.'

'You're kidding me?'

'No, man, it *does*. I get myself a place to stay, and I'm just laying in my room, right? Because there's nothing here to see, or do, or anything, I'm just laying in my room, staring at the ceiling, with the radio on. Like, all day. Waiting for the next sign. And guess what?'

'You hear my show?'

'*I hear your show, man!* I totally hear your show.'

'Yessss!' The car door's lock had finally surrendered to my key.

'Yes!'

'What?'

'Wh— Oh, right. Yesss!'

'Yes.'

Steady now, Rob. Don't blow it on the home straight by making a break too soon. Make sure you open the door very slowly and casually. That's the way. Don't make him suspicious.

'Yes,' repeated Zach. 'I knew right away that I'd been sent here for you.'

'*For* me?' I replied (regretting it instantly, as I imagined Zach throwing back the reply, 'Yes, *for* you – I am to be your bride!' followed by a lunge, a brief scuffle, and then all kinds of unpleasantness).

'That's right. You see, we've both been saved; you don't know why yet, but I know now that *I* was saved to help you find out. It's a quest – like the Holy Grail or whatever it was. You have to go on a quest, and I was saved to help you – to protect you on your journey.'

'*Riiiiight,*' I replied, nodding pensively. '*Yeeeees.*' Not only was the door open now, but I'd also moved around to the right side of it. This was the moment. This was where I would either make a rapid, surprising escape to safety, or be caught. Halfway through. Bending over.

'Hmm—' I began – at first appearing still to be pondering Zach's analysis, but then abruptly cutting off when he'd been fooled into thinking that there were a few more 'm's still to come out, and lurching as fast as I could into the car.

I made it on to the passenger seat and, on all fours, frantically twisted back to grab the interior door handle. It fell right into my hand – which was a fantastic moment – and I yanked the door towards me; it struck the soles of my feet (which were still projecting out beyond the car), bounced free from my grip, and flew wide open again – which was a less fantastic moment.

I scrambled to turn around and snatch it shut again.

'Ee-*yuh*!' I grunted, as I somehow managed – without

Zach stopping me – to reach out, catch hold of the door by that curved storage-well area at the bottom designed for holding discarded sweet wrappers and dirt, and heave it towards me. It swung to with a euphorically satisfying crunch. Without pausing for an instant, I slammed the lock down using a decisive, slapping hand, then frantically clambered across to the driver's seat and stabbed my key into the ignition.

I started the car, punched it into gear, and roared off down the road.

Only when I was actually moving did I risk using up a potentially vital second to take a look at what Zach was doing. I craned around and peered out of the rear window. He was still standing exactly where he had been before I'd started my escape – I don't think he'd even changed posture. Obviously, I'd used speed and surprise to devastating effect. He was, now, just starting to catch up, though, because he began to jab a finger towards me and shouted something. I turned back away from him, and poked at the dashboard with lazy irritation.

'Yeah, yeah, my lights. OK, shut up.'

ELEVEN

'Why didn't he attack you?' asked Jo, yet again.

There was something vaguely unsupportive about this, I couldn't help feeling. Unusually, she had tuned in to listen to the show tonight – 'To see how you got on, babe.' (Translation: 'To see if, with Keith's threat hanging over you, you could actually get through it without beginning to howl at the moon.') At first, she'd been surprised by the drastic change of format, but had soon figured out what must have happened – it was clearly a programming decision, after all, not simply my unilaterally going off on a tangent. This made her feel a little better about my job security. Her worries about that allayed, she wasn't going to sit there listening to some nutter talking about how he'd been a high priest in the court of Rameses II only a few previous lives before his current incarnation as a minicab driver in Smethwick. So, she'd turned the radio off and been happily fast asleep by 12.30. Which – fair enough – meant I'd woken her up in the early hours of the morning for the second night in a row. Still, even so, she could have praised my daring escape a little more. Her delivery of 'Why didn't he attack you?' seemed to carry with it the unspoken addition: 'That's what *I*'d have done.'

'Maybe he was waiting for his moment,' I replied. 'Maybe he wanted to make sure he'd have the best possible chance of taking me down.' This was the adrenaline talking, and Jo smiled into her mug of tea.

That stung a little more than was sensible, to be honest. Jo's type (however much she denied that she had a type) was your rippling and rugged sort. I don't really 'ripple'.

What I tend to do is 'sprain'. Her previous boyfriend had been Pete, of course, which was perfectly in line with what one would expect – whereas the physical gulf between a sports teacher and a late-night jazz DJ took some leaping, in my opinion. I suppose I'd always been a bit over-sensitive about this. I mean, obviously, I'm not saying that any ludicrous voice in my head was hissing that she'd probably rather fancy Zach. That she'd most likely be a little excited by watching some testosterone-stuffed bloke in army gear beat the crap out of me – that she'd get off on it – and probably have sex with him – right there – looking across at me as I lay on the pavement drifting in and out of consciousness – and laughing. No, I certainly wasn't that insecure. I could simply have done without that little smile, that's all.

'What?' I asked. 'What?'

'*What* what?'

'What was that smile for?'

Infuriatingly, she replied to this question with a smile.

'Oh – just go and fuck him, then!' I said, and sat back heavily in my chair.

'What *are* you talking about?'

'*Nothing*,' I sang, sarcastically, and gave her a twisted, bitter smirk. I was pretty much certain that this was the perfect tactic to make her well up with guilt and regret.

She looked at me as though I was a twat.

'I just think,' she said with a shrug, 'that he doesn't sound all that dangerous to me; not from what you've told me. Maybe you're over-reacting a little, babe – you are . . . you know . . . stressed out.'

'You mean fucked up.'

'I mean stressed out.'

'Well, OK, then – tell me this: if he *wasn't* some kind of violent nutter, why did he say he wouldn't bugger me?'

'He said, "I won't bugger you"? Really?'

'Yes, really.'

'God. That *is* a bit suspicious; coming out unprovoked.'

'Well, no, it . . .' I pulled myself up.

'What?'

'Never mind. It's not important.'

'*Tell* me.'

'Well . . . it wasn't exactly "unprovoked". Not in the strictest technical sense.'

'What do you mean? What happened?'

'I asked him not to bugger me, and he said, "OK." '

'Right.'

'Fuck off – don't look at me like that. That's not the point at all.'

'Right.'

'Oh, for f— OK, look: suppose someone said to you, "Please don't bugger me." '

'How would that work, then?'

'It'd work because you're *not* buggering them, OK? And because it's purely hypothetical – stop taking the piss. Suppose someone said to you, "Please don't bugger me," you wouldn't reply, "OK," would you?'

'I couldn't really reply anything but, "OK," could I? Anything else would be pretty obviously an empty threat.'

'Hy-po-*thetical* – for Christ's sake. You wouldn't reply, "OK," you'd reply something like, "What the hell are you talking about?" or, "I've never even thought of buggering you, as it happens." The very fact that he replied, "OK" means that it must have been on his mind, right?'

'Um . . .'

'What?'

'It's all a bit convoluted, isn't it?'

'Of course it is. It's twisted and sinister. You expect him to stride over and reveal his plans by saying, "I'm going to bugger you" straight away? That's a bit of a giveaway for your victim, isn't it? What would you do if someone said to you, "I'm going to bugger you," eh?'

'Who?'

'Does it *matter*?'

'Well . . .'

'Oh . . .' My annoyance lessened somewhat. 'Well, if it was me, for example.'

'Well . . .' she said, thoughtfully.

'Really? You've never told me that before.'

'I didn't say I *would* . . . I'm just saying, you know, I wouldn't rule out the possibility of trying. If I felt . . . you know.'

'Oh, of course . . . Of *course*. No, no – absolutely. Only if you were completely . . .'

'Yeah.'

'Wow . . .'

I spent a little time in silent reflection.

Jo eventually pulled me back to earth. 'All I'm saying, Rob, is that it's all very tenuous. He just seems like a pretty harmless fruitcake to me.'

'Really?'

'Actually, no.'

'Make up your mind.'

'Good choice of words,' Jo said (mostly to herself), before continuing, 'What I meant was that, to be honest, that's not "all I'm saying".' She reached out and took hold of my hand. God. That was a bad sign, right? 'Rob . . .' (My name, followed by a pause – things were *really* looking bleak.) 'Rob, maybe he's right.'

'You reckon God *did* choose him? Hold on, don't answer that yet – let's take it back a step . . . You reckon there's a God now? And he's chosen Zach? That's two pretty impressive epiphanies for one evening, Jo, I must say. Hey!' I hushed my voice. 'Hey – wait a minute; this is just too much of a coincidence, isn't it? There's only one reasonable explanation – Zach *is* God!'

'Finished?'

'Not nearly.'

'Too bad. Listen . . . I think you should really seriously consider whether taking some time out – completely – to work things through—'

'You mean go on a quest?'

'No—'

I grinned.

'OK, then,' snapped Jo. 'Yes – go on a fucking quest.'

'Yeah – right.'

'Listen to me, Rob. You remember what I said before? About your sorting yourself out or us not having any real chance of a future together? Last night, you thought you'd done it – you told me it was all fine . . . but it wasn't, was it? I think we've got to the point where we need to take drastic action – and you refuse to see a therapist – so what does that leave? If you're going to have any chance of curing yourself, I think you need to focus on nothing but doing that for a while. You ought to give it all you've got, if it's a final attempt.'

'A "final attempt"?'

Jo kneaded my hand with so much reassuring affection that it very nearly popped the cartilages out of a couple of my knuckles. But she kept her eyes aimed at the table. 'Where is there to go if this doesn't do any good, Rob? If you give it all you can, and nothing changes?'

'Christ, Jo,' I gasped. 'You can't leave me *now* – not when you've just told me that you're up for anal!'

I could, arguably, have expressed my feelings better there.

Jo began to say something that looked like it might be pretty far-reaching, but I thought it better to clarify my position first and I cut her off.

'I don't mean . . . I just mean, well . . .' I said. 'I know things between us aren't perfect, exactly. But they're not too bad. And not too bad is fine to be going on with, isn't it? Lots of couples last for years and years on not too bad. I think you're being unnecessarily "All or Nothing".'

'How old am I, Rob?'

'You're twenty-eight.'

'I'm twenty-nine, you twat. *God.* How can you not know that? Isn't that, you know, basic stuff?'

'Is it?'

'Er . . .' She pretended to think. '*Yes.* It's remedial-level relationship stuff. Like . . . OK, you're a Virgo. First – basic-level – thing I did when I started fancying you was work out that you were a Virgo. I used to read your horoscope and my horoscope *every* day. You've had plenty of time to catch up by now, so, go on, then: what's *my* sign, Rob?'

'You've *really* got it in for me tonight, haven't you?'

'What's my sign?'

'Um, the one with the dog?'

'*God.*'

'OK, OK, I don't know what your star sign is – and you're going to leave me because of *that*?'

'No, don't be stupid. You know it's got nothing to do with that at all. I'd be fine about staying with you – I'd stay with you in *spite* of that. You just got me side-tracked by *not even knowing how old I am.* OK . . .' She blew out a long, calming breath. 'I'm twenty-*nine*, Rob. I'm not eighteen or nineteen; I'm leaving my twenties now. If you ask me if I fancy you, then, yes, I do. If you ask me if I love you, then, yes, I do. If I were five years younger, then that'd be enough. But I'm not. The person I'm with when I'm twenty-nine – the person I'm *marrying*, in case you'd forgotten – is the rest of my life. I can't say, "Oh, Rob's having a nervous breakdown – but I fancy him, and love

him, and we'll see how it goes for a couple of years."
I have to believe it's got a future; that it can survive
forever. Sure, I can put up with it now . . . but will I still
be able to carry on ten years from now? What about the
children?'

'The children?'

'Yes – the *children*. You've mentioned children – in the
very, very abstract. But think about children in the,
um . . . in the real. What about if it's ten years from now,
and we've got children, and I'm still having to go and
collect you from the newsagent's because you've been
standing there in front of the magazine rack for an hour
and a half, trying to decide whether your buying *What's
On TV* or your buying *TV Choice* will alter the entire
course of history for the bleeding better?'

Jo was breathing deeply and rapidly. It was the only
sound in the room for quite a time.

'So you want me to go on a "quest"?'

'I want you to do whatever it takes. This Zach guy said
you needed to find an answer, and I think he's right about
that.'

'What kind of answer?'

'One that satisfies you.'

'But I don't even know what the question is.'

'Well . . .' She took my hand in hers again. 'Go and look
for that first, then.'

'It's a load of wank, if you ask me,' said Pete.

He stared at me across the table and shrugged, in an
amiable 'but that's just my opinion' kind of way. He had a
foam moustache where the head on his Guinness had stuck
to his top lip; deep-black skin and a bright-white moustache – he looked vaguely like a worrying number of the
other people in the pub, only in negative.

'Yeah,' I replied. 'But Jo's absolutely serious about it.

You know what she's like when she makes up her mind about something.'

Pete nodded solemnly, and then took another mouthful from his glass.

'Do you think I'm a fuck-up?' I asked.

'God yes,' Pete said, supportively. 'I've always thought that. You were a fuck-up in junior school.'

'No, Pete, really. Do you think that I'm too much of a fuck-up for anyone to risk a future with me as I am now? Do you think Jo's right?'

'Jo's always right. She made sure I learned that fact by heart when I was going out with her. There's no way I can make myself believe any different now, even if I try: going out with Jo is like being raised by the Jesuits, isn't it? I think the whole "finding yourself" wank – or whatever wank it is – I think that's a pile of wank. But . . . well, Jo's right about the fact that you need to do something. If she doesn't feel completely sure about getting married, then she's right not to, isn't she? It's not to do with wank and fuck-ups, is it? It's about her not feeling one hundred per cent about it. And she should, shouldn't she? She's right, mate . . . Sorry.'

'Hmmm . . .' I began scratching the writing off a damp beer mat.

'And, you know, if I could start being able to stand at the bar and ask what flavour crisps you want with any hope of getting an answer before they cover the taps, then that'd be pretty special too. So – everyone wins.'

'Right . . . and what do you reckon to this Zach character? Do you think he's likely to kill me and then dress in my skin, or do you agree with Jo? I mean, the most common thing the police find on serial killers is a copy of the Bible, isn't it?'

'It's also the most common thing found on nuns.'

'Do the police conduct a lot of nun searches?'

'Someone's got to.'

'Come on, Pete, straight up – do you think I should be worried?'

'Pff.' He twisted his lips into a casual 'Who knows?'

'Helpful. OK, then – would *you* be worried?'

'Nah. But then, if he did go ape shit all of a sudden, and it were with me, I'd just kick the crap out of him. You don't really have that option, do you?' He grinned at me.

'One day, Pete Saunders, you'll push your luck just a *little* too far, and I'll have to introduce you to a whole world of hurt.'

'Ha . . . Anyway, no one's said anything about having to listen to the mad Yank. There's no reason at all for you to involve him in what you have to do.'

'But what *do* I have to do, though?'

'*Something.*'

I dropped the, now utterly destroyed, beer mat into the ashtray, and slumped back in my chair. 'Jesus. My girl-friend and my best mate are giving me the same advice. That's just *wrong*, Pete – it mocks Nature.'

'So does how you look when you try to play football.'

'I'm warning you – you won't see it coming. Just a blur of movement and – *boomf!* – you'll be down.'

'Ha ha. That's the spirit, mate.'

TWELVE

After I left Pete in the pub, I went home briefly before going to the radio station. Jo was sitting on the sofa in her bedclothes watching TV. She gave me a kiss on the cheek as I left, and wished me a good show, but she did so while juggling a whole selection of meaningful looks.

Jo and Pete's similarly shrugging unconcern had almost convinced me that Zach was probably not dangerous, but I was still not completely sure that they were right. When I parked the car by the station, I scanned all around the area before getting out. And when I *did* finally get out, I darted to the entrance in a series of swift dashes; pausing every thirty feet or so – my back flat against something that both made me less visible and also prevented a surprise attack from the rear – to check that he was nowhere in sight. I also kept my right hand ready in my jacket pocket. I hadn't wanted to be entirely defenceless, so the main reason I'd dropped in at home on the way to work was to find something I could take along as protection – something to repel Zach if he did jump me. What I needed was some pepper spray or a small canister of CS gas. We didn't have any pepper spray or canisters of CS gas around the house, oddly. So I'd had to improvise, and was carrying an aerosol of furniture polish.

I swiftly made it to the front of Central FM without seeing any sign of Zach, or anyone at all for that matter. Outside the doors, I took one last look around. There was an empty coldness – Birmingham's trademark sullen drizzle was sparkling in the air as it fell through the beams of the street lamps, and the wind was barely strong enough to pass a whisper along the trees around the car park; it was a lifeless, deserted, hollow night. I gave myself permission to exhale, spun around, and pushed quickly through the doors, into the station.

Where Zach was waiting, facing directly at me.

'Argh!' I noted.

I made a quick recovery, however, and held one, staying hand out towards him, while simultaneously moving the other hand threateningly inside my jacket and barking, 'Stay back! I'm packing heat!'

Oddly, this *wasn't* the most stupid thing that I could possibly have said. Peerlessly idiotic as it seems, it still pretty easily beats, 'Stay back! I have a can of Mr Sheen in my pocket!'

Zach smiled at me in a way that might have been the precursor to a frenzied attack, or might have been gently indulgent – it was difficult to tell. He didn't come any closer, however. Still keeping him covered so that, if he made any sudden movements, he'd damn well quickly find himself both waxed *and* anti-static, I flicked my eyes over to the reception desk. Geoff looked up in my direction, thoughtfully tapped his teeth with a pencil for a second, smiled with satisfaction, and then scribbled something in the *Daily Mail* crossword.

'I decided to wait inside,' said Zach. He motioned with his chin. 'Geoff said it was OK.'

'Geoff's a diamond.'

'I figured you'd maybe be less skittish if I was here, you know? Bright lights, and company, and all. And, anyway, it's raining out there.'

I peered at him; trying to see if I could find a physical sign – spot something decisively benign or conclusively homicidal: a forensically reliable Harmless Nutter shape to the earlobe, say, or some positioning of the legs that only mass murderers adopted. Nothing entirely unequivocal presented itself.

'Why did you say you wouldn't bugger me?' I asked.

'*What?*'

'I was talking to *him*, Geoff . . . So – Zach – why did you say you wouldn't bugger me?'

'Because . . . Um . . . Sorry, Rob, I'm not sure I understand the question. I mean, I *didn't*, did I? I never intended to. What else should I have said?'

'Well – what about what you just said *there* for a start? "I never intended to." That would have been perfectly natural. Not really weird like "OK" is. *Jesus.* Didn't it strike you as odd that the first words out of my mouth were "Please don't bugger me"?'

'Um, not really.'

'Why the hell not?'

'Because you're English.'

'What the fuck has *that* to do with it?'

'Well, you know . . . Your private schools, and the way you all speak, and stuff.'

'*What?* You think every man in England has to specifically *ask* not to be sodomised by every other man he meets, or else it's pretty much a foregone conclusion?'

'No, no, of course not. I'm sure not *all* English guys are into it . . . you're just, you know, probably *more* into it.'

'More into it than *what*?'

'More into it than we are in Nebraska.'

I tried to find some words to convey the vast sweep of my thoughts, but none seemed to sufficiently capture the precise essence of their many-faceted infuriation. Finally, I simply slapped my own forehead, made a noise halfway between an exasperated sigh and a growl, and pushed past him towards the stairs up to my studio.

'Hey, man – I wasn't judging you or anything,' Zach called to my departing back.

Francine from Cradley Heath was insistent.

'No,' I repeated.

'Are you *sure*, becau—'

'Yes, Francine. I'm completely sure.'

'There's no need to be embarr—'

'Francine – I do *not* hear voices. OK?'

I let out a long, weary sigh and, shaking my head, looked up towards the control room – where I saw that Keith was waving agitatedly and pressing to the glass a piece of paper on which he'd written, 'Tell them you hear voices!'

Francine was even more of an irritation because my mind was elsewhere. When I'd got in, I'd found I'd had another email from 'Beth'. It was brief ('I know how you feel. Your life is in danger. We have to meet'), but, like a collapsing sun, its tiny size gave it more weight. Or more gravity. Whatever – it works both ways. I hadn't replied to the previous mail, so I'd have expected any follow-up to urge me to do so by offering greater detail or making longer arguments. Beth had gone the other way. She'd opted for the clipped style of a telegram: which evoked a feeling of importance and urgency. I wondered whether I should reply. *Against* doing so was that it was encouraging someone I knew nothing about, but who had somehow got hold of my private email address; maybe she was one of those women who developed obsessional romantic fixations for emotionally shaky, Birmingham-based, radio jazz presenters – you know the sort. *For* replying to the email was this: I wanted to.

During the break for the news at 1.30, Keith gave me permission to go to the toilet. I stood at the urinal and – wrapped in its sensible, lemony reassurance – tried to take stock of my life. Time passed.

'You know, it's really difficult to go with you standing there, Keith,' I said at last.

'Is it?' he replied absently, and sucked the innards of a bitten-in-half grape through the mutilating sieve of his teeth. (What kind of man can eat in a public toilet? Really – there's something wrong somewhere if it's even *possible* for you to do that, isn't there?)

'Yes. It is. Can't you go back to the studio? I'm not going to leg it, mid-show. I could have not come in at all, couldn't I?'

'Oh, I'm not worried you'll do a runner. You have to be back after the bulletin, though, and I simply wanted to make sure you didn't get lost, or become frozen with fear because of something you'd imagined you'd seen, or started crying.'

'I'm not a complete nutcase, you know.'

'Did I *say* that?'

'I just can't decide about things, sometimes.'

'Right. Like whether you want a piss or not.'

'I *want* to, Keith – I just *can't* with you standing there watching me.'

'I'm not watching you – why would I want to watch you? You think I'm *watching* you? Do you imagine anyone else is watching you?'

'Ugh.'

'Would it help if I turned on a tap?'

'Yes – yes, go over there and turn on a tap, OK?'

'Right.' Keith loped to the sink and started the water. I could hear it splashing, and hear his grape sucking, and feel his eyes pressing into my back. About fifteen seconds went by.

'Anything coming yet?'

'Will you just fuck *off*?!'

Amazingly, he did. But that turned out to be less than perfect too, because he'd obviously felt the need to share.

When I returned to the control room, both he and Jenny looked up at me; their eyes full of questioning expectancy – I thought Jenny was actually going to ask, 'Well? Did you?' Before she could, however, I marched bad-temperedly into the studio, dropped into my seat, and sat there with my arms folded across my chest with message-heavy tightness.

Finally, Jenny said, 'Out of the news in ten, Rob. There's a caller waiting on the line – show ident, welcome back, then right into her, OK?'

'OK.' I pressed a button on my console so that the caller could hear me. 'Hi there . . .' I waved my hands at Jenny.

'Elizabeth,' Jenny cut through into my headphones.

'. . . Elizabeth,' I continued. 'Sorry to keep you. We're just coming out of the news, and then we'll be on air, OK?'

'That's fine,' she replied.

'Great,' I said, the show's ident playing in my ears.

'I know how you feel.'

The ident finished and I sat there. In silence.

After around five seconds of dead air, I heard Jenny in my headphones saying, 'R-rr-r-ro-oo-ob-b-b-b.' I looked up into the control room and saw that her curious vibrato enunciation was because Keith – while staring fixedly at me with wide, panicky eyes – was impressing upon her the need to *do something* by holding her by the shoulders and shaking her bodily.

I fell back to earth with a slightly disorientating suddenness.

'Right . . .' I said. 'Welcome back to the show . . . everyone . . . I believe we have Elizabeth on the line. Hi there, Elizabeth. Where are you calling from?'

'Does that matter?'

Not remotely, of course. I suddenly felt like an idiot radio presenter. I experienced a brief draught of resentment towards Elizabeth for making me feel like that. Then remembered that I *was* an idiot radio presenter. And experienced a huge gale of resentment towards Keith.

'Well, er, no . . .' I replied. 'I just—'

'Let it fall out of your mouth without any genuine thought because you don't really care about the answer anyway? I can't believe you're interested in where I live. I can't believe you're interested in *anything* that isn't very tightly focused on the one thing that fascinates you utterly: you.'

Already, I was really warming to Elizabeth.

'I don't . . . Well – whatever. So, Elizabeth, you live in a doorway, huddled inside a duffel coat soaked in your own urine, let's say – just so the listeners have something to picture. Do you want to get on with why you called in now?'

'I know how you feel.'

Those words again. And spoken calmly too. Elizabeth sounded a little drunk, or perhaps very, very tired. That was only the very subtlest of colouring in her voice, however. The major hue was effortless assurance. She spoke easily and directly; Elizabeth was in control of herself and the world, it seemed to me. She had a tremendously, um, *English* voice. Not exactly posh, but geographically unplaceable; it was refined, and intelligent, and certain.

'Do you?' I replied.

'Yes . . . And it's wrong.'

'Well, feelings are a very personal thing, Elizabeth. I don't know that anyone's feelings can actually be *wrong*. I mean—'

'Oh, *do* fuck off, Garland.'

'Please mind your language, Elizabeth, or I'll have to end this call.'

I could have ended it right there. We might, possibly, pick up a fine for that 'fuck' alone – I could have cut her off immediately; dumped her back into anonymity with the push of a button, and then made a sarcastic comment at her expense to the listeners. I didn't though. In fact, I made a face and waved at Jenny, just in case she might have been going to cut her off from the control room.

Elizabeth continued without an apology, nor a commitment to stay broadcastable, nor even, come to that, a pause. 'Good Lord. "No one's feelings can be *wrong*." What an impossibly flaccid remark. I suppose everyone is special in their own way too? Let's all join hands, why don't we? Of course people's feelings can be wrong. They can be more than wrong: they can be *obscene*. They can be dark and septic and ignominious.'

'I don't think my feelings are dark, *or* septic, *or* . . .' Actually, I wasn't precisely sure what ignominious meant – better let that one go. '. . . anything like that.'

'Well, some people's are. Yours aren't, no, because they're too scramblingly self-serving to be anything so lucid.'

'I have to say that I don't think you have any right to judge my feelings unless you've been through what I've been through, Elizabeth.'

Though hoping this would land a blow, I was fully expecting it to bounce off her – probably to bounce directly back, and hit me in the mouth. In fact, she surprised me by not replying at all. After a few seconds, I wondered if she was even on the line anymore.

'Elizabeth?' I said. 'Elizabeth? Are you still there?'

'Maybe I have been through what you've been through,' she replied.

'Do you want to talk about it?'

'Absolutely fucking not.'

'Eliz—'

'Yes, yes: mind my fucking language – you mentioned it. What happened to us doesn't matter at all, in the whole scheme of things . . . And it matters even less if you'll be dead soon anyway.'

'What does *that* mean?' I asked, jumpily.

'Got to go now,' she replied, and hung up.

I threw my hand to the console in front of me and banged at the button that took me off air and through to Jenny. 'Get her back,' I barked. '*Call her.*'

'OK,' Jenny replied.

'Tell her she doesn't have to talk on the show. I just want to speak to her – personally.'

'OK.'

'Go on – call her, then.'

'I will.'

'*Now.*'

Keith was pointing at me with the veins on his forehead for leaving the listeners with nothing but hiss. I didn't really care, but simply to maintain the unblemished high level of professionalism that was my trademark, I prodded the console and went back to doing the phone-in.

'Wo-oh, sorry about that. There was a fault with my producer. So, line . . . five. Five? Yes, OK, five. Hello, line five, who are you?'

'I'm Colette, Rob.'

'And where . . . oh, never mind. What have you got to say, Colette?'

'Well, Rob . . .'

'Yes?'

'Yesterday . . .'

'Yes?'

'You're going to think I'm making this up . . . But, I swear to you, Rob, it's absolutely true. Yesterday, I was just thinking about my sister Alice – and the phone rang . . . *and it was her.*'

'God in heaven!'

Jenny tried to call Elizabeth back for the rest of the show, and then I tried when the show was over. No luck. At first, Jenny said, the phone had been left to ring without being answered, then it had been taken off the hook (or engaged for a long time), and then it had returned to being un-answered – though this second unanswered 'ringing' might have been because Elizabeth had disconnected the phone line at the socket.

'Why are you so keen to talk to her?' asked Keith. 'She struck me as deeply unspecial. Even if she could control her fucking, she had a flat voice. She's not very radio.'

'I'm taking two months off: starting now,' I replied.

'OK, OK – we'll get her back!' Keith blurted nervously. 'You can have her on the show; we'll do a time-delay to bleep her or something.'

'It's not that. It's that I need some time to concentrate on things. Concentrate on them *fully* . . . I need to go on a quest.'

'A fucking *what*?' gasped Keith.

'He said a fucking *quest*, Keith,' said Jenny.

'I know what he fucking *said*, Jenny. Christ. Rob – *Rob* – think about this calmly for a moment . . . think about what's really important here. We're getting higher figures than the breakfast show, for God's sake. Do you want to throw all that away? Cast it aside to . . . well . . . what the hell is a quest, anyway?'

'I'm not quite sure yet.'

'There you go, then.'

'But I'm taking two months off to find out.'

'Fuck you – no, you're not!' shouted Keith. 'You'll be in here again tomorrow, or you won't be coming back at all!'

'Then I won't be coming back at all.'

'I didn't mean that,' said Keith – he stepped forward and clasped my hand. He was ashen. 'I'm sorry. I was just thinking about . . . your fans, Rob. Is it fair to desert them to do something else, when you don't even know what that something else *is*?'

'Fans? I don't have any fans. They're simply people with a morbid, voyeuristic interest in witnessing me come apart.'

'Those are the truest kind of fans, Rob. They're not your here today, gone tomorrow faddists: no – their commitment to you is wonderfully pathological.'

'Well, they'll hang around for two months, then, won't they?'

'I think it's a great idea, Rob,' smiled Jenny.

Keith stabbed a finger within half an inch of her face. 'Shut the fuck up!' He turned back to me, and his voice softened to almost a lilting whisper again. 'Don't listen to Jenny,' he soothed gently. 'She's just a mad fucking tart who wants your job. Think of the show, Rob – the *show*.'

'I'm going, Keith. My mind's made up.'

'Oh, for Christ's sake! I thought you *couldn't* make up your mind. Isn't that the whole fucking problem? Now – when it'll fuck me over – you *can* make up your mind, can you? What's the deal, Rob? *Can* you make up your mind or *can't* you make up your mind? *Make up your fucking mind!*'

'Does no one ever listen to a thing I say?' I replied, starting to boil. 'I can make up my mind about *big* things – *big* things are easy. You can see the paths and take a considered stab at where they'll lead with the *big* things. It's the *small* things that are the problem.'

I began, illustratively, pointing an angry finger off in a random direction. 'There was a knife and a fork in the sink today, and I couldn't decide which to wash up first. I stood there for forty-five minutes. Knife? Or fork? Or leave them both? Or do them both together? That could be a life-or-death decision, you know, Keith? It *could*. Every single thing you do is a life-or-death decision. And, when it's "Do I try methadone?" or "Should I get married?" or "Shall I stay around gradually falling to bits, or try as hard as I possibly can to sort myself out?" then you have the important information available. You can work out what's the smart, or at least the smartest, option. But how the fucking *hell* do you decide whether to wash up *a knife or a fork first*?'

Keith chewed his lip and stared at me without replying. He was obviously anxious to say something, but utterly terrified of saying the wrong thing. The brittle silence in the room grew longer and longer, until Jenny finally broke it.

'I'd have washed up the fork first,' she said.

'Ugh.'

Keith used the fact that I was distracted by possibly being about to physically explode to re-engage me in negotiation. 'Look, Rob, all I'm asking is that you think about it. You've only just finished Wednesday's show – at least see the week out. Think about it until you've seen the week out.'

'No.'

'Aeeeeeiiiii!' Keith wailed: a wordless, primal, beseeching cry of pain expressing the timeless agony of the radio producer's lot. He dropped his head forward and grabbed a fistful of his hair in each hand.

I sighed. 'Look – maybe it's better this way: a dramatic disappearance. You can say I've gone AWOL. Last seen running from the building wearing the Manchester United away strip and heavy mascara or something.'

Keith brightened a little. 'Yes . . .'

'I fled into the night – ranting about a quest.'

'*Yes*. People might tune in to hear updates. "How wild has Rob Garland gone today?" We could do daily reports. Could you send back daily reports?'

'No.'

'We'll make up the reports. Christ – yes: this could really work.' He was happy and energised now. 'We could add a forum to the Website. It'd be *buzzing*. Everyone speculating self-importantly, and repeating baseless rumours, and lying outright – it's *perfect* for a Web forum. *Fuck*. There could be a Sony in this!'

'Yes.' I nodded. As though I gave a shit.

'*Yes*,' Keith whooped.

'You'll get even more listeners – it'll take on a life of its own,' I said.

'It's the logical next step!' boomed Keith.

'It'll be great,' I agreed.

'Fan*tastic*!' Keith said.

'And I can fill in on the show!' added Jenny.

'Not a fucking *chance*,' replied Keith, smiling and ruffling her hair.

'That's that, then.' I began to leave. 'I'll take the two months . . . Maybe I won't need that long, who knows? Maybe I'll be back this time next week: all sorted and with my head together.'

Keith stepped forward quickly and laid a hand on my shoulder. 'No, Rob – it'd be better if you came back even more fucked up.'

'Right.'

'I don't want a commitment – I'm not pressuring you. But just promise me that you'll bear it in mind, OK? Keep being even more fucked up open as an option.'

'Take care of yourself, Keith. I'm going to miss you.'

I tapped my index finger rapidly against the side of the mug of tea. It was a nervous thing. Part fear, part exhilaration – the hyperness leaking from my body at an extremity; like electricity spilling and sparking from a trailing cable as it swings across a wet floor.

I stared across the table in the dining room, but I wasn't actually focusing on what was there. I wasn't focusing anywhere, really. Which was a bit troubling.

'You have a nice home,' said Zach.

'What?'

'I said, you have a nice home.' He took a gulp from his mug. 'So, this is real English tea, then? Cool.'

'It's Safeway's own brand.'

'Wow – you have Safeway here in England?'

'Yeah . . . Just for the tourists, really.'

I wasn't *entirely* sure why I'd asked Zach back to our house. I think the best explanation was that I knew I had to do something, but – as I was almost completely inkling-free as to what that something might be – I'd sort of slipped into doing *anything*, as a scrambling second best. Zach was barking mad, obviously, but at least he had direction: Zach knew where he was going. He knew what he needed to do next. If *I* didn't have that asset, my almost-reasoning went, shouldn't I perhaps surround myself with people who did?

'What should we do next, Zach?' I asked.

'Dunno,' he shrugged, and smiled, and drank some more of his tea. 'The light switches work the wrong way here, don't they?'

'Sorry?'

'The light switches, you know? You push them *down* to turn on the lights over here.' He laughed and shook his head in amazement.

'What? Wh— Is that an allegory or something?'

'Huh?'

'Are you trying to tell me something quite deep using a metaphor? Has God commanded you to speak unto me using the Parable of the Light Switches?'

'Huh?'

'Or are you just telling me, for no particular reason, that

American switches need to be pushed up to turn on the lights?'

'Well . . . yeah.'

'How *incredibly* interesting.'

Zach shrugged again. 'So . . . why *do* your switches work downward, then?'

'Why do yours work upwards?'

'Um, because that's the way switches work.'

'Ah.'

I envied Zach. Yes, I also wanted to slap him, but I was still jealous of that kind of instinctive, uncluttered, unquestioning, dumb-as-fuck assurance. Which reminded me.

'You listened to the show while you were waiting in reception at the station, right?' I asked.

'For sure.'

'What did you make of the Elizabeth woman?'

'Was that the one who said that her cat talked to her through special brain waves?'

'No. Elizabeth was the one who swore, gave me a very hard time, and then hung up on me.'

'Oh, right.'

'Well?'

'Well what?'

'Well, what did you think of her?'

'Dunno.'

'John, Jude, Revelation and Dunno. Splendid.'

'What?'

'Never mind. Here's the thing, Zach . . . I need to do something.'

'I'll help.'

'You don't know what it is I want to do.'

'It doesn't matter. My job is to help you. That's why I was sent here.'

'Whatever. Anyway, the only thing I can think of is to

focus on what things have made an impact on me recently, and then follow those up – in the hope that they've touched a nerve for a good reason; even if I don't quite know why yet.'

'K.'

'Maybe it will lead somewhere that'll help me understand everything – if I take it step by step. See what happens, and then react to it, hopefully learning stuff along the way. A bit like word association – you know?'

'Yes.'

'Good.'

'Bad.'

'Sorry?'

'Apology.'

'What?'

'Whe—'

'Shut the fuck up, Zach, OK?' I rubbed my temples for a few seconds, and then continued. 'Right. So – other than Jo—'

'Who's Jo?'

'My fiancée. Other than Jo and Pete—'

'Who's Pete?'

'Is this you shutting the fuck up?'

'Sorry, man – go on.'

'. . . and Pete – who's my mate – only three things have made any kind of a dent recently. You know – really made me think. One is you.'

'Cool.'

'But you're insane. Another was a couple of emails I got from a woman called Beth who, among other things, said my life was in danger. The third was that phone call tonight. She sounded . . . *sure*. She sounded as though she really did know how I felt, but that she saw things more clearly than I did. I felt as though, if she stopped ripping the piss out of me for long enough, she could tell me where

I needed to be; because she'd been where I am now, and had managed to move on. And she mentioned I might be dead soon too. So, you, Beth and Elizabeth are the three things I have to work with.'

Zach looked down towards the table, and nodded pensively. He took a few sips from his tea, and then nodded pensively some more. This continued, I estimate, for close to a minute.

'Hey!' he said, abruptly. 'Hey, hey, *heey*! "Beth" – "*Eliza*beth" . . . It could be the same woman!'

'*No*? You think so?' I rubbed my temples again. 'Of course it's the same woman . . . but that doesn't help much. I need to talk to her.'

'So, call her.'

'I've been trying. She's not answering her phone. Maybe she will at some point, but *she* hung up on *me*, so it's possible she's had enough. She made contact, decided I was a twat, and that's the end of it. She may never speak to me again now.'

'Um . . . email her.'

'If she won't pick up her phone, then she's not going to reply to an email, is she? That's even easier to ignore.'

'Hmmm . . . I don't know . . . visit her, then. Turn up at her door – she can't ignore you if you do that, right?'

'Zach?'

'Yeah?'

'Where the hell is her door?'

'Oh . . . right. They didn't take her address at the station?'

'No. We just make sure we have a landline number to call back on for a good signal.'

'What about tracing her by her email?'

'Can that be done?'

'Dunno.'

'Hurrah – got there in the end.'

'What?'

'Never mind. I suppose I could check with Danny. He sorts out all the station's Internet stuff. He'd know.'

'Cool.'

'*Argh!*'

'Oh – hi, Jo,' I said. She was standing in the doorway, looking like she might well go, '*Argh!*' again. Possibly the noise of us talking had woken her, or maybe she'd simply got up to come down for breakfast – I'd no idea of what the time was. Whatever the reason for her being up, walking into the dining room in her bedclothes and discovering Zach sitting there was obviously a bit of a surprise for her.

'This is Zach,' I said.

Zach stood up. Which he probably did to be polite, rather than to look very large and scary.

'Right.' She nodded tightly. Her arms were strapped across herself: one belted around her stomach and the other reaching up from it over her chest to fiddle with the neck of her pyjama top.

'I was saying that you have a lovely home,' said Zach.

'Thank you . . . Rob? Could I have a word, please?' She smiled at me and I knew I was in trouble.

I left Zach drinking his tea and followed her into the living room. When we were both in, she shut the door, and leant back against it.

'What the hell are you *doing*?' she hissed in a hysterical whisper.

'You mean bringing Zach back?'

'No – I mean to discourage the illegal exploitation of Malaysian timber . . . Of *course* I mean bringing Zach back, you twat. Last night you were telling me he was some kind of homicidal sex fiend, and tonight you bring him home.'

'But you said he sounded harmless to you.'

'Yes, but I *didn't* say, "In fact, Rob, you ought to let him into our house in the middle of the night when I'm upstairs in bed asleep, just so we can be sure," did I? You *twat*.'

'I know he looks terrifying and mental, but I think you were right about him.'

'You think he's *not* mental now?'

'Oh, *God* no – he's mental all right – but he's not dangerous.'

Jo sighed, shook her head slowly, and then reached out and touched my cheek with the back of her hand. 'Oh, Rob . . . You never get it quite right, do you? You're always off the road on one side or the other – wrench the wheel so hard to avoid a ditch that you swing right across to the pavement opposite and demolish a bus shelter.'

'I'm going on a quest with him, Jo.'

'Of course you are.'

'No, Jo – it's a good thing. I'm going to get myself sorted out. That's what you want, isn't it?'

She smiled, slightly sadly, and kissed my ear. (Which would have been an incredibly tender moment, had she not made the kissing noise. That lip smack – when it's *right* there – is like someone firing a pistol directly into your aural canal, isn't it?)

'Ow! Bloody hell, Jo.' I winced, and backed away from her clutching the side of my head.

I'm sure that, pre-quest, Sir Galahad probably did that kind of thing all the time too.

THIRTEEN

'Stay in the car,' I said to Zach.

'But—'

'Stay . . . in the car,' I repeated, warningly: making sure I looked him right in the eyes so he knew I was serious. Much like you'd give the instruction to an excitable seven-year-old you thought might leap out and play with all the pumps while you went to pay for your petrol.

Things had moved pretty quickly.

After a few hours' sleep, Zach and I had gone to see Tech Bloke Danny at the radio station.

'If I have their email address, can I find out where a person lives?' I asked.

'Are you asking me if it's possible to find out an emailer's physical location?' he replied. In a whisper. Staring at me with huge amounts of conspiratorial graveness. And spoiling it by then taking a bite out of a chocolate éclair and getting some cream on his nose.

'That's what I just said, didn't I?'

'*Ahhhh*, well, no, you didn't.' He smiled here, indulgently. 'First of all, you asked if it was possible to find out where a person lives – which . . .' Danny laughed, 'is *very* different from asking if it's possible to find out where the email was sent from.' He laughed again. Danny was having a whale of a time. 'And next, you asked if *you* could find out – which is *very* diff—'

'Can you find out where an email was sent from, Danny?'

'Well, I can trace the IP address in the x-sender header.'

He paused to take a second mouthful of éclair. I waited for him to finish chewing it, in the foolhardy belief that he'd then continue. He didn't. He raised the éclair up to take another bite instead. He was determined to make me ask.

'Will tracing this "Eype E" address—' Danny sniggered at something terribly amusing. I ploughed on. 'Will tracing this tell us where the email was sent from?'

'Yes.'

'Good.'

'And or no.'

'And or no?'

'And, or or, or, in fact, or and or. Yes, and, or or, or and or, no.'

'Danny – this is Zach. One word from me, and Zach will snap your neck like a finger of fucking Kit Kat, OK?'

Zach laughed. Which didn't help.

I continued. 'So, will you please just give me the answer to my question? Ideally, in some language other than "Bollocks".'

'I *am* answering your question,' replied Danny. 'It's simply that, as phrased, it's a very *imprecise* question.' He grinned a smug, éclairy grin. This man had *no* chance of ever getting a girlfriend. I stroked my irritation by soothingly focusing on the fact that he would undoubtedly be the last of his line.

'Right. OK – Danny – just tell me what you can. I'm an idiot. Tell me what you can, while I stand here like an idiot. Fair enough?'

He poked at a few keys on his computer, and went, 'Hmmm . . .' four times, and, 'Ahh . . .' twice. When he'd finished, he turned back to me and smiled. Without saying anything. It was apparent that he wasn't going to budge until I said, 'Well?'

'Well?'

'London.'

'London? Can you be more specific?'

'Nope. London's not one hundred per cent, even. But it is . . . oh . . . ninety-six per cent. Originated at a node in London. If we had the legal powers to access her ISP logs, we could find out exactly who and where this Beth is, but, as we haven't, London is all I can give you.'

'Damn.'

'What about *Eliza*beth?' Zach asked. 'Can we cross-check the intel for Beth and *Eliza*beth?'

I shook my head. 'No – we don't have an email from Elizabeth. We have nothing but her first name and her phone number.'

Danny snorted. 'You have her phone number?'

'Well, yes. But that's no good, is it? You can find a phone number if you know the name and address, but not the other way round.'

'Yes you can,' replied Danny, as though any fool knew that.

'How?'

'There's a computer program. It matches numbers to addresses.'

'Is that legal?'

'It's not *il*legal. All it does is allows you to search through data that's already in the public domain – it's in the phone book. Even without the program, you could search through all the phone books to match the name and address to a number. It would just . . .' he pushed the last of the éclair into his mouth, 'take a little longer.'

'So – we can get this program from some hackers or something, can we?'

'Yes, you can, I suppose.'

'I see.'

'Or you can buy it at Dixons. Or PC World. Or Currys. Or – because, *as I'm sure you know*, all of those are, in fact, part of the same parent company – you could go wild and get it from, say, Amazon. If you think that would be more edgy and exciting.'

'Right.'

'But don't bother. I've already got it loaded on my PC here.'

In under ten seconds, Danny gave us Elizabeth's address. It was in London.

I thanked him, left him to chuckle over my lack of computer skills while his genetic material continued on its journey to extinction, and four hours later, Zach and I were sitting in my car outside Elizabeth's house. Things, as I say, had moved pretty quickly.

I got out of the car. I didn't really want to, to tell the truth. Up to now it had all been a bit unreal. Yes, I was attacking the situation – taking things in hand, moving forward, sorting myself out – but in a way that meant I didn't really have to do anything except wander around harmlessly with a proactive and resolute angle to my shoulders. It was all very theoretical.

It wasn't theoretical now. Now, I had to go up to a real door, press a real bell, and confront a real human being. What the hell would I say? I was calling at the house of a complete stranger, unannounced and unwanted, armed with nothing but a mouthful of needy, maniac speculation. How did Jehovah's Witnesses *do* this? Without feeling like utter pricks? It was only Zach being there that got me out of the car, I have to admit. Yes, there was a slight temptation to take him along: if some woman was going to call me a nutter, then it *would* have been useful to have had Zach standing beside me – I could have simply pointed to him, to put things into perspective. Realistically, though, an unfamiliar bloke turning up at a woman's door out of the blue is potentially intimidating enough; *two* blokes turning up – one of whom is built like a bulldozer, dressed in combat gear and with a 'fresh out of rehab' look to his eyes – was simply taking it too far. And Zach was so excited that I knew, if I didn't get out and ring the bell pretty quickly, he wouldn't be able to hold back from doing it himself for much longer.

I opened the car door and stepped out on to the pavement: one final '*Stay*' and a stern look at Zach, and then I strode up the short garden path with an air of decisiveness that was having to fight tooth and nail to prevent my queasy knees from fleeing from underneath me in opposite directions.

The area of London we were in was Willesden. That location didn't mean a great deal to me. By the look of it, it didn't mean a great deal to the people who lived there either. The house itself was terraced, with a negligible front garden separating it from the street – the lawn looked absently neglected, rather than flamboyantly abandoned (the garden of the house to the right had grass that was a couple of feet high, and incorporated the original use of a broken television set as a central feature to draw the eye elegantly up towards the small, sodden pile of household waste behind the bin). The bay window of Elizabeth's place had taciturn curtains drawn tightly shut – like arms folded across a chest; there was no bell that I could see, but the cheap oak-effect front door had a cheap brass-effect knocker two-thirds of the way up. I took a breath and gave it two hard, I-*am*-confident raps – which nudged two dull, cheap, knock-effect noises out of the soft, sullen wood.

Two and a half seconds passed in which nothing whatsoever happened. This, with an almost euphoric rush, provoked me to think, 'Oh well – gave it my best shot. Better go home and get married now.' I was utterly delighted.

Nothing toys with your emotions like the possibility of a

cop-out, however, and this one ran true to form when it raced away from me, guffawing, as, in the next instant, I heard the sound of someone moving inside.

There was another silence, and so I raised my hand to use the knocker again, but the door opened just before I touched it – leaving me standing there looking at the occupant, with my arm frozen in the 'up' position of 'Can I go to the toilet please, miss?'

She looked at me, and then looked up at my hand, and then looked back to me again.

'Elizabeth?' I asked.

'Yes,' she said, without any particular inflection. 'Yes . . . that's correct – you can put your hand down now.'

I lowered my arm, and then shook it about a bit: as though I was trying to get the blood back into it. I was attempting to indicate that . . . well, I don't know . . . that I had some kind of condition that required I regularly raise my arm for periods of time. Perhaps she'd think I was suffering from an affliction other than stupidity.

'And who are you?' she continued. She didn't seem surprised or anxious. Quite the opposite. If there was anything in her manner, it was vague curiosity poking itself – out of a sense of duty – through weary indifference.

She was older than I'd thought she would be. Her smooth black hair had occasional trails of grey twisting through it, and her face seemed tired in that way that comes not from being awake all night, but from simply being alive for longer than one had expected. Not that it was an unattractive face. No – with some careful lighting and the sympathy of the judges, it might even pass for beautiful. It was more that it brought to mind those photos you sometimes see: Movie Stars Without Their Make-up. And she was thin too. Thin like a figure made out of pipe-cleaners; her long cotton dress fell down with only a few gentle forays away from the vertical. Beneath it her feet were bare, and, at the end of a slender, pale arm, the tendons were stretched and clearly visibly in her hand as it grasped the edge of the door to hold it open.

'I'm Rob Garland,' I said.

'Oh, right . . . yes.' She nodded slowly as she remembered. 'Yes – I called you a cunt on air.'

'Um . . . no, you didn't.'

'Didn't I? *Fuck* – I meant to.'

Oddly, she then stood back and opened the door wider, inviting me in.

There was no hallway and so I stepped right into the living room. In there was an old sofa, that looked like it had probably belonged to someone else before she got it, and an ancient and battered wooden coffee table, that looked like it had probably belonged to everyone else – certainly in London, and possibly in the world – before she got it. A genuine coal fire burnt in the grate with a noise like cracking knuckles, and in the far corner was a sparse desk-and-chair set-up on which, flanked by ashtrays, sat a computer (a screensaver swirled random patterns across the screen). Every other available inch, it seemed, was occupied by books. All the bookcases – and they took up three walls – were crammed full (books piled on top of other books, and wedged in tightly at odd angles: as though the whole thing were a makeshift dam blocking off a river that would otherwise have run through the house). Books lay on the table, on the mantelpiece, and on the floor. It was a frightening swamp of books.

Really annoying books too. Every stinking one of the things seemed to be a book you felt you *ought* to have read. And I don't mean simply books that you would have liked to have read, in an ideal world, but that you can get away with not having got around to: Tolstoy or Dante, say – who's actually *read* the *Inferno*? You can't look down on a person for that – that'd just be taking the piss. But Elizabeth also had all those books that are guaranteed to make you squirm with discomfort if they're brought up and your back is against a wall. Those obvious, (literally) taken as read, standards by Dickens, and Camus, and Melville, and Flaubert. ('Do you know – haha – do you *know*, the odd thing is, for some reason, I've never actually read *Madame Bovary*. Haha! Can you believe that?') Every title looked out at me and stifled a snigger. Elizabeth would almost certainly be a fearfully wounding person to encounter at a dinner party.

She saw me gazing at the tactical nuclear strike of literature that surrounded us.

'Do you read . . .' she paused for a moment to draw on a cigarette, 'at all?'

'I don't get the chance to read as much as I'd like,' I replied. Which I immediately regretted. Ugh. Never mind – maybe I'd get away with having said that.

'You poor dear,' she replied with a smile.

Then again, maybe I wouldn't.

I changed the subject. 'I suppose you're wondering why I'm here?'

'There is that, yes. But first of all, I'm wondering *how* you got to be here. How in the world did you find me?'

'I traced your address from your phone number.'

'Really? Is that legal?'

'Well . . .' I adopted a casual air. 'It's not *il*legal. The data's already in the public domain anyway – in the phone book – and there's a computer pro—'

'I'm sorry, but could I just cut in there? Only, I've lost interest in what you're saying now.' She walked past me and flopped down on the sofa. 'So . . . *why* are you here?'

This wasn't going to be easy. I walked over, coughed lightly and unnecessarily, and sat down on the sofa too. Elizabeth looked at me. She looked at me with the face of a woman who'd say, 'You twat' if the next words out of my mouth were 'I'm on a quest.' I should perhaps work up to that particular announcement via some small talk.

'You like books, then, don't you?' I said, pulling Graham Greene out from between my legs – having accidentally sat on him.

'I like *good* books. Actually, I like fucking terrible books too – in the sense that bad writing infuriates me into something not unlike euphoria. Hatred is a terribly invigorating emotion, don't you find? And durable too. "Hatred is by far the longest pleasure; Men love in haste, but they detest at leisure."'

'Right.'

'Byron.'

'Byron. Yes . . . He had a club foot, didn't he?'

'You've clearly studied the Romantic Poets in some depth.'

Hmmm . . . I wonder what the opposite of 'charisma' is?

'Do you write yourself?' I continued, commendably. 'Is that what you do for a living?'

'What I do for a living . . .' She gazed up at the ceiling as she said this, and smiled in a way I took to probably be ironic, rather than merely annoying. 'No. No, I don't write. I teach English.'

'Where?'

'In a school.'

'A local school?'

'Fairly local.'

'That's good. It's rubbish to have to travel ages to get to work, isn't it?' I wittered. 'It adds to the length of the day.'

'Well, I've been off work for a while in any case.'

'Really? Why's that?'

She leaned forward and stubbed out her Marlboro in the grey metal ashtray on the coffee table. 'You were about to tell me why you were here,' she said, immediately taking out another cigarette and pushing it between her pale lips. 'I hate to rush you, but I'm forty-six years old, and I'm rather hoping you'll have finished talking before my menopause starts. I'd find it terribly wearing to have to deal with both at the same time.'

'Forty-six? Really? You don't look it.' She didn't. Maybe being really aggravating keeps you young. 'I'd have put you, oh . . . mid-to-late thirties.'

'Was that meant to be a compliment?'

'It was an observation. Would a compliment have been a bad thing?'

'Suggesting that forty-six is a fucking awful, guilty thing for a woman to be, but, "Well done, Elizabeth – no one would ever suspect it of you" would be a bad thing.'

'Right.'

'Whereas essentially some breed of "You're quite attractive . . . still", made in the gloriously comic belief that expressing such a notion using a disguising collection of alternatively tired words is dreadfully winning of you . . . that isn't exactly bad. No – that blends "pointless" and "vaguely insulting" in a way that's really quite exciting.'

'Right . . . You're an ugly old witch.'

She looked at me for a second, and then conjured a gentle genie of cigarette smoke from between her lips before letting out a small, but I think genuine, laugh.

'What do you want?' she said.

'I want to know why you said you knew how I felt.'

She turned to flick some ash into the ashtray. 'I have a rich talent for empathy. Really – I simply can't help sensing the pain of others, and taking it upon myself. At one time I was going to be a saint, you know, but my parents didn't approve.'

'I don't think that's it.'

'What? That I was going to be a saint, or that my parents didn't approve of me?'

'I think you know how I feel, because *you've* felt like that too.'

'No, no – I've never felt stupid.'

'I can't help noticing that you're not quite giving me a direct answer. And I can't help thinking that generally you're not evasive. Generally, you seem to be non-evasive to the point of being bluntly, relentlessly abusive, in fact.'

She looked at me penetratingly, without replying, for two deep, slow pulls on her cigarette.

'OK,' she said, finally. 'Let's bond.'

Elizabeth's Story

I was in Bulgaria. I'm still not quite sure why.

The purely superficial skin of the reason was that I was there attending a seminar on Teaching and Appreciating English Literature – some manner of co-production between their state education department and a British–Bulgarian Friendship and Development quango based in the UK; the conference itself doubtlessly funded by the EU, charitable contributions, the Russian Mafia and Virgin Mobile. That much is all very standard and lovely, but how I got to be invited to attend the thing at all is a fucking sightless mystery. I have written a few angry pieces for the kind of English literature periodicals with circulations that, in a good month, amount to their own editorial staff, I do teach our nation's pubescent future with a uniquely sustained weary hopelessness, and I may even have run a finger down the spine of Dimiter Dimov's Tobacco *in Willesden public library once, but that's about it. Maybe Martin Amis was at the dentist's that week. Fuck knows. My best guesses are still: (1) mindless, random chance, (2) administrative error, or (combining the previous two and renaming the result) (3) a government policy initiative – perhaps there'd been a memo somewhere declaring that at least one person on these kinds of lightly disguised free holidays should be picked, paper-from-hat, out of the vast, disgruntled pool of front-line workers doing the job day in and day out. I was, perhaps, the delegate in charge of keeping it real: 'Yo! Listen up 'bout Eddie M. Forster, motherfuckers.'*

To be honest, I really couldn't have cared less. I felt the same as anyone would: I was being offered a week away at someone else's expense, and so I quickly accepted the invitation saying I was grateful, excited about the opportunity to exchange experiences and ideas with colleagues from a sister European nation, and that, if there'd been some sort of mistake about inviting me, then it was too fucking late now, because, if they tried to back out, I'd sue for both the emotional distress and the cost of my 'Bulgarian in Two Weeks!' audio tapes.

So, that was that, and, a few months later, there I was in the country of balalaikas and Soviet-era industrial spillage.

They put us up in a hotel not far from where the conference was being held. It was ghastly place – a hate-crime against eyes. The Hotel Mika: a great, fuck-off boxy construction that looked like it had somehow managed to mock and defy the very logic of time itself so as to be constructed in the 1950s, in a 1970s style, using technology from the 1820s. My room had a combined shower and toilet. That's not a joke. It had a combined shower and toilet.

The only good thing about it was that at least you could smoke. In fact, when I checked in, I asked for a smoking room, and the receptionist looked back at me, blank and bemused; as though I'd asked if I could please have a room with gravity in it. Marvellously cheering. And good for Bulgaria as a nation too, I'm inclined to think. Really, these former Soviet states with their civilised tobacco laws are poised to reap fine rewards, in my opinion. The next European Wirtschaftswunder will take place in the 'smoking economies'. Tourism, you see. A few years from now, I have no doubt, you'll be able to go on smoking holidays. People fatigued and frustrated by living and working in buildings – in entire cities, in fact – where smoking is forbidden and actionable will pay well, and happily, for the simple, age-old pleasure of being able to walk into a bar, sit down with friends and a beer and a whole night of thoughts to share, and light up a cigarette with easy, unfretful naturalness. Delightful evenings in smoky taverns where the official fucking policy of the London fucking Borough of fucking Brent means not a fucking thing – who wouldn't reach into their pocket for that?

Ah, but here I am getting all girlish and sentimental. Forgive me – I dream so ardently only because I love, and I care, and because Brent Council are a pack of joyless cunts.

So, I attended talks and discussions during the day. I listened to papers, entertained myself by coughing loudly every time someone used the word 'pedagogical', and, over coffee, nodded non-committally at a socio-linguist from Plovdiv, while watching the biscuit crumbs gathered in the corners of his mouth slowly become soggy as he spoke about Proto-Indo-European voiced aspirates. In my free time, I wandered around with a gloriously liberating lack of purpose. The hotel served meals – specialising in both goat and the goat-like – but still I was tempted to eat out sometimes; on a couple of occasions, I even had dinner with one of the people who was also in our party – Jane. Jane was from Liverpool, but actually perfectly lovely, and I remember we discussed the Brontës – I told her how Branwell was my particular favourite because, unlike his sisters, he'd had the simple good manners to forgo writing any fucking awful novels in favour of drinking himself to death. I liked Jane. At night she, the rest of the party and I would generally gather in the hotel bar, drink Bulgarian lager, and talk such complete bollocks that you simply would not believe it.

I was usually the last to go to bed after these sessions. I don't sleep well. What I do is lie in bed, looking at the ceiling, and smoking. Or sleeping fitfully, and smoking. Or staring at the television (what's on makes no difference at all – I simply like the sound of voices and the soothing visual movement; it's gently narcotic), and smoking.

This particular night, I went up to my room very late. I'd bought a bottle of red from a supermarket earlier, and deliberately left it on the table by my bed: paid for and waiting for my fancy, whenever that might be – my little merlot gigolo. I flopped down on top of the duvet, opened the wine, flicked on CNN, and lay there watching the world come apart between sips.

I did this until I got really quite drunk.

That didn't matter – I've been on my own and drunk before; I wouldn't make any claims of being an expert at it, but I carry the thing off, I think, with a broad competence punctuated with occasional flashes of real skill. Being pissed in a Bulgarian hotel room is fine in itself, but a chasm of spiritual darkness awaits to sink your soul down into its depths if such Balkan drunkenness results in your clumsily dropping your last packet of cigarettes into the lavatory in positively the latest of the early hours of the morning. When you see your final, almost full, soft pack of Rodopi hit the churning waters of the bowl, then you truly do feel how very small you are in relation to the vastness of the universe.

Fishing a few from the toilet and drying them out with the hotel hairdryer would have been the civilised option, but that was shattered in front of my stretching eyes as they almost instantly disintegrated before my fingers had even begun to reach out: melted away – the paper dissolving and releasing kinked strands of tobacco like seeds from a rupturing pod. Gone.

There's a disbelief that comes over you if you run out of cigarettes when all the shops are closed. Even though the indestructible facts are right there, even though unblinking reality stands directly in front of you, you're utterly unable to believe it. You're compelled – demanded – to think that there must *be a cigarette around the place* somewhere. *In your handbag; far-sightedly placed in a drawer in case of just such an emergency; forgotten, torn and twisted, but still smokeable, in a pocket – fucking somewhere. The despair that's an unavoidable consequence of the truth is so chilling that your mind won't let you accept what is brutally obvious. I imagine the whole experience is very much like how people who think there's a God must feel. So, I went over my room like a crime-scene investigator for a full ten minutes. I looked under, inside, and on top of everything. I checked the bin to see if a crumpled packet hid a carelessly discarded pearl. I examined the ashtray for any butts that might have had enough unburnt white remaining in front of the filter for them to be capable of an encore. However, nothing but fruitless hopes and misery sunk bone-deep were in room 418 of the Hotel Mika.*

'Fuck,' I thought.

Maybe I could go to Jane's room, just along the hallway. She smoked – I could beg a few cigarettes to tide me over. No . . . that was too selfish, even in the midst of a terrible personal tragedy like this. I couldn't wake her up at this hour – mornings were a cruel enough thing, even as a senseless act of Nature; for a person to inflict this time of the morning on another human being for personal gain, in the clear knowledge of what they were doing, would be an act of hedonistic barbarism. Damn and arseholes.

But then, with a sudden orgasm of relief, I remembered I was in Bulgaria. The hotel bar, and any shops, would be shut at this gluey, leaning-half-asleep-against-dawn time of day, but European cities have cigarette machines on walls in the streets. All I had to do was go for a walk to find one.

I argued my feet into my shoes, whirled on my coat, and made my way down to the front of the hotel. I was tingling. The streetlights and the sky were providing about the same level of illumination now, which made everything seem oddly flat; two dimensional – like a movie. I was in a movie. And on a mission. In a mysterious middle-European nation. I was Marlene bastard Dietrich, for fuck's sake. I was pissed, Marlene Dietrich, and off to buy some fags. Does life get any better than that?

It took about a quarter of an hour to locate a machine. They really ought to be marked on maps. Mind you, I didn't have a map, so that wouldn't have helped. They ought to send up flares, then. Shoot signalling stars high into the air every couple of minutes, so that the cigarette-less and frantic and pissed would know where to find them in an unfamiliar city. Eventually, though, I found a machine, using nothing but my tenaciously moving feet; I threw in my coins, tore open the wonderfully delivered packet, sat down on a nearby bench, and smoked two heartbreakingly beautiful cigarettes back to back in an almost teary trance of delight and comfortingly cherished well-being.

Happy and content, I made my way back towards the hotel. The day had crept out much further now. Even though the sky was cloudy – a white sheet marked with occasional blurry streaks of darkish grey; like charcoal lines on paper, smeared by a thumb – everything shone for me with that strange, hyper-vivid, up-all-night bright-ness. The world felt clean and full of energy and, quite simply, right.

After a short walk, I stood in the pretty square opposite the Hotel Mika and watched fifty-three people burn to death.

Well, that's melodramatic, of course. I'm sure that many of them were dead before I got there, and, in any case, the smoke almost certainly killed far more than the flames did. I waited in that square, staring up at the fourth floor, and it was only in my imagination that Jane was trapped in her room: *desperate and frightened and screaming her fucking lungs raw with panic and pain. Most likely the fumes had smothered the life out of her before she even managed to emerge properly from her sleep and reach across to the bedside table for her glasses. I'm flattering myself that I bore witness to a horror that went on out of sight; daydreaming that it was timed for my benefit: that its circular raison d'être was to make me its audience.*

Obviously, I'd like to be able to say that the fire was started by a stray cigarette. That would be wonderful. I could hug an irony like that until my arms ached. It wasn't, though. Faulty wiring. Faulty wiring, a badly maintained alarm system, and everyone on the fourth and fifth floors died, as well as some on the third. Jane; others from our group; people I'd probably seen in the bar; people I didn't know in any way at all. Fifty-three in total – not fifty-four only because it didn't include me: because I'd popped out to buy some cigarettes. Maybe it'd have been less – at least one less – had I woken Jane. Or had I stayed in my room – awake, and thus able to raise the alarm sooner. It probably would have been; almost certainly would have been. But, well, that's life, isn't it?

FOURTEEN

Elizabeth lit another cigarette, and smiled at me.

'Or I could tell you the one about a man who goes to the doctor's with a parrot on his head?' she said.

Her face looked precarious. It was the kind of look you sometimes see on a person who's just been dumped. That forced, cheery acceptance that you know could slide violently away in any number of directions in the very next instant: rage, sobbing, numbness – anything. And, in fact, any one of those things would be less disconcerting than that teetering expression of unnatural ease.

'I knew you'd felt like me,' I replied, gently.

'I didn't fucking feel like you. Or, if you want me to be wildly accommodating out of sheer politeness, I felt like you for a thousandth of a second – before seeing that any such feeling was arrogant, piss-brained twattery. *God* . . . you are *such* a cunt.'

'Oh, come off it. You thought about what you could have done differently. How things might have—'

'Yes, I *thought* about it. I didn't *feel* it, though. Of course one thinks about how things might easily have turned out another way. That's an idea that's going to occur naturally to anyone with even the low-water-mark sentience level of a . . . a . . .' she struggled for a word, then, relieved, motioned towards me, 'a radio presenter, say. The difference is whether you immediately see that Stuff Simply Happens, without meaning or design, or whether you're emotionally teenage enough to conclude that *you* are the crucial pivot whose decisions and actions shape the world. I, or others, could have done things differently, or not done them at all, and then, perhaps, all, or some, of those people wouldn't have been killed – or I'd have died with them. But it's all arbitrary. My actions are of no importance – not really. Your fucking obsessional examination of your decisions isn't sensitivity: it's ego.'

'Right. So it doesn't bother you that those people died, then? You have no problem with that at all? "They died, I lived – pft." Is that right?'

'That's not quite it, no – since you ask.'

'Then what *do* you feel?'

'I wish I were dead.'

That pulled me up sharply. It was because she didn't say it argumentatively, or in the theatrical way that some people use the phrase. She said it calmly and quietly; with the hint, even, of a slight shrug. I opened my mouth to say something in reply, but my lips just hung there, clueless.

She tapped the ash from her cigarette and continued. 'Jane was a good person. A happy, kind person: a better person than me. I'm sure nearly everyone whose life ended suddenly and pointlessly that night was more use to their friends, to their families and to Western civilisation generally than I am. There were respected academics with unique reservoirs of knowledge stored in their heads, children who never had a chance to experience life properly, people – normal, in-the-street people – with enthusiasm, and plans, and new kitchens on order. It's unfair that they died and I didn't. Undeserved. It's simple chance, but that doesn't matter. In the same way as chance isn't the point when a millionaire wins the lottery while someone living in a shitty bedsit with three kids is one number off. I should be dead. I should be dead because that's *the right fucking thing*. Every breath I take is a slur against justice.'

'It's not your fault.'

'Oh, fuck off. Haven't you been listening? Fault has nothing to do with it. It's simply wrong that I'm still alive.'

137

'It's not. And you are useful.'

She gave a tight little laugh. 'Why? Because what? Because I'm a teacher perhaps? Well, I've been off sick for God knows how long, and, even when I wasn't, I was fucking terrible. I wasn't one of those inspirational teachers they have in films – the ones who walk into a classroom and open up new worlds to their astonished pupils. I hated the little bastards.'

'You're useful to me.'

'What? How am I?'

'Because you're sure. I want that certainty. I want to know how you get up in the morning and are able to decide which vest to put on, or—'

'You wear vests? Ha! You ponce.'

'See? *That*'s it. I want to know how you can put aside constant, debilitating indecision in the face of a billion life-or-death choices every minute to be so happily, effortlessly fucking irritating.'

'Woah – I'm being called irritating by a *radio DJ* now.'

'Argh! You . . . you . . . *Argh!*'

'Touché.'

I took a few deep breaths.

'Look,' I continued, when I'd calmed down a little. 'Come with me.'

'Where are you going?'

'I've no idea.'

'How very surprising.'

'OK, then – OK: I'm going on a voyage of self-discovery.'

'Good Lord. That's *heroically* banal. It's the very apotheosis of "life-affirming", by golly – and I applaud your integrity in refusing to be diverted away from the hackneyed in any way at all. You're based on a true story; you're rated "U"; and the box reads "Heart-warming".'

'Take the piss all you want.'

'Really? Only, you know, I wouldn't like to overstep the mark . . .'

'The fact is, I think you need me almost as much as I need you. Why did you call my show in the first place? Eh?'

'I was pissed. I know you'll find this difficult to believe, but when I get drunk I tend to get verbally combative.'

'Bollocks. You *needed* to talk. I think you have problems just as much as I do, they're simply different ones. I think you need help. *And*, by the way, I think you're not as unpleasant as you'd like me to believe.'

She turned away from me and made a very long job indeed of crushing her cigarette out in the ashtray. I couldn't be sure, because the general movement made it difficult to pick out, but I thought her hand might have been shaking. I felt that I'd perhaps hit the target there – sort of *tamed* her. Cracked the hard shell, so I'd now see the softness underneath. I even relaxed for a moment. But when she turned back her eyes were burning and her jaw was aggressively rigid. She glared right into me.

'I'm more unpleasant than you could fucking *dream*,' she said, with cold authority. She continued to look at me for a few, freezing moments, then stood up. 'I want you to go now.'

'I'm . . .' I began, but I didn't really know what I was, so I stood up too, and walked towards the door.

I let myself out, then turned back to look at her. She was standing there stiffly, framed by the doorway, her arms not really folded – more clasped around herself.

'Maybe . . . maybe we could talk again. Tomorrow, perhaps?' I said.

'Tomorrow? No. I don't see myself as being all that chatty tomorrow.'

She closed the door, and I started to go back to my car. Just before I reached the end of her path, however, I heard her shout my name, and, when I turned, she was standing in the doorway again.

'Things aren't your fault,' she called out to me. 'General things, specific things – it's all the same. Things happen around us, not because of us; if one thing doesn't happen, then another one does, and, ultimately, it doesn't really matter if we're there or not. You don't have any real control over those things, and you're *definitely* not responsible for them.'

'Responsible?' I replied. 'Before I can even start feeling responsible for stuff, I think I need to jump the hurdle of being able to do anything in the bleeding first place.'

'Fair enough. Then remember that you're not responsible for the actions of others either – not at all.'

'Um . . . Mind you, I *do* feel responsible when I hold up the checkout queues at Safeway.'

'Meh – they should lay on more staff. And have an "Eight Items or Less, but in Need of Counselling" line. Easy enough to do – "Would you like help packing? Or maybe you just want to talk about your mother?" Put it in the suggestion box.'

'OK.'

'I . . .' Her face leaned itself back wearily into a small, sad smile – she looked incredibly . . . erm . . . *lonely*. It was hard to square that with someone who was obviously so self-sufficient, but that's the feeling I got. 'I hope things work out for you . . . Goodbye, Rob.'

'Goodbye, Elizabeth.'

She closed the door again. I looked at it for a few seconds, for no reason I could pin down, and then walked slowly back to the car.

Zach was sitting in the passenger seat, seemingly calm and happy and content with his place in the world. The git.

'Sorry I was so long,' I said, getting myself comfortable in my seat and putting the key in the ignition.

'No problem.'

'You weren't bored?'

'Bored? No. I was working the geography: deciding the ideal places to locate snipers, or the best way to assault the houses in a hostage situation, or how I'd defend that optician's on the corner using a three-man team.'

'*Right* . . . Of course.'

'So?' asked Zach, eyes like Christmas morning. 'How did it go?'

'Poorly.'

'Yeah?'

'Yes. Her position is that everything is meaningless, so it's idiotic to try to understand it.'

'That's all she had to say?'

'Well, no – I'm summarising: there was lots of personal abuse too.' I clicked my teeth, dejectedly. 'It seems we've had a completely wasted journey.'

'No journey is wasted, Rob. The travelling itself always adds something to your soul.'

'Pff – let's see if you still feel that way once we hit the M6 again.'

I started the car and pulled out – though I didn't really know where I was going. 'Hmmm . . .' I said, 'I'm not sure if we should go straight back home, or stay down here for the night. Or, if we stay down here, *where* we should stay. Or—'

'We'll stay, so you can rest before the drive back, and we'll stay at the nearest Holiday Inn. We can pull over and ask someone where that is.' I looked across at him. 'Sorry, Rob,' he shrugged, 'but . . . you know. We were iced-over for fifteen minutes at the counter of that McDonald's off the freeway on the way down here. Both of us standing there like jerks with you nearly in tears trying to decide whether you wanted to go large or not. If I leave the "stay or not stay?" decision to you we'll still be circling around in this car next week.'

I drove along for a good while trying to pick out anyone at all in North London who looked like they might, just *might*, not be clueless, stoned or certain to car-jack us the second we slowed down. I eventually found a bloke walking a dog (the badge of solid and decent – just count the number of movies where they give Tom Hanks's character a dog), and pulled over so that Zach could wind down the window and interrogate him for intelligence. I tapped the steering wheel and let my mind drift while they talked. There was no use my listening in any case – my brain can't absorb directions. If I ever stop the car to ask for them it goes:

'Left at the traffic lights . . .'

'OK.'

'Then second on the right.'

'On the right – gotcha.'

'Along for about two hundred yards until you pass a pub on the left . . .'

'The left.'

'Then a sharp right . . .'

'Uh-huh.'

'Round the bend . . .'

'Round it, OK.'

'And it's directly in front of you.'

'Cheers – that's great. Thanks very much.'

And then I drive off with a grateful wave, not having a bleeding *clue* where I'm heading.

So, I let Zach get on with it and thought about my fingernails, and life, and Elizabeth. The first two were in a more or less hopeless state, so there wasn't much use dwelling on them, but I wished I'd managed to make more of an impression on Elizabeth. I was sure she genuinely could have helped me, in some way. I liked to think I could have helped her too. And there were definitely tiny flickers during which I thought I'd *almost* got through; when, despite her determinedly acid temperament, we'd very nearly ended up sitting side by side without elbowing each other for more space. It was a bit of a pisser that I hadn't pulled off getting her to spend some time with me – and not least because she was my only lead. What the hell was I supposed to do now?

Zach finished talking to Dog Bloke, thanked him far too loudly for it to translate comfortably into British, and wound up the window.

'So?' I asked.

'It's all cool. There's a Holiday Inn two klicks that way.' He swept his hand down off to the right, like someone demonstrating a slow karate chop.

'Ah . . . two klicks, eh? What's the, um, ETA on that, Zach? Just so you know, this ve*hic*le can do about fifteen klacks an hour.'

'What are you—'

'Never mind. Just tell me when to turn.'

I drove on.

What *was* I supposed to do now? I'd relied on the vague notion of a domino effect of revelations: one idea of what on earth I should do leading naturally to the next, and so on – until everything was sorted out, and I was fully functional again. Elizabeth had turned out to be a dead end. I'd failed. Failed especially gormlessly, come to think of it, because not only hadn't I swept her up into my personal odyssey, but I'd also forgotten to ask all the things I'd intended to. I'd been concentrating so hard on defending myself against her personality that I hadn't even remembered to ask what she'd meant, in her emails, about my life being in danger. Oh well – she was probably being metaphorical, or figurative. Quite possibly, if I *had* asked, she'd have started going on about spiritual existence, or will – thrown Nietzsche at me or something. Phew – actually, I'd dodged the bullet there.

Zach said he thought I should turn right at the next junction. I replied, 'Affirmative – over.'

A thing I've always noticed about films – especially, but not exclusively, whodunnits – is that some random happening has to trigger a main character's realisation. Miss Marple is baffled for days, until she finally has a boiled egg for breakfast and – boom! – suddenly sees, with complete clarity, that the reason that no one could find a murder weapon is because the victim was beaten to death with *one of those chickens*! Maybe it's just me, but I tend not to get lit up with insights or important thoughts because something else I've seen or done has ignited them by association. Mostly, I sidestep the whole phenomenon by simply not having any insights or important thoughts at all, so that could be a factor. However, when I *do* have them, they tend to, well, 'drop on me', for no identifiable reason: they fall – they aren't pushed.

I was driving along the street. Zach, by my side, was talking effusively about how he'd thought London would have fog, and did it have fog? or was it maybe only at night? or just in certain areas? or certain times of the year? because, if it was, then they ought to tell you how likely you were to get fog if you were a tourist visiting London – like they do with snow if you go on a skiing holiday – because London was a bit disappointing without fog, wasn't it? and was it a special fog? or like normal fog, like Nebraskan fog? which isn't that common, but they do have it; it's not like he'd never seen fog before or anything: in essence, pulling many more words out of the single concept 'Fog' than you would ever have thought, or have dearly hoped, possible. I was in third gear. Four teenagers in shiny blue tracksuits were standing on the pavement outside a newsagent's shop, laughing and pushing each other good-naturedly, and looking like they were probably planning to burgle someone's house and shit in their fridge. Up ahead, a Ford Focus with a tail light held in place by gaffer tape and a Radio 1 sticker on the rear window pulled away from the kerb without troubling itself to indicate.

None of these powerfully mundane things provoked me to have the sudden realisation that made me stop the car abruptly in the middle of the road and gasp, 'Oh, Jesus fucking Christ!'

'What is it?' asked Zach, glancing over at me, and then peering through the windscreen (upwards: presumably scanning the sky for attack helicopters).

'How do we get back to Elizabeth's place?'

'Uh, well, I dunno. Backtracking the way we've just come is easiest, I figure.'

I shifted into reverse and began backing down the street – at speed.

'Rob,' said Zach, chidingly. 'Backtracking doesn't mean, you know, literally going backwards.'

'I'm trying to find a place to turn, you twat. *Jesus* – just look at the parking here. Just *look* at it. There are no spaces at all.'

'There was one ahead of you – where that car pulled out.'

'Ugh. Why didn't you tell me that before?'

'Before what?'

'Before I was in this panic, of course! God. You're bloody useless, you are.'

I quickly and insanely reversed out on to the main road, not quite hitting a van coming down it by a distance that was invisible to the naked eye – pretty much missing it at the subatomic level. With a desperate and deafening screech of rubber on tarmac – that sounded like someone had miked up the noise of nails scraping down a blackboard through Aerosmith's PA system – an SUV following

145

the van braked and swerved to avoid slamming into us. While it howled to a halt, I swung the car around ferociously, tail first, so as to be facing the right way. This terrifying manoeuvre very nearly caused us to roll, and its whipping change of direction sent Zach lurching across towards me because of his own momentum – making him bang heavily against the side of my seat.

'This is *great*!' he whooped as I hurled us into first and squealed forwards – ignoring the fact that one of my hubcaps had come off, rolled rapidly across the other side of the road through the oncoming traffic, bumped up on to the pavement, and disappeared through the open door of a discount carpet warehouse.

'It is not fucking great,' I replied. I was driving right in the middle of the road so that I could overtake everything that was in front; every vehicle coming towards us had to hug the kerb to avoid a head-on collision. 'Elizabeth is going to kill herself.'

'How do you know that? How could . . .' Zach became suddenly awed. He reached out to touch my shoulder and, hushed, said, 'Did God speak to you just now?'

'Jesus.'

'*Jesus?*'

'What? No. *No*. Bollocks, Zach. No bleeding deities at all spoke to me, OK? I simply realised it.' The other drivers could see from the way I had my hazards on, and was flashing my headlights, and was stabbing my horn – and also from the simple fact that I was driving in a manner that would have been considered impossibly dangerous even in Italy – that I was obviously in some kind of emergency situation where every second counted. Their selfless reaction to this appeared to be: 'Yeah, well, I'm in a hurry too. So piss off.' Who'd have thought other road users could be so insensitive, especially in London?

'Quick,' I said to Zach, 'reach over and get my mobile.

Call an ambulance. Tell them to go to Elizabeth's house *right away*.' Zach didn't do anything for a second, and then he began patting my pockets. 'No, no,' I snapped. 'My phone's in my belt clip. On the right.' I started to get it myself, but taking one hand off the wheel and twisting to do this resulted in my very nearly failing to round a bend with that specific kind of less than total success that means you end up crashing into a chemist's at 58 mph. Shaking, I abandoned that idea.

Zach unclipped his seat belt, leaned right over, and reached under my arms to retrieve the phone. He quickly located the carrying pouch, but had a little trouble with the fastenings at the top: a fiddling, squirming delay that excellently gave me time to overtake a bus, and for every single passenger downstairs on our side of it to look across at us and visibly conclude that Zach was fellating me as I drove recklessly through Neasden. (That he was dressed in military gear made it *so* much worse, somehow – in fact, had Jo and my mother been on that bus, then the awfulness of the situation would have been scientifically perfect.)

'Why do you think that she's going to kill herself, anyway?' Zach asked my crotch.

'She said she wished she was dead.'

'Lots of people say that.' He finally sat back upright, my phone in his hand.

'Press the Enter and the Hash keys together to take the lock off . . . I know, that's what I thought – 999: ask for the ambulance service – but when I put it together with everything else, it was obvious that it wasn't just a figure of speech with her.'

Zach called the ambulance and gave them Elizabeth's address. There was a slightly tricky moment while he was doing this, because the person on the other end of the phone naturally assumed that we were there with her – and asked for details of precisely what the situation was. Zach put his hand over the mouthpiece and asked me what he should say. Rather than risk dulling their sense of urgency by replying that we weren't there, and didn't actually know for sure that she had attempted suicide, and that they should send an ambulance screaming across London because I had a 'hunch', I instructed him to make something up. Zach nodded, and told the emergency coordinator on the other end of the line that Elizabeth had shouted, 'I'm going to kill myself now!' out through the letterbox, and then we'd heard the sound of machinery . . . possibly a lawn mower.

I thought, in quick succession: (1) that this was the stupidest thing I'd ever heard, (2) that it was so ridiculously intriguing that it might actually be a brilliant thing to have said; the ambulance crew would race there all the quicker now – just out of sheer, appalled curiosity, and (3) that it was perhaps simply the way they did things in Nebraska.

'Put together what?' asked Zach, when he'd finished making the call.

'Eh?' (At that instant, I was smashing right over the top of an unnecessarily high mini roundabout with a crunching directness that had just driven the car's front suspension right up into the base of my skull, and was thus a little distracted.)

'What did you mean when you said you'd put together what she'd said about wanting to be dead with other things? What other things?'

'Oh – *things*. How she was. When she'd talked about my life being in danger, maybe she meant *one's* life was in danger – that missing death for no good reason like we had left you prone to being suicidal. Mostly, though, it was the little "jokes" she was making to herself that I didn't get until now. One of the last things she said to me was that she "didn't think she'd be very talkative tomorrow". I took it as being a deliberately obvious brush-off – like "I'm washing my hair" – but now I'm sure it was really gallows humour.'

'K.'

'See?'

'Oh, yeah, for sure.'

I chanced taking my eyes off the road for a second to look at him. He didn't seem convinced.

'You think I'm wrong, don't you?'

'She made a few bad gags. So, she's going to kill herself.' He shrugged. 'Whatever.'

'Oh, bollocks to you. I *know* it, all right? You weren't there. I know I'm right about this.'

'Hey, man, it's not a problem – really. You're on a quest: my duty is to be by your side to help out however I can. That's the task I've been given. You tell me that you just *know* that Elizabeth is turning into a sea bass this evening, and I'm right there with you, man, holding a net. I'm here to serve you, not to question you.'

You don't often get told you're a complete fuckwit as subordinately as that, do you?

I was about to pick my way through telling Zach that I didn't give a damn that *he* didn't give a damn what I thought, while simultaneously trying not to overturn the car, but the corner I was screeching around was actually the one at the bottom of Elizabeth's street – so it seemed pointless. We were here now. We'd see who was right. (Abruptly queasy, I caught myself – and guiltily told my watching conscience that, in fact, I really hoped that I *wasn't* right.)

Zach and I threw ourselves out of the doors as soon as I pulled up. I simply stopped alongside another car, right in front of Elizabeth's house – without making any attempt to find a parking space. Annoyingly, the road was wide enough that this wouldn't block any traffic. I *wanted* to block traffic. This was important enough to block traffic. I wanted a whiny driver to get out of his car and say, 'You're blocking traffic!' so I could angrily snap back, 'Someone's *dying* here – fuck off about my blocking the bloody traffic.' I'd do it without looking at him. Without even pausing. My focused determination to pursue something genuinely significant completely trumping his petty problems. It'd be rather impressive. Perhaps there could be some onlookers who'd gasp.

I apologised to my conscience again.

Elizabeth's house looked just as it had when I'd walked away from it earlier. There was no reason why it shouldn't, of course, but it was still somehow very wrong that it appeared unchanged. Maybe that's the real reason why people draw the curtains when there's been a death in the house – so that it doesn't look like it did the day before. So that it's clear: Things Here Have Changed. I ran up the path, Zach right behind me, and pounded my palm against the door. 'Elizabeth?' I waited only a moment – '*Elizabeth?*' – and then I banged on the door again. There was no answer.

I crouched down and looked through the letterbox. All I could see was the back wall of her living room (the thought, 'living room', took a bite out of me); it was wild with dozens of books, yet eerily still. I moved across as far as I could to try to get a view of more of the room, pressing my head hard against the door in a pointless effort to improve the angle. I was able to glimpse the edge of her computer monitor (the screensaver still dancing mindlessly on its screen), but nothing else.

I held open the flap on the letterbox with my thumbs, pushed my mouth to the hole and shouted through it so loudly that my voice rasped painfully at the back of my throat. '*Elizabeth!*'

Nothing. My call roared into the house and died

instantly, without even the slightest resonance coming back; it plunged into silence as though it had been dropped into cotton wool. I got up again and turned round. Zach was standing there looking intensely watchful, but entirely in control – a bit like one of those nightclub bouncers who doesn't have a criminal record that you see occasionally.

'Zach,' I said, hearing a warble of fear and panic in my voice. 'Do you think you could break down this door? I'm sure that—'

He didn't seem overly concerned with how I was going to finish the sentence because, before I'd reached the next word, he'd jumped forward and landed a shockingly vicious kick not far below the lock. The bottom of his boot hit the wood like it had the weight of a skipful of paving slabs behind it – the light Yale mechanism didn't so much give in as become embarrassingly irrelevant as a large section of the frame splintered away entirely, leaving a jagged wound in the wood. Shards of the cheap faux oak fireworked outwards as the door was smashed open with such force that it flew back on its hinges, hit the wall behind, and bounced itself shut again. Zach calmly took two steps backwards and, looking at me, held out his hand towards the shattered entrance in a 'There you go' manner.

His actions had been so instantly, explosively violent that I was surprised into shocked, lead-footed confusion for a second or two; I simply stood there staring at him, feeling I ought to say something. Like, 'Well done.' Or, 'Christ!'

I soon shook this off, however, and strode quickly into the house, pushing aside the crippled door.

Elizabeth's living room contained everything it had when I'd last been there, including Elizabeth. Except now she wasn't spitting verbal wasp stings in my direction and exhaling powerful streams of cigarette smoke and savouring little half-smiles at jokes she was making to herself.

Now she was slumped – oddly – awkwardly – back on the sofa, not saying anything, and not moving at all. The skin of her face was wrong: ill and waxy, with tiny dots of perspiration lying all over its bloodless surface. She looked like a sweating doll. She looked creepy. She looked creepy and terrifying.

All of this threw itself, unwanted, into my eyes in the time it took to involuntarily snatch a breath.

I stepped over to her and moved the table out of the way so I could get closer (as I did so, an empty tablet bottle rolled off on to the floor). I knelt down and clasped my hands around her arms. They were clammy. '*Elizabeth?*' I felt sick. I tried to pull her to her feet or at least sit her upright (I don't know why: hysterical denial, I suppose – trying to *make* her be alive). But I was unbalanced, and weak and dizzy with fear and nausea, and I toppled over on to my back while attempting to lift her up; she fell limply on top of me, her head flopping forwards and butting me in the mouth as we hit the floor together.

'Gngh,' we both said simultaneously.

I said this simply because of the perfectly well-known pain and unpleasantness associated with being head-butted in the face by a corpse. It croaked out of Elizabeth's mouth, however, in a groggy, million-miles-away fashion. I rolled her off me and stared down at her.

Was she really alive? Maybe it was just a lifeless expulsion of air; dead breath squeezed from her lungs by the impact of her landing on top of me – like that truly delightful phenomenon of cadavers breaking wind as they lie on their slabs in the morgue. I scanned her face and, wonderfully – euphorically – saw that she was bleeding where her forehead had impacted with my teeth. I was pretty sure dead people didn't bleed. Thank *fuck*.

I grabbed her shoulders and shook her. 'Elizabeth!' Her head whipped about atop her flaccid neck. Argh! Stop! What's that you hear about? 'Shaken baby syndrome'? Where shaking causes a brain haemorrhage or something? Killing someone while trying to see if they were alive is the kind of thing that you'd really regret later, isn't it?

Fortunately, however, my potentially fatal first aid had a positive effect.

'Mhh . . .' She opened her eyes, though doing so seemed to be a tremendous struggle. 'Rob?' she said, puzzled and distant. 'Ahh . . . right.' She let her eyelids fall shut again. 'So, this is Hell, then.'

I felt a hand on my shoulder and looked up. Zach was standing there, reading the label on the pill bottle. 'Let me, Rob,' he said. 'I've done emergency medical training. I at least know how to put people in the recovery position, yeah? Your technique seems . . . well, you know. If she goes into arrest I wouldn't be surprised if you just started hitting her with a chair or something.'

I moved aside slightly so that Zach could kneel down and examine her. He pulled one of her eyelids open and, presumably, examined her pupil (rather than, say, just doing it for a laugh). Elizabeth moaned with sleepy irritation at this and made a completely ineffectual attempt to push him away. The instant he stopped, she let her arms fall back down, and her eye shut again.

'Well?' I asked, nervously.

'Hmmm . . .' he replied.

'For Christ's sake, Zach, do something.' I banged a fist against the floor. 'Where the *fuck* is that ambulance? Jesus – she's going to die while we sit here waiting for it. *Fuck*. She's going to *die*, Zach.'

Zach narrowed his eyes. 'No one's dying,' he said with a cool determination. 'Not on my shift.'

'Eh?' Elizabeth surfaced once more – her body tensing slightly. She looked up at Zach, and then over at me. 'On his shift?' she slurred. 'Is he a doctor?'

'No,' I replied. 'No – he's an American.'

She closed her eyes and went limp again. 'Oh Jesus.'

FIFTEEN

Where do middle-class people go when they injure themselves? When they trip over their brochures for holiday
homes in Tuscany and fall heavily against their Agas, what
do they do? BUPA doesn't have its own casualty departments, does it? So, you'd think they'd have to go to
the same place as everyone else. Yet I've been in A&E a
reasonable number of times in my life, and I'm damned if
I've ever seen any A1s or A2s shuffling around with a wet
towel clasped against a head wound. No, it's always the
same mix of working-class drunks, pensioners, and young
children sitting on orange plastic chairs under the sickly
fluorescent lights in the waiting area; all cradling their
mute, ashen pain in betrayingly febrile hands. Night-
clothes, sockless feet, dashed-out-of-the-house hair, dirty
legs, stains, sweat; fear, embarrassment and strangers. Do
middle-class people *really* go to some other A&E department that we don't know about? One where it doesn't take
six hours to see an Iranian doctor who came over two
years ago and hasn't slept since, but rather a brisk five
minutes before you're in the company of an enthusiastic
senior consultant who smiles, and mends you, and, as you
leave, offers you a complimentary mint. Or maybe the
middle classes simply employ people to be injured for
them. I don't know. But I do know that A&E departments
are utterly bloody miserable. That you feel exposed and
vulgar.

To add variety, the one I was standing in was also
making me feel like a complete idiot.

The ambulance had arrived at Elizabeth's place, and

they'd quickly hurled her into the back of it and raced away: siren howling. As we'd smashed her door down (and what passing opportunist thief would be able to resist the chance of nipping inside and helping himself to all those Henry James paperbacks?), I'd told Zach to remain there:

'Will you be OK to stay here and look after the house?'

'For sure, Rob. No one will get past me. I can go three days without sleeping and survive indefinitely on nothing but bugs and rainwater.'

'Right. That's a bit of luck, then.'

While he'd settled down to guard duty, I'd jumped in my car and followed Elizabeth to the hospital.

Everyone there seemed to be a bit pissed off with me. I suspect that it was partly because they didn't particularly like people who tried to commit suicide. A 'Fffff – haven't we got *enough* work to do without you deliberately creating more for us?' kind of thing, I'm guessing. They couldn't effectively convey this irritation to Elizabeth as she was wilfully spiting them by drifting in and out of consciousness, so I got it due to some weird logic based on association. Not only that, but Elizabeth's being at death's door, ringing the bell impatiently, meant she was rushed straight through to be cared for by a buzzing and energetic circle of medical staff. The other patients – some of whom looked as though they may have been waiting to get a chipped bone seen to since the mid-eighties – gave me a series of stares that told me that they regarded this as tantamount to cynical queue-jumping.

To be honest, though, this wasn't the main problem. Being nominated as the proxy for all the annoyance that Elizabeth was too out of it to receive was a bit embarrassing, but the major personal discomfort was all my own work.

I'd arrived in a worried panic, but they were used to people turning up like that. The trouble was that their long familiarity with nervous friends and relatives led them to make the mistake of confusing me with a functioning human being. They discovered their error pretty quickly.

A receptionist, or some kind of helper, had asked me to fill in a form listing basic details about Elizabeth. I was handed the thing and told to write down what I knew. I should have said, 'I don't really know anything,' and then gone straight back to Birmingham, but I didn't. Because something came up first. The something was the woman who'd given me the form motioning along the counter and mumbling, 'There's a pen over there.'

There wasn't a pen over there.

There were *two* pens over there.

Worse – a thousand screaming times worse – one was blue, and one was black.

I scanned the form frantically. Sometimes forms say (right at the top, in capital letters), 'USE BLACK INK', or 'USE BLUE INK', don't they? Not this vicious bastard. It gave me no clue at all. My intestines constricted. Jesus. My mouth went dry at the same instant as my palms became moist. I could effortlessly and instantly decide, while calmly driving along, to swing the car around and race across London to Elizabeth's house – the options were laughably crisply defined – but how in Satan's arse was I supposed to decide between a blue pen and a black pen? I didn't have access to even the most *basic* information. Which ink was more toxic? Which more prone to fading or smudging? Was the flow better in one pen or the other (which impacted directly on my likely completion speed – assuming rapidity was a plus; the care provoked by a slow or uneven flow might ensure I went back to correct a poorly considered word and thus spotted a crucial mistake)? Elizabeth's life could – conceivably, given only a mildly outrageous set of circumstances – rest on such things. Which of the two seemingly identical transparent plastic shafts actually possessed the greater structural integrity? I was anxious and pumped full of adrenaline: I could easily grip too hard or press too much on an already compromised pen, shatter it, get sharp splinters of it in my skin, and then . . . who knows what? Blood poisoning? It was a hospital pen, so it being alive with methicillin-resistant staphylococcus aureus was a very real possibility – and they can't really do anything very effective to treat that, and it eats your flesh away until you expire of toxic shock, in an isolation room, looking up at edgy medical staff; their eyes wide with fear, their masks moving in and out on their faces with each terrified breath – all glaring down at you visibly thinking, 'For God's sake just *die* so we can get your body out of here and burn it, will you?' Argh! Which pen should I choose? Both my and Elizabeth's lives were on the line here, and I had *no information.*

The woman glanced up at me and frowned with minor irritation at the fact that I still hadn't started filling in the form, but was instead just standing there, shivering.

'There's a pen over there,' she repeated.

'No. No, there isn't. There are *two* pens there.'

'Um . . . right. Well . . . um . . . pick one, then.'

'I'm sorry?' (I couldn't keep a laugh of mocking incredulity out of my voice.)

'Pick. One.'

'Ahhh . . . "Pick one." I see.' This was coming on top of the Elizabeth situation, of course: standing on the shoulders of all that anxiety, terror and sparking nerves. 'And which one should I pick, then?'

'Pardon me?'

'Which one should I pick?'

'It doesn't matter.'

'It doesn't matter? It doesn't . . . *matter*? Are you fucking *mad*?'

She set her face. 'If you're going to become abusive or threatening, then the police will be called to remove you from the building,' she said.

'*Me* become threatening? Christ almighty – *you're* the one who's trying to get me to play Russian bleeding roulette with the lives of two people here.'

'I merely asked you to choose a pen.'

'Yes – *yes*! "Merely." See? It's your unbelievably casual attitude that makes it all the more callous.'

The woman considered me for a couple of seconds in silence and then, in a flat, official voice, said, 'Never mind the form. Go and sit down.'

'Oh, great,' I replied, laughing bitterly. 'Fantastic – give me a *third* option, why don't you? Jesus. Do you know what you are? I'll tell you what you are.'

I hadn't been telling her what she was for very long before some orderlies came along and placed me outside in the car park.

I stayed out there for a long time – watching ambulances come and go, seeing little groups drift out to have a smoke and talk to each other in quiet, worried voices, and thinking about a million things to no useful end. After what was perhaps an hour, or perhaps two, I decided to go back inside, carrying every apology I could think of, and try to see how Elizabeth was. Fortunately, there appeared to have been a change of shift while I was away, and the person who was now on the reception desk was favourably inclined by my selection of half-truths, outright lies and, I imagine, by the fact that I hadn't previously called her a vicious, ignorant fuckwit: she not only gave me an update of Elizabeth's condition, but also allowed me to go and see her.

Elizabeth wasn't dead. Even had I not been told this, it would have been obvious the instant I saw her: a dead person would have looked far healthier. She was lying in a

159

side room on a bed-cum-examination table, propped up into a semi-seated position by pillows. Her eyes were the red of raw meat and her skin dry and pale yellow, like cheap paper that had been kept for too many years.

'How do you feel?' I asked.

She sighed tiredly and let her eyes settle on me. 'Horny,' she replied.

I didn't know where I should stand. What was polite and appropriate? To move closer to show concern, or to stay by the door so as not to intrude? I took a couple of uneasy steps over towards her.

'How do you think I feel?' she continued. 'I've had the contents of my guts sucked out through a big tube. My throat's scratched, I've got an eye-fucking headache, and I'm brimming with nausea . . . Have you got a cigarette?'

'No.'

'Tosser.'

'I don't think they'd let you smoke in a hospital in any case.'

'What better place is there to smoke than in a hospital? They have doctors and oxygen and everything you need here. It's like telling people they can't break their car in a garage. It's arse-brained Puritanism. You know, I think hospitals have become our new churches. Religion has withered because its own untenable premises have finally starved it of sustaining credibility, but people want that ritual: that sombre, clearly defined, arbitrary formality. Hospitals provide a yearned-for framework for small minds: with their doctor/priests, and hushed voices, and special areas, and controlled misery. The medical terms, triage processes and consultations aren't simply a requirement of the business – they're a liturgy. Why didn't you just let me die?'

The last sentence took me by surprise. I'd almost

switched off while she stared at the ceiling and rambled along on her irrelevant, detached monologue about hospitals. But then, without pause, she'd turned to look at me and, suddenly full of sadness and hurt, asked me why I hadn't left her to erase herself quietly in Willesden. I wasn't sure what to reply.

'Um . . . because I wanted you to be alive.'

'Why?'

'Because dying is, er, pretty crap.' I shrugged. It was a good job that I could earn a living as a radio presenter, because I'd never pull in the punters as a philosopher. 'And I like you, I suppose,' I added, by way of a convincingly additional bullet point.

'No, you don't.'

'Oddly, yes, I do. It's unfathomable and disturbing and, believe me, I'm not any more happy about it than you are, but I *do* like you.'

'Christ. You *are* a sick little fuck, aren't you?'

I shrugged again. 'Maybe it's not really weird . . . at least, not all that weird. You're clever.'

'Well, compared to you, yes, I am. But then, compared to you . . .' she pulled at the material by her left breast, holding it out for me to see, 'so is this sick stain on my dress. And, more important, that's not a reason to like anyone. Being clever is like being a strong swimmer or having good teeth. One doesn't like people because of those sorts of things. One likes people because they're good and kind. And I don't have either of those qualities. I'm mean, selfish and worthless. The fact that I'm still ambling about uselessly on this earth when all those people were burnt off the face of it is definitely the point where "irony" upgrades to "taking the piss".'

'You said—'

'Don't go trying to use anything I've said as evidence, OK? The source is ludicrously unreliable – you'll be laughed out of court. I'm shit, Rob. Trying to kill myself again here—'

'*Again?*'

'Yes, again – sorry if that erodes some of the specialness of the moment for you. Trying to kill myself again wasn't the work of a delusional fool; it was the considered action of a rational person who has all the facts to hand. It would have been right and proper for me to have died in that fire in Bulgaria . . . Maybe it's better if you think of me not as suicidal, but rather as tidy.'

'You're mad.'

'No. I'm shit. I'm broken and useless and undeserving and I want to be dead.' She paused and shook her head in irritation at a thought that came into it just then. 'They want me to have counselling, you know?'

'You're kidding?'

'Tch – I abhor sarcasm; it's so cheap.' She swung her legs over so that she was sitting on the edge of the table. 'Yes, they think that they and Lustral are in a better position to make decisions about me than I am.'

'Who's Lustral?'

'Lustral is the proprietary name of the weaselling anti-depressant sertraline. I take Lustral every day, and it sits in my head and argues me out of suicide on technicalities. Well . . . I'm *supposed* to take it every day – I've been giving it a miss for the past few.'

'Ahh . . .'

'Oh, I have nothing but dismissive fucking contempt for your "Ahh"s, Rob. Don't go siding with Lustral: Lustral is merely the latest in a long line of chemical liars. Before it came along just recently, I'd been cajoled by the variously effective mendacity of Gamanil, or Lofepramine, or Prozac, or Zyban, or Effexor. The efficacy of their deceptions has been interestingly diverse; I've stuck with them for different amounts of time – assiduously or not – and a couple have thrown in fucking murderous indigestion at no extra cost, but, in the end, they're all fundamentally the same. They ride shotgun. Take away their interference and sophistry, and I'm left with a clear view of me. And I'm shit. That's the truth – the constant: I'm shit.'

'Jesus, Beth—'

'Please don't call me Beth. My name is Elizabeth.' She stood up, unsteadily. 'You try to call me by the correct, undecapitated version of my name, and I'll try not to slam your fingers in a door while you're asleep, OK?'

'Sorry. I simply used Beth because that's how you signed your emails to me.'

'What? I never sent any emails to you.'

'Didn't you?'

'Of course not. What on earth would have provoked me to make the assumption that you could read? I listened to your radio show on the Web, but I preferred telephoning to tell you that you're an arsehole rather than emailing. It seemed less impersonal somehow.'

'But . . . Well, I had these emails from someone called Beth . . .'

'Two people with the same, very common name contacting you? How utterly inexplicable – gosh, it's almost Fortean.'

'It wasn't just the names. You both had a kind of, um, authority about you . . . and you both said you knew how I felt . . . and you both said my life was in danger.'

'I never said your life was in danger. Or, at least, I did no more than gently imply that it was in danger due to your own perilous stupidity, and perhaps also that *I* might kill you as a blow for the cause of acceptable IQs.'

'Well, no, but . . . um . . .'

'Don't try to think, Rob: it's agonising to watch. Help me out of here, would you? Have you got transport?'

'I'm in my car. But I'm not sure you should leave.'

'*I* am. They can't force me to stay, and I want to go. Take me home.'

'You'd be better off here. They could look after you. And, well, you know . . . you'd have a door.'

'A door?'

'We smashed down your door.'

'How very sweet of you.'

'It was an emergency.'

'Rather than a prank, I suppose? Context is simply everything, isn't it?'

'We couldn't get in.'

'That's the point of doors. And what do you mean by "we"?'

'Zach and me. Zach was the one who saved your life, really.'

'Remind me to thank him for the massively unwanted intervention. Hmmm . . . "Zach", that's a grisly name. Is he American by any chance? I have a watery memory of an American putting his hefty fingers into my mouth in a delightfully violating checking-of-the-airways manner, but I thought it was simply a phantom conjured up by the delirium of the overdose.'

'Yes, he's American.'

'Outstanding.'

'He's a good bloke.'

'Not only good, but also a "bloke"? You simply *must* introduce us.'

'He's still at your house now, in fact.'

'Then what are we waiting for? He'll think I have the most appalling manners. Here I am indulging myself in hospital, while he has to hang around making himself comfortable in my home with access to all my private things. What must he think of me? *Fuck* – am I blushing, Rob? I can feel myself blushing.'

'Zach *saved your life*, Elizabeth. You should—'

'Be grateful?'

'Well, *yes*. And, anyway, you should show him some respect even without that.'

'Why?'

'Because he's damn near as barking fucking mad as you are.'

SIXTEEN

Zach had jammed the door shut using an improvised wedge made out of a copy of Joseph Heller's *Something Happened*. He wrenched it out of the way to let us in when we knocked, and I half thought that Elizabeth was going to give him a hard time for damaging one of her books. But she just glanced down at it (avoiding Zach's eyes entirely) and muttered something about it being a reasonable idea, because having to get through that particular novel was sure to drain all sense of urgency out of any would-be intruder.

Elizabeth stood and looked around her living room, like someone visiting a place where she'd lived many years before: disinterested but vaguely curious to see what had changed.

'How are you feeling, ma'am?' Zach asked the back of her head.

'Rather less fucking dead than I expected to be,' Elizabeth replied distractedly, without turning round.

Zach, seeming uncharacteristically ill at ease, continued. 'I'll fix that door for you tomorrow.'

'That'd be lovely. It'd be helpful for it to be ready, in case anyone wants to break it down again in the future – I'd hate to seem a lazy hostess.'

Zach looked at me. I shrugged.

'I'll repair it so as it's more secure,' he assured her.

'Indeed. Why not set yourself a challenge,' she replied.

'How about I make a cup of tea?' I offered. Both Zach and Elizabeth looked at me for a second with something approaching pity, but then Zach replied, 'Sure – sounds cool,' and Elizabeth turned back to letting her eyes drift around the room and said, 'The teabags are in the cupboard over the sink – there's a hammer around here somewhere, if you'd prefer to smash it open to get at them.'

I spent as long as I possibly could in the kitchen. There was a collection of old mugs – no two the same – and half a carton of milk in the fridge. (I guessed that Elizabeth didn't take sugar, based on the fact that I couldn't find any sugar.) When I returned to the living room, Zach was running his fingers along the splintered wood of the door frame with the look of someone who knew all sorts of fascinating and important things about timber, while Elizabeth was sitting at her computer smoking a cigarette.

I handed Zach his tea, and then placed Elizabeth's down beside her; she was half-heartedly going through her email.

'Hmmm . . .' I said. 'Could I check my mail too? Would that be OK?'

'Well,' she replied, 'I'm rather anxious to find out what amazing thing *Teen Slut Tammi and her Hot Girlfriends* want to show me on their Webpage, but I've been disappointed like that before – so, go ahead.' She moved aside to let me sit down.

I went on the Web and typed in the address of Central FM's site. It came as something of a shock (though I suppose it shouldn't have) to see myself staring out from the main page. The usual station info had been squeezed down to the bottom to make way for the Rob Garland Circus. Links to background stories, downloadable sound files of my most entertaining moments of trauma, etc. – the whole wonderful, amusing phenomenon that was me – were listed alongside a large photo of my face. Or, rather, a photo that had originally been of my face. It seemed they'd dug out one of the pictures that had been, rightly, discarded after the publicity photo-session I'd sat for years ago. If I remembered correctly, just as the photographer had taken this particular shot, I'd started to sneeze. With this as an excellent starting point, they'd altered it in some kind of image manipulation programme: so my eyes were artificially wilder, my eyebrows looked vaguely demonic, and my ears stuck out in a manner that suggested many generations of fastidious inbreeding.

Suspecting I'd regret it, but unable to prevent myself, I clicked on the link to the forum. Keith had recently posted an update. (I had, it seemed, been spotted prowling in woodland near to Wenlock Edge: '. . . according to some reports,' he said, 'semi-nude.') However, what unsettled me more than Keith's cynical, self-serving inventions – which were at least *predictably* depressing – were the comments of random people, from all over the world, whom I didn't know. People I'd never met, and who, only a few days ago, had most likely never even heard of me, felt qualified to dissect my psychological state completely and in obsessive detail. Creepier still – dotted among the general madness, smug attempts at humour, disjointed rambling and so on – was a small, but persistent, vein of pure, visceral hatred. 'The fucker should have died with all the others.' 'Burn in Hell, Garland.' 'He'll get what's coming to him, and I'll hold a party when he does.' What kind of bitter, lonely weirdos would be driven by the need to post that kind of stuff? I found it pathetic, unfathomable and, to be honest, a little unnerving.

Eventually, I stopped picking at this online scab, made a conscious effort to shrug, and moved away to open my Webmail – that was, after all, the real reason I'd gone there in the first place: I wanted to send an email to Beth. If Elizabeth was telling the truth (and I could see no reason why she'd be lying), and she and Beth really were two completely different people, then Beth was a person I needed to talk to. She had said she knew how I felt – and said it convincingly – just like Elizabeth had. Maybe *she* could help me sort things out in my head so that my former life would come home, and Jo and I could work things out, and we could get married, and I'd be happy and content and normal for evermore. (And wouldn't, instead, simply spend the rest of my days alone; immobilised with panic and fear every time I had to choose a Liquorice Allsort.) Maybe, in fact, Beth was the *ideal* person to help: perhaps she'd turn out to have the insight born of personal experience that Elizabeth had, but without Elizabeth's tendency to go all Sylvia Plath on me. What's more, Beth, unlike Elizabeth, had seemed eager to help me. And, finally, but possibly most gnawingly, I wanted to contact her because she'd mentioned that small matter of my life being in danger. OK, I'd misread Elizabeth's allusion to her own death as referring to mine, but Beth's warning had been unambiguous: Beth definitely had been talking about *my* life.

So, I was very keen to get in touch with her. But perhaps only slightly more keen, it appeared, than she was to get in touch with me.

There were four emails from her waiting to be read. The first two were essentially resends of her previous mails. The third said simply, 'EMAIL ME!' The fourth, however, seemed to be almost shaking with concern and anxiety, and included a phone number. 'This is my mobile,' it said. 'Call me. Call me *now*.'

I leaned back in the chair and stared at the words, not quite sure how I felt. On the one hand, this was good. Zach wanted to help me, but he was certifiable. Elizabeth probably *could* help me, but she wasn't very interested in doing so – and, even if she did feel like offering advice, it was possibly going to be difficult to hear it clearly sometimes because of the muffling effect of her head being in the gas oven. Here, however, was the promise of an ally and supporter who was both more than willing to help and was also not a complete lunatic: at this stage, those two personality traits alone combined to make her the dream ticket. Yet . . . she, in a sense, carried something that threatened my life: a knowledge of something about which I was, right now, (relatively) blissfully unaware. Did I want to know what it was? I mean, of course, I wanted to know. But . . . well, did I want to know? Yes, obviously I did. Possibly.

I took out my mobile and stroked the number pad thoughtfully with my thumb for a while – the keys glowed a pleasing green, and I savoured the comfort of an obviously, unquestioningly, weighty decision. Finally, I tapped the pad, briskly.

'Hi, Jo – it's me.'

'Rob?' She sounded oddly surprised, or wrong-footed, or, well, something in that area. Perhaps she'd been reading Keith's fabricated reports on the Central FM Website and hadn't expected me to telephone owing to my being preoccupied by being nude and feral.

'Yes. Rob Garland. The UK's most psychologically damaged radio presenter.' (A pretty impressive claim, considering some of the competition, but I had only meant it as a joke.)

'Oh – hi, babe. How are you?'

'I'm OK.'

'What have you been doing?'

'Oh, nothing much. Saved a life, some minor breaking and entering – you know the sort of thing.'

'What?'

'I'll tell you when I get back . . .' (Elizabeth glared at me.) 'I can't really talk about it right now.' (Elizabeth glared at me harder, and pounded her cigarette out viciously in an ashtray.) 'So, anyway, are you OK?'

'Me? Yes. I'm fine.'

'What have you been up to?'

'Nothing at all.'

'Right . . . well . . .' I tried to think of something else to say. I could ramble on all night professionally, but it was a completely different matter privately. Generally, I was happy to let Jo do all the talking. She could speak for hours without ever appearing to be handicapped by having a point to express that would naturally mark the end of things once she'd made it. Sometimes, I'd listen to what she was saying too. But, even when I wasn't, I still found her voice in the room to be quite a soothing background noise – a bit like the effect of trees in a heavily built-up area, or the sound of sea birds in the distance: an unobtrusive but clear and steady reminder that the world was there. That it was alive. That it had uncomplicated life in it. 'So . . .'

'Pete's here, if you want to say, Hi,' she said, throwing me a lifeline.

'Yep – put him on.'

There was a brief pause while the baton of the phone was passed.

'Hiya, Rob, you complete fuckwit.'

'Pete! You tosser! How are things?'

'Not too shite. I was just dropping back those CDs you insisted on lending to me. What with their being not only fucking awful to listen to, but also a cause of embarrassment whenever anyone saw them in my house, I thought it was unfair to keep hold of them any longer.'

'Thanks, mate – I owe you one . . . Pete?'

'Yeah?'

'How's Jo?'

'OK, I think. I mean, as far as I can tell . . . It's her boyfriend I worry about, to be honest. He's a twat. Do you reckon there's a chance of him fixing that any time soon?'

'He's working on it.'

'See that he is . . . Right, I'll pass you back.'

'OK.'

'Sort yourself out, will you?'

'Yeah. First me, then you.'

'Fuck off.'

'You fuck off as well.'

Jo returned. 'So . . .'

'So . . . I've got another lead to follow.'

'Good. That's really good, Rob.'

'Yes. Yes . . . I'm trying, Jo.'

'I know, babe.'

'Right . . . I'd better get on with it, then.'

'OK.'

'Um . . . I love you.'

'Yes . . . You too.'

'Bye.'

'Bye.'

'Bye.'

'Bye.'

I pressed the key to end the call and looked down at the phone thoughtfully. I felt that there was something I ought to have said, but I didn't have a clue what that thing might have been, and so I simply sat there for a time in that peculiar melancholy that sometimes falls on you immediately after a phone call.

When I looked up, I saw that Elizabeth was staring at me – drawing on a cigarette as though she were sucking thick syrup through a straw. She didn't say anything, but I felt uncomfortably uncovered in front of her; almost as if my thoughts and feelings were effortlessly easy for her to see; as if, for her, my head was made of glass.

Deliberately shrugging her eyes off me, I glanced at my email once more (to check the phone number), and then dialled Beth's mobile. I was still adrift – I needed guidance. I was clearly not going to be able to fix myself on my own, not without instructions to follow. I had no idea whether

Beth could provide anything of the sort; but, however thin that possibility, I was going to make damn sure I looked for it. Eternal or not, hope springs internal, you see: it comes from inside, and you merely 'share it out'. If you have lots of options, each is given a moderate amount of hope; if you have only one, then *all* your hopes get hung upon it. The way the intensity – the desperation, even – of hope is down to the number of places available to aim it, rather than the wisdom of doing so, might be called the British Tennis Players at Wimbledon Effect.

The phone rang. It rang again. And again. Then again. Once again, it rang. I felt myself becoming nervous. Not for any sensible reason either – even though there were many of those to choose from. It was simply the ringing. The human mind is built to cope with only three unanswered rings. If the stranger you're calling picks up after the third ring, you can launch into the conversation still prepared and confident. The fourth ring injects uncertainty, and you're no longer anywhere near so cocky. When the fifth passes near-panic sets in: maybe the person you're calling is deliberately not answering. Perhaps they're trying to hold all the parts of a complicated piece of arithmetic vital to their tax return in their head, or are asleep, or are in the middle of having sex. Should you hang up now? Escape before they finally, bad-temperedly answer and discover that you're the person who's broken their concentration, woken them up, or crashed into their orgasm? What will you say if they answer after five rings? You can't get away with the planned, light and casual, 'Hi there,' any more – not after you've been insistently nagging at them to pick up for that number of rings. You'll have to improvise. You're on the spot. You move the phone away from your head to hang up. But, as you do so, you think that you don't hear the next ring. Have they picked up now? You quickly put the phone back to your ear. Gah.

No – it's still ringing. God, you're an idiot. Right: wait for one more ring, and then you'll *definitely* hang up. Hang up and give thanks that you can call again later, when you've collected yourself. This was the point – a thousandth of a second before that ring of psychological closure – when Beth answered.

'Bethany speaking. Blessed be.'

I was in a terrible state by now, and this final shock – her voice pouncing out on me the instant before I escaped – was simply too much.

'Sorry,' I blurted. 'Were you on the toilet?'

'Rob,' she replied, confidently. (Which, obviously, was a tremendously worrying thing for her to do: it almost implied that it pretty much *had* to be me – that I was well known for calling up women I'd never met to ask them if they were on the toilet.)

'Er, yes. Well – yes, it's Rob. Rob *Garland*,' I said – subtly distancing myself from this other Toilet Rob with whom she was apparently confusing me.

'Yes. I knew it was you. I knew it *would be* you.'

'How?'

'I can perceive things. Or, rather, some things are shown to me.'

She sounded Welsh. In fact, I'd go further, and say that she was actually Welsh.

'You're Welsh.' Crap. That came out as though I was surprised that she was Welsh. As though I found it freakish. 'I mean, that's fine, and everything. I don't think it's weird that you're Welsh. And I don't really want to know if you were on the toilet either,' I went on, deftly rescuing the situation.

Elizabeth called across the room to Zach. 'Is it just me that'd pay a hundred fucking pounds to have this conversation on speakerphone?' she said.

'Is there someone there with you?' asked Beth. She suddenly sounded a little anxious.

'No,' I replied. 'Not really . . . Just some woman with a big mouth. And an American fixing a door. Wait a second: I'll move to somewhere I'm less likely to be interrupted.'

I hurried out of the living room, pausing only to let Elizabeth know that I thought she was tremendously immature (which I did by pulling a face at her).

'OK,' I said, when I'd shut the door behind me and got myself composed.

'Where are you?' asked Beth.

'I'm standing in the kitchen.'

'I meant more generally. Are you still in the Midlands?'

'No. I'm in London.'

'Really? What are you doing in London?'

'Um . . . I'm standing in a kitchen.'

'Right. Well – that's good, I suppose. There's tremendous power associated with areas of food preparation. The hearth. Home. Protection. Safety.'

'I see . . . There isn't actually a hearth here, though. There's just a gas cooker.'

'The power lies in what it represents, not in its purely physical incarnation.'

'Right . . . There's a microwave as well.'

'What wattage?'

'Erm . . .' I stepped over to read the writing on the front. '650.'

'650? That's rubbish.'

'The capacity's only point five of a metre too.'

'Ffff.'

'Beth? Who are you?'

'That's a very good question, Rob. It's an instinctive question – I think you probably have great intuition. Not well developed and trained, maybe, but great *natural* intuition.'

175

That impressed me. You see: it was true. I felt I *did* have very good intuition – or, at least, better than most people's. I'd never really voiced this, though. I didn't go around telling everyone that I had good intuition; so it was quite startling that Beth, who'd never even met me in person, had picked that up so quickly. Impressive. Almost spooky, in fact.

'You probably try to push aside your intuition, don't you?' she continued. 'To question it: to hear its voice but make yourself resist what it's saying. You look for dry, mechanical facts to support or contradict it, so you can tell yourself you're making . . .' She laughed. 'Good decisions. Decisions based on logic. I understand that. Intuitive people are creative, and modern society hates creativity. Modern Western society is based on order and conformity: it regards creativity as the path to chaos, and it protects itself by ridiculing those who display it. So, you hide how you feel. You keep it to yourself. Hardly anyone knows how creative you are, inside. You're frightened to let them see it. You rein in your own potential because you want to fit in . . . Even though, deep down, you *don't* want to fit in.'

(Wow. That was spot on. How was she managing to see this? And in such detail? What else might she be able to see about me? And was she so piercingly perceptive with everyone? I listened to her even more attentively now. Maybe she wasn't a slim hope after all: maybe she was a really, really fat one.)

'Well – now – I want you to trust your intuition, Rob. You need to open your mind and listen to yourself. Attune yourself with the element of Air – that'll help. Do you have any aventurine quartz there?'

'Um – I'm afraid not.'

'Topaz? Amethyst?'

'Not on me, no.'

'OK. That's OK. Just imagine the scent of lavender, then. And, if you can, face east.'

'I'm not sure which way that is.'

'Intuit, Rob.'

'Well, I think—'

'Don't think – intuit. Feel for the cardinals with your spirit.'

'Right . . .'

'OK?'

'Yes. I'm looking at the fridge. I think — I *feel* that the fridge is east.'

'Fantastic. I *knew* you had the gift.'

Perhaps it was a reaction to the stress and fear I'd experienced lately, or a symptom of my lack of sleep, but her voice seemed almost magical – both reassuring and uplifting. Maybe it was that Celtic lilt to it: the Welsh accent rolling through its native green hills and valleys. There was a calm wisdom there. A beautiful peace and timelessness borne of her background.

'Where are you from in Wales, Beth?' I asked.

'Lampeter.'

Oh well. It was clearly a purely personal quality of Beth's, then.

'I'm from Birmingham,' I replied, hoping to convey a feeling of empathy.

'It doesn't matter,' Beth said kindly. 'You are you, Rob. You're you, and you're very special.'

'I am?'

'Yes. I knew it the instant I first heard your voice. The moment I tuned in to your show on the Web, I knew.'

'Wow.'

'I knew I could trust you. And now, I need you to trust me. I'm going to tell you some things that you'll find easy to believe, and that will make it extra hard for you to believe them. You'll instinctively feel that I'm someone you can trust completely, and that spiritual certainty will trigger the socially conditioned part of your brain to reject it. It'll urge you to be suspicious; it'll try to maintain control – convention's foremost characteristic is fear, Rob. What it can't explain it can't control, and what it can't control makes it afraid. Do you feel ready to stand up to it and listen to me?'

'Yes.'

'It won't be easy. You'll need to be strong.'

'I'm ready.'

'OK . . .' She paused for a long time, and then, abruptly, began talking quickly and confidently: a brisk, smooth stream of words – assured, careful, without hesitation or qualification.

'In 1997 a man called Joseph Belkin was interviewed by the local media after a houseboat being used for a party on Lake Cumberland, Kentucky, sank resulting in the deaths of fourteen people – everyone who had been on board. Belkin himself had been due to attend as well, but had – literally – missed the boat because the idea was that everyone had to bring along a six-pack of beer and a CD, and he'd lost track of the time while trying to decide which Judas Priest album to take: *Ram It Down*, or *Jugulator*. Six months later, Joseph Belkin was killed in a random drive-by shooting in Louisville.

'Earlier this year, Sophie Pichette was found dead in Marseilles, apparently after having fallen from the balcony of her fourth-floor apartment. It was judged to be nothing more than a terrible accident. Though an accident made all the more bitter for her family as Pichette had escaped death just three weeks previously. She had been due to go on a work's outing but had been too late to catch the coach because she'd locked herself out of her flat during the brief panic provoked by being surprised by a moth in the hallway. Pichette, it seems, had a thing about moths. Anyway, while she stood in her neighbour's apartment in her night-gown – cursing moths and waiting for her mother to arrive with a spare key – the coach carrying her colleagues on their trip lost control rounding a bend on Mont Sainte Victoire. Of the twenty-two people on board, eighteen died at the scene, one was dead on arrival at hospital, and none of the remaining three survived the week.

'To my certain knowledge, in the period between Belkin and Pichette, seventeen people in Europe and the Americas – people who were known to be sole survivors of accidents – have died suddenly. That might not sound a lot, but when you consider how rare it is for only one person to escape death through some odd quirk of – let's say – fate, when many others are killed, and for such an event to be reported in the media, then it starts to look like being a survivor is a very dangerous occupation indeed.'

Beth paused again. While she paused I thought this was all a bit stupid. You can find anything if you look for it, can't you? Just take the interminable conspiracy theory wanking over the JFK shooting: it's become an industry – one of the world's largest employers of idiots. Stare at any random collection of dots for long enough and you'll start to see a picture. I mentally dismissed Beth's words as, at best, silly and, at worst, paranoid.

I did this while she paused and while, simultaneously, all the hairs stood up on the back of my neck.

Beth let me absorb what she'd just said for a little longer. 'Are you still there?' she asked, at last.

'Yes. I'm still here . . . Are you suggesting that these people were meant to die? That they somehow clumsily missed their deaths, but were then living on borrowed time?'

'No. In fact, that's almost the precise opposite of what I'm saying.'

'Oh. I see . . . No, actually, I don't see. Not at all.'

'Are you still facing east?'

'Yes.'

'Good.'

I heard Beth take a deep breath. She was preparing herself for part two.

'Do you know how some fundamentalist Christians in America deal with the old problem of "Why does God let bad things happen to good people?" Rob?'

'I haven't a clue . . . Though I bet it involves a fat bastard on talk radio in some way.'

'They resolve it by saying that it doesn't happen. For example, AIDS is targeted, by God, at homosexuals and drug addicts. Sometimes someone who isn't either will be killed by it – due to a blood transfusion or after being infected by an unfaithful partner, say – but that's *not* collateral damage. That person also deserved to die. We don't know *why* – we can't see what sin he or she is guilty of, because we're not God – but there *was* a reason why Jehovah struck him or her down: it wasn't a mistake. When a plane falls out of the sky, everyone who dies had it coming: that's the Fundos' line.'

'You're kidding?'

'I wish I were. Check it out if you don't believe me. These people don't keep their theories to themselves. They're not embarrassed by them – they're *proud* of them.'

'Fuck,' I said. Then, after a moment's reflection, added, 'Fuck.'

'If you're not meant to die on that plane, then God will send you a warning: a dream, a premonition, foreknowledge, some kind of gut feeling . . . Quite possibly, he'll appear in the middle of the road and stop traffic, if needs be. But he won't leave the final passenger list to chance. He'll make sure you *know* you shouldn't board the flight, that – however indefinably – you sense it in some way.'

'But I didn't have any kind of premonition, or even a vague feeling, about the crash at the pub. I was just taking some towels back to a discount shop.'

'Exactly. That, in their view, makes you doubly guilty. Not only are you a sinner who deserves to be dead, but you've also thwarted God's plan – gone against his will. You've escaped: avoided your just sentence of death through nothing more than stupidity, or acting on arrogant whims, or impossibly dumb luck. It's a bit like the process alluded to bitterly in the saying "You can never make anything fool proof, because fools are so inventive." Not only should you be dead, for reasons beyond mortal understanding, but you've also thumbed your nose at God using casually-arrogant, wilfully-human means. You're a chicken whose neck he didn't wring, purely because you flapped around so senselessly and unpredictably that you slipped from his perfectly-wise grip.'

'So, he's pissed off and catches up with me later? Is that the situation?'

'What's your guess?'

'My guess would be "No." I mean, the problem is: God doesn't exist. Which kind of ties his hands, follow-up-wise.'

'A philosophical point that we don't even have to debate . . . because the fundamentalists most definitely *do* exist. And fundamentalists tend to hold in their heads, very easily, the two opposing ideas that (a) God is all-powerful and (b) they need to help him out – that God controls the world, but *they* have to ensure the election of politicians who'll control the world for him, for example. It's fear, again. Extreme belief – being utterly convinced – expresses itself as terrified insecurity.'

'Are you saying . . . Hold on. Are you saying that these people go after the ones that God "missed"?'

'Yes. I'm saying exactly that.'

'That's insane.'

'How insane would you say it is? As insane as bombing family-planning clinics, or as insane as murdering doctors who perform abortions? As insane as banning the teaching of the theory of evolution from schools, perhaps, or as insane as preaching that the Secretary General of the United Nations is the Anti-Christ?'

'But . . . Um . . . *How?* How would they do it?'

'However they can. You simply need to be killed. Some acts are seen as part holy retribution and part "sending a message" – killing a doctor is a warning to other doctors that they should stop. With you escapees, there doesn't need to be any message. They're not concerned with making an example of you. You just need to be made dead, that's all.'

'Bugger.'

'And it's not too demanding either. The hardest murders to solve are those that are committed by people completely unknown to their victims. If there's no connection between the victim and the killer, and – as far as the police know – no motive either, then any investigation has nowhere useful to start. All the Fundos have to do is to keep a watch out for escapees, and, when a likely candidate appears, they drop by and take care of business. If they can make it seem accidental, so much the better: that exposes them to even less risk of being found out.'

'I know I've already said this, but "Bugger".'

'It gets worse.'

'It can't possibly.'

'It does. You see, the prime source of information for the Fundos is the Internet. Occasionally, they might get lucky and see a story in the press or somewhere, but that's unlikely – that media haystack is too big to have any real chance of finding their particular needle – and it also requires lots of work. On the other hand, a targeted keyword search on the Internet can do a pretty passable scan of the entire world at the click of a button. A mention in the online version of a local paper, an anecdote told in a chat room or newsgroup, an official accident report put up for public viewing – the search has a good chance of catching any of them. So, you can see that when the story has the Net profile that yours did, it's rather like you walking into the line of fire with a Day-Glo "Shoot me!" T-shirt on.'

'Oh . . . *Bugger*.'

'And it gets worse.'

'Stop *saying* that.'

'You encouraged feedback from your listeners – listeners who, via the Web, were all over the world. You'll be likely to draw out escapees the Fundos would otherwise never have known about, because their stories were never re-ported anywhere. You're both prey and bait. Going after you means they'll probably pick up others as well . . . they might even torture you for information first, so they can look for your contacts afterwards.'

'They wouldn't have to look far. I'm in a house in Willesden with two of them right now.'

'Really?'

'Yes.'

'Bugger.'

This all seemed too crazy to be true. Yet, as I looked at the fridge, my intuition told me (just as Beth had suggested it would) that it *was* true.

Partly, it was Beth's conviction: the unqualified solidity of her belief gave what she was saying weight. If it weren't true, how could someone – and someone as smart and perceptive as Beth too – believe it? And she wasn't merely giving an opinion. She was backing it up with names and dates: with solid facts and tight reasoning. Also, however, I was affected by what it said about me. Oddly, I'd always sensed I was . . . well, I can't quite say. Perhaps, 'part of, or going to be part of, something bigger'; I hadn't known what that bigger something was – and I was less than overjoyed to find out that it was something like this – but I'd felt I wasn't simply a person alone, unconnected, and unremarkable. I had too many thoughts, and too many feelings, for that to be possible. To be insignificant but not to *feel* insignificant inside wouldn't make sense, would it?

Unfortunately, none of this immediately helped with the fact that I knew I'd still hit a wall if I opened the refrigerator now and found I could choose between butter and margarine, nor – slightly more pressingly – that some religious nutcases were quite possibly out to kill me. I'd found my drama, but it was going to be less fun than suddenly being recognised as the most perceptive jazz critic of the last fifty years, and therefore being courted by the media, beloved and admired by the general public, and having my phone constantly ringing because film stars were calling up to ask if they could hang out with me. For example.

'We have to meet,' said Beth, wrenching me back from a celebrity party in LA to a kitchen in Willesden. 'There's more to tell you, and it involves the others you've found as well, obviously. You should bring them along too . . . Who are they, anyway?'

'Oh, a clinically depressed English teacher and a brain-fried ex-army bloke who thinks he's been put on earth to be my personal bodyguard.'

'Right . . . Right. Well, give me your number, and I'll call you tomorrow. I'll sort out a place for us to meet up.'

'You could just come round here.'

'No, that's far too dangerous. I don't think the Fundos are on to me at the moment, but I can't be sure – I don't want to lead them to you if they are. And they might very well already be on to *you*: they could be sitting outside watching right now. If that's the case, then I'd be exposing myself completely if I turned up there. It could even be a trigger, come to that: they could be satisfied to wait for a little longer – simply following you around – but the four of us in the same place would be too tempting a target to resist if it was placed right in front of them.'

'Why are they after you?'

'Like I said, there's more I need to tell you . . . Have you ever heard of Professor Osbourne?'

'No.'

'What about the Servants of Azrael?'

'Are they a jazz-funk four piece?'

'They aren't.'

'Then I'm out of guesses.'

'I'll call you tomorrow. Be careful. Be very careful indeed.'

SEVENTEEN

'Well, what do you think?'

I glanced back and forth between Elizabeth and Zach. While sitting in front of the computer stabbing search terms into Google, I'd summarised Beth's call to them both – as best I could.

'Well,' I repeated, 'what do you think?'

Zach shrugged. 'I don't think anything, Rob – you know that. I'm here to facilitate the implementation of your decisions, not to formulate them.'

'Aww . . .' said Elizabeth, looking at him with her head gently inclined. 'Such prescribed phrases tumbling from such an inchoate understanding. It's the *most* darling thing, isn't it, Rob? Couldn't you just eat him up?'

'Leave Zach alone,' I said to her sharply. (Zach let out a little laugh, presumably at the thought that anyone would worry that Elizabeth – who looked comically tiny and fragile next to his muscular vastness – was bullying him.) 'What do *you* think, then?'

'What do *I* think?' she replied, placing the flat of her hand on her chest and widening her eyes in faux surprise. 'Well, *I* think – for what small worth you're generous enough to allow it – that it's the biggest pile of shite I've heard in a very long time indeed.'

'Why?'

'Why? *Why?* I'm dreadfully sorry, but I can't answer that question adequately without recourse to hitting you in the face with something heavy, brass and scourgingly elaborate. *Why?* Never mind its fucking intestinal con-volution – the sheer amount of folding contortions needed to create such a fanciful theory from such prosaic facts – no: discard that aspect of it as you would a troublingly passable level of intelligence. No, no – just consider the source. She's obsessive, obscurantist, delusional, drunk on mysticism, and fucking Welsh.'

'She seemed clear-headed and convincing enough to me,' I snapped back. 'And I don't think the fact that she's Wel—'

'Chk,' Elizabeth cut in. 'Allow me the petty prejudice for the sake of rhetoric, please. I, personally, have nothing whatsoever against the Welsh, but it would be mean-spirited of you to deny me such an obvious weapon when attacking someone, wouldn't it? You, for example, are stupid and self-pitying, but what civilised observer would censure me for mentioning that you have a big nose too?'

'I *don't* have a big nose.'

'See? That's my point. The efficacy of an arbitrary personal attack is that it clears a path for the important issues. You have allowed "stupid" and "self-pitying" through unopposed, because they were riding on top of your big nose.'

'I do *not* have a big fucking nose!'

Elizabeth didn't reply, but simply lit another cigarette and leaned back on the sofa, smiling. I took a few deep breaths to steady myself, and then continued, addressing both her and Zach.

'And, in fact, I—' (I stopped at this point because Elizabeth silently mouthed, 'Big nose,' at me; I bit down on my lower lip, closed my eyes for a second, and tried to focus on not killing her. And took another deep breath or two.) 'And, in fact, I've been searching on the Web, and *look* . . .' I flicked my fingers towards the computer screen. Zach came over, followed a couple of haughty seconds later by Elizabeth.

'There you go,' I said, 'www.servantsofazrael.com.'

They both peered at the page. 'So, Beth is clearly not making all of this up, is she?'

'I didn't say she was making *all* of it up, did I?' replied Elizabeth, reading the screen with more interest than she wanted me to notice. 'Fantasists and conspiracy-theory nuts incorporate reality into their fictions: that's a vital fucking part of the whole process, *obviously*. Without one and one lying around, they'd get no satisfaction out of saying, "Hey, everyone – this makes five and a half. And I was the only one clever enough to see it." However . . .' she took a long pull on her cigarette, 'being magnanimous by nature, on the basis of this new evidence I'll allow the promotion of her story from "shite" to "specious".'

I looked at the site again. The whole thing was rather untidy and random. It seemed to have been put together in a hurry – to have been constructed by people who were so feverishly excited about getting their ideas down for the world to see that they couldn't bear to waste a single moment on planning or design. There were lurid pictures scattered about the place, and biblical quotations, and righteous barking in the direction of thought that Beth had told me about. There were links to dozens and dozens of other Websites; taking the Servants of Azrael as a starting point, just a few clicks in any direction would have you lost in a rolling storm of rhetorical raging – on behalf of God – against almost everything imaginable: from homosexuality, the media, day care and gun control, to Harry Potter, Catholicism, psychiatry and the Teletubbies. There were countless pages claiming to be providing breaking news on the rapid approach of Armageddon too, and site after site packed with the decrypted messages and signs that revealed current events were biblical predictions or warnings. A striking thing about all of this – from the Servants of Azrael outwards – was the similarity of tone. It was always an odd combination of paranoia and supremacy. The writers never failed to see themselves as simultaneously persecuted, abused and beset on all sides by evil, cunning enemies, but also as powerful, favoured and unstoppable; the thrust flipped back and forth erratically between these two positions. If you had to attempt to pull a coherent view out of it, it'd probably be something like, 'You're making us suffer right now, but you're *really* going to regret it tomorrow.' It was the kind of mindset you'd expect in the fracturing teenage psyche of a nerdy student who'd be coming into school the next day with his dad's gun to 'get his own back'.

True, none of this was completely conclusive. It wasn't unbreakably hard evidence. The Servants of Azrael site itself could have been done by a group of organised fanatics with access to the money needed to fund their cause, or (like most of the rest of the Internet, I suspected) it could have been done by a sexually frustrated fourteen-year-old boy alone in his fetid Texas bedroom. It scared the crap out of me, though. And, on this one, I was for putting aside any glib cynicism, and listening to my crap.

I turned my head from the computer screen. 'But they're out there, and they're as mad as fuck – you can't deny that,' I said to Elizabeth.

'Yes. "Some Nutters Found in America." Well done, Rob— you've certainly stumbled upon a carefully guarded secret there.'

I looked at Zach for some support.

'Zach?'

'Dunno.'

Well, I didn't see *that* coming.

'OK,' I continued, 'forget about the Servants of Azrael for a moment . . . Have a look at some of the things that have been sent to the forum on the Central FM site.'

I showed them what I'd seen earlier. I'd been made to feel uneasy by the cold savagery of the comments the first time I'd read them, but, with the knowledge I had now, they went well beyond 'troubling' and simply screamed 'sinister'; they weren't merely unpleasant, they were threatening.

'See?' I said, getting up and motioning for Elizabeth to sit down in the chair in front of the PC, so she could examine things herself. 'These messages – which have been coming in from all over the place, it seems – were disturbing when I originally saw them, before I'd even spoken to Beth. The only difference is that now I can see just how scary they *really* are, because they have a context.'

Elizabeth blew smoke at the screen. 'They also have the context of the Internet,' she said. 'Which is a madhouse.'

'Joe's folks,' said Zach, nodding slowly.

'What?' I asked.

'Oh, nothing.' He shrugged. 'I was just thinking about how you don't know who these people are that are writing this stuff – what their situation is. I went to see Joe's folks when I first got back to the States. To . . . well, whatever – to say how he'd been a great guy and how sorry I was, kind of thing. They were polite and stuff, but you could feel it: they're looking at me and thinking how come I was in their house drinking a soda and sweating through my shirt, but their son was dead. Why couldn't it have been the other way around? Me being alive, just sitting there, was like taking their loss and rubbing it in their faces, you know? So, I suppose what I'm saying is that these people might be upset for reasons that have nothing to do with you, Rob. Maybe the doctor has given them six months, or their mom had a heart attack that morning. They're just venting, you know? It's nothing personal.'

'Or,' added Elizabeth, 'they've hated you for absolutely fucking ages, but this is the first chance they've had to tell everyone about it. Maybe, if you'd started this forum three years ago, the first message would still have been "Fuck off and die, Garland." Let's not fall into the trap of over-looking the fact that you *are* a wanker, after all.'

They both continued to read the entries – for quite a time. On one level, this was a little aggravating, because they clearly wanted to keep on going through the posts: it was obvious that they both found looking at savage and graphic physical threats aimed at me to be really rather moreish. On the other hand, though, I understood. I don't know why, but there *was* something strangely addictive about reading them. Even I found that – and it was me they were specifically hoping fell into a wood chipper. The most important thing, however, was that I knew the farther Elizabeth and Zach read, the more they'd see – as I had – the sheer extent of the murderous ill will out there.

Elizabeth occasionally scrolled down to reveal yet more of the messages. She also occasionally let out a little laugh (though, I noticed, the more she read, the less frequently she did this). I paced the room, allowing the two of them to get on with it, so that they could absorb the implications without interruption. Then, suddenly, I had a thought that brought me to a dead stop.

'Jesus,' I breathed. 'Zach? Do you remember the night I left the radio station? The second night you were there?'

He turned away from the computer screen and gave me a shrug. 'Um, yeah.'

'Do you remember that car? Just before you grabbed my shoulder, there was a car coming across the road, straight at me. I thought it was simply some bloke who was lost . . . but maybe it wasn't. Maybe the driver was waiting: waiting to run me down as I came out, right there in the street. He was all ready to do it – had actually *started* to do it – but then he saw you. Suddenly, he was faced with having to be sure of killing two of us; if he didn't take *both* of us out – and he had no 'just' reason to kill you anyway; he wouldn't know you'd dodged death too – then he was only a phone call to the police away from a real risk of being caught as he tried to make his escape. So, he decided not to chance it – or lost his nerve – when he saw you, and he sped away to wait for a better opportunity. He could have been waiting the next night too. I wouldn't have known – I didn't even see what model of car it was: just the glare of its headlights. But – because of you, Zach, ironically – I was quick and careful about getting into the station, then we left together, and I haven't done the show since.'

'Well, I saw a car there . . . for sure.' He scratched his chin.

'Yes,' I said. 'See? Elizabeth? This isn't just idle talk on the Web – it's solid, physical stuff. It's a car pointing right at me in a Birmingham street, revving its engine as the driver decides whether to mow me down there and then, or to bide his time and wait for a safer moment.'

I looked at them both in turn, waiting for a response. Neither of them spoke.

'Elizabeth?' I said, finally.

She shrugged.

'Zach?'

'Dunno.'

Oh, bloody hell. This wasn't getting us anywhere. I needed to put my foot down.

'Well . . . *bollocks*!' I declared. (Definitively the noise of a foot coming down.)

It was all very well for them to be casually dismissive of the mounting circumstantial evidence – to demand unequivocal certainties before even starting to take things seriously. But I had the feeling that they wouldn't be quite as, 'Show me a maniac actually pointing at the Servant of Azrael tattoo on his forehead with one hand while ripping out your intestines with the other, and then we'll concede that there might be something in this, Rob,' if *they* were so directly and immediately in the firing line.

'I say we at least meet Beth and listen to what she has to tell us,' I announced. 'The very worst that can happen by following this up is that I'll be wasting my time. When we compare that to the worst that can happen by my dismissing it all, then it wins out by a clear six points of "not being unexpectedly kicked to death in a back alley by lunatics". And, even if Beth *is* mistaken here, I'm sure she's still got an awful lot of insights that might help me get my head straight. She's a *hugely* perceptive woman. So . . . I'm going to meet her. Listening to what she has to say is clearly the sensible option. You'll come with me, right, Zach?'

'For sure – I wouldn't let you go without me, Rob. It's my job to stand by your side and watch your back.'

Elizabeth snorted. 'Careful you don't crick your neck.'

'And you're coming too,' I told her.

'Am I fuck,' she replied with a laugh. 'An international conference of shriekingly irritating mad people? I've simply nothing appropriate to wear.'

'Fff. Come as you are.'

'Oh – *so* close to being funny, Rob, that the tragic almostness of its failure tugs at my heart horribly . . . I'm still not coming, though. Fuck off.'

'Yes, you are. For a start, Zach and I are both going, and I am *not* leaving you here on your own. I can't trust you not to be dangling from the ceiling when we come back.'

'Why should you care?'

'I can't think of a single reason that you wouldn't take smug pleasure in ripping to pieces. But I *do* care about you. Tough shit. You're just going to have to choke the fact down.' I paused for Elizabeth's mocking reply, but she just sat there and looked away. I was wrong-footed for a moment, but then continued. 'What's more, I want you there with me. You're clever: clever in a very, very grating way. I need you to meet Beth too, so you can ask her things yourself, and then tell me what you think. I'm no fool . . .' (involuntarily, I paused again here in expectation of a remark from Elizabeth, but again she let the opportunity pass), 'but I know I'm a bit fucked up and vulnerable right now. That's me: a little shaky. And Zach is . . . Zach. But *you* bring something that we'd be missing if you weren't there. This, quite simply, is a mission that needs a gob-shite.'

Elizabeth – still without turning her eyes back to mine – remained silent for a few seconds, and then shrugged. 'Fine.'

I was a bit taken aback by her being so agreeable. I'd expected more of a fight; in fact, I'd been all ready to extend my solid refusal to leave her here alone into out-right threats of dumping her back at the hospital – telling everyone she'd made another suicide attempt and needed strapping to a bed for a week under twenty-four-hour observation or something. Perhaps she'd guessed as much. Or perhaps, underneath the facade, she actually wanted to come – to be dragged along, willingly, while still holding on to the image of cynicism. She needed help as much as I did, if not more. She was just too proud to been seen to be looking for it.

'Glad to have you with me,' I smiled.

She turned to look at me, briefly, then lowered her eyes, shrugged again, and turned away once more. 'I suspect I don't have much of a choice,' she said. 'So it's more dignified – in the words of Thomas Mann – to show myself to be "in harmony with the inevitable".'

She wanted to come. She wanted to come, and it really pissed her off that she did – I could tell.

So, that was everything settled.

We decided to get some sleep. Zach suggested everyone stayed together in the living room, for safety. ('Absolutely,' Elizabeth agreed. 'Otherwise Charlie could take us all out, one by one.') I arranged some cushions on the floor, and Elizabeth curled up on the sofa. Zach positioned himself 'So as to cover the entry points', leaning against a wall, eating a Snickers by cutting it into sections with a huge knife he'd pulled from his backpack and slipping the slices into his mouth straight off the blade. He looked like he might well have decided to stay up like that all night. I remained awake for a little while – longer than Elizabeth, certainly. I watched her lying there on the sofa: semi-foetal and with her eyes screwed shut. After a time, she began to breathe more slowly and steadily, and her face unclenched – it relaxed, and became almost gentle. Shortly after that, I drifted off myself.

The noise of Zach moving around woke up both Elizabeth and me around mid-morning. I forced open my reluctant eyes just as she was sitting up. She looked across at me and said croakily, 'Wow . . . a vision made to lure envious angels down from heaven.'

I was lying on my side, facing towards her. A silvery trail of spit was running across the cushion under my face, as though a slug had slid slowly over the material and up into my mouth during the night. My left arm was hooked around my head, flattening my nose. My right arm was reaching down so as to allow my right hand to cup my crotch.

Elizabeth raked a sleepy hand through her hair and had a little cough. 'Ugh,' she said, scrunching up her face and smacking her lips. 'My tongue tastes like a rancid fucking dustbin.'

She lit a cigarette.

Zach was peering out of the doorway into the street. 'I'm just going for a quick recon,' he whispered. 'Sit tight, guys: I'll be back in two.'

'Zach,' Elizabeth called, her voice pulling his head

around the door to look at her. 'When you return, knock three times.'

'OK, ma'am,' he replied, nodding approvingly.

'Then leave a two-second pause,' she went on. 'Then knock twice more. Then fuck off to the shops and get me eighty Marlboro, would you?'

Zach clicked his teeth, rolled his eyes at me, and disappeared through the doorway.

There was an awkward little vacuum, and then – standing up, brushing myself down and recapturing my dignity – I spoke to Elizabeth. 'Did you sleep OK?' I asked, quite formally.

She shrugged and tapped her cigarette against the ashtray. 'Meh. I failed to clutch my genitals and I completely forgot to gob on any soft furnishings, but otherwise I think I did reasonably well.'

'Um . . . I'm sorry about the . . .' (I searched for the best possible word) '. . . saliva,' I said, and pointed at it.

We both looked at the trail in silence for a while.

Finally, Elizabeth tore her eyes away from my drying spit, rested her cigarette in the ashtray, and stood up too. She gave a tiny yawn and stretched – latticing her fingers together and raising her arms up above her head: looking a little like she was practising a ballet position. 'I'll have a shower, and then I should get something to eat and take another Lustral,' she said. 'I'd rather not embarrass myself by going wacko on you again too soon.'

'Yes. That'd be good.' I shuffled uncomfortably. 'The pills do work, then?'

'Yes. Mostly. They work, but sometimes I don't work even harder. I'm too broken for the glue to hold without the occasional failure, I'm afraid. I can function perfectly acceptably for quite some time, but then . . .' She shrugged. 'Well – something will bump into me, and I shatter.'

'I'm sorry,' I said.

'There's no need to be.'

'There is. Listening to me gabble on about my situation on the radio was what bumped into you this time, wasn't it?'

She didn't reply.

'So,' I continued, 'it was my fault.'

'No. It wasn't. It was mine. I'm responsible for my own actions, however irresponsible they are.'

'I'm still sorry.'

'Still don't be . . . *Really*.' She looked down and let out a long sigh, then took a deep breath and raised her eyes to me again. 'Look, Rob, I ought to tell you—'

Zach burst back into the room just then, and we both turned to look at him.

'All right, guys,' he said enthusiastically, 'we're five-by-five. I can't see any sign of hostiles, so I'll go get some stuff to fix this door, OK? I won't be long and, like I say, I reckon it's clear out there, but you all lay low until I get back, K?'

He dashed out again.

'That's *lie* low, you fuckwit!' Elizabeth shouted after him. 'And don't forget my fags!'

Zach was the only one who could settle during the rest of the day. He fixed the door (attaching so many bolts and chains and padlocked clasps and reinforced hinges to it that I was certain no one would be able to break into the house in the future, but was not at all sure whether Elizabeth would ever be able to get out of it in the future either), and then did a lot of peering out of windows and flexing himself, ready for action. The very fact that we were all – quite possibly – under serious physical threat seemed to make Zach happy, fulfilled and content.

Elizabeth and I, on the other hand, were fidgety and

tense. She spent most of the time reading a book, but most of that time she spent not reading it: I saw her thoughts frequently drift away to other things. Her eyes would slide out of focus and her book would absently droop in her hands, before she shook her head with irritation and – back from wherever she'd been – made another attempt to concentrate on the page.

I browsed the Internet. A quick glance at the Central FM forum revealed there'd been hundreds more posts since I'd last looked. They were mostly nothing but variations on the angry ranting and addled irrelevance of the previous messages, but one did stick out. It was from 'B. M.: in the US of A'. B. M. didn't actually say anything himself. To the uninformed observer, it might have looked as though he'd accidentally sent his message to the wrong place, in fact. All he'd posted was a line that read, 'The *Atlanta Morning Post*. Saturday 09/22/2001,' and, next to it, a link. Clicking on this link led to what looked like a scan of a newspaper clipping. It reported an incident that had occurred the previous night at a local venue where a talk on Statistical Prescience, Freewill and Self-Actuation had been due to be given by 'controversial travelling speaker Professor J. Osbourne'. It seemed there'd been some sort of disturbance, and the police had needed to be called out to control the situation. Several people had been injured – 'one seriously' – and the building itself had suffered several thousand dollars' worth of damage. No arrests had been made, however, and the police said they were still investi-gating and appealed for witnesses. Actually, B. M. *had* written something besides the reference and the link. It was this: ;-). I wriggled uneasily, and then moved away from the forum and began travelling down the endless, infinitely branching paths that began with links on the Servants of Azrael site; this was less like intelligent investi-gation, to be honest, and more like the phenomenon of simultaneously not wanting to, but being somehow unable not to, look at a road accident. Other than paring away at my nerves in this fashion, all I did was almost telephone Jo a couple of times (but not do it: if I was supposed to be sorting *myself* out, I decided, then I needed to make at least a little effort to stick to doing just that – not keep phoning her every other minute), and basically hang around anxiously waiting for Beth to call.

Her call didn't come until quarter to one in the morning. (I'd tried to ring her a few times before that – after about nine, when I couldn't bear the waiting any longer – but there was never any answer.) When the call did come, she was terse and rapid: as though she had time only to state the facts and nothing else. She told me to drive to an address in East London (it was a deserted factory, apparently: 'There's no security – it's totally abandoned. Just go in through one of the gaps in the fence,' she said), *making absolutely sure that we weren't followed*, and she'd meet us there. When the call ended, I thought for a moment, and then went for a pee.

It turned out that I didn't really need a pee; it'd just felt as if I'd needed one. I stood there in the lavatory, looking down at my non-peeing penis with irritation and impatience. 'Oh, *come on*,' I said to it, and gave it a small, threatening shake – a warning of the throttling it could expect to receive if it didn't sort itself out and start to pee pretty damn sharpish. It knew I was bluffing, of course. My penis has always been the psychologically stronger of the two of us. A few small drops trickled out eventually, but the sheer, risible paucity of the amount made it clear that it did that as mockery rather than compliance. I sighed angrily, and pushed it back into my jeans with deliberate roughness – telling it we'd be having a serious talk about this later and it shouldn't kid itself otherwise.

Having thus prepared myself mentally, Zach, Elizabeth and I all hurried out to the car.

We drove for quite a while. The place was difficult to find, and (at this time of night, in the dingy backstreets far away from Central London, and also, I'm sure, because it had begun to rain) no one at all was around to ask for directions. The roads were poorly lit and deserted. Everywhere seemed featureless and forbidding. In fact, we passed the building at least twice before we realised that it was the right place.

It was smaller than I'd expected – not a vast factory like a car plant or something which had once housed a huge production line that disgorged a refrigerator a minute. It was actually the size of only three or four houses joined together. The area around it had been cleared: it was probably the only remaining building where there had at one time been an industrial estate. Now it stood alone on waste ground, surrounded by a chain-link fence that – possibly after losing all self-respect because it was effectively guarding nothing at all, and it knew it – had really let itself go. Grey concrete; rubble; the angry, glass-toothed maws of broken windows; a discarded carrier bag caught on a broken bit of wire struggling to free itself in the wind; darkness; decay; desolation.

I turned the engine off and peered out at the place through the rain-mottled car window. 'Christ,' I whispered uneasily, 'we could be in Walsall.'

There was a sudden glow from behind me as Elizabeth, sitting in the back, lit a cigarette. 'Let's get on with it, then,' she said. 'The sooner we meet this woman, the sooner I get to tell you what a stupid fucking twat you are for dragging us out here to meet her.' She banged on my headrest a couple of times to encourage me to move so that she could fold my seat forward and climb out. Zach picked up his rucksack and got out of the car too.

Finding a section of fence that we could get through was far easier than it would have been to find a section of fence that we couldn't get through. The main defence against trespassers seemed to be the pointedly depressing nature of it all – I almost wished there *were* a couple of attack dogs there to savage me: it would have raised my spirits. Not far beyond the fence was the building itself. We gingerly stepped through the nearest doorway (the door that had presumably once filled it was lying, extensively charred, a few feet away), and – as though hoods had suddenly been placed over our heads – sank into a disorientating, pitch-black sea thick with the smell of mustiness and stale urine.

Elizabeth drew on her cigarette. As the tip burned more brightly, it illuminated her face; her disembodied head, lit up in eerie amber, floated alone in the abyss. Somehow, I didn't whimper. (This place was already making me nervous without having creepy, ghost-like visions added to the mix.) After taking this final drag, she cast the cigarette on to the floor and thumbed her cigarette lighter on. This pushed back enough of the darkness to show us that we weren't missing much. Around us lay bits of brick and plaster, broken glass and some beer crates. Beside the crates were half a dozen crisp packets that looked like they'd probably been used for sniffing glue. (Sitting on a plastic beer crate in an abandoned, piss-stinking factory sniffing glue out of an old crisp packet . . . Tch – young people, eh? In our day we had to make our own fun.) Elizabeth's flame didn't produce enough light to see very deeply into the room, so it was impossible to say how far it stretched back. Some dark, fuzzy shapes – old machinery, perhaps, or barrels, or damned souls frozen in poses of unearthly torment – were just about visible, but whether they were against the far wall or simply dumped in open space, it was impossible to guess.

'Jesus,' I said. 'What a shit-hole.'

'Oh, I don't know,' replied Elizabeth. 'A touch of paint, a few throw cushions – use your imagination.'

'I don't like this, guys,' murmured Zach.

'Oh, Zach, don't be so impolite. This is Rob's treat. You ought to at least make an effort, or he might never take us out again . . . Fuck!' (The last bit was Elizabeth carelessly burning her finger on the overheating lighter, and marked us being sucked into darkness again.)

'I'm going to recon the AO,' Zach's orphaned voice said from somewhere to my left. 'You two stay here, K?'

There was the sound of rapid shuffling, and then, briefly, Zach's exiting silhouette caused the faint eye of the doorway to blink.

'What do you think an "AO" is?' I said to Elizabeth.

'For me, half the thrill is in the not knowing,' she replied, her words seeming to come out of the air itself.

'It really freaks me out, not being able to see you,' I admitted. Without admitting that this was only one of a growing number of things about being there that were beginning to freak me out.

'Hmmm . . .'

'What?'

'Faces.'

'What about them?'

'How fucking powerful they are. You're uneasy because you can't see mine . . . but the covering of our faces often uncovers us. One will write, or even say on the telephone, things that one never would were one, literally, face to face with the other person. And, what's more, wearing masks is often all that's needed for people to be able to behave in ways they otherwise wouldn't dare to. Those masked balls people used to hold fermented impropriety not because the masks worn really hid any identities, but simply because they allowed the guests to cover their own faces and feel released from the restraining gaze of others, don't you think?'

'So?'

'Pertinent. Incisive. Top marks, Rob.' She sighed. 'I was simply musing about the way that the physical is still so important to us. We're physical creatures: our actual presence can change everything. Perhaps, that's why international politicians fly out to meet each other, even though they could surely say whatever they needed to more efficiently and easily via other means.'

'Oh, right. I thought you were musing about "the polite masks people wear"; the way that they hide our real selves.'

'My. How achingly trite. No, I leave that kind of thing to you. Maybe you could do a show on it?'

'But, more, um, *pertinently*, I was wondering why you were bothering to say it at all, rather than our simply getting out of here – to somewhere you can see what's two inches ahead, and that doesn't stink of piss.'

'It's raining outside.'

'Getting a bit wet is better than breathing in urine fumes in the dark.'

'No. Breathing in urine fumes in the dark is merely a passable metaphor for life in general, whereas standing in the rain messes up my hair.'

'Oh, I suppose you—' A noise from deeper inside the room abruptly kicked the rest of the sentence back into my mouth. I lowered my voice to a whisper. 'Did you hear that?'

'Yes.'

'What do you think it was? Do you think it was Zach? Maybe it was Beth. Do you think it was Zach or Beth?'

'Hello?' she shouted. 'Zach? Beth? Is that you?'

'Shut up!' I hissed.

'Why?'

'Jesus fucking Christ – I thought you were a book addict. Haven't you ever read *The Rats*? By James Herbert?'

'I'm embarrassed to say that I haven't, no.'

'It's about these rats.'

'Ahhh.'

'There could be a whole bastard horde of rats in this place. And there you are telling them right where we are. They'll swarm over us in the darkness; tearing us to bits with their lacerating claws and needle-like, pestilent teeth.'

'Fuck me. How dreadfully lurid of them . . . *Zach? Beth?*'

'Shut the fuck up!' I hissed again, and made a grab for where I thought she was: my hand swept through the air and came back Elizabethless.

'Calm down, for fuck's sake,' she said. 'If it's Zach, there's no problem. And if it's Beth, she needs to know we're here . . . And, if it's killer rats, we'd be dead before we made it back to the car anyway.'

'Oh – very fucking funny,' I spat back, bitterly. 'It's easy to be brave when you're suicidal, isn't it?'

There was another noise from the darkness. It was the same non-specific, short scraping sound – although, I thought, it seemed to be coming from a little further away this time. The fact that whatever it was appeared to be moving away soothed my pounding heart just long enough to give it a run-up to the lurch into overdrive that was triggered by Elizabeth firing up her lighter again.

'Argh!' I yelped. 'Now they'll be able to *see* us!'

She twisted her head round and gave me a chiding look. 'Don't make me have to slap you, Rob,' she said with a sigh. Then she turned back to face the fearful black void that lay further into the room, and began to walk towards it.

'What are you doing?' I asked, using a clever blend of amazement and panic.

'I'm going to take a look.'

'*Jesus*. You're going to do *what*? You've never read *The*

Rats, and now you're actually doing the "I'll go and see what that undead groaning from the cellar is" thing? Has popular culture *entirely* passed you by? You're fucking asking for it. Fucking *asking* for it . . .' I made little fists. And shook them. 'Why don't we start having sex, just to making absolutely bastard *sure* we end up dead?'

'Ha. Given who you're talking to, Rob,' she replied, glancing over her shoulder, 'that's effectively a chat-up line, you know?'

She continued to move deeper into the factory – carefully checking her footing with each step. I spun my head around to peer at the doorway: a beckoning rectangle of blue-grey against the darkness – leading outside and only three or four steps from me. And then I turned again to look at Elizabeth inching away into the black, rat-filled bowels of the cursed Ghost Factory that had surely been built over the grave of a Satan-worshipping child murderer using bricks forged by big spiders in Hell.

I *really* wanted a pee. Why hadn't I been able to pee before? This couldn't all be new pee, generated since we'd left the house. No, I'd been fucking lied to back then. Shit – I *knew* I'd been right about needing a pee. *Bastard*. I hated my urinary system more than I had ever hated it before.

Awww . . . Fuck it.

'Elizabeth? Wait. Wait for me.'

She didn't, of course, but she wasn't exactly racing forwards and so was still close enough for me to be able to be beside her in a few seconds.

She flicked a look at me. 'Rats are more scared of you than you are of them, you know?'

'No they're fucking not.'

'Yes, you're right – they're fucking not. But I tried the line on you, at least, yes? That shows my heart's in the right place, doesn't it?'

'Fuck off.'

We moved another half-dozen paces into the room, past what did indeed turn out to be barrels – or canisters, at least: small plastic canisters stacked so as to perfectly mimic something unspeakably evil, when viewed from a certain angle, in near darkness, through my eyes.

'Zach? Beth?' Elizabeth called out, and I punched her arm. Not hard. Certainly not hard enough, anyway, because she went ahead and called out, 'Zach? Beth?' yet again.

It turned out the room was L-shaped. Rounding the corner meant that the doorway we'd entered through was now completely out of sight, but, fortunately, its faint glow of hope was replaced by that from another exit, about ten yards ahead of us. This one was a window rather than a doorway, but it was low down and easily big enough for us to climb out of it.

'I have to put this light out for a while,' said Elizabeth.

'*No!*' I advised.

'I have to – the lighter's too hot. I'll burn myself if I don't.'

'No!' I reiterated. '*I'll* hold it if you can't!'

The flame disappeared.

I made a grab for the lighter in the total darkness.

There was a small skidding sound off a distance of 'God knows' to the right: almost as if someone had knocked a lighter out of someone else's hand and sent it spinning away in a manner that ensured it'd take hours and hours to ever find it again in a pitch-black factory.

'Hmmm . . .' said Elizabeth thoughtfully, before adding, 'You cunt.'

'Sorry.'

'You sorry cunt.' She sighed. 'Ffff . . . Let's just get out of here – take hold of my hand. I'll help you keep your footing.'

OK, I may have been scared shitless by now, but

I did have some pride left. 'No – *you* take hold of *my* hand.'

'I'm sorry?'

'Take hold of my hand . . . I'll help *you* keep *your* footing.'

'Chk. Just take my hand, Rob, there's a darling. We'll help each other, OK? It's all the same.'

'If it's all the same, then you take hold of my hand.'

'I'm starting to leave now, Rob. And my hand's leaving with me.'

'Christ, you're immature – give me your hand . . .' I snaked an arm around in the darkness, trying to find a palm. 'Where is it?'

'Here . . . *Here* . . . No – breast.'

'Jesus – sorry.'

'Don't allow it to trouble you. I'm forty-six years old: I've had my breasts groped in the dark before.'

'But I—'

'Forget about it, Rob.' Our hands connected. She held mine in hers and, with her other hand, patted it. 'Just promise me you won't brag about it to your friends, OK?'

We began to pick our way towards the window, stumbling about three times with every step. The ground was scattered with unseen things that had probably lain in wait for years, solely for the opportunity to unbalance or trip us. Each time my foot caught or slipped or twisted, it made me even more impatient to get out, and my impatience made me even more prone to have my feet catch, slip or twist on things. Elizabeth fell full against me at one point and nearly brought both of us down. It probably took us under thirty seconds to reach the window, but it felt like I'd achieved something incredible; people would talk about me in the same breath as Edmund Hillary or that bloke in *The Guinness Book of Records* who'd eaten a whole bicycle.

I scrambled out first (gallantly – to make sure everything was OK out there), and Elizabeth was about to follow me when my mobile rang. I reached out my spare hand to answer it, while my other was helping her out through the hole. 'Hello?'

'Rob? Where are you?' asked Beth, sounding unusually tense.

'Where am I? Where are *you*? We're all in the factory waiti—'

I didn't get to finish my reply, because two things happened simultaneously.

The first was that Elizabeth slipped as she was getting over the wall below the window frame. Because I was standing in front of her, wisely tugging on her with my entire weight, her losing her balance sent us both tumbling backwards. She shouted, 'Argh!' which meant her mouth was wide-open (teeth bared) when she fell on top of me – her head slammed down on to my crotch (teeth, let me repeat, bared).

The other thing that happened was more alarming. And, for reference, you truly know that things are alarming when they're not simply 'alarming', but rather 'alarming when compared to a middle-aged woman suddenly and unexpectedly sinking her teeth into your testicles'.

It erupted from the window. I'm not sure whether I heard the dull, percussive *Whummph!* a fraction of a second before it appeared, or whether they both occurred at exactly the same instant. I suspect the explosion sent a jolt through the ground too, but I can't be certain of that either, because it would have happened just as I was landing on my back anyway, and so I couldn't separate the feeling of my hitting the earth from that of the earth hitting me. But those things are details, however. The important thing was the fire.

The great, billowing vomit of orange flame that surged through the window was angry and scorching and stank of acrid chemicals mixed with volatile vapour. It burst out into the air, just a couple of feet above our fallen bodies. Pinned supine, I felt its sharp heat on my face and instinctively flung my arms up to protect myself. Fortunately for Elizabeth (though she later, somewhat ungratefully, failed to explicitly state how lucky she felt about this), she had her head buried in my crotch. That, combined with her being closer to the factory – which meant the wall under the window more directly shielded her from the flames – provided some protection. Without those things, I'm sure that, at the very least, the clawing fire would have caught in her hair and set it alight.

I watched the burning cloud twist up into the sky above me without a single thought in my head. I can't even say I was frightened at that point: I was simply dumbfounded. Having a quick mind, however, in the next instant I'd pulled myself together so that I could be very, very frightened indeed.

'Elizabeth?'

The brightness of the fireball had left an obscuring blind spot in the central two-thirds of my vision.

'Elizabeth?' I shouted again, sitting up and reaching down between my legs for her. I was aware of a stony clattering and, from the sides of my eyes, I saw that it was the sound of the walls of the factory collapsing. The explosion hadn't been sufficiently powerful to blow them apart, but it had pushed and contorted them outwards so severely that they could now no longer bear the weight of the building they'd been supporting: it was beginning to crash downwards under its own weight. My arms swung around frantically in the swirling, glowing blindness ahead of me until they at last found Elizabeth.

'Elizabeth!'

'I'm OK,' she replied, 'I'm OK.' She sounded confused and shaken.

I took tight hold of her and, dragging her with me, began to scramble backwards – trying to get away from the factory, with its crumbling walls that could easily topple over on to us. The heels of my feet skidded and slipped across the wet ground as I furiously tried to back-pedal the two of us to safety.

After a few long, thrashing seconds, the mass of phantom light that had been blinding me had paled sufficiently so that I could see the partially destroyed building we'd been in just moments before and – the shoulder of her dress clutched in my hand – also see Elizabeth trying to get to her feet. I judged we were far enough away from the factory by now and let go of her. She struggled into an unsteady standing position, and I leapt up to join her. Her clothes were torn and muddy and she smelt of singed hair; I stood there speechless and shaking – mute and palsied with adrenaline.

'What the *fuck*,' she said, 'was that?'

'I think it was an explosion.'

'Well, I didn't think it was the call-waiting alert on your fucking mobile, Rob. I wasn't asking in quite so generalised a way. "The fuck", Rob – there's your clue. What the *fuck* was that? See?'

'How – how the *fuck* – should I know?' I replied, not all that calmly.

'So, it wasn't your fault?'

'How in Christ's dancing arse could it be my fault? Bloody hell. Some East London factory I've never seen before in my fucking life suddenly explodes out of the blue, and your first bleeding instinct is to blame *me*. What are you? My fucking girlfriend now? *Jesus*.'

'There must have been some reason for it.'

'Obviously there must have – but I've no idea what it

was. Are you suggesting I called in an air strike or something? Maybe . . .' I waved my arms about idiotically, to convey how hastily cobbled together and arbitrary any suggestion I might make would have to be. 'I don't know, maybe the place was full of chemicals that had been dumped in there: there were plastic canisters lying around, weren't there? And lighter fuel and glue from the local sniffers. Maybe something just set them off. The heat from the cigarette lighter we lost, say.'

'So it *was* your fault!'

'It was not my fucking fault.'

'You knocked the lighter out of my hand.'

'Yeah, sure – *I* knocked it out of your hand, but *you* . . . *you* . . . but *you* are so fucking *irritating*. Do you know that?'

I turned away from her in a manner that you'd call 'huffily' had I not been so gloriously in the right on a million levels, and peered at the wreckage of the factory once more. A few feet away from it, I noticed a green glow. My mobile: I must have absently dropped it when distracted by nearly being killed unexpectedly in a colossal, fiery explosion. I jogged over to retrieve the thing. There were a few, scattered flames still burning in and around the rubble, but mostly it was oddly still and unimpressive – there simply wasn't much there that could sustain a fire. As I got closer, however, I could hear the rain hissing as drops fell against hot metal, and that caustic, chemical stench scratched at the back of my throat. Also, faintly, I could hear my name being called.

'*Rob? Rob? Rob, are you there?*'

I picked up the phone. 'Beth? Yes, I'm here. Elizabeth and I are both OK.'

'Then get out of there!'

'I think—'

'Don't think, Rob – what have I told you about thinking?

Just get out of there. I'm in my car in front of the factory. Get here as quickly as you can!'

I spun round. 'Elizabeth! Come quick!'

'What is it? Why do I need to come?'

'Christ – just come quickly, will you? Why can't you just come without wanting me to explain first? Just do as I ask for once. What about if there was a sniper pointing a rifle at your head with his finger already pulling on the trigger, and I was trying to get you out of the way, and you were standing there asking, "Why? What is it? Why? *Why?* What is it?" You'd be full of high-velocity bullets before you'd finished your damn quibbling.'

'*Is* there a sniper pointing a rifle at my head?'

'I don't know – *possibly*. And, even if there isn't now, it'll happen. You're way too annoying not to be targeted by a sniper at some point or other.' I let out a wordless, exasperated growl at the sky. 'Christ – just *come quickly*, will you? *Fuck*.'

She began to move grudgingly towards me, but I hurried back over to her far faster and grabbed her hand. Then I ran in the direction of the fence at the front of the factory: Elizabeth, half trotting, half being pulled, behind me.

I could see a car parked on the road – the falling rain flashing like TV static in the beams of its headlights. With renewed tugging on Elizabeth's arm, I increased my pace over the uneven, debris-littered ground and speed-hobbled unsure-footedly forwards until we reached a gap in the fence we could struggle through.

Beth pushed the passenger's side door open as we approached; I leapt inside – Elizabeth, breathless, flinging herself into the back seat just after me.

'We have to get out of here,' said Beth. Her voice was steady, marked by a reassuringly robust self-assurance, but she was staring at me out of eyes sprung wide with intensity. 'I've been driving around for twenty minutes. I just this second pulled up here. I thought I'd lost them . . . Maybe I had. It doesn't matter. The main thing is – we *have* to get away from this place. *Now*.'

I had no idea what she was talking about, but what should have been worrying incomprehension about that didn't hold my sadly male attention, I'm afraid to say. My mind was suddenly elsewhere. There are dozens of things I ought to describe and explain about the situation I found myself in at this moment. But there's one thing I really must stress, even if I forget to mention everything else: Beth was absolutely *gorgeous*.

She was probably in her late twenties or early thirties. As she was sitting down, I couldn't be sure exactly how tall she was, but my guess, instinctively, was that her height would be round about 'lovely'. She was wearing a long black dress – slit high, high up the sides – with a sort of bodice top to it; laces drew together a front made from a deep purple, velvety material, and ended just below breasts so wonderful that I just stared at them in humble, reverent silence. They weren't huge breasts by any means. (But then, I don't favour huge breasts – what's the point of them? What are you supposed to do with huge breasts? I know you're *expected* to do something with them – 'Christ! Your breasts are *huge*. You'll be wanting me to make a point of doing something with them, then, eh?' – but I don't have any very appealing ideas as to what those things might be. In fact, it was a slight niggle – just a slight niggle, you understand, but a niggle – for me that Jo's breasts were larger than they really needed to be for any logical reason.) No, they weren't huge . . . but they were impossibly perfect. Firm, and round, and buoyant, and *there*. There was surely not a person on the face of the earth who could have set eyes on Beth's breasts without instantly wanting to put one of them in his mouth and go, 'Mmmmm . . .' Even in the limited illumination provided by the interior light of the car, her wet hair shone blue (a rich, bright blue, like the colour of a tropical ocean – the result of a vibrant and vivid dye) and, set into a smoothly curving oval face, was not one, but *two* of the greenest eyes I'd ever seen. Almost the very first second I saw Beth, an image of Jo charged into my mind: charged in at the head of a roaring army of accusatory guilt. That's how gorgeous Beth was.

'OK,' I replied. Not really sure what I was replying 'OK' to – what she'd just said to me was half lost in the noise of her gorgeousness.

'Right,' she replied. 'You drive – I'm shaking like a leaf: I'm not sure I could even steer properly.'

With that she began to scramble out of her seat. I thought for a second that she was going to climb over the top of me, so we could change places. Had she done so, I'm pretty sure that I would have blacked out from arousal. However, she actually clambered away into the back seat. Doing this placed her arse (which, it turned out, was gorgeous) only a few magnificent, unbearable inches from my face. I let out an involuntary gasp.

As quickly as I could, I moved myself across the car – hampered by the clinging of my rain-wet jeans, and by a fear-fuelled clumsiness, and by an erection that threatened to pole vault me straight out through the driver's side window. When I eventually got into position, the seat felt warm against my buttocks, and I knew – knew in a surging wave of throbby desire – exactly where that warmth had come from.

'What about Zach?' asked Elizabeth, breaking into the communion that was taking place between me and Beth and Beth's arse.

'Christ – yes: I forgot abou—'
Thwump!
'Arghh!' shouted Beth and Elizabeth together, as Zach

pitched himself out of nowhere – or, at least, out of nowhere we'd been taking any notice of – right on to the bonnet of the car.

'It's OK,' I reassured them. 'He's forever doing that.'

I jabbed a finger towards the passenger door. He nodded, rolled over, landed on his feet on the pavement, and swung himself inside next to me.

'This is Zach,' I said to Beth.

She looked at him as anyone would look at a massive, clearly half-mad bloke dressed in combat fatigues, caked in mud, and with all his eyelashes and eyebrows burnt off.

'You must be Beth,' he said, offering her his hand.

After the briefest of hesitations, Beth took it. 'Yes. Blessed be, Zach . . . It's good to meet you. I can sense your energy. You're vital. Primal. Your spirit has the strength of something controlled, yet still powerfully animalistic.'

Zach nodded blankly, then shrugged. 'Cool.'

Beth smiled at him. He smiled back.

'And I'm Elizabeth, by the way,' said Elizabeth, looking out of the window.

'Yes,' replied Beth. 'Rob – go. *Go!*'

I fired up the engine, and we raced away from the kerb with a quite colossally pleasing squeal of tyres.

'If you send, you know, a tracer round into where the enemy has stored the gas for their vehicles, the whole thing can go up. Go up, like – *boom!* – right? Real rock 'n' roll. Was it like that? Did it have the signature of a gasoline explosion?'

'How the hell should I know, Zach?' I said, looking across so as to give him the benefit of the expression on my face. 'I present a jazz show on a local radio station. I hardly ever send a tracer round into an enemy fuel dump – at least, not any more: there was a memo . . . But . . . I don't think it was a petrol explosion – or not *only* a petrol explosion. It reeked of chemicals. I think it was an, unfortunately unstable, chance collection of industrial waste and glue-sniffers' rubbish.'

'Right.' Zach nodded, (in a way that, were it any other person, I would have labelled) thoughtfully. 'Well, I can't give you any high-confidence intel, so, whatever you say. I finished my recon and came back to where I'd left you guys. You weren't there, but I could hear you talking, off inside someplace – Elizabeth was saying something about you groping her.' I flicked my eyes up to look at Elizabeth in the rear-view mirror, but she was still staring out of the window. Zach continued without a pause. 'I decided that the easiest thing was to skirt the outside of the building and catch up with you around back, right? As I did that, I stuck my head through each window I passed to take a look-see – just in case I happened on anything I'd missed before. Around the side, I poked my face in, and this blast came right back out at it. I must have been well away from ground zero, but it was still kicking enough to knock me right back – excuse the language – right back on my ass. If I'd been inside, I reckon I'd have been upstairs knocking on the gates for sure. Man, that thing was hotter than hell – and I guess I caught a bit of flying debris too.' He reached up and touched his forehead. There was a bruise the size and colour of a plum on it. (Zach's general aura meant that he was the kind of person who could have an injury caused by a chemical explosion sitting on his face and you simply wouldn't notice it until your attention was drawn there.) 'I think maybe I blacked out for a time. Anyways, the next thing I know, I'm laying on the ground, I look up and see this vehicle, and see you getting into it. So, you know, I haul ass – sorry – I haul myself over here ASAP.'

'Well,' I said, 'at least we're all OK. That's the main thing. It's still a bit crappy, though, don't you think? Us getting caught up in an accident like that? I mean *us*. Of all people. What are the chances? It's like we're being picked on: as though Death has taken our still being alive personally or something.'

Beth had remained completely silent while Zach and I had been gabbling. I'd glanced at her in the mirror a few times: she'd been sitting there with her eyes closed and her hands raised up, two fingers resting on each of her temples. As though she were deep in some form of Eastern meditation, or had a migraine. Now she spoke.

'It was no accident,' she said, calmly. I looked at her in the mirror again. Her face was still: focused but serene. 'I was sure I was being followed when I drove here, that's why I was late – I was trying to lose them. I thought I had. That's when I called to check that you were still there. But I think now that you were followed too, and you didn't notice.'

'*I*'d have noticed,' replied Zach immediately.

'Hmmm . . . yes.' Beth nodded, slowly. 'I believe perhaps you would have, Zach. Your animal senses would have picked up on that.' She placed a hand on his shoulder. 'One can't easily slip past the spirit of a jungle cat,' she whispered, before leaning back once more – her fingers slowly trailing off him as she did so.

Great, so Beth went for big, muscular types too – just like Jo. I thought women were supposed to be utterly indifferent to all that? Don't they keep telling surveys that they're mostly interested in sensitivity? 'Sensitivity and a nice smile.' Well, I smile, sometimes – and I'm as sensitive as fuck. Either there's some statistic-warping lack of honesty going on somewhere, or, by a really curious coincidence, I keep meeting the wrong women.

'OK,' Beth continued, having finished feeling up Zach's deltoids for the moment. 'So that means that they had to have been there already. In fact . . . If we look at this logically, step by step, then it's obvious that they *must* have been there already. Explosives and the triggering devices for them are easy enough to make – any number of Websites will tell you how to do it using stuff that's easily obtainable. They could have prepared the materials days ago, just in case an opportunity arose for them to be used: that'd have been easy, quick, and would have increased their options. But they'd still have needed a little foreknowledge to be able to set things up at that factory – to have it all in place ready to get us when we arrived. Realistically, it wouldn't have taken long – they merely had to drive there and dump it in the rooms – but they would have needed to have known where we'd be meeting at least a *little* before we actually arrived. They could perhaps have made final preparations after we'd got there, but they couldn't, even optimistically, have had a plan that relied on setting *everything* up after we'd turned up to show them where it was. So, I can think of only one explanation that fits the facts . . . they're monitoring either your mobile phone, Rob, or mine, or both.'

'Electronic surveillance,' said Zach, in an incredibly hard-bitten tone, and then clicked his teeth.

'Yes, they were eavesdropping on our calls using some form of listening device. Though I suspect that the equipment they'd have access to would have a very limited range.'

'For sure – but that makes it even worse in a way, doesn't it? If they had to be close in to listen, then we've got to assume that they were right outside one – maybe both – of our places. We've got to assume that those locations are compromised.'

'Yes.'

'Hold on, hold on,' I said. 'Let me make absolutely sure that I understand what you're saying here. You mean that the explosion was caused by a bomb of some sort? That it

was the result of these Servants of Azrael nutters deliberately trying to kill us?'

'I believe so,' replied Beth.

I swivelled my head round quickly to look at Elizabeth.

'See? I *told* you it wasn't my fucking fault!'

She glanced at me and sighed.

Beth continued. 'They must have panicked when they
lost me. They worried that it was all slipping away from
them . . . They'd have been close by, though, still able to
monitor your phone. When you answered my call and said
that you were all in the building – which was just a figure
of speech for you, but they didn't know that – they took
the snap decision to detonate and at least be sure that you,
Zach and the woman were taken out.'

'Christ,' I whispered. 'Yes, I see.'

'The important thing now is that we get well away from
here. My parents have a farmhouse in the north of
Ceredigion. They rent it out to the English in the summer,
but no one will be there now. It's pretty secluded – so we're
more likely to spot strange people hanging around than
we are in the city – and I can't see the Fundos possibly
knowing about it. We should go there.'

She reeled off the directions. Which, of course, I
instantly forgot, but, as she was sitting right behind me,
I trusted that I could ask again if I needed to.

I felt pretty good about not being murdered by a bunch
of nutters, Beth – with a clarity of thought and breadth of
knowledge that I found impressive and reassuring and
horny – carried on speculating about how this Azrael lot
must have set things up, and it generally all went a long
wonderfully for about – oh, let's see . . . perhaps a good
five or ten minutes. Yes: until a T-junction on the A10, I
was on a roll. When I pulled up at this junction, however, I
casually asked Beth, 'Which way? Right or left?'

And Beth, catastrophically, replied, 'Erm, either – it doesn't matter.'

Instantly, I was drowning. Fear had me. And it wasn't the same kind of fear I'd experienced a short time earlier: the buzzing, pumping, empowering, fight-or-flight fear that whips about inside you in response to immediate danger. This was the cold, constricting, immobilising fear of unknowns, indecision, desperation and doubt.

It was obvious to the world's biggest fool that which way I turned the car was not remotely something that 'didn't matter'. Of course it mattered. Or, at least, it *could* matter. It could *easily* matter. Shitting gibbons – did everyone but me think that the impossibly intricate, criss-crossing chains of circumstance that connect us to the mundane, to the fatal, and to everything in between were somehow more forgiving (or perhaps even breakable?) just because we *happened to be sitting in a fucking Volkswagen Polo*? I could see at least a quarter of a million ways in which turning in one direction (or the other) would save (or kill) us. And that, of course, wasn't even the terrifying bit: the terrifying bit was the twenty million ways I knew I *couldn't* see.

'What kind of a fucking dim-witted hippy *are* you?' I shouted – all thoughts of Beth's arse now, shamefully, flung from my mind. My hands were gripping the steering wheel so tightly, and shaking so much, that you'd have suspected it had a thousand volts going through it. 'How can I list all the dangers here? Where do I start? Do you realise, for example, that even the very action of turning the wheel this way, or that, uses different muscles? Muscles clustered around the neck and shoulders, where – it's not inconceivable – they could twist awkwardly and trap a spinal nerve? Those things happen, you know? Those things happen. "Ffff – turn either way, Rob . . . Oh dear, you appear to be suddenly paraplegic: no problem – I've got a heart-lung machine in the boot." *Jesus*.'

I could feel perspiration beginning to seep out of my skin, body wide. Not just under my arms and on my forehead and across my back, but everywhere: I could feel my shins sweating. Our vehicle seemed suddenly hot, ensnaring and airless; I had no room to move, there were too many people, everything was confused; in some way I couldn't explain – but which was frighteningly real nonetheless – it felt as though there was a stampede inside the car.

'Whoa, Rob. Cool it,' said Zach. 'It's OK.'

'It's not fucking OK. It's not . . . fucking . . . OK. *Jesus*. You know what everyone's like? They're like that person in those old movies – those old, silent comedy movies – who sleepwalks through traffic and off bridges and along twelfth-floor window ledges. And it all works out fine. Something luckily happens at each surely-fatal moment and he doesn't get killed. That's what everyone's like: happily blundering about mentally asleep, trusting to chance to save them. Except, *I'm* awake, *I* can see the dangers, and – instead of anyone saying, "Oh, yes – nice one, Rob," and then helping me avoid them – everyone says, "Pft – just close your eyes, mate. Everything's fine if you close your eyes." Well, I don't want to close my fucking eyes!' I was shouting with every lung I had now. 'What I want is some better fucking glasses!'

'You must find your centre, Rob,' said Beth, soothingly. 'Find your centre. Visualise it. Then let the negative energy there discharge into the Earth.'

'Arggh!'

'Listen to me,' said Elizabeth matter-of-factly, and speaking for the first time in a good while. 'Get out of that fucking seat and let me drive.'

'But—'

'A-ahh – no buts. I'm sure that whatever thought you have primed and impatient in your mouth would awe and delight us even as it challenged our picayune notions of consequence, Rob. However, the important point to focus on right now is that you are unable to drive: so you need to swap places with me – and you need to do that some time in the six seconds before I manage to take my shoe off and begin striking the back of your head heavily with its heel.'

I let go of the steering wheel with a delicious slumping exhalation, and opened the door.

'Um, guys . . .' said Zach, when I'd got one foot outside the car and Elizabeth had begun pulling on her door handle. 'What's the feeling here about having the car driven by a suicidal person?'

'You're suicidal?' Beth said to Elizabeth. Her tone displayed a trace of surprise but mostly it was simply cool curiosity.

Elizabeth flopped back into the seat. 'Fine. You drive, Beth – you're probably spiritually in contact with GLR's traffic desk anyway, yes?'

Beth shook her head. 'I'd prefer not to, really. I'm still disrupted.'

'Ah, right – so that's what it is. I thought you were merely completely fucking—'

'*I* can drive,' cut in Zach, before Elizabeth had a chance to provide us with the adjective she'd chosen for Beth.

'You?' scoffed Elizabeth. 'Surely you're not old enough to hold a fucking driving licence? You're not in Texas now, you know. Here you don't get a driving licence, a gun and your cousin's hand in marriage as soon as your balls have dropped.'

'I don't come from Texas, ma'am: I come from Nebraska. And I'm qualified to drive armoured personnel carriers, even.'

'*Without* stabilisers or . . . ?'

'I think Zach should drive,' said Beth. 'I'd feel safer being driven by someone whose vital energy is attuned to sensing danger.'

Everyone looked expectantly at Elizabeth for her verdict. 'Fuck it, then – let the boy drive,' she replied with a shrug, before returning to slouching against her door and looking moodily out of the window. 'I suppose his driving us *is* largely preferable to his sitting here in the back constantly asking, "Are we there yet?" '

Zach and I swapped places. He took a few seconds to look around – familiarising himself with the controls for the windscreen wipers, lights and so on – before indicating left, swinging the car around the junction and roaring away up Old Street with an expert, easy confidence that was marred only by Beth, Elizabeth and me, in near-perfect unison, screaming, 'Drive on the left!'

Eventually, when we'd left all the London traffic behind and the comforting, womby rumble of engine and tyres combined with the steady beat of the windscreen wipers seemed to have relaxed everyone a little, I turned around to Beth. She was leaning back in her seat, looking lovely.

'So, Beth . . .' I said. 'Who are you?'

Bethany's Story

I think that you're born twice in every life. The first time is your physical birth: a thing of Earth. A moment when your corporeal self is given breath. It's a passage into the world paid for with pain and blood and all those ancient, vital energies that are the domain of Woman. The second birth – one that is yours alone – is the birth of your spiritual self: it is a thing of Air. Just as powerful, but more elusive and more diverse. This second birth could happen at any time . . . or it could never happen at all. The two births are entirely separate, but complementary. And without the second, the first is only a shade: an existence, not a life.

My sister is three years older than me, but we look so similar that we could almost be twins. Though, I have to admit, I have always copied Julie a little, which is probably a factor in how alike we seem. Older sisters are something to aspire to, I've always felt. Older brothers seem to have only one purpose: to kneel over you, pinning you down, and then let the spit string out of their mouths towards your face – sucking it back up at the very last moment . . . or misjudging it and failing to. It's almost as if they're taken aside by their parents as soon as they're old enough to understand language and told, 'OK, your responsibilities are to torment your little sister and to make your bedroom smell – off you go: see you again when you're twenty.' Older sisters, on the other hand, blaze a trail for you; showing you what it's possible for you to become, and also taking the heat of all those firsts on the way – if you stay out late, say, you at least come back to ground prepared; fathers already softened up, anger now second-hand, because your older sister has been there before you.

And Julie has blazed an awful lot of trails, I can tell you. She's reckless and wild – not in a selfish way, though. She's constantly unthinking, but never uncaring. No, it's almost as if she's so full of life – so bursting with it – that she can only possibly deal with its demands moment by moment; when the now is that intense and joyful it consumes everything – the present makes so much noise the future can barely be heard. And everyone who meets her picks up on the strength of her life force too: just being around Julie makes you feel happier and more alive. She broadcasts vitality, and you can't help but tune in.

It's the way her wonderful energy interferes with her ability to think more than two minutes ahead that's crucial to what happened.

She was staying with me, and she ordered an inflatable man off the Internet.

This was eighteen months ago. I was living in Manchester and I'd already been working as a Web designer for quite a few years. Julie was between jobs and had come to stay with me for a while. On the day I'm describing, I'd popped into a client's office to go over a site I'd created: it was meant to be only a very brief visit – because I had to fly out to Switzerland for a conference on SSL in the afternoon – but I'd got bogged down explaining the whole of the Internet to them. (It's always the worst possible situation when the company's managing director is there. Having a managing director give opinions on the corporate Website is like asking a primary-school pupil to draw a picture of a moon rocket: you end up with something that has no fuel cells, but three bunks beds, a tree house, and a big ray gun poking out of the side.) The previous night, when I was already asleep, Julie had come back from a club, full of Pernod and horse tranquillisers, and started *surfing the Web on my PC. In her chemically altered state – and with my credit-card-containing purse lying temptingly close by on the table – spending close to one hundred and fifty pounds (plus packaging and priority 'Rush it to me!' postage) on* Lumber Jack *seemed not just inviting, but both absolutely vital and worryingly urgent.*

When her prosthetic man arrived the next day, I was already out at my meeting. Julie was there, but in bed: sunk way down in a post-rave sleep and immune to all human doorbells. The package, of course, was too large to push through the letterbox. She shuffled downstairs in the afternoon and found the card that the postman had left – the standard 'You were out. You can collect the item from the sorting office. Please bring some form of identification' slip.

That would have been the end of that, had I not been flying to Switzerland that day. But, because of the trip, I'd prepared my suitcase and left it in the hallway for a quick getaway. Julie realised that it contained my passport. So, she figured, she could go to the sorting office with that. The name matched the one on the credit card – and therefore also the one on the parcel – and she could easily pass for me if they checked the picture; so, she could simply take a taxi across town and pick up her vinyl lover (which she wanted to take out clubbing with her that evening – as a cheap, nude date and conversation piece). She was cutting it fine if she wanted to be back in time for me to grab my stuff and hurry off to catch my plane, but Julie always errs on the side of optimism.

As it happens, the taxi was late arriving, which cut things even finer. And then the driver started to have an allergic reaction to the long-haired Maine Coon cat that the previous fare had been taking to the vet: his eyes became watery, then inflamed, then blindingly swollen. He struggled on bravely, before hitting a pedestrian refuge on Glebelands Road (fortunately just missing an old woman from Prestwich but, a little ironically, killing the old woman's cat). The upshot of all this was that Julie didn't make it back home in time for me to catch my flight: it left without me.

The aeroplane went down near Basel. Instrument failure. There were no survivors.

Just before this all happened, I'd started to become interested in Wicca. At first it was simply a vague desire to find something more fulfilling than Welsh Methodism: something with a more direct spiritual connection to the Universal Force and a better range of jewellery. But then it started to become an increasingly serious passion. After the plane crash, I told my story in various online forums devoted to the ancient magicks, and everyone agreed that it was no accident that the growth of my faith had accompanied such a fortunate escape. It was an invitation – a message that full acceptance of the old gods would guide and protect me.

For the next year I gave myself up totally to the study of Neo-Pagan, Heathen and Reconstructionist religions: Kemetism, çsatrœ, Strega, Dynion Mwyn (of course) – the whole spectrum of 'alternative' belief systems. I took the Wiccan name of Bethany; abandoning 'Linda' – which had never suited me anyway, in my opinion. It was during this period (the period of my Second Birth) that I came across Professor Osbourne.

Professor Osbourne is a Canadian mathematician: a brilliant Canadian mathematician. In the 1990s, while teaching at a university in Colorado, he began to look at numerology. At first, he did this out of nothing but idle curiosity, but he was soon amazed to discover its depth and power: to discover, in essence, its Truth. He started teaching numerology to his students. Predictably, the establishment of the university was uncomfortable with such radical thought and, under the cover of some trumped-up charges of sexual misconduct with seventeen of his students between 1996 and 1998, dismissed him from his post. This only spurred him on. He applied his amazing mind fully to the discipline and, ultimately, made a wonderful discovery: using his complex analytical techniques, he was able to decipher the Akashic Records – *the first person to be able to do this since Edgar Cayce (the famous Sleeping Prophet of Virginia Beach)*.

He published his findings on the Net, and offered to teach his techniques – and thus psychic perception – to others. You will, I'm sure, have already picked up that the timing of this meant that he was making himself highly visible precisely when the Servants of Azrael were becoming active. They quickly targeted the Professor. He hadn't side-stepped the death sentence of God like the group's usual victims, but he was, in some ways, even more of an obscenity in their eyes. Not only was he preaching an entirely different view of Destiny, but he was also offering to reveal its secrets to others. He was a cartographer making maps of how to skirt God's will.

After three attempts on his life – one of which left him partially bald – he went underground. He now lives on the run, somewhere in England.

Only seven people know his whereabouts. I am one of those people.

I sought you out to warn you of the dangers you face. But I'm merely an acolyte: it's Professor Osbourne you must meet in order to find the answers you seek.

EIGHTEEN

'Wow . . .'

It was all I was able to say. My skin was prickling as though I was totally exposed in the presence of a powerful source of static electricity. Standing naked by some nylon curtains, say.

'Wow,' I repeated, and wiped my hands through my hair – worried that the sheer size of the astonishing information I now possessed might burst my head. I peered over at Elizabeth, who was *still* gazing out of the window into the darkness (as she had been the whole time Beth had been talking – I'd been too transfixed by what I was being told to look away from Beth all that much, but I had found myself glancing at Elizabeth every so often, and she'd never met my eyes). 'So?' I asked. 'What do you think *now*, Elizabeth?'

She didn't turn away from the window. 'Oh . . . there isn't enough swearing currently in the world to fittingly convey what I think now,' she replied.

I sighed loudly, and twisted to look at Zach. He was staring with eager attention at the road. 'What do you think?'

'What do I think about what?'

'Oh, for f— . . . about what Beth has just said, of course.'

'Ahhh – that.' He paused for a time, and his forehead creased with thought. Finally, he nodded slowly and replied, 'Dunno.'

Beth smiled. 'Everyone chooses to find the path at their own time, Rob,' she said. 'Some are not ready to look yet . . .' She reached forward and stroked Zach's shoulder, gently. 'Others . . .' She let me see her eyes flick towards Elizabeth. 'Simply don't want to see.'

That was *so* true. 'Hmmm . . . yes,' I said. 'Deep.'

'Christ in a bucket,' sighed Elizabeth, to no one in particular.

I continued to chat to Beth in an excited, conspiratorial whisper for the rest of the journey. Elizabeth didn't say another word or even (I kept glancing over at her to check whether she was looking) change position. Zach carried on driving without any indication of being interested in what we were saying at all (breaking his focused silence only to ask what some road sign or other meant, and then, after we'd told him, grinning at us. 'Really? Ha – cool').

I'm not sure what time we arrived at Beth's parents' cottage, but I'd guess it was somewhere around five in the morning. Only Zach – with his Siamese twin of a rucksack – had anything with him but the clothes he was wearing. That wasn't as big a problem as it might have been, however, as the cottage turned out to be well stocked. There was food, towels, bed linen and all we immediately needed – even a drawer full of spare toiletries. In fact, it wasn't really a 'cottage', as I'd imagined it, at all. I'd pictured a tiny, grey-stone hovel where countless generations of shepherds had lived while tending their flocks and, sitting in front of a rustic hearth, gone gently mad with boredom. In reality, it was a fairly modern house with a kitchen, a quite spacious dining room and, upstairs, a bathroom and two double bedrooms.

Almost as soon as Beth let us inside (after retrieving a key that was hidden in a hanging basket by the door), I went for a quick wash – as much to wake myself up a little as anything. Well, I intended it to be a quick wash, but I'd forgotten that I was now in Wales and therefore had to deal with the kind of ultra-soft water that exists in

Birmingham only in ancient folk tales used to frighten unruly children. No amount of the stuff seemed to have any effect at washing the soap off me – so I didn't wind up feeling clean, but instead just highly lubricated. I returned to the others no fresher, and barely more awake, but possibly in a far better condition should I be suddenly called upon to slip through an air duct.

They were all in the dining room, discussing sleeping arrangements. Beth was suggesting that she and Elizabeth shared one bedroom, while Zach and I used the other. Elizabeth wasn't too happy about staying with Beth ('Tell me – will there be an *awful* lot of chanting?'), but mostly, I thought, only as part of her general inclination to be not too happy about anything. She did no more than make a few comments and glare, and then acceded with a shrug. Zach, however, was insistent that he sleep downstairs on the sofa rather than upstairs with me.

'Homosexual anxiety?' asked Elizabeth, putting a cigarette in her mouth.

'I'd prefer it if you didn't smoke in the cottage,' Beth cut in.

'I'm not smoking. Rob lost my fucking lighter.'

'Oh. OK.'

'Have you got any matches?'

'There are some in the kitchen. I'd prefer it if you didn't smoke in the cottage.'

'OK.' She wandered off towards the kitchen.

'No, ma'am, not homosexual anxiety,' Zach replied as she passed him. 'I don't think Rob would try anything.'

'She meant you, Zach,' I clarified.

'Me? I'm not a homosexual.'

'Neither am I.'

'Oh, yeah, right . . . I remember you said now.'

'I'm *not*.'

'I've got nothing against homosexuals, Rob. It's cool if you're partially . . . that way.'

'Yes, but I'm n—'

'I told my mother I was a lesbian,' said Beth.

Elizabeth returned from the kitchen, smoking a cigarette. 'Lord – what have I missed?' she asked.

I wrenched my eyes away from Beth, forcefully ejected a surprisingly detailed image from my mind, removed the big grin that had somehow crept stealthily on to my face, and glanced over at Zach – he was busying himself in his rucksack and looking embarrassed.

'I called her and said, "Mother: I'm a lesbian." She let out this long, relieved sigh and replied gently, "Yes, Linda. I know." I was furious. "What the hell do you mean, you *know*?" I said. "I'm not a lesbian! I was just trying to shock you – to see how you'd react. God . . . I can't believe you think I'm a lesbian! Why do you think I'm a lesbian? Put Dad on the phone!" There was a pause – I could hear that they were talking, but only got muffled noises because she had her hand over the receiver. Finally, my dad came on and told me to calm down and that it was OK that I wasn't a lesbian.' She bit her lip. 'I felt such a failure.'

'What a lovely story,' said Elizabeth.

'I really would prefer it if you didn't smoke in the cottage.'

'Thing is,' said Zach, 'if I bed down on the sofa, then I can guard the whole house. If I sleep upstairs, then the first floor might be penetrated without my knowing it.'

'This is the ground floor,' Elizabeth replied. 'Upstairs is the first floor.'

'Sorry, ma'am?'

'*Upstairs* is the first floor.'

'Why?'

'Because we're in England, that's why.'

'We're not in England, ma'am, we're in Wales.'

'Well, it's the first fucking floor in Wales too.'

'OK, ma'am. If you say so.'

'I do. And will you stop calling me fucking "ma'am"? Are you perhaps under the impression that I'm the Queen?'

'No: I kind of think that the Queen of England probably uses the F-word less.'

'Boiling piss and arseholes – are you dissing my vocabulary now, *dude*?'

'It's none of my business, ma'am. It's only that you do curse a real lot for an older lady.'

'Cunt.'

Zach visibly flinched at this, but then continued softly. 'It's maybe a sign that there's a lot of hurt inside.'

'No.' Elizabeth took a deep, deep, deep draw on her cigarette. 'No. It's actually a sign that I'd prefer to use the full richness of the English language, rather than paint with your priggishly restricted palette. *That*'s the reason. You tit-witted, shitty cattle-fucker. Why don't we call the police?'

The last sentence had me briefly confused, until I realised that she was directing it at Beth.

'I apologise,' she went on, 'if the question makes everyone think me disastrously bromidic – and that on top of being guilty of louche speech too – but I simply can't cork my curiosity any longer. If a shadowy sect is heaven bent on murdering all of us, then why don't we simply call the fucking police? The police would be the people I'd go to first if someone stole my television, so I think there's a passably fair case to be made for going to them when a gang of fanatics tries to kill me by blowing up an entire fucking factory.'

Beth smiled – smiled sadly. 'Except . . . you don't believe what I've told you, do you, Elizabeth?'

'I think it's stretching credibility somewhat, yes. Bethany.'

'And that's the problem,' said Beth, looking back and forth between Zach and me. 'The reality is so extraordinary that even someone who very nearly lost her life to it only a few hours ago still has trouble accepting that it's true. Imagine going to the police claiming you're being targeted by a group of religious fundamentalists called the Servants of Azrael who are out to kill you. I doubt they'd immediately set up an operations room and cancel all leave. It's hard enough to get anyone to believe it; let alone to believe it when it's being claimed by you, Rob – fresh from famously breaking down live on the radio. Or you, Elizabeth – with a recently failed suicide attempt in tow. Or you, Zach – who's . . .'

'American?' suggested Zach, smiling.

'No. Sorry – I only hesitated because Rob didn't tell me about you as fully as he did about Elizabeth . . .' (Elizabeth threw a scalding glance at me here.) 'But I do know you've lost comrades in action, and I know you've given yourself the mission of guarding Rob, whatever the cost to yourself. That would look obsessive and delusional, would it not? To a stranger? To a weary police officer used to hearing any number of drunks and drug addicts and hysterics make wild accusations day after day?'

'And what about you?' asked Elizabeth.

'Yes, you're right.' Beth nodded, solemnly. 'Prejudice against witches is as old and ingrained as it is ill-informed. It's almost impossible for someone from our community to be treated with respect.' She sat down and parted her dress so she could begin removing her boots – which were black leather, high and fastened with criss-crossing laces, I noticed. 'I'm not saying you shouldn't tell the police – it seems to me that you *must* tell them; you have to try that. Perhaps . . .' She twisted her lips and appeared to allow herself to hope: like someone seeing the possibility of success after repeated frustrations. 'Perhaps, if we went separately, the four of us – one after the other – we might be able to push them to take us seriously. Rather than dismissing us, in one go, as a single group of hysterics. It's definitely worth a try. I'm simply saying that we need to be realistic about our chances. The police are really unlikely to believe us, and it'll make no difference to our position if we go to them in a few days' time. And, right now, the most important thing is to stay safe and out of sight so that you, Rob, can speak to Professor Osbourne.'

'We can meet him soon, then?' I asked.

'Yes, that's my plan. I hope I can persuade him to come and talk to you. If I can do that, I know it will change your life – *all* your lives. It changed mine.'

'Right.'

'If you just keep your heads down and stay invisible for two or three days, then the Professor won't feel so exposed meeting you. You can speak to him, and then we can still do whatever we would have done anyway. How does that sound?'

Zach, Elizabeth and I looked at each other.

Beth had managed to remove her boots now. She ran her hands up and down her legs, stroking and massaging them, as anyone might do after taking off their footwear at the end of a long day.

'Listen to the voices of your spirits,' said Beth. 'They will guide you.'

Elizabeth took a final pull on her cigarette, tossed the end into the fireplace, and immediately lit a second one. Beth glowered at her slightly.

'What?' Elizabeth asked, looking innocently around at everyone. 'My spirit guide told me to have another fag.'

'OK, Beth,' I said. 'It seems that we've got nothing to lose and everything to gain by seeing the Professor. It'd be great if you could arrange that for us.'

Beth smiled. 'OK.' She put the back of her hand to her

mouth to mask a yawn, then stretched her arms above her head, sleepily: unintentionally pushing her firm nipples against the tight fabric of her dress. My eyes moved from them, to Elizabeth. And then, reluctantly, back to them. 'I'll see what I can do,' said Beth. 'But first, I really need to get some sleep . . . Blessed be.'

She glided across the room and made her way up the stairs. Zach slapped my shoulder for no reason I could think of other than that he hadn't done it for a while and probably thought it was about time he did, and then he began to arrange the cushions on the sofa into a more suitable sleeping configuration. Elizabeth had left the room again – disappearing into the kitchen. I went after her.

She'd opened the door and was standing outside, one arm banded across her stomach with the other, the one with the hand holding her cigarette, resting on it at the elbow. The rain had stopped and there was virtually no wind, but it was very cold. She glanced back at me as I approached.

'Smoking outside as soon as Beth has left? It's almost as if you were only smoking in there to annoy her,' I said.

She looked at me carefully as she drew on her cigarette. 'I don't like her.'

'You don't like anyone, do you?'

'Pff.'

'Most of all yourself. In fact, I almost think you hate other people only *because* you hate yourself. You're a bit like those serial killers who have a refrigerator full of bodies due to low self-esteem.'

She appeared to ignore this. (Tch – that's the last time I try to be charming.)

'I don't like her because she isn't . . . right,' she said.

'None of us are right.'

'I prefer "none of us *is* right" – but I'm sure that's merely my being dreadfully old-fashioned. But, yes: you, Zach and

I aren't right. That, however, is down to simple fucking madness or idiocy. You – as you must be aware – are a twat, for example: Beth, I don't trust.'

'I trust her.'

'Well, perhaps my perception is a little off because the Lustral is ebbing from my bloodstream. I think that effect is negligible at the moment, though: there's a while yet before its influence is shallow enough for me to become truly barking. *Your* perception, on the other hand, is distorted by your wanting to fuck her until her eardrums burst.'

'Says who?' I asked, indignantly.

Elizabeth answered this question with nothing but a smirk and a pair of raised eyebrows. That reply was sufficient, unfortunately.

A mental photograph of Jo barged into my mind. It wasn't a specific memory – more a composite of many images assembled into a defining ideal. She was standing in front of the bathroom mirror: her lips pushed into a practised pout, applying lipstick in preparation for the two of us going out somewhere – an evening with friends, perhaps, or a family birthday. She was wearing a pair of pastel-coloured jeans and a pink top, and her hair had a clean, Laboratoire Garnier gleam to it. She was pretty, and kind, and I stared at her with a sense of gentle contentment. While all around me life was dangerously uncertain and chaotic, here with Jo I felt myself to be that most reassuring of all things: part of a couple.

'Well,' I continued, carefully turning my righteousness down from ten to six and a half, 'OK. I do find Beth physically attractive, yes. But I already have a girlfriend, remember? One I'm going to marry soon – one I'm doing all this *so* I can marry soon. I have a girlfriend.'

'I'll not dispute the impressively unwavering sexual focus of men for fear of alarming the fuck out of you,

Rob. My point is only that it might possibly be easier for you to keep your eye on the ball if the ball were down Beth's top.'

'Oh, bollocks – you can't even see down her top. It's too tight.'

'I am shot, and descend in flames. But, for the sake of argument, let's put all that aside – it's nothing to me if you're pubescently inflamed by her, after all.'

'Well, er, no . . .'

'Or that she knows it.'

'No she doesn't. And I'm not. And . . . well – *Fff*. I bet Beth thinks I spend half my time staring at *your* arse.'

'That's not very likely, is it?'

'Who knows?' I replied sharply, sensing victory. 'Maybe she does. I've stared at your arse lots of times, when I've had the opportunity – *and* I was staring at your tits just now; I couldn't stop myself – your nipples are hard as peanuts. I even tried to look up your dress in the car once!'

'OK,' Elizabeth replied quietly, with a single, accepting nod.

I took a moment, during which I rapidly felt very much less pleased about proving my point than you'd imagine.

'So . . .' I began. And, at the same time, finished.

'So,' said Elizabeth. 'Let's put you to one side for now, and concentrate on the choking amount of shit that Bethany talks. Not the fairy-speak – that's a detail: distracting merely because of its sheer, bowel-twisting awfulness. What about this professor? Is it possible to imagine anyone who sounds more like a bull-shitting chancer and charlatan? I bet he's not an academic at all; I bet he's really just a newspaper astrologer gone bad. And gone bad, moreover, from the starting point of being a newspaper astrologer.'

'I'm sure Beth would know if he'd completely made up his past. She's a computer whiz, after all – she wouldn't have found it hard to check up on his basic details, surely? And, even if he is a little dodgy, that doesn't mean he's got nothing at all to offer. Insights and sensitivity aren't tied to irreproachable personal purity, you know. Just think of poets.'

'Why was her hair wet?'

'What? What are you talking about?'

'Beth said she'd arrived at the factory only moments before she called you, and that she'd done nothing since leaving her place except drive around in her car. So, if she hadn't been out in the rain, why was her hair wet?'

'I . . . um . . . well, maybe she was, I don't know, just really sweaty.'

'Brilliant and unexpected, Rob. Thank God you weren't around during Nuremberg – Hess would have walked.'

'Oh, piss off. So her hair was wet. So what?'

'So, I think she had been out of the car. I think *she* blew up that factory. As you've just said, she's very familiar with the Internet, and, if the media are anything to go by, that small part of the Internet that isn't devoted to child pornography is set aside for telling people how to make bombs. Shy teenage girls who feel powerless and insignificant watch a few glossy American TV shows, buy some extra mascara, and decide they're fucking witches, don't they? Beth's no different: she's a woman who felt inadequate, and overshadowed by her sister, and was desperate to be special. On teetering top of that, she's a fantasist – or at least leapingly eager to buy into other people's fantasies. Means, motive and opportunity.'

'That makes no sense. You're saying that Beth was sitting there one day and she thought, "Hmmm . . . I've seen *The Witches of Eastwick* – blowing some people up is the next logical step"?'

'I didn't say she meant to blow us up. All she wanted to do was spectacularly explode the factory. Doing that, she imagined, would convince us that these Servants of Azrael were a real threat. When she called you just before the explosion, that was probably to double-check that we were out of harm's way . . . but she fucked it up – got the timing mechanism wrong, or knocked her flabby arse against the detonator button, or . . . I don't know. Fucked it up. Simply fucked it up. Fucked it up like an inept, delusional, Wiccan fucker.'

'Wow . . .' I stared at Elizabeth in amazement. 'You're *really* jealous of her, aren't you?'

'Amusingly – because of the legal definition of responsibility – when my medication wears off, I'll probably be able to breaks your shins with a hammer while you sleep and not serve a day in jail.'

She turned and began to march back inside.

'Oh, come *on*,' I said, reaching out and grabbing her arm. 'Are you telling me that you could have come up with something as wild as that if Beth had fat ankles and a face like a shovelful of mud? Try to tell me that there isn't some jealousy at work here.'

'Rob?'

'Elizabeth?'

'Why do you want me to be jealous of her?'

'I . . .' I let go of her arm. 'I didn't say I *wanted* you to be. I was simply asking if that wasn't a factor.'

'Right. I'm going to bed now. With Beth – adorably. If I'm not here in the morning, it won't be because I've fled while you slept due to tormenting jealousy, OK? It'll be because the lunatic woman has killed and eaten me. Good-night.'

She swung around once more, and strode back into the cottage.

'If she eats you,' I said quietly to myself, 'she'll have indigestion for the rest of her bleeding life.'

NINETEEN

Zach examined the doors and the windows. Only he and I were still up; I sat on the sofa and watched him move around the ground floor double-checking bolts and arranging furniture. (He even found a box of cornflakes which had been left on the kitchen table and emptied it in front of all the potential entry points – to 'deny intruders silent movement even if they manage to get inside without making any noise': it was like *Black Hawk Down* meets *Home Alone*.)

'Do you fancy Beth?' I asked, as he strode across the living room rehearsing a tactical withdrawal to the coat rack.

'*Fancy* her?'

'Do you think she's attractive? Would you say that it's a normal opinion – unremarkably normal – to think she's shaggable?'

'*Shaggable?*'

'Christ. Don't you speak *any* English in America? Is Beth a babe? Yes or no?'

'Dunno.'

'Ugh. You better call in more Kellogg's support, or *I* might very well attack you during the night, Zach.'

'Well . . . if she sorted out her hair and got herself some normal clothes, I suppose she'd be OK. But I guess I haven't really considered it.' He glanced at me briefly from the edges of his eyes. 'Why would you be? Jo's a very fine woman. I wouldn't have thought you'd even be thinking about how Beth looked.'

'I didn't say I was.'

'What with you getting married, and all.'

'I didn't say I *was* thinking about how Beth looked. It was simply a question.'

'Right. Whatever.'

'But . . .'

Zach stopped his preparations and waited for me to continue. I didn't really want to continue, to be honest – I'd have been happy to leave it there – but his oppressively artless gaze pushed at me to carry on.

'But you don't . . . things aren't simple and neat, you know? Just because you ask one woman to marry you doesn't mean all other women become invisible. It's nothing to do with Beth. It could be any woman.'

'If you say so. But, when the time comes, I reckon I'll make my decision, and that will be it.' He shrugged. 'Maybe you ought to remember that you *have* asked Jo to be your wife. Focus on that, rather than allowing yourself to forget how you felt when you did it.'

'I felt . . .'

Zach didn't move, and his eyes remained insistingly on me.

'I felt . . .' I was forced to carry on, 'lots of things.'

Zach sat down on the coffee table in front of me. Oh, Jesus: I'd made the mistake of wandering too far into the open, and now the only way Zach would allow me to retreat was by paying him for safe passage with more of an explanation.

'In the movies,' I said, 'blokes plan their proposals. They spend weeks – months, maybe – arranging everything. Then they pop the question during a special dinner at a fancy restaurant, or have it appear on the display screens at a concert, or pay for an aeroplane to write it in the sky with smoke at exactly the right moment.' I laughed. 'Maybe writing it in smoke is the wisest thing.' I smiled at Zach. He looked back at me with an expression that

243

reminded me of the amiable 'Haha – yeah, that's right' one I use if I'm in the audience at a loud gig and someone says something to me and then grins – but I haven't heard a bloody word they've said. I pressed on. 'For me, though, it wasn't that calculated.

'Jo was in the kitchen one evening, putting extra toppings on a pizza before she took it over to the oven. She isn't keen on pizzas, really. I couldn't live without them, but she prefers stuff that isn't actually food: salads and the like – all the pointless odds and ends you leave on the side. There's even this whole weird idea she's got about, oh, I don't know, "visual composition", or something. She'll say, "I like a bit of colour on the plate." I've tried to compromise. I bought a tartan dinner service for us once – I found it in Netto. That way, I thought, we could get on with eating our pork chops and roast potatoes without having to add something ridiculous like courgettes to keep her eyes entertained. She thought I was joking. Can you imagine that? She's serving courgettes, and she thinks *I'm* joking. Anyway, as she's not keen on pizzas, she always makes a big deal about preparing them. She can't just stick them in the oven: she always has to spend ages amending what the scientists at Iceland have carefully developed – like a teacher looking at a pupil's work, sighing wearily, and setting about correcting the spelling.

'So, she was pointedly doing repairs to what had come out of the plastic wrapping, and she cut herself while slicing the salami.

' "You little, pork-based fucker," she said, and sucked at her finger as she hurled the knife into the sink. Suddenly, from nowhere, I thought, "This could end."

'It was mundane. *Beautifully* mundane – wonderfully everyday. There was nothing special about it at all, but how special it *was* hit me out of the blue – hit me like an unexpected punch in the stomach. Standing there hammering things down into the bin so I didn't have to carry the bag outside and put in a new one, while Jo made the tea in a bit of a huff, *wasn't* necessarily how it would always be. It was familiar, yes – so familiar that I would usually never have thought about it – but, abruptly, I realised that it could end at any moment. The very next day was no more than an assumption: in twenty-four hours the world might have shifted to a place I'd never seen before; had never even dreamt existed. A place where everything was different: a place without this kitchen, without this Wednesday pizza, and without Jo.

'I could barely speak – my throat had swollen: it felt as though I'd swallowed a bee. "Marry me," I said.

' "What?"

' "I'm asking you to marry me."

'She rolled her eyes and replied, "Stop taking the piss."

' "I'm not taking the piss," I insisted. "I want to be with you. Forever. In this kitchen."

' "In this kitchen?"

' "Metaphorically."

'She turned away from me and fished the knife back out of the sink.

' "You're talking bollocks."

' "No. I am completely bollock-free. Marry me. It feels good here – solid. Marry me and let's stay as we are now, always."

' "I've cut my finger."

' "We'll get an Elastoplast. With a bit of luck and an Elastoplast, you won't bleed to death for another fifty years. We'll have had children, raised them, and they'll have semi-detached homes in Edgbaston before the blood loss finally takes you down. Let's grasp the opportunity."

'She looked at me for what seemed like a thousand years. On and on: just staring, in silence. My palms started to become sticky. I could hear the hissing of the flames in the oven, and smell oregano and mozzarella mixing with the bright, chemical zest of economy washing-up liquid. I tried to read her face, but it was like trying to climb a wall of wet glass. It wasn't that it had no expression: it was far worse than that. It had every expression. When a face can appear to say *anything* – to fit equally well with whatever emotion you search for in it – you realise that you can't distinguish between what its owner might be feeling and what *you're* feeling as you look at it; you can no longer tell the difference between a window and a mirror. All I could do was wait.

'Finally, gazing down at the chopping board, she smiled.

' "OK," she said. "OK."

'I moved over to her, and we made love across the work surface. By the time we were finished the pizza was squished halfway up her bottom. We called out for Chinese.'

Zach rubbed his chin and squirmed slightly.

'I would've been fine with you finishing a couple of sentences earlier there,' he said.

'I'm just trying to show you that life isn't Lego. Things aren't all simple and discrete – tidy little blocks with all the edges defined and fixed.'

'K.'

'I'll tell you something else.'

'You don't have to.'

'And I'm not simply being defensive here.'

'I didn't say you were being de—'

'Physical attractiveness isn't something you base a long-term partnership on.' I looked at him, demanding agreement. 'Yes?'

'For sure.'

'In fact, an intelligent, sensitive, mature person considers it a very minor factor indeed. It would be foolish – *shallow* – to give it any real meaning. Looks are almost irrelevant when it comes to serious, committed relationships, wouldn't you agree?'

'Yeah. I guess.'

'A-ha!' I had him now. I'd subtly outflanked him with logic, insight and sheer, undiluted brilliance. 'So, as you've admitted that looks are immaterial, you have to accept that I could think some woman besides Jo was as hot as fuck, and it wouldn't affect *anything*. I could decide hundreds of other women were gorgeous – I could walk around with a near-constant erection throbbing to bursting point at practically every woman I saw, and it wouldn't mean a damn *thing*.'

Zach shrugged. 'It's not a real pretty picture, though.'

'But neither is it in any way, um . . . "telling". That's the plain truth, and you can't deny it.'

'Whatever.'

'It'd be far worse, as it happens, for me to want to be around a woman who *wasn't* obviously in possession of blazingly fantastic tits and an arse that could be the basis of a new religion, right?'

'If you say so.'

'I do. I absolutely do . . . what *would* be a cause for concern is for brains to be the issue.'

'What?'

'Brains. Having a thing about brains. Not simply thinking, "Wow – I'd like to shag her brains *out*." You know, it being a personality rather than a purely physical thing. Quite honestly, if I told Jo that someone I'd met had legs that set my scrotum rolling, I expect she'd say, "Phew." That's the real point, isn't it?'

Zach looked at me, and then drew in a long breath.

'Maybe you should go to bed, huh?' he said.

I did feel terribly tired. I wouldn't say that I suddenly felt tired; it was more that I had been wide awake, and, at some point while I was too busy to notice, I'd become so exhausted I could hardly move a finger.

'Yes . . .' I replied. 'Perhaps you're right.'

I struggled to my feet and began to drag myself up the stairs. Halfway, I paused and looked down. Zach was still sitting on the coffee table, watching me.

'Goodnight, Zach.'

'Goodnight, Rob.'

I didn't sleep very well.

I wanted to – I wanted to so much I could have wept – but the troubling and dangerous reality I was inhabiting swept into the room and fell on me like a dead weight as soon as I lay down in the bed. The cottage creaked, and every creak sounded to me like the signalling weight on a floorboard of a religious fanatic approaching with a cutlass. But, even without the nagging possibility of ritual slaughter playing on my mind, it wouldn't have been easy to settle. My head was gooey with thoughts. I was sure I'd followed things through steadily, one step at a time, to-wards a clear goal – at each point simply choosing the most sensible and promising side of the fork in the road to go down. Yet, only a few days ago, I was safely looking at jazz play lists with a man who disfigured grapes, and now I was in a forest in Wales, hiding out from God's hitmen, with a hot witch, *Guns and Ammo*'s Mr October and Woman Interrupted.

I hadn't called Jo. I must call Jo. And I mustn't call her too. I knew I should, and also knew I shouldn't. (Let me tell you: the very worst time to have to perform a balancing act is when you're unbalanced.)

I tried to herd all the things roaming wildly around in my brain so that they were in some kind of order. If I could do that, I thought, I'd be able to see them properly and therefore understand and control them. But too many of those things were erratic, hazy or outright conflicting. There was no tidying it: my brain was a midden.

There's a theory that dreams are the mind's way of assimilating and organising the events and ideas of the day. If that's true, the couple of times I fell asleep might have provided me, via my subconscious, with a settling, revealing structure. In fact, the first time I drifted off for a few hours I plunged down so rapidly and so deeply that it was black, and mute, and utterly dreamless. The second time I dreamt that I was having sex with Kristin Scott Thomas over the counter of Travellers' Fare at New Street train station. And I don't think that was especially relevant: I have that dream fairly regularly.

When I shuffled downstairs later (not vastly refreshed, but having given up on fitful dozing), it was already dark again, and everyone else was up. Elizabeth was sitting in an armchair, smoking; Beth was talking in a commanding manner; Zach was standing by the window, looking coiled. I slumped down on the sofa.

'Hiya, Rob,' said Zach, cheerfully, and holding his hand up as though he wanted to show me something on his palm.

I nodded back at him, and then turned to Elizabeth. 'You were inedible, then?' I said.

She glared at me for a second; her eyes (a muddy olive green, but with a brighter circle of almost-amber ringing the irises) sparked with the approach of a heavily armed reply – and it even got as far as managing to half open her mouth – but then, remaining silent, she looked away from me. I felt a little scratch of guilt. She seemed tired, and – under the veneer of ferocity – vulnerable. I almost reached out to touch her arm and give it an apologetic squeeze, but then lost my nerve. She was a bit like an old tiger slowly fading away under the weight of some chronic illness: still regal, and beautiful, yet also tremendously sad. The trouble with hugging old, sad tigers, though, is that they might well turn round and tear your head off.

'I was just telling Zach and Elizabeth that I'll drive down to meet Professor Osbourne later,' Beth said. 'I want to talk to him personally about coming to speak to you all. I don't feel secure using telephones after yesterday. It's a long way for him to come, but I think I can get him to visit tomorrow – the day after at the latest: the situation is quite urgent, and I'm pleased with the temporal energies too. That's to say, the timing is favourable – I did a reading just now.'

Elizabeth exhaled a gentle geyser of smoke. 'You missed that,' she said (I assumed to me, though her gaze was directed up at the dissipating cloud). 'It pushed all sorts of boundaries.'

Zach rubbed his head. 'I'm starving. What rations do we have?'

'There are some pulses in the kitchen cupboard,' replied Beth.

'*Pulses?*' Elizabeth gasped. 'Then prepare them – prepare them immediately.'

'In fact, a vegetarian diet is more beneficial, Elizabeth: it works in parallel with life's governing forces, not against them.'

'In which case, *you* must be full of life, Bethany . . . Though, there is that distressing laxative effect too. Hmmm – I wonder what that means you're also full of, then?'

'That doesn't even make sense – Elizabeth – because, if they're a laxative, then I'm *not* full of it, am I? Because I'm . . . you know.'

'I do indeed – *Bethany* – and the image of yourself that you evoke there is so subtly fucking adorable that you'll have to forgive me if, from now on, I can never look at you without thinking of it.'

'I'll start boiling some water,' said Zach.

As they seemed to have sorted out the cooking arrangements, I decided to wander back upstairs and have a shower. My mobile phone made a thud as I dropped my jeans on to the floor of the bathroom, and reminded me again that I still hadn't called Jo. I took it from its holder, switched it on, and scrolled through the address book to her entry. Her name came up, and I pressed Call, but, before it had even finished dialling the number, I hit the Cancel button. I scrolled a little further along and pressed Call again.

'Pete?'

'Rob – where the fuck are you?'

'I'm in Wales.'

'*Wales? Why?*'

'I'm going to meet someone. It's a sort of secret rendez-vous.'

'In Wales?'

'Yes.'

'But you were in London. Couldn't this person have met you there? Wouldn't that have been quicker?'

'London's too dangerous for us right now.'

'Dangerous?'

'Yes. Look, never mind all that – my battery is running down and I don't have a charger, so just listen, OK?'

'But . . . Oh, OK. I'm listening.'

'I need you to go and stay with Jo for a while.'

'Why?'

'Just as a precaution. I'm sure it'll be fine, but there are some crazy people around.'

'Crazier than you?'

'I'm not joking, Pete.'

'Neither am I, Rob.'

'Just do it, will you? There are some crazy, dangerous people around, and I think it'd be better – just in case – if

251

you were there. I don't think they'll come after Jo . . . not really. But it's lots more likely that they won't try anything if, if they *do* turn up, they see that you're there.'

'What the fuck does that mean? Why me? Because I'm black?'

'Eh?'

'I'm the ultimate deterrent, am I? A big scary black guy. "Back off, everyone – she's locked down, gangsta style." Unbelievable.'

'What the f— Are you accusing me of being racist? Where did *that* come from? After all these years, you think I've suddenly gone BNP?'

Pete sighed slowly and unhappily. 'Oh . . . it's . . . Look, Rob, it's just that I thought you were going to sort yourself out and get back here quickly to be with Jo. Well, you don't seem sorted – you're at the "having secret rendezvous" stage now, for Christ's sake – and you're definitely not back here.'

'Which is why I need you to take care of Jo for me. Just for a few more days.'

He sighed again.

'OK?' I said.

Another sigh. (Considering that *I* was the one having exploding factories thrown at me – while he was simply hanging around in a Birmingham comprehensive making sullen schoolboys weave footballs between traffic cones in the rain – I thought he was being unfairly tetchy about this.) 'Yeah . . . OK,' he replied, at last. 'And what am I supposed to tell her?'

'Anything. Tell her I've asked you to stay there and help her pick out bleeding corsages – that'll make her day. I don't want to frighten her. Especially as, like I say, I'm sure it's all going to be fine.'

'Is it?'

'Maybe.'

I heard Pete achieve his sighing hat-trick. It appeared to help a little, though. He was a bit more, well, 'Pete' when he spoke again. 'You're *such* a wanker, you know?'

'Yeah, yeah – and you're over here taking all our jobs.'

'Arsehole.'

'Fucker.' I glanced at the power level on my mobile. 'Look, I've really got to go: I'll turn off the phone now – I want to save the battery.'

'OK.'

'Thanks, Pete.'

'Yeah.'

With an icy and ruthless calm, I continually held down my mobile's power button until the lights went out and it expired – like suffocating someone under a pillow. I felt a little better. Looser. Lighter. It didn't feel so much like I'd abandoned Jo. Well, 'abandoned' was probably the wrong word – I was fully intending to go back to her very soon, after all; there was, absolutely, definitely, no other possibility in my mind. But I felt that she wasn't alone and uncared for now – that she would be OK without me.

That sorted, I carefully placed my clothes in a big crumpled pile on the floor, undressed fully, stood in the bath, and turned on the shower. Cranking it up to full blast produced an enormously invigorating dribble of tepid water, but I stayed there for three hours. Only about twenty minutes of that was strictly intentional, however. After twenty minutes – feeling clean and perky – I went to step out of the bath.

So . . . should you step out with your strongest, most dextrous leg (for me, my right) first, or go for leading with your weaker side? The former leaves an – easily fatal – moment of balancing, on wet plastic, on your B-team foot. Yet the latter option puts the burden of balance management on the counterweighting abilities of your least skilful leg. And it's not an idle consideration either. Don't most accidents occur in the home? And isn't the bathroom the second most likely location for those accidents? I know it is. (I'd taken the Morbidity and Mortality Survey for England and (tellingly) Wales – produced by the government's chilling National Statistics office – out of the library three weeks ago.) Christ. *I was right on the front line here*. My mind buzzed and skidded. Soon, I was well beyond the area of implicitly reckless considerations such as which leg it was better to step out with: Hell's ball-smashing hammers – it was sheer bloody madness to risk moving a leg *at all*.

I shook, and tried to stop shaking. Shaking was the last thing I needed when only my ability to hold my balance against gravity (that's, 'against the force being exerted by the *entire fucking universe*', there) was keeping me alive. I clawed and curled my toes against the bath beneath me in an attempt to get some kind of life-saving extra grip, but they slid punily – frantically, Hitchcockianly – across the sleek, watery surface. I imagined losing my nerve. Like that person in disaster movies who screams, 'I can't stand it anymore!' and – with no space for the hero's, 'No! Don't be a fool!' in his panic-filled ears – runs wildly out of the door, to instantly sink under lava/fall eighteen floors from a crumbling ledge/be eaten by bears. I imagined myself making a desperate, random-legged leap from the shower towards the safety of the bathmat: my reason cast aside by cowardice and fear and self-delusion. In sharp, slow detail, I saw my feet aquaplane across the bone-white, killer polypropylene and swing up to shoulder height. I saw my upper body plunge past them – hands flailing at the fragile shower curtain, merely dragging it down with a rapid drum roll of popping fastening rings. I saw the weight of my whipping head drive the cold, gleaming metal of a tap into the soft flesh of my temple. The motion suddenly increased to real time for the final dead, wet thud of my corpse coming to rest in the bath. Glassy, lifeless eyes harassed but unblinking under the indifferent rain from the shower head; blood thinned and dissipating in the water as it rolled over my skin towards the plughole.

Had we agreed on something sensibly microwave or boil-in-the-bag, I would have had to endure this stay on death row for only a few minutes. But, because we'd decided on eating bloody pulses, no one came to find me for two and a half hours, as it took three hours for the bloody things to cook. Only when the meal was ready did Zach search me out, to tell me it was time to eat.

He broke down the door (of course). As I'd responded to his shouted questions with nothing but, 'I'm trapped!' I could tell that he was a little surprised to find me simply standing in the shower (surprised and, I thought, a little disappointed). He allowed himself a brief, hopeful glance around the room for laser tripwires and motion-sensing detonators, but then gave in to the saddening reality of the situation, reached across to turn the water off, and lifted me bodily out of the bath.

I felt utterly wretched. I was naked, wet and trembling in the rescuing arms of a huge American soldier. I felt utterly ashamed, and crushingly homoerotic. If I absolutely *had* to be nude and vulnerable and glistening in the company of a near stranger, then Zach was just about the last person I'd have chosen to share that moment with. And I could see from the way that Zach handed me a towel that he was silently asking God why he couldn't have been spared this ordeal and merely have been called upon to throw himself on a grenade instead. It was a horrible place for two heterosexual men to be standing.

'Zach. I didn't . . .' I began, staring at the water pooling around my feet.

'It's OK, Rob,' he replied. And then cleared his throat.

'But I *really* didn't.' (I checked myself for erections. Mercifully, I was clear.)

'It's OK.'

'You go. I'm fine now. I'll be down in a minute.'

'For sure.'

He left without looking at me.

Being a straight man is a burden that people who aren't straight men will never understand. It's the most demanding role in the world: a full-time occupation of incalculable complexity – raked minute to minute by danger. Not for the first time in my life, I pondered how very much simpler things would be if I'd been born a lesbian. Lesbians have it all.

'Christ,' I thought, as I dried myself. 'I hope he doesn't tell Elizabeth.'

Having, only minutes before, stared both death and unintentional gay subtexts in the face, I was still a little shaky when I went down to join the others at the table.

Beth was enthusing about Professor Osbourne again.

'The universe is like the mind – only a tiny proportion of it is used by most people. A genius taps into the unused potential of the mind; a sage and visionary – like Professor Osbourne – taps into the overlooked or hidden potential of the universe. He can see patterns where almost everyone else sees nothing but chaos. He can touch and interpret the most basic forces of eternity. He hears the tides of time and space.'

'Fuck, but these beans are execrable,' said Elizabeth. 'It's like consuming the sodden droppings of some huge, lumbering beast. Ahh – Rob: returned from the shower . . . Drained – your appearance seems to indicate – by onanistic excess. Sit down and try this, and tell me if it isn't the most emotionally upsetting thing you've ever put into your mouth.'

'It's not really very good of you to criticise, Elizabeth, when Zach and I did all the cooking.'

'No, that's where you're wrong. Or, at least, one of the many places where you're wrong. Had I helped, then my impartiality could have been called into question. Without the inoculation of shielding disinterest, it could be thought that my stating that these beans are a fucking calamity that physically debases the eater was nothing but my being gently self-deprecating.'

I sat down and got myself a bowlful of the stew-like mixture. It was, like any vegetarian meal, certainly not something you'd eat for fun, but I suppose it could have been worse.

'You really ought to work on eliminating your negativity,' Beth said to Elizabeth.

'Oh, please, *do* fuck off.'

Beth shook her head, compassionately. 'Ohhh . . . you poor, troubled spirit.'

Elizabeth pushed her food away, leaned back in her chair, and lit a cigarette. Beth continued.

'Look at Zach. See how powerful he is? He's learned to harness the force of positive energy streams. Haven't you, Zach?'

'Well . . . I dunno.' He shrugged. 'It just kind of seems to me that there's no sense focusing on all the bad stuff. You've got to focus on the good stuff. Mostly, things are pretty good, anyhow.'

'Sweet Christ in a wok – see? *This* is what fucks me off. This obdurate fucking optimism. This foot down, lights off, juggernauting American belief that everything's pretty fucking good, all told. And that – would you fucking believe it? – it's pretty much all going to be even fucking better tomorrow. Given a little vim and a cotton-cloth-covered basketful of looking on the bright side, every fucking thing in the entire fucking world will be fucking wonderful.'

'What's wrong with things being wonderful?' asked Zach.

'But they aren't. They *aren't*. They're unquantifiably shitty.'

'No they're not.'

'Yes they fucking *are*. Everywhere you look the planet is bloated with misery and suffering and stupidity and seeping, prosaic evil. Everything's falling over and fucking up and dumbing down. People are selfish: driven by greed, jealousy and petty vendettas.'

'That's not true. Most people are good, given the chance.'

'Bollocks.'

'And, anyhow, it's still better to figure like things are going to work out for the best.'

'It isn't when it's pure fantasy. Seeing things as they really are is far better than bovine sanguinity. You're an enthusiastic accomplice in deceiving yourself.'

'I'm not. But, you know . . . whatever. What I am works for me.'

'You think?'

'Well, I don't get suicidal when bad stuff happens.'

'Fuck you.' Elizabeth's eyes welled up. 'Fuck. You. What do you know? You're still a child. You can't understand anything about me.'

'All I'm saying is that my way of thinking means something bad happens, and I get past it – take it on board, but get past it: stronger. Something bad happens to you, and it messes you up.'

'Well, that shows how fucking penetrating *your* analysis is, then. Nothing "messed me up".'

'Sorry, ma'am, but I think attempting to kill yourself after that hotel thing is really kind of that way.'

'But I tried to kill myself *before* that too. You fucking twat. I've been on medication for nearly thirty years – I didn't watch all those people die, and then try to take my own life: I'd tried to take my own life several times *before that ever happened!*'

A silence so solid and heavy that it could have been used as the foundations of some vast municipal building crashed down on to the table and lay there like a dead weight, pinning all of us to our chairs. After half a dozen uncomfortably-obvious heartbeats, it was broken by Beth.

'Um . . . but doesn't that just make you even *madder* than we thought you were originally?'

Elizabeth stood up sharply – sending her chair toppling backwards on to the floor – and scurried away, off up the stairs.

I glared at Beth. She looked back at me with a kind of wounded and indignant innocence.

'But, well – it does, doesn't it?'

I rose and began to follow Elizabeth, but then returned and looked at Beth again. 'Why was your hair wet?' I asked her.

'I'm sorry?'

'You said you'd been in the car all the time – when you met us at the factory yesterday. You said you'd been in the car all the time, but your hair was wet.'

She squinted at me – surprised and vaguely confused that I should be asking the question. Then she turned to look at Zach, and gave him the same expression, questioningly. 'Well,' she said finally, and paused to give an as-if-it-matters curve to her lips before continuing, 'I'd washed my hair. It was wet when I came out . . . and I *did* pull over and step out of the car a couple of times – to check if I was still being followed. So, I suppose *that*'s why my hair was wet. Does that matter? I'm sorry: I thought that telling you about other things – and getting away quickly – had a higher priority that being nit-pickingly accurate about every single movement of my body up to that point.'

I remained wedged in peering mode for a moment, and then sighed back to reality. 'Yes. I'm sorry – never mind.' With a quick, apologetic wave to her, I turned around again, and ran upstairs to Elizabeth's room.

Outside the bedroom door, I paused and knocked.

'Fuck off, Rob.'

I accepted the invitation and entered. She was sitting on the bed, a shaking hand putting her cigarette to her lips. Tears were creeping from the corners of her eyes.

'How did you know it was me?' I asked.

'Well . . . Well, who said I knew it was you?'

'You shouted, "Fuck off, Rob."'

'I shout, "Fuck off, Rob," every two or three minutes, whatever's happening – even when I'm alone. Sometimes one just gets lucky.' She took a final, draining pull on her cigarette and dropped it into a teacup on the bedside table. There was still three-quarters of it left: I think that, at that moment, the symbolic action of dumping it was more important to her than the comfort she'd have got from smoking it.

'Are you OK?'

She gave a humourless little laugh. 'I bet that, even now, you're kicking yourself for asking something of such erupting idiocy, aren't you?'

'Yeah.'

'Can I kick you too?'

'If it'll help.'

I sat down next to her. 'It's OK,' I said.

'Oh, *really* . . . It looks like the Lustral has finally seeped away. My chemical scaffolding's been dismantled, and this fucking wreckage is what I am without artificial support. It's far from "OK". I think that "OK" has now left town on a swift horse without a glance back.'

'Is that what it is? Your medication's worn off?'

'Yes. So, I'm an embarrassing, useless pile of shit again.

This is the real me. My only viable personality comes in a blister pack.'

'You don't really think that.'

'I do . . . No – you're right: I don't. Without my medication, things are uncontrolled. Sometimes they're bad, sometimes they're fine – though, they're not fine for very long. The drugs keep things steady: it's not really that I'm always fine with them and always hideous without them.'

'There you go, then.'

'Yes. Actually, I'm essentially hideous whatever the circumstances. The drugs are merely cosmetics – emotional beauty products: they give me the appearance of not being a fundamentally shit person.'

'You're not a shit person.'

'I *am* a shit person.'

'You're *not*.' I put my arm around her shoulders.

'I *am*.' She rubbed some tears from her face with the back of her hand, and let her head fall exhaustedly against my chest. 'You are without a fucking clue when it comes to my shitness. You've deluded yourself that I'm crotchety, perhaps. That's all, though: a little saturnine, irascible and prone to leap from bridges every now and then, but basically not too bad. I've just told you that I didn't become suicidal after Bulgaria – that I'd been a depressive for years before that – and you still can't see the nauseating vileness that's sitting here next to you. I . . . am . . . shit.'

'Christ, Elizabeth.' I gave her a squeeze. 'So you were a depressive before that hotel thing. That's nothing to beat yourself up about. So you were ill before it happened, rather than being all bright and chirpy up to the point when you were traumatised by a tragic event. So what? It doesn't matter that those people dying wasn't actually the thing that made you feel bad.'

'Those people dying made me feel *good*.'

She pushed herself up away from me and looked at my face. Her eyes were sad, but at the same time also glowing with something very like anger.

'As their lives were taken away from them, I could have *sighed* with relief. I could have danced and bought drinks. "Oh, how *gorgeous*," I could have squealed as I read down the list of victims. "The perfect gift!" That's how I felt. All those years I'd been depressive – suicidal sometimes – in shame. I wasn't abused as a child; I didn't live in poverty or fear; no opportunities had been unfairly denied me because of race, or background, or physical disability. I was an educated person in a rich, Western democracy: able-bodied, intelligent, the casual recipient of a life full of kindnesses and blessed by fate in almost every way. And there I was: a depressive. "Pull yourself together, woman." "How many people are in *far* worse situations than you, yet they don't need prescription medicines to keep them off the railway tracks?" "What have *you* got to be depressed about?" Well, now, at last, I *did* have something to be depressed about. Now, I had a reason to want to die. Now, I was a casualty, not a malingerer.

'That's how sick and obscene I am, at my deep, fetid, suppurating core, Rob. The feelings and thoughts too fundamentally me to be prevented from existing by the policing disgust of the person who likes to pretend she's Elizabeth are utterly repellent. I'm soft, camouflaging flesh covering the bones of a perverse monster.'

She'd let her head drop forward. She was still, but tears were pouring down her cheeks and dripping into her lap from the tip of her nose. I took her face in my hands and tilted it up so she was looking me in the eyes again.

'You're no monster,' I said. 'You think I haven't felt glad that other people died when I didn't? Yes, if you asked me to calmly explain, I'd say that I wished *no one* had been killed in the crash. But that's not the instinctive thought.

The instinctive thought ignores everyone else and simply says, "Phew, I'm glad I didn't die there *too*."'

'That's not the same thing. That's hardly more than a semantic stumble. It's not being secretly happy that innocent people burned to death because it makes one seem more deserving of one's misery – hiding from tutting disapproval by consciously wearing a lie other people have paid for with their lives. You're not shit. I am.'

'No you're not.'

'Yes I am.'

I wiped away some of the wetness from her face by running my thumb lightly across her cheek. And then I leaned forward, and kissed her mouth.

Her lips were gentle and warm. Salty from the tears. The palm of her hand curled itself around the back of my neck, and she began to reach up into my hair – fingertips pressing hard, sharp nails moving slowly across my skin. I slid my tongue over her teeth, and hers came out to meet it, just as keenly. My hand slipped over her shoulder and explored its way down to the small of her back. I pulled her closer – pulled her with an intensity driven by a desperate, deafening desire not simply to have her close to me, but to have her in me; for there to be no distinction between us.

TWENTY

There's sex, and there's sex. And then there's *sex*.

The first is pretty damn good, but all fairly standard – if post-watershed – stuff. The second is wilder, top-shelf material: the sponsor of grinning memories and salacious, theatrically hushed pub conversations that begin, 'Well, this one woman I was with . . .' The third you wouldn't admit to if you had your feet in a bowl of water and the person asking you was toying with a couple of exposed electrical cables. It's way beyond impressively, anecdotally kinky and into the realms of 'Holy *Christ*!' You'd *never* confess to the things it involves, not even to your closest friends: and just the vague rumour that you'd actually done some of those things would, quite frankly, kill your mother stone dead. While having the first two, you might, in a sexual way, say that you felt 'hot'; while having the third, you feel as though you could, at any moment, incinerate entirely – right down to a powdery ash. When having *sex*, you're almost past emotions of sexual arousal and erotic desire – those are merely whispers heard at the edges of your mind: distant music. With *sex*, the feelings hurling your buzzing, twisting body around the room are more like fear. It's beautiful terror. It's sinning and screaming for sin. It's like dancing on the edge of death. It's intimacy let off the leash and rabidly out to show how much deeper than mere sex it is by driving you to places far beyond where mere, vapidly boastful sex would ever go. It's love speaking through the medium of excess.

Um, OK – I got a little carried away with the words, there. But that's because words were never meant to describe this. It doesn't transcend words: it exists underneath them. Somewhere deep, deep down – in a place older than words, where desire and action aren't separated by thought: where countless, blurring, merging, insistent hungers are intense, all-consuming and nameless.

Damn. Went over the top again, didn't I?

So, anyway – *that*'s the kind of sex Elizabeth and I had. And it damn near destroyed half of the furniture and fittings – the bed sheet alone was rendered a shameful disgrace, and, well . . . well, if anyone else so much as glanced at that decorative candleholder in the future I would simply have to flee the room with my face glowing crimson.

When, after a ludicrous amount of time, it finally finished, I lay next to Elizabeth in the bed; pleasantly tired, if also sore and extensively bruised. The sheet was dumped in a discarded heap on the carpet (awaiting – at the very least – a hot wash, and, ideally, being ritually burned on a hilltop after exorcism by an especially steely nerved priest). I held her beneath the bare duvet – she lay on her back with her head cupped in the curve of my neck and shoulder, having a cigarette and sending spumes of smoke up towards the ceiling.

'Well . . .' I said – articulating every thought that was currently able to survive in the blasted landscape of my head.

Elizabeth took another draw on her cigarette, and spoke with words entirely realised in tobacco smoke. 'A penchant for sexual extremes is a well-documented trait of my depressive illness.'

'Right.'

'I thought it worth mentioning. Not really out of any hope that you'll respect me in the morning, but perhaps so you'll be less inclined to have me arrested in the morning.'

'Yeah, well, much as you'd love the easy cop-out, I'm

not prepared to give you a "Depressive" T-shirt and see you as nothing but a collection of symptoms.'

'Suit yourself . . . I imagine you're already enthusiastically committed to having me wear a "Sub-Dom" T-shirt anyway.'

'Nah – it's not a T-shirt.'

She laughed. Perhaps the first time I'd heard her laugh completely happily: without there being some trace of bitterness or irony or sorrow in there too.

My hand rubbed thoughts against my cheek. 'I would never have guessed you'd be so . . .' I gave up trying to think of a word for it, and settled for simply blowing air out between my lips. 'I mean, you read books. You're "bookish". Aren't books and sex pretty much an either-or choice?'

'A notion that could only possibly have gestated in the low-ceilinged brain of someone who doesn't read enough books. Just think of Emily Brontë, for example: psychotically bookish – but was there *ever* a woman screaming out so loudly for a good fucking? I even suspect that's why *Wuthering Heights* carries on decades too long, rather than sensibly drawing the curtains a little after Cathy's death. It was Brontë saying, "Look – I'm simply going to keep on writing this stuff until someone comes and shags me raw."'

'I think you'd like James Herbert. I'll buy you *The Rats* – it can be the start of a new collection I'll gradually build up for you: Books Normal People Read. I mean, I've had to plough through some genuine literature in my time – I did go to school and everything – but it's not much fun, is it? I'd like to introduce you to fun. That can be my first task.'

Elizabeth let out another laugh, but now the undercurrent of sadness was back again.

She sat up in the bed. Not exactly moving away from me, because we were still touching, but . . . hmmm –

266

disengaging slightly. Strange. In this new position, her breasts were uncovered and her sliding up over my hand meant that it was now on her arse. Strange: strange that a woman spontaneously both exposing her tits and putting her arse into your hand can suggest, unmistakably, that she's doing it because she's backing off. Body language is full of irregular verbs.

'You had a slip, Rob,' she said from her new attitude. 'Your legs were understandably shaky, and you slipped on the moment. You don't have to apply the soothing salve of hinting at some small future of *any* sort of association between us beyond the next day or so. It's OK. I'm all grown up now.'

'Are you dumping me?' I asked with a smile. But my suddenly swelling throat made sure I knew it was a back-door smile. It was a serious question that wanted a serious answer, but given a grin and a jokey style of expression as an escape route in case the answer that came back made me want to pretend I'd simply been kidding.

'I can't dump you. I've never had you,' she replied, and then leaned over to the bedside table and stubbed her cigarette out: *clear* punctuation via physical movement – calculatedly throwing her bodyweight behind the suggestion that she'd answered my question, and that was the end of it now. Slippery. But, being a man, I'd performed similar manoeuvres many, *many* times myself. And they had never worked bleeding once – so I was damn sure I wasn't going to let Elizabeth get away with it here.

'You haven't answered my question,' I prodded.

'Haven't I?' she said, under a frown of surprise, before shrugging innocently and adding, 'I thought I had,' with a mixture designed to contain equal measures of honest casualness and blocking finality. Then, immediately, she began to poke around in her cigarette packet. 'Fuck. I wish I'd brought another twenty with me. I wonder if there's a shop anywhere near this place. Did you see a shop when we drove here?'

Infuriating. 'Ugh,' I thought to myself. 'Men are such swines – why do they do this to us?'

And pretty much instantly knew that I was going to spend the rest of my life trying to convince myself that I had, in fact, *never* thought that.

'So, you *are* dumping me,' I said, nodding slowly.

'What? What are you talking about? Gah – there aren't enough cigarettes here to kill a tiny, asthmatic child. I really will have to find a shop.'

'OK. As long as I know you *are* dumping me, then. That's OK. I simply want you to be honest about it. I'm fine, just as long as I know.'

Christ – where was this *coming* from? These words were using my lips without consulting me. (I wondered if this is how it works with women too: they don't mean to say this kind of stuff any more than I did now – it just falls out of their mouths while they're distracted with coolly and rationally thinking, 'Hmmm. As I have a grip, what I'll say in a moment is . . .')

Elizabeth sighed. 'What do you want me to say, Rob?' she asked. No, she 'said': it wasn't really a question. 'I can't . . .' she smiled sadly, '*spurn* you, because you're not mine to spurn. You're . . . um, what's the girl's name?'

'Jo.'

'That's the one. You belong to Jo, not me. She's your fiancée: I'm just some woman you repeatedly penetrated in a moment of weakness. And I'm already quite horrifically guilty about that, incidentally. It was a selfish, and cruel, and . . . well, and an utterly un-British thing for me to do. Mad or not, I ought to have had more self-control.'

'Now you're taking the piss.'

'No. What I'm doing is being deliberately flippant about

it to keep it at arm's length because, really, I do feel absolutely *dreadful* about allowing it to happen.'

'Yeah. I can understand how dreadful it must be to have sex with me. Ineffectual fuck-up that I am.' (God help me, but I think I may have pouted as I said this.)

'Ahh, wallowing in over-dramatised self-loathing: fuck off, Rob – you're in my seat. But anyway, you know perfectly well that I meant I felt terrible about having sex with someone else's fiancé, not about having sex with you, per se.'

'It was more than sex for me.'

I don't want to suggest that the sex wouldn't have been awe-inspiring in its own right: that would be a cruel and wholly unfair slur on the sex. But it really was only an aspect of something far bigger. The sex was like hitting the water: it was like hitting the water at the end of a long, long dive from a high, high cliff. You need that moment of impact before a dive is a dive: until that happens it's simply an accelerating fall after standing on the edge, looking down with your stomach tight from fear, then leaning forward and allowing yourself to drop. The splash is a confirmation, and a spectacular one, but the heart of a dive is the falling.

I wondered when it was that I'd fallen . . . No – there's no getting away from the word: I wondered when it was that I'd fallen in love with Elizabeth. The very first time I'd seen her I'd thought she was physically attractive – in an oddly distinguished, dissolute librarian kind of way. I'd found her intriguing too. But I'd certainly been in love with her far less than I'd wanted to push a trifle into her face. I asked myself when the change had come about. Myself shrugged. More disappointed with the lack of trust it demonstrated than anything else, I told Myself that the specific timing probably didn't matter but that, as I'd thought we were so close, Myself might have at least *mentioned* it to me, once it knew. Myself looked a bit sheepish and mumbled that it was sorry.

'Well . . .' Elizabeth replied. 'Well, on top of your already wobbly mental state, there's been the dangling threat of shadowy assassins, and exploding buildings, and a fucking *horrifying* bean casserole – your emotions are bound to be on something of a hair-trigger.'

'So, it was nothing but sex for you, then?'

She made a large and intricate job of pulling a Marlboro from her packet and lighting it.

'Was it?' I asked.

She tapped the cigarette on the edge of the teacup, to very carefully remove all the entirely imaginary ash.

'Yes,' she replied, without looking at me. 'Yes, it was.'

Late the next morning, I went downstairs to make myself a cup of tea (leaving Elizabeth asleep in bed). Zach, who was standing by the kitchen window eating a piece of cheese in the style of a lieutenant in the Special Forces, watched me wordlessly. I could feel his eyes hosing me down with reserved, Nebraskan disapproval.

I was briefly indignant – I mean, he didn't know what Elizabeth and I had actually done the previous night. (I hoped to God that *no one* would know specifically what Elizabeth and I had done the previous night, *ever*.) For all he knew, we could have just talked. Talked through why she was upset, perhaps – then maybe discussed our favourite books. Where did he get off jumping to conclusions?

But then I realised that there had probably been a degree of noise. Yes. There'd have been those noises. Come to think of it, I believe I may have shouted a few things too: and not the type of things that would generally be shouted by someone who was staffing the phones at the Samaritans or a person chatting about *Mansfield Park*.

'Where's Beth?' I asked, brazening it out.

'She left last night. While you were—'

'Right . . . Right.'

'She's gone to get a hold of this Professor Osbourne guy. She said she figured she'd maybe be back today. Today or tomorrow.'

'Right.'

I held the mug of tea in my hands, noticing that they were cupped gently around it with my fingertips touching: take the tea away, and it'd have looked almost as though I had my hands together in prayer. I changed to a one-handed grip.

'It's not what you think,' I said.

Zach shrugged. 'I don't think anything.'

'Normally, I'd have no trouble believing that statement completely, but . . .'

'People do crazy things when they're at war. It's not the people, it's the situation.'

'We're not at war.'

'Aren't we?'

'I love her.'

'OK, Rob. If you say so.'

'I do.'

'For sure. I mean, she's real lovable, right?'

'Yes – in fact – she is. OK, on the surface she's snotty and insufferable, but it's only because she has problems with herself that she has trouble dealing with. When people don't think they deserve to be liked, they often seem to go out of their way to make themselves unlikeable. She's not nasty: she's hurt, and sad, and lonely. Lonely most of all, I think. But, underneath the hard show, she's kind and wonderful . . . Um – like Mr Rochester.'

Zach did something with his mouth.

I sighed. 'Mr Rochester is a character in a book. Not a bit of rough I fancy back in Birmingham.'

'Oh, right.'

'He fucking *is*.'

'No, no – I believe you.' He scratched himself a little. 'And she loves you?'

'Well . . .' I waved arbitrarily towards the draining board. 'Pfff – you know how women work.'

'Not English women.'

'I suspect English women are the same as Nebraskan women.'

'Not from what I've seen.'

Fair point.

'Oh, fuck off,' I snapped. 'What do you understand about anything?'

'Nothing. And it's none of my business anyway, man. Like I say, I'm just here as your physical guardian. A good soldier follows orders. I'm purely tactical – I leave the strategy to the Man Upstairs. He's the only one as can see the big picture . . . So, when are you going to tell your girlfriend?'

'Weren't you supposed to be fucking off?'

He held up his hands – 'OK' – and strolled away towards the door out of the kitchen. 'I'd better check up on the situation outside . . . You keep away from the windows and do your best to secure the entry points,' he said. 'I'll try to maintain a perimeter.'

'Jesus, Zach. You do know you're going straight to video, right?'

He left.

I went back into the living room with my mug, sat on the sofa, and thought about one thousand two hundred and seventeen things.

Long after my untouched tea had gone cold, Elizabeth padded down the stairs behind me. I felt her walk over and stand at my shoulder.

'Where are Zach and Beth?'

'Beth's gone to get Professor Osbourne. Zach's in the trees defending democracy against enemy rabbits.'

'Splendid.'

'I should call Jo.'

Elizabeth didn't reply.

'I ought to tell her about . . . things,' I continued. 'It's only fair.'

'Things?'

'Us. Well . . . me.'

She came around the sofa and crouched down in front of me, putting her hands on my knees. 'Rob?' she said. 'I know this is a complex idea for you to absorb, but I think you should try not to be a stupid cunt.'

'She has a right to know, Elizabeth. I want to be honest with her.'

She stood up. 'Do you fuck. You want to confess because it'll make you feel better to unburden yourself. What you want isn't honesty – it's absolution. Don't be so fucking selfish. If she never knows, she'll be fine: you're the one who'll have to live with it. Trying to shirk the guilt is understandable, but characterising it as noble . . . it's nothing but disguising cowardice as bravery. Take responsibility, Rob. I know that you're basically decent, so behave like it: you did something impulsive and ill-advised, and the price you have to pay is to keep your fucking mouth shut about it forever.'

'That's such a pile of shit.'

'No, it isn't. And you know it.'

'Is . . . Is *so*.'

'Jesus.' She folded her arms and turned her back to me. But, after a moment, I saw her shoulders drop, and her voice was quieter when she spoke again. 'I hope that it's just craven idiocy that's causing you to talk about telling Jo, Rob. That, at least, is acceptably unacceptable.'

'I don't know what you mean.'

She turned to face me once more. 'I mean that the alternative interpretation is that you're raising the possibility deliberately to put pressure on me. Like a man's mistress threatening to call his wife: not because she wants to tell her, but simply to force his hand – to make him accept, or confirm, that their relationship isn't trivial or subsidiary.'

'Now, that *is* a pile of shit. I mean, the other thing was a pile of shit, but that . . . that is just *a pile of shit*.'

'OK . . . Good. Because it really wouldn't work between us, Rob. There are *so* many reasons why it wouldn't work that it'd take the rest of our lives simply to count them. So, let it go. It's a cul-de-sac, there's no driving through it – *whatever* you may mistakenly think you feel for me, or whatever I may feel for you.'

'Whatever you feel for me?' (She might have just said some other stuff, but that was the only bit I heard.) 'So you *do* feel something, then? What d—'

The sound of Zach coming in the kitchen door cut me off. My eyes were explosively blown in that direction by detonating frustration and fury. Elizabeth quickly moved three yards away from me and stood with her arms refolded across her chest, gazing out of the window at whatever pointless collection of leaves and sky and who-cared-what had been dumped outside as a view. Her intention was obviously to create a tableau that spoke evocatively of a room in which nothing was happening.

Zach marched through the doorway, saw Elizabeth and me were there, faltered almost imperceptibly (his gaze flicking rapidly between the two of us), and then dropped his head like a fourteen-year-old boy who'd walked in to find his parents fucking while both dressed as cheerleaders.

Just in case we weren't all as uncomfortable as possible, he then cleared his throat, mumbled, 'Um . . .' and stared at his boots.

Someone had to speak, or the sheer weight of the embarrassment was likely to form a black hole that would suck in and destroy all of Wales, killings thousands. So – working hard to ensure I kept any trace of irritation out of my voice – I snapped bad-temperedly at Zach, 'Well? Did you see anything?'

'Oh, no – *no*,' he replied, concussively mortified. 'Honest – I didn't see a *thing*.'

'I meant did you see anything *outside*, you dog's arse.'

'Oh. Right.'

'You *couldn't* have seen anything in here. Because nothing was happening. To see. In here.'

'No. For sure.'

A pause full of lead.

'Well?' I asked.

'Um . . . Fine – I believe you.'

'Oh, for Christ's sake . . . "Well, did you see anything outside?"'

'*Riiight*. No, no, I didn't. It's all clear. Our position is a defensive nightmare: extensive cover for attackers, approachable from every angle, exposed . . . but I reckon there are no hostiles in the vicinity at this time.'

'Phew. I'll drop back to Code Orange, then, if that's all right?'

He nodded thoughtfully. 'Code Orange would be m—'

'I was taking the piss.'

'OK.'

Elizabeth turned to speak to him.

'I don't imagine you found a newsagent's anywhere near here, did you?'

He replied without being able to meet her eyes. 'A newsagent's, ma'am?'

'A shop. Somewhere I can buy some cigarettes.'

'K – got you. No. It seems as we're kind of isolated here. Wooded terrain all around us. A couple of tracks, but

275

Beth's taken the car and I found nothing as far as I went on foot.' (This reminded me again that I'd left my car outside a bombed factory in East London. Oh well. It might still be OK; at least it wasn't parked in Birmingham.)

'Great,' said Elizabeth, twisting back to look out of the window again. 'So, I'll run out of cigarettes, then . . . You'll both have to forgive me if I become a little testy.'

Zach opened his mouth to make some reply, but I vigorously shook my head at him and he pulled himself up.

TWENTY-ONE

Elizabeth avoided me for the rest of the day – something she achieved by staying close to Zach. I could see that this situation didn't really make him any less inclined to bite through his own knuckles than, for different reasons, it made me. Elizabeth didn't appear to enjoy it either: in between his patrols – on which she accompanied him – they'd stand in the kitchen in a state of grim, knotted awkwardness. Zach would occasionally say something carefully calculated to be comprehensively innocuous, and thus profoundly redundant; Elizabeth would stare at him, tut, and then roll her eyes in reply. After this, they'd fall into an itchy silence again.

In the evening, Zach reheated the leftover casserole. It looked like something you'd see pouring into the sea out of an exposed pipe close to an Italian city. I decided not to risk it, and had a Cup-a-Soup instead: chicken and vegetable with croutons. As the brief given to the developers of chicken and vegetable Cup-a-Soup with croutons almost certainly read, 'Should taste OK, but be visually indistinguishable from sick – and absolutely *always* have a mucus-like sediment at the bottom,' it wasn't exactly the most appetising dinner table you could imagine. Elizabeth said she wasn't hungry at all. Instead, she found a bottle of wine – which she declared, 'flagitiously ghastly,' and which she drank entirely in twenty minutes.

I wanted to go to bed with Elizabeth. I don't mean I wanted to have sex with her. Well, I do mean I wanted to have sex with her, obviously. But what I *needed* was to talk to her. So, my hope was that some entirely natural moment would come about where she (or I) would yawn and say, 'Well, I'm going to call it a night,' and then I (or she) would stretch tiredly and reply, 'Yeah . . . I think I'll turn in too,' and we'd go upstairs together. However, I was sensible enough to guess that, if *I* did the first bit, then it was very unlikely that she'd chip in with the second. I'd leave, and she'd simply remain there. Then I'd be left lying awake in my room; pushing my ears out to catch the sound of her feet on the stairs or trying to pick up anything she might be saying to Zach while I was away.

So, there was nothing to do but wait her out: for all three of us to sit in the living room, breathing, until she cracked.

I should have been used to being awake during those grim hours when the day is dead – when it loses all the romance of night, and just lies there like a cold corpse; I usually worked until 3 a.m. every weekday, after all. But it didn't feel like I was used to it. Maybe it was simple tiredness, maybe it was the wearying tension I'd been living with, or maybe chicken and vegetable Cup-a-Soups with croutons wisely contain a chemical designed to make you want to sleep . . . and forget – I don't know. Whatever it was, it made for an ordeal. My eyes dried out. First, blinking stung. Then it reached a point where I was almost scared to blink at all, because I was worried that my lids might actually stick to my eyeballs.

Eventually, Elizabeth declared, 'Christ – I need a piss' (an announcement that pushed Zach back into his chair with discomfort), and she plodded away up the stairs. After about ten minutes, I realised she wasn't coming back. The piss story had possibly been nothing but a clever ruse. My God, she was a sly one.

So, I laid on a yawn for Zach, and said, 'Well, that's enough partying for me. See you in the morning.'

He wished me goodnight, and said that he'd keep guard

downstairs – adding that, if he *were* overpowered by intruders, he'd shout, 'The wolves are free!' as loud as possible as a code phrase so I knew, and might therefore have a shot at escaping through an upstairs window. I asked him why he didn't simply go with shouting, 'I'm being overpowered by intruders!' He replied that code phrases were always better, as they eliminated the possibility of misinterpretation. And that, in any case, he'd feel a fool shouting, 'I'm being overpowered by intruders!'

'But you wouldn't feel a fool shouting, "The wolves are free!"?'

'No. That's our agreed code phrase.'

'Goodnight, Zach,' I said. (I'm wise enough to be able to spot an argument I can't win.)

The bathroom door was ajar, and the light was off. I peeked inside, just to make sure that Elizabeth wasn't still in there – having fallen asleep on the toilet or something. Finding it empty, I moved along to her room.

I stood outside in what I believe is known as a quandary. After standing in it like an idiot for quite a while, I reached an arm out of this quandary and tapped my knuckles against her door.

'Elizabeth?' I whispered.

There was no reply.

What did that mean? Was she asleep? Was she deliberately ignoring me, hoping I'd go away? Was she making it clear that she wanted me to enter by emphatically not calling back, 'Fuck off, Rob'?

I knocked again. 'Elizabeth?'

The same inconclusive silence was the reply.

What should I do now? It felt disgustingly creepy to simply open her door and peer inside. She could be asleep, and might wake to see me 'sneaking' into her room. That would be terrible. She might even scream, 'What are you doing in my room, Rob? You fucking pervert!'

Zach might then run up in response, and think I was a pervert too.

No, hold on – he wouldn't do that because 'What are you doing in my room, Rob? You fucking pervert!' hadn't been agreed upon as a code phrase.

I tried once more – 'Elizabeth?' – then, having again received no reply, I gently eased the door open.

There was a tiny, glowing dot in the darkness. That solitary light was expanded easily in my mind, and labelled the Constellation of Elizabeth Sitting Up in Bed Smoking a Cigarette. I froze. The dot glowed brighter. This was followed by the sound of smoke being exhaled, and then Elizabeth said, 'If you're coming in . . . then come in.'

I felt that, clearly, the best thing to do was say, 'Sorry,' close the door, and go to my own room.

I didn't say anything, entered her room, and closed the door behind me.

Trying to be as unencroaching as possible, and also to avoid banging my shins on anything in the darkness, I slowly moved over to the bed, and lowered myself down next to her.

She took another drag on her cigarette – the orange glow of the burning tobacco briefly illuminating her face.

'It really *wouldn't* work, you know?' she said. It sounded as though she'd been insistently repeating this phrase to herself in the darkness, long before I'd arrived.

I lifted my shoulders and stuck out my lower lip. As it was almost pitch-black in her room, I guessed that a few of the many irrefutable levels of this considered counter-argument might have gone over her head.

'It really wouldn't,' she continued. 'For a start, you're a radio presenter – which is appalling. OK, so you're actually more intelligent and less narcissistic than I'd imagined . . . But you're still a radio presenter. Which is *appalling*.'

'I present a jazz show, on local radio, between midnight and 3 a.m. So, it's not like I have listeners or anything. Just think of me as some bloke who talks to himself.'

'Which is the first sign of madness, is it not?'

'I don't know. I think we're probably both too far along even to remember what the first sign is.'

'Which brings us elegantly to another point: I'm a depressive, Rob. I'm not "a bit glum". I don't have some kind of "captivating depth". I'm a fucking nutter. You might think it's all very gothic and excitingly intense when you've only dipped your toes in the water, but, long term – immersed in the sea of me with the beach a fuck of a long swim away – it's actually inexpressibly tedious. Woundingly boring: attritionally wearisome. You can't see that . . . Or, even worse, you have some arsehole notion that . . . Fff – I don't know – that "the power of your love will cure me".'

As my eyes had become more accustomed to the low light, I had gradually been able to see Elizabeth better. She'd faded in before me; like a ghost melting out of the darkness. She looked so sad that I could hardly bear it.

'I don't think that.'

'Don't you?'

'No . . . But I do think I could help, at least a little.'

'A perception based on insufficient data. Gathered, I should add, from observation of me under conditions that wouldn't apply in the real world. Your methodology is shite.'

'You can't be sure that's true.'

'Yes I can. I can because I have long – horridly long – experience of me. And there again we have a bridge to the next point – rather like one of the links you use on the wireless to join items together and provide the illusion of narrative flow. What's the technical name for those links?'

'Links.'

'Really? How very disappointing.' She pulled hard on her cigarette again – presumably to numb the pain of this discovery. 'Anyway,' she continued once she'd composed herself, 'I have long experience of me because, despite my best efforts, I've stubbornly hung around taking up space for such a long time. How old are you, Rob?'

'I'm thirty-one.'

'Thirty-one. Christ. I'm *forty-six*.'

'So? So, it's fifteen years – so what?'

'It's fifteen *colossal* years. You're still trying to clamber up one side of the curve: I'm skidding rapidly down the other.'

'Oh, come on. You can't possibly think I'm too young.'

'I admit you're not Zach – for all his size, he's really little more than a boy; still panting and excited from the playground. But you're not old. I'm *old*.'

'You are not.'

'In terms of options I am. You have a whole decade full of choices and opportunities lying ahead; all my choices have already been made.'

'Ha. Choices – just what I need.'

'Pft. Forget about that. That'll pass, I'm sure. It'll wear out, if nothing else: your particular stymieing indecision doesn't exactly gleam with the unmistakable quality of a timeless classic, does it? You're more like a cheap, Korean knock-off version of Hamlet. The point is the potential you still have in you. You're spilling over with possibilities: all I bring to the table is access to rapidly approaching offers of cheaper car insurance.'

'Don't be melodramatic. If I were fifteen years older than you no one would even mention it.'

'I doubt that. And, more to the point, it's qualitatively different in any case: a man's being fifteen years older than a woman will raise an eyebrow – a woman's being fifteen years older than a man will raise a smile. That's the way of things.'

'I wouldn't have thought that you gave in to the way of things.'

'Perhaps I don't, generally. But is it remotely fair of me to allow the coming about of a situation that would mean you got to have some manner of Oedipal tag fastened to your forehead? Or perhaps even the general assumption that you were fucking me for my money?'

'Have you got any money?'

'I live in Willesden.'

'There you go, then. People will easily be able to work out that I'm fucking you without any money at all changing hands.'

'Outstanding. So I'm confirmed as a penniless Jocasta, then . . . Hmmm: Jo/Jocasta. Dear me – how very unfortunate.'

I didn't really know what she was talking about here. 'That's bollocks,' I said. (Always the best reply when you don't really know what someone is talking about.) 'All people will think is that I'm fucking you because you're hot.'

'Ugh.'

'You're gorgeous, then. People – as if I give shit – will think I'm fucking you because you're gorgeous. And *I'll* know that I'm fucking you because I love you. If we love each other, that's all that really matters.'

'Ha! My apologies for assuming you were an unusually callow thirty-one-year-old man, Rob. I see that you're actually a fuck-witted thirteen-year-old girl.' She stubbed out her cigarette.

'Oh, fuck off, you aggravating cow: do you love me or not?'

'That's not the point, you simplistic arsehole.'

'Arrgh. Just answer the fucking question. Christ – you're such a condescending shit.'

'Moronic prick.'

'Arrogant bitch.'

'Shithead. Yes.'

'F— What?'

'Yes. You wank-brained twat.'

'Then shut the fuck up.'

I rolled over and kissed her.

This time it was tender. Our lips moved slowly and gently. My hand touched her face in the semi-darkness, and hers came up to meet it; stroking it, holding it closer against her cheek, and then gripping it tightly, so that our fingers latticed together.

This went on for the longest, sweetest time.

Then we had *incredibly* dirty sex again. Jesus – if this was going to be the future, then we really needed to invest in a gallon of lubricant, lots of antiseptic gauze, some broad-spectrum antibiotics and possibly our own personal air ambulance.

Beth didn't return that night. This was probably quite lucky. Had she come back and walked into what she'd assume was her and Elizabeth's bedroom, she'd have probably taken one look at us and thought she'd stumbled across the scene of a particularly grisly murder.

When I awoke at a little past noon, I sat up in bed. The movement caused me to feel a raw, burning sensation in a part of my body that I'm ashamed even to name. I sucked air in sharply between my teeth. And then smiled at the memory. Elizabeth lay beside me, still asleep. She looked peaceful, and heart-breakingly beautiful. I leaned back, propping myself up on my elbow, and simply stared at her lying there, sleeping, for close to an hour.

Finally, she half opened her eyes, saw me, and smiled.

'I love you,' I whispered.

'Yeah. I'm afraid I love you too.' She sat up with a creaky groan. 'How are you today?'

'Fine. You?'

'Fine. Well . . . I could probably do with sitting on an ice pack for a day or so, but other than that: exceptionally fine.'

We stayed in bed for a while, talking, before eventually getting up and hobbling downstairs together. Zach was there, rummaging around in his backpack. He glanced up at us and his accusing eyes made my sore, throbbing nipples want to shrink away under my top, lest he somehow discover their shame.

'Good morning, Zachary,' Elizabeth said, brightly. 'What's the news from "Ops"?'

'All quiet,' he replied, fastening his backpack and putting it aside. 'I've done a couple of patrols, and observed no activity.'

'First class. Right – I'm going to get something to eat. What do you fancy, Rob?'

'Oh, anything. I'm open to whatever you suggest.'

'Hmmm . . .' replied Elizabeth, grinning.

'I'll do another patrol,' said Zach.

It was a wonderful day. Zach kept as low a profile as he could without actually burying himself under several feet of earth, and Elizabeth and I lounged around the house together, rambling about whatever came into our heads. There was a portable TV in the living room, but Wales is rightly famous for having television reception that consists of three channels of static. We did watch the news in Welsh in the early evening, however. Enjoying the stream of serious, utterly unintelligible mouth noises out of which erratically bobbed the odd recognisable word – 'Gwyen Ilan nwgg rhllyggnnffon NATO bwrryd yrngg iffyn,' or,

'Cydymffurfinethyll rywnn bwydd llenyth dyd nffync-wydrr iathynaegg cwmyll ithallyff wyneth nyn: *The Rolling Stones.*' We made up our own news reports that were spontaneously invented gibberish punctuated with tantalising fragments of English: stories that, in some gloriously hidden way, involved traffic congestion, bear-baiting, rubber stockings and the Prime Minister of Canada. In essence, we enjoyed being six years old. And, marvellously, Elizabeth was much better at it than I was.

Around teatime, I switched on my mobile – just to check if Beth had called with some important information. I didn't think she would have (not after what she'd said about our phones possibly being monitored, but it was best to make sure). There were no messages from her. But there was a text from Jo. 'how r u? hope ur better, we should talk, call me x.' 'Yes,' I thought, 'we really *should* talk, Jo. But that talk isn't going to be anything like what you'll be expecting, I'm afraid.'

Now, I'm fair, and deeply, deeply honourable. The proper thing to do, in the circumstances, was to tell Jo about the situation. Elizabeth's earlier insistence that virtue demanded I never tell Jo, ever, only made sense in the context of a fling. (An odd word for it – 'fling' – I've always thought. Who came up with that? Of all the phrases you could choose to mean a brief sexual encounter, 'fling' hardly seems the most obvious – I mean, if you simply *have* to go in that direction, then even a 'toss' is better, isn't it?) To be a valid argument, it relied utterly on Elizabeth and I being an isolated typo in a life that other-wise had Jo written right through it. But it wasn't that. I did not intend for Elizabeth and I to end soon, to the extent that the very idea of us ending at all was unbearable. This was no fling: it was a leap. Given that I'd be staying with Elizabeth, then, telling Jo was important and urgent.

However painful it would be for me – and, come to that, for her.

Still . . . well, there was no sense being an arse about it, was there?

It was unthinkable to tell her via a text or two, and my battery was so low that it might manage only thirty seconds or so of a proper call before it died. The line going silent on her in the middle of *that* conversation? That would be a cruel thing indeed. So, I decided, I *had* to overrule my instinctive decency for the time being, in the service of a greater good: I shouldn't take risks with Jo's feelings, simply to serve my desire to be noble. It was best to wait until I got back: to tell her face to face. Quietly cursing the course of action realism had forced upon me, I turned the phone off again, without replying.

In the evening, Zach did a few more patrols, and I watched TV with Elizabeth: she lay in my lap, and I stroked her hair and tried to convince myself this wasn't all a dream. I couldn't believe how lucky I was. Partly this was a result of watching *EastEnders*: seeing the endless trials life throws at the unfortunate inhabitants of Albert Square really does make you count your blessings. Mostly, though, it was sheer, grinning amazement that I'd found Elizabeth, and that she – unfathomably – wanted to be with me. When the two of us went to bed that evening, we said goodnight to Zach at the same time, and climbed the stairs together.

'This is madness,' said Elizabeth, her head on my shoulder and her hand moving gently over my chest. She smiled. 'Quite apart from the three to eighteen hundred prosaic levels on which it's madness, how can we dream of it lasting? And I'm not simply talking about our feelings: how can we be such fools as to build hopes on something as frail as life? We both know *very* well how fragile and brittle it is. Death comes rapidly, indiscriminately and without warning to people day after day after day. It makes no sense for you to invest in me, when I could be gone in the very next moment. Even if we can somehow miraculously avoid your fiancée stabbing me through the eyes, then a bug, a bursting blood vessel, or a bleeding bottle opener could have me mortally uncoiled in a tick of the clock.'

'No. You won't die on me.'

'Really? Oh, that's all right, then.' She slapped my chest. 'Tch.'

'Honestly – you *can't* die in some sudden, random way. I've thought about it, and it simply can't happen.'

'Phew. Thank Christ I didn't get taken in by that sweet-talking life-insurance salesman last year.'

'No, listen . . .'

I paused for a time.

'Well?' she asked.

'Oh, sorry – I was just savouring the unique experience of you actually listening.'

She slapped my chest again.

'OK,' I continued. 'Do you know the old joke about getting killed in a terrorist attack on an aeroplane?'

'No. Which is odd – because it certainly sounds like my kind of joke.'

'The idea is that, if you're frightened about there being a bomb on the plane you're catching, then the safest thing you can do is to take a bomb on to the plane yourself. You see, the chances of there being a bomb on a plane are millions to one. But the chances of there being *two* – unrelated – bombs on the *same* plane are so ludicrously high as to effectively make it a statistical impossibility.'

'I see . . . Oh, and I'm laughing on the inside, by the way.'

'If we expand that idea—'

'And, to be frank, how could we possibly resist doing so?'

'If we expand that idea, then we can say that the chances of you dying, for some arbitrary reason, just like,' I clicked my fingers, 'that, are pretty small. But the probability becomes *microscopically* tiny if we try to imagine this random happening will be the trigger for *two* deaths. And it would have to be. Because I couldn't live without you: if you died, it'd kill me too.'

'Awwww . . . that's dreadfully sweet, Rob. Utter shit, self-evidently – and actually quite sickly – but very, very sweet. You're sickly sweet.'

'I prefer to think of myself as "rich".'

'Indeed . . . Poor jokes and flawed mathematics aside, though, we're still clinging to fantasy, you know? This isn't real life. It's a shipboard romance; where the ship is full of lunatics; and not unlikely to be torpedoed at any time. Once you stop racing around the country – believing you're under the threat of death – you'll go home to Jo and realise that's where your heart is. I work only when your world's in disarray. She's the one you'll choose when you have the space to be rational again.'

I thought about telling her then.

I'd nearly told her when she was struggling with her guilt about Bulgaria. I'd nearly told her again last night, when she was unwilling to believe that I knew my own feelings about loving her. Both times I'd pulled back. And I pulled back again now. Things were good between us. Elizabeth had doubts – but they weren't threatening; they were just sad anxieties. So, why risk telling her now? I mean, the problem was . . . Well, it was a double-edged sword, *that* was the problem. Rather like if you confess to a lie. If you come clean, admit an uncomfortable truth, be open and honest, and confess to a lie, what does that confirm you are?

A liar.

Now wasn't the time to tell her. The time to tell her, if ever, was when she was holding my hand as I lay on my deathbed; her face lined but still beautiful, her black hair no longer detailed with isolated threads of grey but completely white; two grown-up children and a loyal mastiff quietly distraught at my feet; perhaps one of the tracks that Lester Young recorded with Rene Urtreger playing achingly in the background. Yes, that would be the right time. Otherwise, trying to demonstrate I was lucid now might end up only confirming to her that I was long-standingly flaky.

I didn't tell her.

'No,' I said. 'I love you.' And I kissed her on the forehead.

'I love you too. Fucking idiot that I am.'

I traced my fingers across her face.

'Hmmm . . . do you fancy doing that thing again?' I asked.

'What thing?'

'That thing with the . . . I nodded towards the curtain pull.

'You didn't think . . . I was worried you might have thought that was going too far.'

'Oh, yeah – it was going *way* too far . . . Fancy doing it again?'

'Abso-fucking-lutely.'

TWENTY-TWO

I awoke to the smell of burning. 'Oh,' I thought . . . um, actually, let's not say what I thought. What I *didn't* think, initially, was, 'Bicycling Christ! The fucking house is on fire!' After a second, however, I grimaced, wrinkled my nose, insisted my eyes open, and looked around. The room was still dark, which made the glow easily visible under the door. I also became aware of a crackling noise outside. And heat. And how really very, very acrid the air around me was. Finally, I jerked upright in bed and (better late than never) thought, 'Bicycling Christ! The fucking house is on fire!'

I turned, and shook Elizabeth.

'Elizabeth! Wake up! We're *on fire*!'

She groaned sleepily and mumbled. 'I know, Rob. But can't you wait until tomorrow? I'm dreadfully sore.'

'No! No – I mean – no – we're on fire! *The fucking house is on fire!*'

She sat up too, and said, 'What?' Then, '*Fuck!*'

I leapt out of bed and slapped at the light switch. Nothing happened. Maybe the electrics had already been burned through and shorted. The curtains were pulled completely away from the window, however (for reasons we needn't go into), and enough moonlight was coming in for us to be able to see reasonably well.

Elizabeth scrambled to her feet, and I ran to the door.

'No!' she shouted. 'Don't open it!'

'Why not?'

'They say you shouldn't.'

'Who do?'

'*They*. Haven't you ever seen one of those government information films about fires?'

'Govern— What? No – of course I fucking haven't. I've never seen any "government information films". I wasn't even *born* in the 1950s.'

'Neither was I, you cunt.'

'Well, you seem to be very familiar with instructional shorts from the Ministry of Fires.'

'Oh, *right*. So now it comes out. You *do* think I'm an old woman. When push comes to conflagrational shove, it all comes out. Wanker.'

'I don't think you're an old woman.' I yanked my boxers on. 'I'm simply less familiar than you with a cinematic tradition developed during the Blitz.'

She pulled her dress over her head. 'You are such a tosser. Go on – open the fucking door, then. Mr fucking Sky Digital.'

I dashed across to the window and wrestled it open. Below was some soft-looking grass. In between the window ledge and the soft-looking grass was about fifteen feet of cold, empty air.

What's more, I could see the bright, flickering light of the flames blazing behind the window directly below ours.

'I think we may have to make a rope out of knotted bed sheets.'

'Oh – so you know *that* one, then?'

'Everyone knows that one.'

'Everyone knows— Oh, never mind. Knotted sheets are sadly not an option open to us, however. We only ever had a single sheet – and even that's now downstairs in the washing machine. All we have left is a duvet.'

'Fuck . . . OK: we could cut it into strips and—'

'Both choke to death while you pretend to be the Count of Monte Cristo.'

She was right. We didn't have anything to cut up the

duvet with, the crackling and splintering sounds from beyond the door were becoming extremely loud, and the room was now half full of smoke.

'We'll throw the mattress out of the window, then. Use it to break our fall.'

'The window is eighteen inches wide. The mattress is the size of Wessex. All we'd succeed in doing is blocking our only exit with a mattress.'

'It's so easy to find fault, isn't it? At least I'm making suggestions.'

'We can do only one thing, Rob: jump and hope for the best.'

She was right again.

It really pisses you off to have all your survival tactics effortlessly trumped by someone who's suicidal. I know that, in the circumstances, that shouldn't have mattered. But it did. So, I'm petty – and you're perfect, are you?

I leaned out of the window again, and peered down.

Peering back up at me was Zach.

'We have a fire situation,' he said.

'*No?* Really? What's your source on that?' I shouted at him.

'Climb out on to the window sill, let yourself down as much as you can, then drop. I'll try to catch you. That'll decrease the force of your impact.'

I turned around to Elizabeth.

'Zach's outside. He wants us to jump on him.'

'For fuck's sake do it, then. *I'll* do it. I'd jump out of a first-floor window on to him even if there weren't a fire, in fact. Just let me find something heavy to hold.'

'OK – you first.'

'Why me first?'

'Because I want you to get out first.'

'Just fucking do it, Rob. Don't fuck around wasting time. I'll be right behind you.'

'I . . .'

We couldn't afford to wait – the smoke was already making my eyes stream – so I stopped trying to persuade her to go ahead of me and began to get out myself. I clambered through the window, lowered my feet as close to the ground as I could, and let go.

My arse collided with Zach's upturned face at what I guessed was something like the re-entry speed of an Apollo space capsule. He grunted out the word, 'Ngh!' directly between my impacting buttocks, and – I have no doubt – exhilarated and refreshed by the experience, toppled backwards with my splayed body on top of him.

Without any kind of pause for reflection, both Zach and I moved *tremendously* quickly to remove his nose from my bottom, and struggled up on to our feet. Elizabeth was already trying to climb out above us – smoke overflowing from the room behind her. Now I was standing up, I could feel the heat pumping harassingly from the window on the ground floor; it pushed at me like a flat hand. In the next moment, the intensity of this heat increased tenfold when, with a sound like a boot stamping down hard on a scattering of snail shells, the glass in the window shattered and flames – insane with delight at their escape – began streaming out. This surge of fire threatened Zach and me, but (nauseously worse) it also poured and pawed upwards, towards Elizabeth: putting an angry blanket of flame directly between her and the ground.

I knew she was going to die.

The course the next few seconds would take plunged into my head as though it were already a memory. It was a vision of what was yet to happen, but it felt like a recollection of the past because I knew it couldn't be changed. I could see with agonising clarity Elizabeth's dress catching fire; the thrashing, twisting, screaming fall of her burning body; I could hear the crack of her neck as it hit the earth.

I tried to shake the terrible future from my head, and I called up to her – howling as loud as I could, my throat fighting against both the noise of the fire and my own surging need to drop to my knees and retch at the ground with sick horror.

'Jump!' I shouted. 'Try to push away from the house!'

Oh, sweet Jesus – to lose her now. Why hadn't I made her jump first? This was more than I could stand. To find her, and then to lose her again the very next moment. The swamping horror of it swallowed me up – engulfed me completely. I was pathetically small in comparison to it. I hated the whole fucking world. Let it all fucking burn. The whole fucking cruel, fucking vicious, fucking lot of it.

Elizabeth lowered herself as much as she dared (the heat surging up over her must have been intense; tiny flames were already beginning to take hold of the bottom edge of her dress). She paused for an instant, and then let go – kicking against the wall at the same time. The fire spread over her completely as she fell backwards through the air.

Zach and I lunged to where she was heading; each of us with a speed and predictive accuracy that ensured we collided full on in an ugly, heavy crash of bodies and skulls – like two footballers, each unaware of the other, both running to head the same ball. Our outstretched, cushioning arms were lost in the tangle; our preparedly sprung knees undone by our impacting legs. There seemed to be a single, tranquil microsecond of the two of us standing, stymied there together – immobile and enmeshed – and then Elizabeth landed on our combined faces and chests, like a sandbag dropped from a dive bomber. We buckled under the force of her body, and all three of us hit the ground in a heap made of bruising flesh, banging bones, two 'Fucks!' and a 'Gee!'

Winded and stunned, we rolled apart into separate groans. I felt like . . . well, like someone had fallen out of a first-floor window on to me. Even the physical (and psychological) discomfort of Zach's nasal bone having recently been driven into my rectum was forgotten as I struggled frantically to get a single breath of air inside my flattened lungs. Elizabeth lay on her side, coughing and holding her back (but at least not aflame – her speed through the air must have put out those parts of her dress that had begun to catch alight). Zach grimaced while gripping his neck, but soon recovered enough to somehow push himself up on to all fours and bark hoarsely, 'Call off!'

I couldn't speak. I assumed because my tongue was hampered by the fact that my brain had been knocked down into my mouth.

Zach shouted again. 'Call off. Rob? Rob – are you OK?'

'Yes. Yes, I'm fine,' I somehow managed to splutter. 'How's Elizabeth?'

He moved over to her. I struggled on to my stomach and, coming from the other side, slithered there too. She was still coughing and writhing.

'Elizabeth?' I asked, desperately. 'Are you OK?'

'God's weeping bollocks,' she said, her voice wheezy and crackling. 'Is that fucking catching me, then? Is that the fucking famous male hand-eye coordination? For fuck's sake. I wasn't asking for the Australian wicket-keeper – I don't expect you to be able to put your hands on the ricocheting blur of a cricket ball and snatch it effortlessly out of the air – but how can you possibly miss a forty-six-year-old woman, who's *on fucking fire*?' She coughed again. '*Jesus*. You pair of useless cunts.'

'She seems unaffected,' said Zach.

We slowly grunted ourselves to our feet and moved back to a safer distance away from the cottage.

'What happened?' Zach asked, looking at the burning building with boyish curiosity.

I shrugged. 'No idea. I woke up – luckily – and – unluckily – the place was on fire.'

Zach glanced over at Elizabeth. 'Right.'

'What? Why did you look at me?'

'No reason, ma'am.'

'My battered arse no reason. What are you implying?'

'Nothing . . . It's just that, you know . . . stray cigarette, is all.'

'Well, you can push that "is all" back up the bodily canal from whence it came. It was nothing to do with me.'

'She's right, Zach,' I said. 'The fire obviously started downstairs. We hadn't been down there for hours.'

'Right.' He nodded. 'Who knows, then? Maybe it was electrical. Did you switch the TV off?'

'*You* were down there last,' Elizabeth replied icily. 'Did *you* switch the TV off?'

'OK, OK,' I cut in, trying to be authoritative and provide a sense of stability and leadership (which is an uphill struggle when you're standing there in only your underpants). 'Let's not argue about it. Let's just be happy we're all OK. It's lucky you were here, Zach.'

'Though,' added Elizabeth, 'arguably less lucky that you weren't downstairs to spot the fire starting and put it out before it set the whole building ablaze.'

'I was out on patrol,' Zach replied. 'I went out on patrol. I've been doing patrols all night, at irregular intervals: always better tactics – don't let them have a pattern to rely on.'

'Them?'

'Observing hostiles, ma'am.'

'Oh, yes, sorry. Please – do go on: you were talking shite.'

'So, a little ways in, I thought as I heard an engine.'

'Stuka?'

'A car engine. But I couldn't see any glow from headlights and, what with all the trees muddying the path of the sound, I couldn't tell which direction it was coming from real well either. So, I did some wide sweeps to check it out. After a time, I'd still found nothing, but then I spotted the light coming from here. For a second, I thought it was maybe from Beth's car, or that you two had decided to turn the lights on . . . for some reason. But it was the wrong colour. Not white. Kind of orange, you know? So, I hauled back here, full speed. I couldn't get in downstairs for the flames. Came around back, and saved you two. That's it – I'm debriefed, man.' Zach looked at the fire again. 'Reckon we should maybe call someone?' he asked.

'I've got an aunt in Stadhampton,' said Elizabeth. She shrugged. 'But we don't talk much. And, anyway, I don't think this is her kind of thing.'

'I meant more the fire service. Or maybe Beth. I know she said to maintain radio silence – and I was fully behind that decision – but she might want to know about this anyhow.'

'It's academic anyway,' I said. 'My mobile's up there in that burning bedroom.'

'Darn,' grimaced Zach. 'Why didn't you bring it out with you?'

'Well, things were a little hectic, as you ask. That's why I'm standing here with no trousers on.'

'Too bad you didn't take a second to grab your pants – that would have brought the phone along too.'

This, I thought, was all very simple for someone who hadn't woken up in a blazing house to say in the easy, unthreatening calm of retrospect. 'Well,' I replied testily, 'that's where you're wrong. It *wouldn't* have meant I came out with the phone as well.'

'No? But don't you keep your phone on your belt clip?'

'Yes I do. But it just so happens, smart arse, that earlier tonight I removed the belt from my jeans for something.'

'For what?'

'That,' I said, 'is none of your business.'

I saw Zach's eyes flick sideways.

'Don't you look at Elizabeth,' I warned. 'It's just none of your business, OK?'

We stood gazing at the back of the cottage a little, then wandered around to the front. And gazed at that. It was also on fire. Elizabeth sighed lightly beside me. My mobile, my clothes and my wallet were burning as I watched; I was bruised from falling, and being fell on; it was October; I was standing in Wales in my underwear.

'Well . . .' Elizabeth said. 'It could be worse.'

At that moment, we were all scanned by a powerful beam of bright white light. 'Ahh – that'll be alien abduction,' I thought. 'It's pretty much the only place that today's got left to go.'

I twisted to look. It turned out not to be a party of Grays on a probing safari, but actually the headlamps of Beth's car panning across us as she swung up to the end of the track leading to the cottage. She got out and, seeming rather dazed and distracted, walked over to where we were standing.

'You've burnt my parents' cottage down,' she said, in a sort of breathy, distant voice.

'Yeah . . .' replied Zach. He clicked his teeth, and then gave her a loose, sympathetic, matey slap on the shoulder. 'Sorry.'

'You've burnt my parents' cottage down.' Her eyes were wide and locked on the fire.

Elizabeth leaned closer to me and hissed, 'I can see *everything* with your wearing only those pants, by the way. If you reveal the merest hint of tumescence when you're looking at Beth I *will* tear out your spleen.'

'Aww . . .' I pecked her on the check. 'That's lovely. Don't worry, though, I'm not interested in her at all. She's not you – she's just . . . fff, you know . . . just really attractive.'

'Ugh. You transcend abysmal.'

'You've burnt down . . . my par—' Beth began again.

'Actually,' I cut in, 'it wasn't us. It, well . . . it just happened.'

'How can *that*,' she pointed at the house, presumably to emphasise the aspect of its being completely ablaze, 'just happen?'

I shrugged. 'Not sure . . . We think it might have been an electrical fault.'

'An *ele*— Hold on . . . Hold on – did you see anything suspicious while I've been away?'

She looked at us each in turn. We all shook our heads.

'You've seen no one?'

We all shook our heads.

'And you've made no phone calls?'

We all shook our heads.

'Well . . .' I replied, moving unobtrusively from a vigorous shake to a mild nod. 'I made *one*.'

'*What?*'

'It was only a little one.'

'Rob . . . *Rob*. Don't you know that it's possible to locate a mobile phone's position if you have its number and it's used? And – if we assume that they were monitoring you at the factory – we can assume they'll have got hold of your number: it's encoded with the signal.'

Zach frowned. 'You've got to have access to some serious equipment to do that kind of tracking, though.'

Beth threw up her hands. 'True enough. But we don't know *what* these people have access to. The fact that there's so much that we don't know about them is what makes them so dangerous. If they did track Rob's phone to the cottage, and saw you three, they might easily have assumed that I was in there too. Presented with that opportunity – out here, miles from anywhere – then burning the place down with all of us inside would have seemed like a gift.' She paused, put her hands together with the index fingers raised and touching, and closed her eyes.

After a few moments of us all standing there gazing dumbly at this, Elizabeth sighed heavily, looked up into the air and called, 'Grandma? Grandma – are you there?'

Beth ignored her. Half a dozen seconds later, she exhaled fully while spreading her arms wide, and declared, 'OK, OK, I'm centred again.'

'Well – that's one fewer problem, then,' replied Elizabeth.

'OK,' said Beth, falling into a whisper and now back to her usual, commanding self. 'They might well be still about somewhere. That's bad enough, but it's really, really bad with Professor Osbourne here.'

'Professor Osbourne is here?' I asked, looking around.

'Not *here* here,' replied Beth. 'We've learnt to be incredibly cautious about everything we do – that's how we've stayed alive this long. I didn't bring him directly here to speak with you all. He's waiting for us in an old woodman's hut, about a mile and a half that way.' She jerked her head to indicate the direction. 'So, let's get out of here. We need to get there as quickly as possible.'

'I'm in my underpants,' I said.

She smiled and touched my cheek. 'That's all right, Rob. Professor Osbourne sees your inner spirit. He doesn't judge people by physical appearance.'

'No, that's not the point I was making, actually. It was less a spiritual thing, and more a thing about it being October, and you asking me to walk a mile and a half through woodland in only my underpants.'

'Well – you can't stay here.'

'At least it's warm here,' I snapped back – waving (possibly a little insensitively) at her parents' burning cottage.

'Rob . . .' Now she took my face in both hands (beside me, I sensed Elizabeth's body tighten). 'I know this isn't easy. I know that facing the end of a journey can be difficult. Even when the destination is somewhere you've strived to reach, arriving there still has a finality to it. It's the fear of knowing. While you're travelling, you always have hope: you know that you'll lose that at your destination. You risk hope, without any sure guarantee of peace. But, trust me, it *will* be worth it.' She kissed my forehead. 'It's not the underpants really, is it? The underpants are just a crutch . . . To find rest – *true* rest – you have to let go of your underpants.'

Somehow, with Beth looking unblinkingly into my eyes and speaking softly but with absolute assurance, this didn't sound as completely fucking mental as you'd imagine. I suppose you really had to be there.

'This is almost certainly your last chance, Rob,' Beth continued. 'The agreement, for safety, is that Professor Osbourne will only wait for us for two hours. After that, he'll slip away. And he's leaving Britain soon – it's too dangerous here now. In a couple of days he'll be somewhere in Asia, and even I won't be able to get in touch with him – not for who knows how long. This is your one chance, Rob. Take your chance. *Grab* it, while you still can.'

'Um . . . OK,' I said. 'OK: take us to him.'

Beth released my face. 'Good – let's get going, then.'

'But it is *partly* the underpants,' I insisted.

We started off, but after only a few strides Zach pulled up.

'Hold on,' he said. 'I've left my backpack. I took it off when I was catching Rob and Elizabeth. It's still around the back of the cottage somewhere. Give me a second, guys – I need to run and get it.'

He sped off.

Beth, Elizabeth and I stood there waiting, a little awkwardly – like people at a party who've not only run out of things to say, but have also suddenly *realised* that they've run out of things to say.

'So . . .' I offered. And then blew out some air.

Beth glanced at her watch impatiently.

'I'm sure he won't be long,' I said.

'Yeah – Godspeed,' Elizabeth muttered, reaching down to brush some mud off her dress.

'Sorry?' said Beth.

'Never mind. I was merely making a feeble joke: Zach's got Godspeed going for him if anyone has.'

'Sorry? Sorry – I still don't see what you mean.'

Elizabeth waved distractedly – more concerned with the state of her knees. 'He's God's man on the ground, isn't he? That's his thing.'

'What are you talking about?'

I sighed and shrugged. 'Zach believes that he didn't survive by accident. He thinks God lifted him away from death for a mission. That mission being me. He tracked me down when he heard the radio show: he's on a holy crusade.'

'Sacred sisters! I *bet* he is!' Beth's eyes expanded. 'I mean, I was aware he's American, obviously . . . but I thought you'd known him for ages. All you said was that he'd lost friends while in the army in Bosnia, and you thought he was trying to compensate by looking after you. But – apparently – he actually believes Jehovah has chosen him, personally, for a holy mission. And you never thought to mention that to me?'

'It never came up.'

'Right. So, let's go through this list. He's come over from America – the homeland of the Servants of Azrael. He's certainly got some military skills, whether his story is completely true or not. He tracked you down. He insisted he follow you everywhere. When I arranged to meet you at the factory, it nearly kills you two – but he's not around . . .'

'He was outside tonight,' admitted Elizabeth, though not happily. 'We were inside – if Rob hadn't woken up, we'd have died. But he was outside.'

'Oh – come on,' I said. 'He could have killed us at any time, if he'd wanted to. He saved your life, Elizabeth. And *both* of our lives tonight.'

'Think chaotically, Rob,' Beth insisted. 'Empathise. Don't rely on cold logic: that's not the way humans behave. Imagine he wanted to get us all – perhaps me especially. Elizabeth is weak . . .'

'Fuck you, Sabrina,' said Elizabeth.

'I'm not being mean, Elizabeth – but you are. He could kill you whenever he wanted; and that's assuming you didn't kill yourself first and relieve him of the trouble. Saving you to gain Rob's complete trust would seem a good move. Once he'd got us all together, and after he'd failed at the factory, he'd want to pick his moment. He's strong and fit, but things can always go wrong. Military strategy is to play the odds – "overwhelming force at specific points". Imagine he got impatient tonight – maybe worried that I wasn't coming back with Professor Osbourne at all – and decided to cut his losses and take you two out. Fine if you quietly burn to death, but when that doesn't happen and the situation returns to having to face the two of you at once again, he slinks back to playing the Good Samaritan. Was he out of your sight after I called to arrange the first meeting?'

I tried to think. 'I can't remember. Well, he went out to get some things to repair Elizabeth's door . . . and do some patrolling . . . but . . . ugh. I can't remember the exact order of things. But . . . no – Zach? I can't believe it . . . Elizabeth?'

'I don't . . . I don't know, Rob. He certainly has that over-wound, rigid morality that lends itself happily to all sorts of evil, and isn't he the one who encouraged you to seek out people like yourself in the first place? But . . . No: I just don't know.'

'It all fits,' said Beth. She was now very agitated indeed. Quite honestly, I was getting pretty agitated too. 'This is his chance – the one he'll risk everything for – as much as it is for you, Rob. The three of us *and* Professor Osbourne within reach . . .' She froze. 'What has he got in that backpack that's so important?'

There was a numbing moment. A moment when all three of us stood there looking at each other in incredulous, horrified indecision. Into this moment sprinted Zachary Patrick Thufvesson. He appeared from behind the cottage. He was running over to where we were – the flames of the burning building as his backdrop: like a demon speeding at us straight out of Hell.

Slung over his shoulder was his backpack.

'Shhh!' Beth hissed. 'We can't let him suspect – we don't even know if he's alone. Let's wait for a chance . . . maybe I can think of some way to lose him. At least I know these woods.'

Seconds later, Zach was among us again.

'Phew – sorry,' he said. 'It was way hot back there. My pack was too close to the flames to pick up. I had to go find a branch and drag it away . . . So? We all OK?'

There was a terribly elongated, suspicious pause. Elizabeth, Beth and I looked at each other nervously. Nobody spoke. The silence rapidly became hugely conspicuous.

'Oh, yeah,' Elizabeth said at last, 'we're fine. I was just saying that I have no knickers on.'

'Oh,' replied Zach – he hung his head and kicked at the ground.

While his eyes were off us, Elizabeth raised her hands and contorted her lips at me to convey a feeling of 'Well, what was I supposed to say? You just stood there like a twat. Why didn't *you* say something? You fucker.' Even her facial expressions were verbose.

'OK,' said Beth. 'We've lost enough time. Come on.' She led us away from the open space and warmth and light in front of the cottage, and into the claustrophobic, cold, dark trees.

TWENTY-THREE

Beth appeared to know exactly where she was going. Given the circumstances, I doubted that she was genuinely heading for the hut where Professor Osbourne was waiting, but she was nevertheless doing a fantastic job of striding purposefully through undergrowth – even if, as could easily have been the case, she was simply steering us in circles to buy some time while she thought things through.

She was out in front, leading the way. Zach – unnervingly (it made my shoulder blades worry) – was at the back. Elizabeth and I were in between the two of them; I tried to stay alongside her, holding her hand, but we often had to let go of each other and walk single file because of obstructions. Being almost entirely naked, I should have been a lot colder than I was. What kept me warm were exertion, fear and pain.

The pain came mostly from being barefoot. The floor of the wood was largely soft and mulchy, but every so often I trod on a sharp stone, a pointy twig, or something or other that made me wince and half wish I'd chosen to put on my socks rather than my boxers. I was learning a lesson the hard way. However much you might want to convey an air of eroticism and elegance in front of a woman, a man's natural instinct is to undress his feet last, and dress them again first. I realised now that this was obviously the result of evolutionary pressure: in terms of natural selection, men who briefly look like a complete fool stand a far better chance of survival than those who – if a sudden exit is called for – end up with blood poisoning from a footful of filthy thorns. I'd defied Nature, and this was my punishment.

It was made worse by the fact that I couldn't complain. Elizabeth, in nothing but her thin dress, was barefoot too, but she was putting up with it aggravatingly well. I kept trying to nudge her into having a little moan – 'Are your feet OK?', 'How are your feet holding up?', 'Are you sure you can go on? I'm worried about your feet' – but she was annoyingly brave and never responded with anything but plucky assurances that she was fine. Naturally, if she didn't whinge, then neither could I – not without looking like a complete ponce. And I wasn't about to look like a complete ponce in front of a woman I'd recently fallen in love with, and another woman I hadn't fallen in love with, but who was very attractive nonetheless. It was all a bit unfair. Maybe her feet really weren't hurting? Maybe all women over forty naturally grow thick, leathery soles that you could nail horseshoes on to without their feeling a thing. If you go into Superdrug, there's certainly that whole shelf in the foot-care section devoted to abrasive stones, fearsome graters and terrifying razor-like implements created for the purpose of shaving away excess tough, horny skin from the bases of increasingly woody feet – and that area is never free for long from the scavenging baskets of women over forty, is it?

Yes. That must be it. It was Nature at work again. Women over forty develop hard pads to protect their feet for the day when they hit the menopause and run – barefoot, howling and disorientated – into the street.

I began to worry that I was, perhaps, obsessing about feet.

I didn't know how long we'd been walking for. It seemed like hours, but when you're wandering around in woodland in only your underpants it's easy to lose all sense of time. Now, however, Beth had stopped moving. She was standing motionless in the semi-darkness, looking uneasily down at the ground.

When I drew up alongside her, I was able to see that she wasn't looking at the ground at all. Or rather, she was, but it wasn't the ground at her feet: it was at the ground a worrying distance below them. Directly in our path was a medium-sized stream. Nothing problematic in itself, but it was on a lower level of the woods. Its effects, plus general erosion from rain and wind, meant that it lay at the base of what it would be dreadfully overstating the case to call a 'cliff', but which was unarguably a nasty, almost sheer, crumbling drop of perhaps thirty feet or so.

Everyone peered down reflectively for a moment – as you do – then moved cautiously back away from the edge.

'We need to get down there,' said Beth.

'Can't we go around?' asked Zach. 'Or at least move along to where it's less steep?'

'No,' replied Beth emphatically. 'It's like this for quite a way in both directions, and we've already lost enough time. Professor Osbourne won't wait for long, remember. It'll be OK. I have a feeling we're in favour with the ancient spirits of the wood – they won't let any harm come to us.'

'Hmmm . . .' Zach said, stepping back and taking another look down. 'I don't know nothing much about wood spirits, but that obstacle is a real hazard for civilians to negotiate.' He took off his backpack, knelt down, and began to feel around inside it. 'Easy to lose your footing on something like that . . . And, if you're laying badly injured down at the bottom of it – all the way out here, well . . .' He drew in air between his teeth. 'That wouldn't be good for you. Not good at all . . .'

The next two things happened incredibly quickly.

The first thing that happened was that Zach's hand emerged from his backpack holding a knife.

I remembered that this had looked pretty damn big

309

when I'd seen it the first time, at Elizabeth's house. Now, it looked like it had been created specifically for the man who quite often found himself in need of gutting whales. I know size doesn't matter: just the first inch of the vagina is sensitive; you can drown in three inches of water; a blade only a little longer than the vagina's tiny functional section – and far shorter than the potentially fatal depth of water – can penetrate the chest deep enough to pierce the heart. Somehow, however, when someone whips out a fucking huge knife, your instinctive reaction is less, 'Pft. You could kill a person with something less than a *quarter* of that size,' and more along the lines of, '*Arrrgh!*'

Gripping the – bleeding massive – knife in his hand, Zach sprang to his feet and lunged at Elizabeth. In the process of doing this (and I couldn't help thinking that this was somehow wonderfully English – maybe he'd been in the country too long), he tripped over an exposed root and fell flat on his face.

'Ugh.'

Then came the second thing. Such was its speed that he hadn't even managed to push himself two inches back up off the ground when this thing – the thing that was the stocky branch of a tree smashing down heavily on to the back of his head – occurred. This wasn't the work of the ancient spirits of the wood: the branch that had clubbed him was wielded by Beth.

Zach was knocked back down on to his face by the force of the blow. Had he lain there unmoving, all this would have been horrible enough, but he didn't. Somehow, despite a big piece of tree having been smacked hard against his skull, he struggled quickly, if groggily, to his feet again – the knife still clutched in his hand. It was truly, queasily unpleasant. I don't know why, but someone getting up – battered but breathing – when you really have every right to have expected them to be stone dead, is a dozen times more eerie and distressing than their simply lying there lifeless. I was very nearly . . . well, 'angry'. It was almost as if Zach was doing it just to creep us out.

Once upright, he staggered backwards a little, his eyeballs swimming around in a gruesome manner, and then briefly achieved a precarious balance. Not for long, though, as Beth thwacked him with the branch again – this time full in the face. The sound this made was indescribably horrendous. A combination of the attack's brain-jolting effects and its sheer force caused him to topple backwards, lose his footing, and then fall away out of sight into the gully.

Elizabeth, Beth and I ran over to the edge and looked down at him lying at the bottom of the deep, muddy trench in an untidy heap.

'Jesus,' Elizabeth breathed quietly.

I looked across at Beth. 'Christ, but you were quick there . . . I didn't have time to think, let alone find anything to whack him with.'

'Oh, I'd already got the branch in my hands,' she said, still peering down at Zach. 'I came here deliberately. I thought I'd say something like, "So, how deep do you think it is, then, Zach?" And then, while he was having a look, I'd clobber him and push him over the edge.' She glanced across at me. 'I did consider casting a spell – maybe Veil of Darkness – but then I decided that clobbering him would be quicker.' She turned her eyes down to Zach's body again. 'I didn't know he'd decide to go for Elizabeth: it was simply a lucky accident that my escape plan saved her a stabbing . . . If you believe in luck, that is. Or accidents. Which I don't. Like I said, the spirits of the wood are with us.'

'He's moving,' whispered Elizabeth.

Incredibly, he was. Not very much, and with obvious effort, but he *was* moving. He was trying to get up.

'Oh, yes,' replied Beth, nodding coolly. 'He's a tough one all right. Ffff – I should have used a bigger branch . . .' She shook her head, like someone dismissing a reverie, and was once again sharp and decisive. 'OK – let's get out of here. I wouldn't bet that he won't recover, be able to scramble his way back up, and be after us again before long. Unbelievable. It's like trying to kill Freddy Krueger.'

She spun around and started off. Elizabeth and I were still flat-footed.

'Well – come on,' commanded Beth, pausing and glaring back at us. 'Professor Osbourne is waiting.' She began trotting away again, and this time Elizabeth and I fell in behind her.

'She's not exactly the *whitest* witch one could possibly imagine, is she?' Elizabeth said to me in a low voice.

Beth's arse weaved and wriggled in front of me as I follow-ed her quickly through the woods (she was moving at an impressive pace – Elizabeth and I could barely keep up). The really quite delicious gloriousness of this view made me feel good about the world – but not in the usual way that a woman's arse will do that. Beth had returned from her journey to get Professor Osbourne wearing jeans. This cost some of the mystique and effortless allure that she'd had in her soft, slitted, spidery dress, but it did mean her arse was on display more comprehensively. (Jeans may have been better suited for running around in woodland too, but that's probably coincidental.) It was now easy to confirm that, from any number of angles, Beth's arse was as close to gluteal perfection as it is possible to imagine. If there were a National Museum of Arses – and I'm strug-gling to come up with a reason why there isn't one already – then Beth's is the one they'd use in the posters for it on the Tube. It was superb. Ideal in shape, size and propor-tions: one glance at the thing would stiffen egg whites. And yet, as I looked at its magnificence, this is what I thought: 'Phwoar . . . awww – Elizabeth.' The instant it started to elicit the slightest hint of strong feelings, I shifted from thinking about it to thinking about Elizabeth; because that was where any truly strong feelings I had came from, and went to. *She* was everything I wanted: *this* was just a bottom. The truth of the matter was that looking at Beth's arse simply caused me to think of Elizabeth's face. I made a mental note never to mention this to Elizabeth. (Romance is a very personal thing.)

After we'd been running for what seemed like a fortnight, Beth came to a halt and held up her hand – indicating that we should stop too. I was delighted to follow her instructions. My legs had been extensively scratched and mauled by the dash through the woods, and my feet were in a truly terrible state. I reached down and pulled a thorn the size of a mouse dropping out of my instep. (I'm fully aware that a thorn 'the size of a mouse dropping' sounds pretty unimpressive, but I assure you that you'd modify that assessment if it were your fucking instep you were pulling it out of.) I turned round to Elizabeth. (I was going to say, 'Look!' and show her the thorn, but then I thought it better not to show her, and instead to simply grimace bravely, say, 'Ack – a thorn,' and then hurl it away, unseen, but with a grunt of exertion that suggested that it probably weighed between ten and twenty pounds.) She was gasping for oxygen.

'Je . . . *sus*,' she managed to say, between racing breaths. She put her arm out and leant against a tree, letting her head drop back – rasping desperate lungfuls of air out of the sky. 'Jesus . . . I can feel all those cigarettes now . . . *Christ*.' She took half a step forwards and, still panting, bowed her forehead down to rest on my shoulder. 'Fuck . . . Ugh – my chest . . .' She lifted her eyes. 'Rob: look at me. I want you to promise me right here that –

however much I rage and protest – you will *never* let me run again.'

'Shhh!' hissed Beth angrily. She was looking around, her eyes narrowed. After a few seconds she seemed satisfied that we were alone. 'OK,' she said, 'come on.'

She parted the low branches of the tree ahead of us, and I was then able to see that just beyond was a hut. It was small – little larger than a big shed, really – but with walls made of heavy, irregular-shaped stones. The roof had long since collapsed, though a few beams remained to suggest that it had probably been slated at some point. There wasn't exactly a clearing, but the area around the hut was clear*er*; it was covered with long grass and low bushes rather than trees.

We all walked forwards but, four or five yards before our destination, Beth turned round to Elizabeth and me and raised her hands; the way a priest might do, for some reason or other.

'Wait,' she said. 'Wait here. I'll go inside and speak with Professor Osbourne first; after that you can come and meet him too.' She smiled and touched my cheek. 'It's almost over.' Then she spun briskly on the spot, walked away, and disappeared in through the doorless doorway of the building.

'You really think this *is* going to be the end?' Elizabeth whispered.

I moved around and stood in front of her. 'Yes,' I replied.

'You honestly believe that meeting a Canadian charlatan in your underpants will produce inner peace? Or provide you with whatever it is you need exactly – give you the key to yourself?'

'No. This isn't the key to myself. I already have that key, now. Looking up at you earlier – watching you fall into those flames – I finally realised I had it. This here –

314

Professor Osbourne and seeing things through to the end – this isn't any kind of key: this is simply closure.'

'Right . . . So – much as I'm sure your answer is going to make my brain vomit – what exactly have you persuaded yourself is the k— Oh, fuck *off*!' Elizabeth directed the final bit over my shoulder, towards the hut.

I turned around quickly, and saw that standing just in front of the doorway was Beth, pointing at the two of us, with a shotgun. Elizabeth sighed powerfully – a hissing blast of air full of weary irritation – looked heavenwards, and shook her head at the sky.

'Christ, Beth,' I said. 'Watch where you're pointing that, will you? It might go off.'

Beth rolled her eyes. 'Duh,' she replied.

'Lord, that takes me back . . .' said Elizabeth with an odd smile on her face. 'Do you remember, Rob, when saying, "Duh," was still a reasonably fresh and amusing thing? Ahh – memories, memories . . .'

'Shut up – you smug hag,' Beth spat. A little unkindly, I thought.

'No, really, Beth,' I said. 'Point it at the ground or something. You never know, it could—' Then I had a slow dawning in the brain. 'Ohhhh . . .' I nodded my head gently. 'I get it . . . OK. I understand how very protective you are of Professor Osbourne. But you should realise that *we*'re no threat, surely? I just want to hear what he's got to say, then go. So, point the gun away, yeah? If it makes you feel any better, you can keep hold of it, OK?'

'You are such a moron,' she replied.

I wrinkled my forehead, confused, and glanced across at Elizabeth.

'You *are* such a moron,' said Elizabeth.

'Wh— Look: I'm cold, I'm tired, I'm bleeding and bruised, and I'm three-quarters naked. Can we just have less of the calling Rob a moron, and more of the speaking to Professor Osbourne and going home?'

'There *is* no Professor Osbourne,' Beth said, with more than a trace of mockery in her voice.

'No Profess— Hold on, hold on: I don't understand. If there's no Professor Osbourne, then *who* . . .' (I raised my voice and pointed dramatically here), 'is in that hut?'

'Unbelievable.' Beth shook her head. '*No one*'s in the hut, you idiot. The only thing that's been in this hut for who knows how many years is this shotgun, which I put there earlier today.'

'But, then . . . why did you do that?'

'Well – du—' Beth pulled herself up; her lips twisted briefly in annoyance. 'Well – *obviously* – so I could kill you with it, if I needed to.'

'Um . . . And why would you need to do *that*?' I asked.

'Fffff.' Beth's jaw tightened: she was certainly losing her patience with *someone* here tonight. 'I'd need to do that, Rob, if – after Zach screwed up my plans to quietly and anonymously run you over after I'd driven all the way up to the bloody Midlands in the middle of the night, and then your somehow failing to die in a factory explosion that I worked *very* hard to set up – you ran true to form and annoyingly remained alive even when I burnt an entire house down around you.'

'Are you saying . . . Are you saying that *you*'ve been trying to kill me?' I said. I pronounced the words very carefully. It seemed the thing to do.

'Yes. Obviously. *Yes*. You – and Action Man – and *this* sour-faced old crow, of course.'

'So . . . then . . . Profess—'

'There *is no Professor Osbourne*!' shouted Beth. 'Bloody hell – how difficult is this to absorb? I invented Professor Osbourne. I invented a whole ridiculous conspiracy just to get you where I needed you. That you believed it – even for a moment – is an object lesson in how gullibly suggestible people are when you tell them things that make them feel special – that and the fact that idiots desperately looking for something are laughably happy to believe almost anything they're shown. So, I simply used a little flattery, a few skilful persuasion techniques and a bit of improvisation – but the result was that I might as well have had you on a lead.' She smiled. 'My degree is in psychology, you know.'

'Ahhh . . .' Elizabeth said, nodding.

'What?'

'Oh, sorry. Only I had wondered why you dressed and behaved the way you do. I thought it showed that you probably craved sexual attention in a rather embarrassing, overtly needy way. Now, I see it was *really* a ruse to take in the boys – a skilful persuasion technique.'

'I *don't* crav—'

'No, no – it was a psychological ploy. I realise that now.'

'I do *not* crave sexual attention.'

Elizabeth merely hummed and looked up into the branches of the trees.

'I'm *really* going to enjoy killing you,' hissed Beth. '*Loads*.'

'If I could just jump back in here,' I said. 'I'm afraid that I still don't see why you feel you need to kill us *at all*.'

'Because you should be dead already. You *deserve* to be dead.'

'No, we don't. I think you've got that all wrong,' I replied, helpfully.

'You do!' Beth roared, with sudden, incendiary anger. The abrupt, explosive nature of it, and the hot and teary look in her eyes, was almost more frightening than the fact she was pointing a gun at us. 'Things happen because they *must*. There's an order to life, and death. When I decided I was too busy with work here to go to Switzerland and suggested that – rather than sit around the house all day watching TV with an inflatable sex doll – Julie should go in my place and bluff herself a free holiday, what was that? When I insisted and insisted, and pointed out how easily she could travel on my passport, what was that? Was that me *killing* her? Am I responsible for her death? Am I her murderer because I practically made her go – made her *die* – in my place? Is that what you're saying? It probably is, isn't it? If, obviously, anything that isn't directly to do with you even registers in your brain at all. *God!* Can you imagine what it was like for me to sit there listening to your show on the Web? Julie gone – torn apart: bits of dead flesh scattered across a field; her last moments spent with total strangers – and you snivelling on and on. "Poor me. I'm a bit indecisive. Oh, the pain of it." It made me sick to my stomach.'

'OK, fair enough . . . But that's got nothing to do with Elizabeth. This is just an issue you've got with me, right?'

'That's how it started, but I couldn't really resist the chance to rid the world of a few more whinging losers or arrogant pricks who shouldn't still be here in the first place, could I? Not when the opportunity was dropped right into my lap, unlooked for. It was pretty much an insult to Julie's memory to let *any* of you live. And, anyway, what other reason is there for all of you to be placed in front of me, if not for me to deal with *all* of you? Things don't happen for no reason. You think it's an accident that I was presented with the three of you together?' She let out a short, derisory laugh. 'What happens *must* happen. I don't know why, but Julie had to die – it wasn't my fault. And I have to kill you all – it's why I was put here. The only bit of chance involved is that luckily I'll have great fun doing it.'

'But . . . how did you . . . ? I mean, the Website and—'

'Ugh. Hardly anything annoys me more than people who, in this day and age, are *still* clueless about the

Internet. I'd be happy to shoot you for that alone, in fact. Any idiot can buy a domain and put up a Website in five minutes. I had much longer than five minutes, so I could not only do that, I could also look into explosive devices, and scout out a good location to plant them, and, well, everything else I needed to do, basically.'

'So, it was you who posted all those angry messages on the Central FM forum too, then?'

'Ahh, I posted a few – the faked newspaper clipping, for example. But the vast majority of those writing in to say they hoped your whiney, undeserving arse died as soon as possible were nothing to do with me at all. That's pretty telling, isn't it, eh?'

'Right . . . But how—'

'Bloody hell – what am I? Blofeld? I'm not going to stand here explaining *everything*, detail by detail. Figure it out, can't you? No, in fact, don't bother trying to figure it all out. Not much point – as I'm going to blow your moronic English head off in about two seconds.' She brought the gun up to her shoulder.

Ahhh . . . So, now – *now* – I can piss really easily, then. Fucking ace.

'Ohhhh,' said Elizabeth, very conspicuously. 'I see.'

'What?' spat Beth. 'What do you think you see now?'

'The real reason behind all this.'

'The *real* reason? What are you . . . ?'

Elizabeth bowed her head slightly, brought her hand up to her brow, and began rubbing her temples. An act of casual, weary superiority that, actually, hid her face from Beth. From under this cover, she looked over to where I was standing – widening her eyes, jerking her eyebrows and doing all sorts of things with her lips. I really thought that this wasn't the time for her to be flirting with me. Then I realised that she wasn't flirting – she was telling me that I should move away to the right, without Beth noticing: she was telling me that she was going to create a diversion and that I should take advantage of it.

Elizabeth raised her head and looked at Beth once more (idly moving off to the left a little – I moved across to the right slightly, equally idly). She smiled in the most irritatingly patronising manner you could imagine: any salesperson in any mobile-phone store in the country would have been proud of a smile like that. 'Your adjectives betray you, I'm afraid, Bethany,' she sighed.

'Eh?'

'What additional label did you choose to apply to Rob's moronic head just now? Hmm? *English*, Bethany. How very, very telling.'

I was edging farther and farther around. Elizabeth, on whom Beth's eyes were furiously fixed, was edging around too, but in the opposite direction. Already Beth's side was towards me: if she maintained her focus on Elizabeth, and our gradual movements continued without her realising it, then pretty soon she'd have her back to me and her attention fixed elsewhere. When that time came, I could make a run for it and leave Elizabeth to be killed.

No, of course I wouldn't do that.

It was like I'd said when I was talking to Elizabeth about her misplaced guilt: you can't stop yourself having these thoughts. Having terrible, cruel thoughts doesn't make you a terrible, cruel person. It's simply the way we're made. It's probably even a good thing that we have them – that they come from within us, to disgust us; make us actively claw ourselves back towards what it means to be decent. At some personal risk, the Marquis de Sade opposed all death penalties during the French Revolution and insisted on hearing every case individually – at a time when his fellow judges were sending prisoners to the guillotine, cases unheard, in job lots. Yet didn't lots of concentration-camp guards say that they thought about nothing during the day but their gardens or what they were going to buy their children for birthday presents?

Naturally, the thought came into my head. But I would never actually have acted on it. I preferred that *I* get shot and killed in that wood, rather than Elizabeth. Though, obviously, not nearly as much as I preferred that *neither* of us would get shot and killed. Neither of us getting shot and killed was still very much my first choice.

Elizabeth continued. 'This nonsense about order and destiny, and who's to blame for what, and who might or might not be more deserving than whom – the whole thing: it's simply a convenient excuse, isn't it?' she said. 'Your real problem with us is that we're English. It's that old, old Welsh chip on your shoulder.'

'I cannot *believe* the arrogance of you people,' growled Beth, visibly shaking with rage. 'That's completely bloody *typical*. I'm standing here, about to brutally kill you to honour my dead sister and serve universal justice . . . and all you can do is shrug, "Oh – it's just some silly Welsh thing." We are the only country that's ever—'

'Pardon me,' Elizabeth cut in. 'Are we talking about Wales here? Only – as I'm sure you're aware – Wales isn't a country: it's a principality.'

'We are the only *country*,' replied Beth, jerking the gun threateningly towards Elizabeth, 'that's ever had to put up with this amount of shit. No other country on earth has had to take the sheer volume of shit from anyone that we've had to take from the English. I grant you, other countries may have been invaded, or decimated, or reduced to slave states or some such . . . But at the level of simply *putting up with shit* – arrogant, haughty, dismissive, pompous *shit* – then we get the gold medal.'

'So . . . are you confirming or denying that you want to kill us because we're English? Your argument seems a little confused.'

I was almost all the way behind Beth now: behind, and perhaps only fifteen feet away from her. If I was going to try to jump her, it had to be very soon. Maybe I could get into a position where I was directly facing her back – completely out of range of even the outermost, glancing edge of her peripheral vision – and I could sneak in a little closer, but that didn't matter. I could see that Elizabeth's goading had been so effective that Beth might snap and shoot her at any moment. She was fizzing with anger – insane with it. And, as she was obviously insane before the provocation had even started, there were way too many levels of madness with their fingers on the trigger of that shotgun.

I took a deep breath, and began my run towards her.

She knew before I'd completed even a single step.

She might have heard the noise of my foot sweeping quickly through the long grass, or she might have seen Elizabeth's eyes involuntarily dart over to me when I began my move. Who knows? Maybe she sensed my bleeding aura. It didn't matter. All that mattered was that she started to spin around to train the gun on me.

Ironically, in a way, everything was clear at that moment. I didn't have to suffer facing any kind of numbing unlucky dip of possibilities. I *knew* that she would easily complete her about-face before I was remotely within striking distance of her. I knew also that she wouldn't bark, 'Freeze!' or, 'Stay there!' or, 'Ha! Nice try, Garland – but I was way ahead of you. So, just calm down and take a few steps back now, would you?'

No: she was going to shoot.

Because I somehow *knew* that, I didn't even try to pull myself up – to stop and raise my hands. I was sprinting towards her. She was going to shoot. We were both committed to our actions: all that was left was to see them through.

I'm not sure if I consciously considered whether the impact of the blast would blow a hole straight through me or not: but I do know that it seemed somehow ludicrous – *impossible* – that I was going to die. That, in a second, I was *really* going to die. Does everyone – everyone who has the chance – think that just before they die, I wonder? 'It's *impossible*.'

Her gun levelled itself right at my face. I saw Beth's finger tighten on the trigger (or my mind imagined I did), and I became aware of an unrestrained roaring scream. I can't tell you how surprised I was when I realised that it wasn't coming from my mouth.

Beth's eyes widened in shock, and she continued her spin. The line of the gun swung past where I was standing, and on around to Zach, who had emerged from somewhere beyond the side of the hut, and was now throwing himself towards her, bellowing at lung-splitting volume.

He was no more than three feet away from her when Beth (as much out of panic as anything, I suspect) emptied both barrels full into the centre of his chest. It couldn't have been the case, of course – not with the thunderous, gravelly boom of the shotgun swamping my ears – but I thought I heard all the breath get punched out of him in a sharp, percussive, sad sigh in the instant that he was hit. His forward movement stopped completely, and he simply buckled: folded in half like a ventriloquist's dummy about to be put back into its box. Then, legs twisting – legs that were now no longer providing any support, but were nothing more than limp, fleshy things under his body – he slumped to the ground, almost comically. I heard a cracking pop as his shoulder hit – it was probably the noise of it dislocating: he didn't utter a sound as it did.

I was hypnotised by his body for a moment. Transfixed by the oddly unremarkable horror of a dead person: this simple heap of clothes on the ground made terrible beyond words purely because it used to be Zach.

I got a hold of myself again pretty quickly, but not as quickly as Elizabeth had got a hold of herself, it seemed. She'd probably started towards Beth as soon as Beth had begun spinning around towards me. My mind back in my head, I turned to see she'd already snatched the, now empty, shotgun out of Beth's hands. Beth looked confused and desperate – her eyes were darting all over the place.

'Quickly! Tie her up!' I called to Elizabeth – at almost exactly the same moment as Elizabeth used the shotgun as a makeshift club to hit Beth on the top of her head very, very hard indeed. Beth – lights out – fell to the ground like someone who'd suddenly had all her joints greased.

'Sorry?' Elizabeth turned to me and asked. 'What did you say?'

'Never mind.'

I limped over and hurled my arms around her, holding her as tightly as I could. She held me too, her hand at the nape of my neck, before leaning back, looking at me in a vaguely sorrowful way, and kissing my cheek.

There was a low, gargling groan from behind me.

'Fuck me,' I whispered, letting go of Elizabeth and turning around. 'Zach's still alive.'

'Alive?' said Elizabeth, smiling broadly. And then, her expression changing, '*Alive?* After being hit full on by a double-barrelled shotgun from three feet away? That's impossible – it'd take a mirac— My God. My God – if he's alive, he's going to be absolutely *insufferable*.'

We both ran to where he was lying, and I gently turned him over. Blood was spilling from his mouth, but not, curiously, from his chest where the gunshots had hit him. I parted his camouflage top, and saw – massively battered – a flak jacket underneath.

'Standard issue,' he coughed.

'Have you been wearing this the whole time?' I asked. 'Jesus – I thought you'd just let your upper body run to fat a bit . . . Um, not that I spent a lot of time thinking about your muscle tone or anything.' (Ugh – I really must get over this gay angst thing.)

'Fuck my ears,' said Elizabeth. 'You've had that contraption on, under your fatigues, ever since you met Rob? Good *Lord*, but you must stink.'

'I'm so glad you're OK, Zach,' I said. 'Partly, I've got to say, because it gives me the chance to ask you what the hell's going on. Why did you try to attack Elizabeth?'

'What? I didn't,' he replied.

'Yes, you did. You lunged towards her waving a knife.'

'No way, man. I was *holding* a knife is all. I took my knife out to cut some things for us to use as, you know, kind of makeshift rope and stuff. So we could climb down that bank more easy. I got out my knife, started to hurry toward some likely-looking material, my foot caught on something, and I fell over. Next thing, Beth is hitting me in the face with a big branch.'

That's the power of suggestion for you, I suppose. If you're hyped up and looking for danger, then a simple trip seems like a murderous lunge.

Zach sniffed contemptuously before continuing. 'Man – if I'd have *wanted* to knife Elizabeth, then she'd have been *knifed*, you know what I'm saying?'

'Unless you fell over on the way,' Elizabeth pointed out. 'Then got taken down by a tiny Welsh woman.'

Zach replied, 'That wouldn't have happened if I was zoned in on a kill,' and then pouted a little.

I began to tug at his flak jacket, trying to get it off.

'Arggh!' he cried.

I let go of it. 'What?'

'You don't know a whole lot about Kevlar, do you, Rob?'

'Well, oddly, no, I don't. Not much call for it, you see: I'm jazz, not rap.'

'For sure, for sure . . . You see, it's like this: a vest inhibits penetration and dissipates the force of the impact . . . but the force doesn't completely disappear, yeah?' He coughed again, and more blood bubbled out of his mouth. 'Two scatter-gun barrels at that range, well . . . my ribs are messed up for certain. And I kind of think one of them might have pierced a lung or two, you know?'

'Fuck . . . I—'

'Get help,' said Elizabeth. 'Get help *now*, Rob. Check to see if Beth has her mobile with her – and cut the straps off Zach's backpack to tie her up with while you're at it. If she has her phone, give it to me. I'll call from here; you head off and try to find a house or a shop or fucking *anything* with people in it – that'll double our chances of getting someone here quickly.'

'Right. Yes – of course . . .'

'*Now*,' snapped Elizabeth.

Beth didn't have her phone on her, so I randomly picked a direction to head off in – hoping I'd happen across someone or something before it was too late. Elizabeth stayed behind with Zach. I briefly glanced over my shoulder at them before I ran off into the trees.

She was kneeling beside him, and holding his hand tightly: a shaky smile on her face. 'It's OK, Zach,' she was saying, softly. 'You're going to be fine . . . You're going to be fine. Come on, now – talk to me . . .'

I was worried I might run for days without seeing a single person or chancing across any building at all. Blind luck, however, put me on a road after about fifteen minutes of racing desperately through the woods. Even better, I emerged within sight of a pub. It was closed, of course, but I knew the owners would be asleep inside.

I was briefly worried that I'd have trouble persuading them to phone the emergency services. Given the wild story I had to tell, how keen would they be to believe me and call an ambulance and the police? Well, here's a bit of information you can have courtesy of me: if, as a total stranger, you turn up at someone's house in the early hours of the morning – shouting your head off up at their bedroom window and dressed in only a pair of underpants – they are actually *amazingly* keen to pick up the phone and dial 999.

TWENTY-FOUR

It was a bleak October morning in a bleak Cardiganshire Accident & Emergency department, but I felt chipper. I don't think, in all my life, I'd ever so much as considered using the word 'chipper' before – about anything. But now, instinctively, it popped into my head, and I knew that I was it.

There had been some explaining to do to the police, and there was surely going to be a lot more, but right now Elizabeth and I were sitting quietly side by side on those orangey plastic A&E chairs. I couldn't help thinking that it was, in a fashion, our first date. Yes, we'd had deeply – some might say 'invasively' – intimate sex already, and yes, come to think of it, I had been to A&E with her before. But this felt, in some cosy way, like it was our first proper trip out together.

We were waiting to be checked over, just as a precaution. Beth – massively concussed – was in hospital too, but not with us: she was elsewhere, accompanied by two watching police officers. Zach had been taken to surgery. They said that his lung had indeed been punctured, and he also had a dislocated shoulder, and various kinds of head trauma, and his eyebrows and eyelashes appeared to have been burnt off – but they expected him to be OK. I thought so too. As they lifted him into the ambulance, he'd certainly been well enough to suddenly reach his hand out and grab my arm.

'Rob,' he'd pleaded. 'Rob – promise me that, whatever happens, you won't let them give me any of that gay Limey blood.' Then he'd laughed up a load of blood. The fucker.

Elizabeth had insisted on travelling with him in the ambulance.

The A&E waiting area was the standard realisation of purgatory: dull, wordless misery to the soundtrack of a television bracketed high on the wall. Waiting. Dried blood and daytime TV. Elizabeth was very quiet. I tried to make conversation several times, but she evaded all my attempts with single-word replies or simple shrugs. The impression I got was that she couldn't be with me right now, because she was needed back at her own thoughts. It had been a bit of an unsettling night, I had to admit, so I eventually decided to leave her alone with her silence.

After about half an hour of sitting there without any kind of indication that we'd be seen while we still had our own teeth, Elizabeth sighed and got to her feet.

'Christ, this is noxiously tiresome. I'm simply not severely injured enough to bear the wheezing dreariness of it. I'm going outside for a smoke.'

She hadn't got any cigarettes with her, but she managed to scrounge one ('Nurses, Rob – nurses always smoke'), and we wandered out into the car park.

She took a massive opening pull on her Silk Cut, held in the smoke – unmoving: like someone suddenly frozen while playing a game of statues – and then let it all out in a collapsing, cleansing whoosh.

'Rob . . .' she began, before deciding to return to her smoking rather than continue.

'Yes?' I said. I reached over and curled my fingers around hers. She looked down at our hands, squeezed mine tightly, and then let go of it – folding her arm across her stomach and turning away slightly.

'We have to end this now,' she said coolly.

That, coming from nowhere, hit me like a punch in the throat.

'End what?' I asked. I knew full well what, of course.

'You know full well what.'

'No, I don't.'

'This. The stupidity. The idiot us.'

'There's nothing stupid about it. I love you.'

'No, you don't.'

'I think I'm the best person to make that decision.'

She turned her eyes to me. 'You're the *worst* person to make that decision, Rob. You're confused, over-tired, and you've probably got more adrenaline screaming around inside you than anyone from Birmingham even dreamt existed. You're in no state to make rational choices: you haven't been for days – possibly months. Which means that the right thing to do is for me to make the choice for you. I'm a forty-six-year-old depressive who hates the entire world, starting with myself. You're thirty-one and have a young woman waiting at home to marry you.'

'But I don't want to marry her.'

'You say that now because you're not thinking straight.'

'I *am* thinking straight.'

'No, you're fucking not.'

'Yes, I fucking am.'

'No, you're fucking *not*. The situation has taken an egg whisk to your brain – and you'll realise that before long. I realised it when I was staring down the barrels of Beth's gun. That little nudge made me let go of all the fluffy fantasies: all this fucking childish pretending we're a couple – let alone a *viable* couple. It forced me to focus on the basic, unchangeable facts. And those facts don't work. You go back to Jo, never mention anything about us. Settle down; be happy – this is your second chance. Second chances are precious, Rob. Don't blow yours. Take your second chance, go back to Jo, and have a good life.'

Now. Now was the time to tell her.

'That's bollocks,' I said. 'It's not *this* situation that's the problem. It's . . . Jesus. Look: I asked Jo to marry me two

330

days after I didn't die in that crash. We'd been going out for a while, and it was OK, but I know I'd never have . . . Everything was so uncertain after the accident, so fragile. I wanted something that was solid: something that put down a deposit on the future. I confused fear with love. I was wrong. Somewhere deep down, I've known that for a long time – I sometimes think Jo has too. We focused on the wedding, we tried to convince ourselves that it was right by sheer repetition, but we knew. I'm sure we hoped that we'd both be let off on a technicality. We'd committed ourselves to marriage, but we secretly longed to run into a problem – be offered an escape route. We'd *try* to keep our promises, but be given a reprieve at the last moment because the blood tests came back badly, or we couldn't find the right kind of doilies for the reception, or the other person saved us by backing out, or . . . something – *anything*. You want to give me a second chance, and that's what I want too. *You* are my second chance.'

Elizabeth looked at me in silence while she sucked on her cigarette, and then slowly blew out the smoke from between pursed lips. She flicked the half-finished Silk Cut off across the car park and shook her head.

'No,' she said gently, but resolutely. 'In her own homicidal, Wiccan-nutter fashion, Beth was right. Sometimes there's a way things should be, and we know it: the reason they should be that way is *because* we know it. Most of the time we can't do anything about that, but we still know what's right and what's wrong. You and I are wrong. When you have time to calm down, you'll see that.'

'That's simply your lack of medication talking – your depression is crawling back into your head and distorting how you look at things. It's the shock of what's just happened landing without the cushion of your pills. That's all this is.'

'Fff. I see your bid of depressive illness, Rob, and raise

331

you a puppyish episode of naïve self-delusion brought on by stress and danger. My realism is possibly a little grim, but it's realism nonetheless. A bit of pre-wedding nerves and a few attempts on your life have knotted up your thoughts: once you have the chance to unpick them, you'll realise that it's Jo you love, not me.'

'I will fucking not.'

'You will. Trust me. Give yourself some time.'

'I won't let you go.'

'You have no choice. I'm going to do the right thing. And you won't be able to stop me doing the right thing for once in my life, Rob: I have the zeal of a convert. Go back to the real world, and make a go of it.'

She turned and began to walk back inside.

'Stop,' I shouted after her. She carried on walking, without looking round. 'Stop!'

TWENTY-FIVE

Jo didn't have her December wedding.

With everything that had happened, it would simply have been too soon. Elizabeth was correct: you do need time. The annoying thing about time is that it takes time . . . but no amount of it is too long to wait through when you're waiting to be sure. However much we might believe, and wish, it were true, you can't really be sure of what you feel however intensely and seriously and constantly you examine your thoughts and emotions. You can be really sure only by forcing yourself to wait: time alone can tell you what will last.

The wedding wasn't until the following July (that was still too soon, some might say – but, in this case, I wouldn't be one of them). Jo had originally longed for snow – a frosting of white over everything in the photos that'd make them look like they were taken in a fairy tale. Now she fretted that it wouldn't be sunny; that Birmingham – the acknowledged drizzle capital of Europe – would behave as usual; that there'd be mud everywhere, and dresses would become soggy, and her hair would collapse until it looked as though she had a small, distressed dog sitting on her head. As it turned out, though, on the day, the sun was a blinding disc burning a hole in a sky that was an unbroken blue from horizon to horizon. Perfection.

The church wedding had been abandoned too. Impressively, this had been Jo's idea. 'What's the sense in two atheists getting married in a church?' she'd said. A civil service at a local hotel would be just as good – because it wasn't the setting that was important. All the silly, expensive, distracting, burdensome paraphernalia and 'rules' were nothing but an unimportant sideshow: it was the vows that mattered.

'Do you, Joanne Alison Rayner . . .' said the registrar. She was a middle-aged woman in a conservative, light-brown skirt and jacket – she looked like the slightly formidable headmistress of a well-regarded primary school.

I was wearing a hired suit. And worse: hired shoes. I wondered how many weddings these shoes had attended; the latest in a timeless line of wedding shoes – dutifully inflicting misery on men's feet to emphasise the gravity of the ceremony until they finally grew too old, and became comfortable, and had to be retired.

Jo, on the other hand, looked completely at ease. As serene as if she were wearing her battered Garfield slippers under that tumbling, pearl wedding dress. And not only serene, but beautiful too. I know it's a cliché, I know it's what everyone says about the bride, but I genuinely don't think I'd ever seen her look as completely, faultlessly stunning as she did on that day.

She was trying hard to concentrate all her thoughts on getting the words out perfectly, but she caught my eye, and smiled. I smiled back.

I thought of how she'd looked when I'd proposed to her. I thought of how I'd been on that day, and during the whole boiling, confused river of days afterwards. And how I was now. I don't think I resurfaced fully from my thoughts until I became aware of the registrar saying, 'I now pronounce you husband and wife.'

There was a slight pause. No one could quite believe that this was it. *It*. It was done. Husband and wife. The registrar softened, grinned, and spoke in a way that was almost an affectionate nudge. 'Well – if you *want* to . . .' she said, 'you may kiss the bride.'

Jo beamed, leaned forward, and (to the sound of a room full of cheers) sank into a long, near-pornographically deep kiss with Pete.

Zach, sitting beside me, mumbled, 'Man . . . I'm welling up here. I'm terrible at weddings.'

Elizabeth, seated on my other side, said, 'Meh – I give it six months.' But then she smiled and started applauding with everyone else.

Both Jo and Pete had been hammered by guilt at first. They'd never genuinely let go of each other (despite the time that had passed, really, I'd got Jo on the rebound – and it was easy to see, now, that the way she'd needed to bounce was back to Pete). With me half mad and away on some dick-headed journey of personal discovery – and actually phoning home to *insist* that they spent nights holed up in the house together – it was almost stupidly predictable that they'd fall back to each other. As this suited me perfectly – and I had been doing some furiously under-the-counter-level infidelity of my own – it was no problem. Still, just for the look of the thing, and to make them feel better, I had made the effort to call Jo a tart and to fume at Pete for fucking my fiancée – in my bed – the second I popped out on a quick quest. That was just a brief formality required by etiquette, however. I was happy for them – and even happier for myself.

St John Rivers nobly took himself abroad to die as a missionary, leaving Jane Eyre to find true love with Mr Rochester. Times have changed, so I wished Pete and Jo all the best, leapt into my car and, at illegal speeds, racingly transported my tumbling joy and a thunderous erection down to Willesden. It was basically the same thing.

I stood before Elizabeth's door in the special, intoxicating semi-darkness of North London: the sound of E4 seeped at a muffle out of thin windows; watery streetlights were a silver flicker behind towering, unkempt privets; the air was full of the smell of bins and southern fried chicken. I took a second to absorb the romantic energy of the atmosphere, and then knocked. Three solid raps. Certainty. Resolve.

She answered looking tired, and annoyed, and knee-bucklingly beautiful, and, when she spoke, I couldn't help but feel a tingle – just from hearing the sound of her voice again.

'How big a fuckwit are you, exactly?' she said. 'Did I not tell you, explicitly, to piss off forever?'

I stepped forward and, smiling, grabbed her hand. 'I've got some *wonderful* news, Elizabeth . . .' I took a breath. 'My fiancée has been shagging my best friend while I was away.'

'Well, well . . .' She nodded. 'You lucky sod. Most people would think themselves fortunate with nothing better than having their gearbox break or getting conjunctivitis.'

'You know what I mean. You wouldn't believe me when I told you that Jo and I weren't right – were never right. Now that's not even an issue, because *now* there's no Jo and I at all.'

She pulled her hand away from mine. 'Fff – Jo and *me*. But that's only half – *less* than half – the issue, Rob. With your fiancée or without her, I'm still wrong for you. Wrong, calamitous and *stupid*.'

'Can I come in?'

'OK.'

Elizabeth had tried to maintain her stance. She'd rejected my arguments, and dismissed my reasoning, and, quite often, spent whole evenings replying to everything I said with simply, 'Twat' . . . but, slowly, I'd worn her down.

'It's no good,' I'd finally said to her, after she'd yet again stated how we simply would not work, long-term. 'You're the person I want to spend the rest of my life with. You're either going to have to be with me, or kill me.'

'How amusingly optimistic,' she'd replied, 'that you think I can't do both.'

Under the words, though, she'd given in. She wanted to give in. It just took time.

Zach had come back over from America especially for the wedding (I'd invited him – somehow, it seemed only fitting that he be there). After he'd recovered sufficiently from the many physical injuries that Britain had inflicted upon him, he'd returned to the States and embarked upon some kind of rock 'n' roll 'Do I have a witness?' tour of Evangelical churches. He told how God had revealed Himself to him in a mysterious way. A really fucking mysterious way, I was inclined to think – and (though, I admit, I'm not sure of the biblical precedent here) by means of a somewhat excessive number of blows to the head. Astonishing. It (almost) made me doubt my atheism – like that philosopher said: if God didn't exist, it would be necessary to invent him to explain Zach.

In fact, he was so busy with preaching appointments that he'd arrived only the night before – jet-lagged and disconcertingly civilian in a T-shirt and jeans – and had crashed out on the sofa at our flat. Elizabeth had warned him sternly that we'd just decorated the living room, so any burning bushes in there and he was going to get a fucking slap.

Yeah – 'our flat'. Elizabeth and I had been living up here for several months. It was a bit of a Catch-22 situation: on the one hand, she got to leave the London Borough of Brent; on the other, she got to leave it for Birmingham. Still, the fact was that she could do a little supply teaching anywhere, but my job was with Central FM.

I did news reporting as well as the late-night jazz show now. It was Keith's idea. My return to sanity had almost broken him: he'd started smoking again, and would often spontaneously burst into tears. He just about held it together by arranging for me to cover local stories. He kept sending me to motorway pile-ups and industrial accidents – clinging, white-knuckled, to the dream that one of them would tip me over the edge again. It didn't work, but, sometimes – just to give him a reason to hope, to ensure he could still get out of bed in the mornings – I'd return from an incident and briefly affect a twitch.

'You OK, man?' Zach asked me, as I watched Jo and Pete continue to snog each other towards asphyxiation.

'What? Oh – yeah. I'm fine.' I waved an easy hand towards them.

'Oh, no, I meant, you know, generally, and stuff. You functioning?' He picked up the menu from the table. 'I see there's a choice of two starters – you're going to have to decide between them. Should I get a defibrillator ready?'

'Ahhh – that world-famous Nebraskan humour. No, I'm all right. The occasional moment, but it's rare. You see, it only took a protracted period of insanity, a couple of fires, a shotgun pointed at my head and – most of all – facing the possibility of losing Elizabeth for me to realise that I had everything arse about tit.'

'Cool. Cool . . . I have no idea what that means. But, you know: cool.'

'I mean I was seeing things backwards. When you do all that fixating on what microscopic decision could lead to your death, you have it wrong. The fact is, all those minuscule, mundane decisions actually lead to your life. You take hold of life, moment to moment, by making those choices: and every time you choose, you win – because you choose to carry on. You decide to live life, instead of it living you. Not only that, but also the odds are against us every second of every day – there's simply such an unbelievable number of ways for disaster, hurt and death to happen: and, in the end, death *is* going to get us anyway, that's certain. The correct way to look at it is to be amazed at each moment you beat the house: arrogantly, bloody-mindedly stick two fingers up at chance and whoop at your continued winning streak. Laugh at the fact that you're being so jammy as to pull it off – because it *is* incredible that you are: life is a succession of tiny miracles. I finally realised that, and it helped me to change . . . I suppose we've all changed because of what we've been through.'

'I haven't changed,' said Elizabeth. 'I still think life is a random, often casually fucking cruel, string of arbitrary events that ends meaninglessly at the grave.'

'Um . . .' added Zach, 'I don't reckon I've changed either. I thought God had chosen me for a reason, and what happened totally confirmed that to me.'

'And Beth simply ended up in a secure mental hospital,' Elizabeth continued.

'Yeah, well . . .' I shrugged. 'Well, that's just proves I'm way deeper than the whole fucking lot of you.'

Elizabeth leaned over to Zach and said in a loud whisper, 'You see? I can't help but love him – he's just *so* three-dimensional.'

Zach sat back in his chair and smiled. 'So . . . what about you two? Do I see the sound of wedding bells?'

Elizabeth sighed. 'Jesus. "See the sound." If Washington had known that the price of freedom would be the American public-school system then I'm inclined to think he'd have thrown up his arms and gone back to growing tobacco. There's a lesson for us all there, in fact: neglect tobacco and intellectual decline is the inevitable result.'

'I don't know,' I said to Zach. 'I keep asking her, but . . . well, we'll see.'

'Give it time,' Elizabeth said. 'When you're old enough to use scissors, Zach, you'll realise that time is sensibly measured in years, not the gaps between commercial breaks. And, anyway, why risk it? Just for a start, I'm not sure that people continue to have the kind of sex we're having once they get married.'

Zach opened his mouth to comment, but Elizabeth cut him off before he could speak.

'Don't even try to debate the issue,' she said. 'I'm thinking specifically about the kind of sex we're having. Do you want me to tell you, specifically, about the kind of sex we're having, Zach?'

'No,' he replied, looking down at his shoes. 'No, ma'am.'

'Taking my medication regularly makes a real difference; and now Rob's there to remind me to do that – or to cajole, con or bully me into doing it. What's more, if I have a bad few days despite the pills, he's *still* there, and – fuck it – I can't think of anyone I'd rather be clinically depressed with. As for the rest of the time . . . well, basically, I simply want him there: full stop. He doesn't just make me feel good . . .' Elizabeth laughed. 'Our being together is actually good for the world in general, I reckon: I'm a better me when he's around. Marriage? Meh – who cares? I just want him to keep on being there.'

'I will,' I said. 'It's everywhere I want to be.'

The hotel waiters had begun to circulate. The meal was next, and then my best man's speech. Pete had thrown that little bastard right back at me. Christ, but he was going to pay for doing that. The notes were in my pocket, and even he couldn't imagine the embarrassment bomb that was going to explode in his face thirty minutes from now. He was going to wish he'd never been born.

I caught his eye and gave him an affectionate thumbs-up sign. Savour these last moments, Pete Saunders, you're a condemned man.

I reached over and squeezed Elizabeth's hand.

'I'm happy,' I said.

'Yeah, me too . . . I wonder exactly how many people had to die for that? Be crushed or burnt to death so that we would end up meeting. Happiness has a high body count.'

'Jesus, you're a miserable fucker.'

'Pft – you're captivated by my fascinating darkness. Admit it.'

'Oh, yeah. That bleak stuff hits the spot every time.' I squeezed her hand again. 'I love you.'

'Yeah, well . . . I love you too. You twat.'

TWENTY-SIX

My name is Robert. I'm alive . . . And counting days is for idiots.

Acknowledgements

Boh! Good evening, good evening. Bless my soul: that you should keep your appointment to visit my humble Victorian mental asylum on a night like this! Braving such foul weather, and on All Hallows Eve too. Please – come in. Come in, shake the cadaverous cold of the moors from your shoulders, and allow your jittery coachman to whip his wild-eyed horses away into the swallowing darkness.

I have a few inmates to show you. Unremarkable by your big-city standards, I'm sure, but perhaps you may find in them some small diversion. At least until . . . Hmm? What? Oh, nothing – never mind me. So, here, first of all, we have Ali Gunn. She's a new guest of ours: a literary agent by trade, and really most impressive. Um, I'd advise you to stay behind that line there: before Ms Gunn arrived, our turn-key – One-eyed Thumbless Jim – was known simply as 'Jim'. It's Ms Gunn's way.

If you'd be so kind as to move along, I can introduce you to Ms Helen Garnons-Williams. Ms Garnons-Williams is an editor – the finest in the business. During the afternoons, we free one hand and she edits as she always has done: uninterrupted by her incarceration – perhaps even aided by it. Here, we like to think, she feels secure and focused. Also, her penchant for swearing and flamboyant nudity is less of an issue than in St Martin's Lane. As it happens, this particular cell – and I mention this partly to mitigate the shameful state of it – was previously occupied by another editor: Ms Sara Kinsella, who was very lovely and, unrelatedly, afraid of pigeons. Many editors end up here. We have an Editor Wing, in fact.

Over in this annexe is what we call our Communal Facility. These inmates have performed various tasks or services, or are simply pleasant to have about the place, but have done so without any financial reward whatsoever. Naturally, we therefore press them all into this big room with no chairs and let them fight over a single bucket of gruel. There – with the teeth – for example, you can see Margret. (She has only one name. Like Bono. But not like Edward de Bono.) I really don't know what I would do without Margret. Though I suspect it would be something rather unhygienic. Ms Carol Jackson and Ms Stephanie Thwaites are also here, toiling underground (in fact, they *do* receive payment; but, by the terms of their contracts, no recognition, by anyone, ever). 'Dean Hoff, SSG, US Army' and 'Lucas Miller, Sgt, USMC' – yes, they both include the quotation marks in their names – are two inmates who have been most gracious in answering my questions. Which was especially polite of them as, while I was sitting in my favourite armchair packing my pipe during these rambling exchanges, they were lying in a desert with people shooting at them. Still, I'm very pleased that they have provided me with some accurate information, which – like all good psychologists – I've then airily distorted as required to suit my own ends. Ms Emily Dubberley has certainly been helpful too. She was here when I originally purchased this asylum. In fact, I suspect they may have built the asylum around her. There are various others in the Communal Facility – Nash, Griffiths, Whyman, etc., etc. – but I see you grow tired and oddly moist, so let us move on to The Final Room.

The Final Room conceals our most, hmmmm . . . *interesting* inmate. An amusing creature: desperately pleading sanity to all who pass – yet sure to die within these walls. Let me open the door so that you may look within – perhaps you will recognise the face . . . What's that you say? There's nothing in there but a mirror? Haha! Hahah—

Oh, hold on – you're right: I released the fellow last week. Mad as a flute he was, but I needed the space to store that mirror. Ack. Righto – that's your lot, then. The exit is through that door there, via the asylum shop. We sell a selection of souvenir pencils, keyrings, toffee and so forth. Please come again.